The Children of Eve

*"A Tí clamamos los desterrados hijos de Eva;
a Tí suspiramos, gimiendo y llorando
en este valle de lágrimas."*

Para la felicidad de ella

CHAPTER 1

MIKE TOOK HIS EYES from the book in his hands and hunched down to peer out the window. The clouds were shredding away as they descended, and he could see now the mountains below, covered in jungle.

The plane trembled in the air and he stuck his hand out to brace himself against the back of the seat in front of him.

The man beside him moaned, half-opened an eye, and smirked. Mike frowned back at him.

"No, that's okay," the man said, straightening up from his slouch and rubbing open his other eye. "You're right to be afraid. This is the second most dangerous landing in the world."

"What?"

"That's what they say, anyway." He was in his early twenties, good-looking, with thick features and long blonde hair. "Short runway."

"How short?

"Awful short. Godawful short."

"That's great, Lonnie," Mike said. "I might have been interested in that bit of information before I signed up for this adventure of yours."

"Ah, but if I'd told you before, Mikey, you wouldn't be here with me right now, would you? I know how you are about airplanes. But you know what they say, air travel is the safest —"

"Yeah yeah yeah."

" — the safest way to travel."

"I've heard all that before."

"Well, it's true."

The plane yawed and dipped in the unsettled ocean of air. Mike turned back to his book:

> *It was the perfect weapon, there beside me. It had cost me a mint to get my hands on it, but there it was now, finally, and it was perfect. Sleek and dark and dangerous, created with one end in mind – to be the ruin of men, men who were not careful and what man was?*

"What is that you're reading, anyway?" Lonnie said.

"Nothing."

God shouldered the plane aside again. Mike cursed.

> *… who were not careful and what man was?*
>
> *"So you got the plan down?" I said.*

"Yes, I have the plan," she answered. She lowered her voice and made with a stupid accent. "I got the plan down," she said. She was mocking me, but that was okay.

"That book won't save you." The man slid down again so that his shins pressed against the seat in front of him. He crossed his arms and closed his eyes.

Mike glanced out the window again. They were falling rapidly now, and he could see tiny white veins twisting their way up through the foliage below, worming along the ridges and into little clearings in which he could make out the roofs of small square buildings. As he watched, a black speck came out of one of the huts and started along a path, a tiny animated comma bounding back and forth in front of it.

Mike pressed his forehead against the window. What kind of beings were down there? Where were they going? Where was there for them to go in that mess of green?

Gadgets on the wing began grinding, and the plane banked sharply left and straightened out.

...but that was okay.

"And when you see I'm in position —"

"I've got it," she interrupted.

"— when I'm in position, you really turn it on."

"Turn it on, huh?" she said. "Really turn it on."

"Tinaco," a passenger across the aisle said. Mike leaned over to look around Lonnie, but through the window on the other side of the plane he could see nothing.

"It looks so peaceful from up here," the passenger said in Spanish.

Mike turned to his own window and bent down to try to catch a glimpse of the city over the edge of the wing, but could see only more mountainside with more *casas* sprayed carelessly about.

The plane shivered and slipped in the air.

> *"Turn it on, huh?" she said. "Really turn it on."*
> *"That's right," I said. "Turn it on."*
> *She was, after all, the perfect weapon.*

"Let me see that thing," Lonnie said, and he grabbed the book from Mike's hand. He surveyed the cover. "'Murder in Reverse', huh?" he said. "'A Trent York mystery'." He scoffed and began reading aloud:

> *She gave the rear-view mirror a twist and tipped her chin up to look at herself. She shook her head in disgust, though to me she looked good, real good.*
> *"I look like a twenty-dollar hooker," she said.*
> *"Oh no, honey. Don't sell yourself short," I didn't say.*

She glanced down at herself and tugged on the hem of the little red dress so that it covered nearly half her thighs.

I liked it better the other way, but I didn't say that, either.

"Hey, this ain't bad after all," Lonnie said. "A bit pornographic, but…"

Mike reached for the book, but Lonnie held it away from him. He read again, a bit louder now, for the edification of the other passengers:

She looked at me and I averted my eyes and I don't avert my eyes for much.

"It's just a job," I said, looking straight ahead at the brick wall of the tavern. At the top of the wall a neon blue sign flashed "Terminal Bar", except that the last two letters had gone dark.

"Some job." She opened the door, swung her gorgeous, naked legs out and lifted herself from the car, slamming the door shut, like she had something to be ticked off about.

"Easy there, girl" I said. "This is a —"

"A classic, yeah, so you told me."

"That's right. '69 GTO ragtop."

Mike made another try for the book, but Lonnie blocked him with his shoulder.

> *As she crossed in front of the car she shook her head. "Whatever," she said.*
>
> *"Just so long as you know," I whispered to myself.*
>
> *She walked towards the door of the tavern, and I could see she was trying to restrain it, but really – how could it be restrained?*
>
> *The perfect weapon.*

"All right, so it's not so much obscene as it is pornographically stupid."

The plane dipped again, glided for a moment in suspense, and shuddered hard, its left wing dipping sharply before the pilot straightened it out. Mike cursed again and reached for the seat back.

Lonnie laughed. "Don't worry," he said, flinging the book back down in Mike's lap. "The last time a plane crashed because of turbulence was in nineteen…nineteen something. And some people say even that wasn't really turbulence, but a column of ice."

"A column of ice?"

"That's right."

"In the air?"

"It happens."

Mike thought for a moment. "I don't believe you," he said.

"It doesn't matter if you believe me. The columns of ice don't care."

Mike scoffed. Still, though, if it could happen once…And what would that look like, anyway, a column of ice? He looked out the window but saw only more mountains, closer now - too close – and sprinkled with *casas*. He had a better view of the miserable structures now. They were tiny; there could not be space for more than a room or two inside any of them. Their doorways were open and their windows grilled over, without glass. Their flat rooftops were cluttered with debris - rainwater barrels, makeshift clotheslines, chicken pens, dogs curled up in the white sun.

In a moment they entered the bowl of the city. Now the shacks on the mountainsides had multiplied and were stacked on top of each other to the height of three or four stories. It looked to Mike as if a single push in the right spot would send the entire interlocking mess collapsing to the valley floor below in a nightmare avalanche of rock and shattered adobe, rough-cut unplaned boards, rusty corrugated sheet metal, scraps of blue tarp.

The streets were obscured by the overlapping tiers, so that no people could be seen other than two small stick figures kicking a ball on one of the rooftops, and it seemed to Mike as if the place had been abandoned and allowed to fall apart, with only these two children left to tell the story.

Mike checked to see if Lonnie was taking any of it in, but he was already back in oblivion, slouched down with his arms folded, his legs extended under the seat in front of him, his head tipped down so that his bangs hung over his eyes.

Something in the bottom of the plane banged and Mike jumped. A little grin appeared on Lonnie's face. Mike heard hydraulics working and felt the drag of the tires as they peeled down. The plane heaved to the side, made a sharp right turn and straightened out, so that Mike could finally see the city proper.

It was covered with rooftops and laced with busy streets, an occasional odd-shaped island of green wedged into the angles. Steeples poked up here and there, and in the center was a cluster of larger structures that must have been the downtown. The distance was sufficient to give it all the illusion of order and even of cleanliness, though a bluish cigarette haze hung over it all.

The plane accelerated. The city disappeared behind a row of cream-yellow apartment buildings stuck atop a ridge. A gravel pit shot by, and Mike glimpsed half a dozen workers idling around a loader and a dump truck, safe and smug on the ground. A modern-looking interchange with a sparse traffic of semis, SUV's, and taxis. Rows of condominiums that in their newness looked out of place.

"Let's get this damn thing down," Mike said.

Lonnie, his eyes still closed, smiled.

The plane dipped, rose, dipped again. The pilot corrected once, twice, three times, before finally slamming it down against the very front edge of the runway, as if having done with it once and for all. There were gasps. The plane bounced once high, once low, then stuck to the black surface. The engines reversed and the plane broke hard; the grinding hell of it filled the cabin. Mike was pressed against his seatbelt and the book slid off his lap and fell to the floor.

Finally their momentum slackened. The plane let go one more dying spasm before easing back and going limp.

The passengers, who had up until now maintained a pretense of detachment, began clapping as one. Lonnie joined in the applause with his typical dog-like enthusiasm, tinged with mockery.

"They do this every landing," he said, and he clapped one last time, after all the other clapping had died away, so as to get the final word. "I read about it."

The plane pivoted off the runway and Mike saw, barely a hundred feet further along, the chain-link fence that bounded the airport, and just beyond that, the edge of the plateau onto which the runway had been shoehorned. He imagined the hidden side of the cliff beyond, strewn with metal and plastic and bone, the remains of aircraft and passengers that hadn't been as lucky, whose pilots had made some simple error, suffered some momentary lapse, or just hit the wrong gust of wind at the wrong time.

"All right," Lonnie said. "Adventure one, complete - the landing."

Mike dug in the pocket of his cargo pants for his notebook. "I have the number of the hotel," he said. "We can phone from the terminal."

"Bah," Lonnie said. "We don't need a hotel."

"It's almost 3:30. Your uncle was pretty clear about it. We're supposed to stay in town if it's later than three." He flipped through the pages of the notepad.

"Give me that," Lonnie said and reached for it, but Mike turned away to block him.

"Don't let your life be guided by little pieces of paper, Mikey."

"Your uncle Marco doesn't strike me as the kind of guy to be messed with."

"Don't worry about him."

"I'm not worried. You're the one who needs that signature."

"I'll get it."

Mike leaned his head back. "Just imagine - if he won't go along with it, you'll actually have to get a job."

"No Mikey, that's you – you're the one who needs to find a job," Lonnie said. "Become a productive member of society. Stop all this reckless globetrotting."

"But just think —"

"No. I refuse to think. You're already thinking too much for the both of us."

"You'll have to eat. Pay rent. And your travelling days? Gone."

"I don't think so. Nothing will distract me from my goal. Man's got to have a goal, Mikey. Gives life meaning."

"Some goal."

"I travel the globe to meet people. I'm like an ambassador."

"You travel the globe to meet women."

"Women are people."

"And not just to meet them."

"To do what men and women do, Mikey, to do what they do." He elbowed Mike as one would one's accomplice. "I'm at seventeen now. That's not bad, is it, for a guy of my tender age. You know how many countries there are in the world?"

"Enlighten me," Mike said.

"Two hundred or so, depending on what you call a country. They even count this one, believe it or not."

"You're a font of fascinating geographical information."

"*Gracias. Gracias.* And I'm going to them all."

"If you get that signature, that is. If you get that signature, you're going to them all."

"A mere formality."

"We'll see what your uncle has to say about that. There's a reason he's making you come here."

Mike stashed the notepad back into his pocket and reached beneath his legs, fishing around until he found Trent York. He rose and from the overhead hold lifted out his backpack, stuffing him inside a side pocket. He hoisted the bag over his shoulder.

"Yup," he said as they waited for the door of the plane to open. "All that money, just outside your reach."

"Not for long, Mikey, not for long. Just a couple more years, and then no more of this chasing after monks in convents."

"It's a mission, not a convent. They call it a mission."

"Whatever."

"A convent is for nuns."

"Just behave yourself there. None of your highjacks. Remember - the signature, then hie we to the beach."

"Hie we to the beach, huh?"

"That's right, to the beach. How do you say 'beach' again?"

"*Playa. La playa.*"

"*La playa.* Hie we to *la playa*. First, the signature, and then —"

"It was a stroke of genius, though, wasn't it, not giving you control of that cash? A guy like you. Your parents were wise." But he immediately regretted bringing up the subject of his parents, and Lonnie turned away.

"We should really get that hotel room," Mike said.

Lonnie glanced back at him and shook his head, the smile once again on his face.

"You've just got to learn to trust me," he said.

CHAPTER 2

"DID YOU SEE THOSE houses?" Mike said.

"What houses?"

"From the plane."

"No. I wasn't at the window."

They were following the crowd through the airport, Mike trying to rush things along as much as possible without being unseemly. When they arrived at customs he started towards the end of the middle queue, which was shorter and where the people were speaking Spanish, but Lonnie put his hand on his shoulder and stopped him at the nearest line.

"Less people in that one," Mike said. "If you really still want to go all the way to Jocotenango ..."

"Of course we do. But there's always time for interesting people," Lonnie said and tipped his head up the near line, where, sure enough, interesting people stood, a group of them, twenty or so in number, wearing identical sun-yellow t-shirts. About half of them were in their mid to late teens, most of these, the ones of most interest, of the female variety. They faced each other in twos and threes and fours, talking and gesticulating as they waited, passports in hand.

Slanting across the backs of their shirts were blue screen-printed crosses, applied roughly as if by two slashes of a paintbrush. Beneath the cross were the words:

When I Was Hungry, You Gave
Me To Eat

And on the front left breast, more lettering:

Birch Creek Church of the Holy
Spirit
Cortes Mission Trip

"Oh sure, they're heretics, all right," Lonnie said, "but not unattractive ones."

The group had been seated at the front of the plane, the younger members filling the air with their laughter and enthusiasm; they did the same here in line. Between them and Mike and Lonnie, wearing the same t-shirt and standing as if on guard, was a chubby, nervous, freckled man, maybe fifty years old, with a khaki safari-hat on his head, its string hanging in a loop under his fleshy chin. He turned and nodded as Mike and Lonnie came up behind him, appearing relieved to have someone to speak with who was not a teen-aged girl.

"Quite a landing, huh?" he said.

"The pilots handled it well," Mike said nonchalantly.

"It's the second most dangerous landing in the world," the man said.

"So they say."

After an uncertain pause the man asked them where they were headed.

"A place called Jocotenango," Mike answered. "How about you?"

"Here in the city somewhere. On the outskirts, I guess. Pretty bad place, they say, but...Have you guys been here before? They say it's pretty bad." He looked up to them as if for comfort.

"Well..." Mike said, since this is what he said when he was at a loss for words.

"Yeah. Pretty bad, especially where we're going."

"Is that so?" Lonnie said. He was standing on his toes and looking past the safari man, to the interesting people beyond.

"Dirt, disease..." the man said.

"Hmm mmm."

"Malaria. Dengue. AIDS."

"Sounds to me like you need a new travel agent," Lonnie said. He clapped the man on the shoulder as if in sympathy, keeping his hand on him to hold him in place as he slipped around and sidled up to the two girls ahead of him in line.

The man watched him go past and turned to Mike.

"It's probably not as bad as it sounds," Mike said, because that appeared to be what the man wanted to hear.

"I don't know," the man said.

The girls were tanned and healthly, wearing sandals and short pants that hung almost to their knees, with wide cuffs and pockets on the thighs; their calves were lean and strong. Slung on their shoulders were backpacks stuffed full, with water bottles bracketed to them. Lonnie smiled at them and said something.

"Hunger, they say," the man continued. "Malnutrition."

"It is pretty poor here," Mike said.

The man nodded. "And stabbings, too."

Lonnie was standing now with his legs cocked, his arms folded, his head tipped slightly to the right. Mike had seen the pose before.

"Shootings."

Mike pointed a finger in the air. "Excuse me a moment," he said, and shifted around him to Lonnie's side.

"So that's where we're going," one of the girls was saying. "To the city dump."

"Landfill," the second girl corrected her.

"The city landfill. Have you heard about it? It's enormous…and it's…well, it's a landfill." She giggled.

"Val," the other said. Val glanced down at her feet.

"Why in the name of…" Lonnie said. "Why would you want to go there, Val?"

"Well, that's where they are."

"That's where who are?"

"You know, the poor," she said.

"The poorest of the poor," the second girl said curtly.

"That's where they live," Val said.

"Okay," Lonnie said, casting a cold eye on girl two before turning again to Val. "So they're poor. Understood. But why —"

"They live there," she said. "Can you imagine? That's how they live, by scavenging."

"Picking," girl two said.

"Picking, right. They call it 'picking'. They're 'pickers'," she said. Here she made a motion like picking something out of a pile, and giggled.

"Physical abuse. Violence," the man said from behind them.

"Anyway, that's what they do, they dig stuff out of the garbage," Val said.

"What kind of stuff?" Lonnie said, leaning in towards her, as if interested.

Val looked up again with her open expression. "Anything. Anything they might be able to eat or sell. Bottles, cans…"

"They eat cans?"

"No. They sell them. And old pieces of cardboard, whatever. Stuff you wouldn't even…and whole families do it, little kids even. They sell the stuff for nothing, for pennies."

"*Centavos*," girl two said. She had her arms crossed tightly in front of her and directed her words exclusively to her friend, as if desiring only to ensure accuracy and completeness, as if Lonnie and Mike were not there at all.

"*Centavos*. So they can eat. And they live right there, right by the garbage piles."

"On them." Girl two again.

"*On* them?" Lonnie said. "You mean, on top of them?"

"Yeah, right on them. Right there in the middle of them. And they dig caves in the…in the stuff, and they live in them."

"I see," Lonnie said, in a manner that a young girl might take as concerned.

Val nodded and smiled at him.

"Alcoholism," said the man behind them. "Drugs. Lots of drugs."

"'Pickers'," Val said again, as if to herself, smiling wanly and glancing at girl two.

"We're building a church there," girl two said, looking over her friend's shoulder at the wall.

"That's awesome," Lonnie said.

"Parasites. Especially there, where we're going."

18

"I don't know, we just felt called to come here and help," Val said with a shrug. "We know we can't save the world, but —"

"But we can give them a little joy they wouldn't otherwise have," girl two said, as if repeating something she'd been assigned to remember.

"That's right. We can give them a little joy." Val glanced at her friend before continuing. "Just think – if we can save just one of them…"

"Save them from what?" Lonnie said.

Val looked at girl two again, then back at Lonnie. "You know. Save them."

"That's really nice," Mike said. "That's admirable."

"Admirable," Lonnie said.

"Are you on a mission, too?" Val asked.

"Oh, you could say we're on a mission," Lonnie said.

"Actually, we're just here for a visit," Mike said. "But some day, maybe," he thought it polite to add. "It would be a good thing to do."

"An admirable thing to do," Lonnie added.

"Well, maybe you could come with us."

"Val!" girl two said.

"No, no thank you," Mike said. "That's a generous offer, but we're all set."

"Or maybe next year."

"Write that down, Mike," Lonnie said. "For next year. The Birch Creek Church of… what is it again?"

He leaned in towards the girl's breast as if to see the lettering better. She stuck her chest out innocently.

"The Holy Spirit," she said.

"Nice," Lonnie said.

Girl two wrinkled her brow.

"Where are you guys going?" Val said.

"We have a place rented up north."

"Oh really? Where?"

"On the beach," Lonnie said. "The *playa*. But first we're going to see my uncle in some town named Joke, or Joco, or —"

"Jocotenango," Mike said. For some reason, he had wanted to mention neither the beach where they were going for the last seven days of their trip nor the city where they were to spend their first two or three, nor with whom they were going to be staying.

"Joco," Lonnie said. He dipped his chin and lowered his voice. "He's a monk, my uncle is, and he owes me money." In an even more secretive voice he continued, "We're Catholic."

"Oh," Val said.

"It's okay, though," Lonnie said. "We don't actually go to church or anything."

Val looked tentatively over to her friend to see if a Catholic was okay, as long as it didn't go to church. The girl said nothing in return, but simply stared blankly back at her.

"But thanks for the offer, anyway, Val," Lonnie said. "I'm pretty sure we're called to do something else, though."

"Well, that's the important thing, anyway; to know what you're called to do."

"*Exacto.*"

"*Exacto?*" Mike said.

Lonnie bowed his head and made a quick, sloppy sign of the cross in the air in front of him.

"Oh, we don't do that," Val said.

"You don't do what?"

"That sign thing…with your hands."

"Well why the hell…why on earth not?" Lonnie said. "What do you do, then?"

The girl shrugged.

"Come on, Val," said the second girl, and she motioned with her head to indicate that it was time now that they move forward and close the gap that had opened between them and the next pair of healthy, tan girls ahead of them in line, and widen the one between themselves and the two intruders.

Val turned back to Lonnie. "Well, maybe someday, then," she said, and followed her friend forward.

Mike grabbed Lonnie's shoulder to hold him back. "Geez, Lon," he said. "Don't you ever turn it off?"

"Don't you ever turn it on?"

"Maybe you could at least wait until we're out of the airport?"

"All right, all right. I just want to know why they don't…," Lonnie said, tracing another lazy cross in the air.

A soft voice cleared itself behind them. Mike apologized and stepped aside. The man in the safari hat passed, whispering, as if to himself, "Parasites," and took up his position behind the two girls.

* * *

Mike checked his watch frequently as the customs line whittled itself away. Finally, the man in front of them was called forward to one of the kiosks, where a small, serious, well-groomed clerk waited.

"Hey, Livingstone," Lonnie called after him. He pointed an imaginary pistol at him and pulled the trigger, making a click with his tongue. "You watch yourself out there," he said.

The man hesitated for a moment, as if considering a dash for it, back out to the plane, but finally he nodded at Lonnie with a resigned expression, pivoted, and started forward towards the kiosk.

CHAPTER 3

THE AIRPORT SEEMED LIKE occupied territory, with police stationed everywhere. They strolled about in pairs or stood guard in front of closed doors, fit, trim, well-groomed and rigid, decked out in crisp uniforms of dark blue and stiff baseball caps of the same color, black rifles pinned diagonally across their chests. All of them, men and women alike, wore identical expressions - attentive, serious, unapproachable. Lonnie dubbed them "Watchers", and with a nod of the head he pointed them out to Mike as they moved through the crowd toward the front of the terminal.

They came to a stand with a rack of newspapers on the counter, tended by a young woman in a neon blue and white nylon soccer shirt. She smiled sweetly at them as they approached.

"Which one do you recommend?" Mike asked her in Spanish, pointing at the papers.

She leaned over the counter to see their front pages. "This one is to the left," and she pointed to the top paper, which had a full-color picture of a limp female body sprawling face down on the edge of a sidewalk. "And this one is to the right," and she indicated the middle paper, featuring a corpse dumped in a riverbed, hands bound behind it. There didn't seem much to pick between them, mayhem in the country of Cortes apparently having no political preference.

"Which side are you on?" Mike said.

The woman smiled. "And that one is sports," she said, pointing at the bottom paper, which featured no violence at all, only a normal photo, a photo of a normal-looking soccer game, as if it did not know the country from which it originated.

Mike picked out the one with the liberal violence, for no particular reason, and to prolong his time with the woman, he leaned over and peered through the glass-covered counter to the shelves below, littered with a thin stock of traveler's stuff - candy, chips, pain-killers.

"A pack of gum, please."

She stooped down and pointed.

"This one?" she said.

"*Sí*," Mike said. "*Eso.*"

She stood and their eyes met, and she looked down.

"American dollars?" he said.

"*Sí.*"

Mike handed her a five, and she gave him back a fistful of limp blue and red bills together with two tiny silver coins.

"Pretty girl," Lonnie said as they walked away.

"What's that?" Mike said. He was walking slowly now, holding the paper in front of him, examining it.

"I saw you eyeballing her," Lonnie said.

The woman was crumpled up oddly, as only the violently dead can be, her feet pigeon-toed, her legs stretched out behind her, one arm folded awkwardly under her chest. Her head was twisted sharply away from the camera, and black tentacles of hair reached out from it as if to slither away. Something dark ran from beneath her body, spilling down the curb into a puddle on the street below - more liquid than Mike thought a body could possibly hold.

"What was that?" Mike said.

He flipped the paper over. On the bottom fold, more trouble: a Watcher in the middle of a field, his face masked, bending over two bulging plastic garbage bags, pointing a flashlight at them.

"I said I saw you sizing up that girl," Lonnie repeated. "I told you they'd be pretty here." He leaned towards Mike to glance at the paper. "What's all this unpleasantness about?" he said.

"I don't know. Drugs, probably. Lots of drugs in this country."

"What does that word mean?"

"*Descuartizado*? That means chopped up, I guess."

"Yeah, I guess."

"I think we better get that hotel room."

"Nonsense."

* * *

The bus station was at the far corner of the terminal. There were two pairs of benches facing each other; scattered about them were a couple dozen folks, sitting motionless, staring silently and blankly down at each other's feet. The only exception to the mood of stunned patience came from two nuns in nut-brown habits who sat in the middle pair of benches, talking, laughing, and glancing about, as if they were on their first trip outside the cloister.

Lonnie made for the benches as Mike went to the ticket counter, a booth set into the far wall with a small Plexiglas window separating the supplicants from the vendor within - a huge *hombre* wedged into his chair. Mike asked when the next bus to Jocotenango was scheduled.

"Four-thirty," the man said. His breath was wheezy and sticky.

"Then how long to get there?"

The man forced in another breath. "Almost two hours," he said. He pushed the air out.

Mike cursed and turned toward the benches. Lonnie had set himself down on one of them, directly opposite a woman with dark skin and black kinked hair. He was talking across the gap and the woman seemed to understand him, which was not good. Mike hurried over and sat next to him.

"What's it like in Belize?" Lonnie was asking her.

"Belize beautiful," she said in English. Across her lap lay a baby, asleep, a pacifier in his mouth. He was a year old at most and had his mother's black skin.

"You speak English," Mike said.

She nodded. "Where you go?" she said.

"Us? Jocotenango."

"Now?" She looked at her watch.

"Right now," Lonnie said.

"His uncle lives there. We're going to stop by, just for a couple days," Mike said. He wondered why he seemed to be apologizing for it. "Then we're going to *Las Palmas*, to the beaches," Mike said.

"The *playa*," Lonnie said.

"We're going to spend a week there."

"Mmm hmm," the lady said. "But must be very care here nighttime, you know, when dark."

"Got that, Mikey? Put that in that little notebook of yours – be care nighttime. But why? Why be so care?"

"Gangs here bad. In Belize, where I be, they play to be gangs. They rob, yes, and hit on your head. But here, kill you. Like that. They don't care nothing."

"They don't care nothing, huh? Write that down, Mikey."

"They hire someone, kid, maybe fifty dollar. Kill you. Like that." She snapped her fingers together. The little boy in her arms moaned and shifted his weight.

"Fifty bucks, huh?" Lonnie said.

"And not even *dolares*. They pay drugs."

"They pay them in drugs?"

"Little kids, *drogas*. So cost nothing to them."

"We should get that room," Mike said.

"Uh uh," Lonnie said without moving his eyes from the woman.

"*Los malos*," the woman repeated, shaking her head. "Their life mean so little to them, how much you think you life is?"

"Nothing." Lonnie elbowed Mike again. "You life nothing."

Mike took out his notebook and flipped its pages.

"Yeah, put that down," Lonnie said.

"I'm getting the number for the hotel."

"Don't worry about it. They always exaggerate these things," Lonnie said, again without shifting his eyes from the Belizean.

"No," the woman said. "No exaggerate. Everyone know. Ask all of them." She gestured with her free hand to indicate the entire waiting room and all the silent souls waiting there.

Mike looked around. No one made eye contact. All looked passive, almost robotic, as if disinviting, by their very aspects, any such question.

Through the large windows in the wall beyond the benches he could see an old bus idling at the curb. Above its windshield were the words "Tinaco – Valera", and beneath it, in fancy lettering, the words "Christ the King" in Spanish.

"Month ago, they go in bus and start shooting, women, kids, everything, just to send a message of something, I don't know. They crazy here."

Lonnie looked over at Mike again and gestured towards the notepad in his hand. "They crazy here," he said.

"So now have soldier on some buses, but he just be shot too, I think. Is crazy here. Is for that I say have care," the woman said.

"But we have to get to what's-its-name," Lonnie said.

"Jocotenango."

"I just tell you," the woman said with a shrug. Then, as if remembering an important point, she added, "They steal people, too."

"Steal people?"

"And say, 'money'," and she held out her hand, palm upward.

"They kidnap people?"

"*Sí*. Steal them. And if no pay…" She shook her head. "No more person. It crazy here."

Another bus lumbered up and pivoted into place alongside the first. It was blunt-nosed and massive, long and narrow. The words "Tinaco – Jocotenango" were painted along its top, and beneath it, "*Gracias a Nuestro Señor*". A decal of the Virgin Mary was pasted directly onto the glass, three quarters of the way up on the passenger side, so that for a moment it looked to Mike as if she were just another passenger on her way to catch the next flight out, having had her holy fill of Cortes and all its works.

About half the people who had been waiting on the benches rose as one and with surprising rapidity and determination rushed out the exit and bunched up at the door of the bus, leaving Mike and Lonnie behind. They stood and gathered their bags. Mike nodded at the lady from Belize. "Well…" he said.

She motioned him over and he went, torn between the pleasure of getting closer to such unbounded beauty and the fear of what else she might say.

She laid the tips of her fingers on his arm and instinctively he flexed.

"You big," she said, almost whispering. "Big guy. But someone say give money, give him – all you have. Even if think you can hit him, and beat him."

"That's how I was thinking of it, yeah," Mike said.

"Because it not for him worry. It for friend in seat behind, with gun. Understand?"

Mike nodded. He understood. He had the newspaper to help him understand.

He straightened up and nodded, smiling as if grateful for the small talk. He followed Lonnie towards the door.

As they waited to exit the building, Lonnie looked back. "I want," he said.

"You want everything," Mike said.

"She's beautiful."

Mike nodded. "And interesting."

"And beautiful."

"And interesting."

"How far is Belize?" Lonnie asked.

"We aren't going to Belize."

"Okay. All right. It's going to be a good trip, though, isn't it?"

As they exited the terminal, the heat enveloped them, thick and sweet. Lonnie took a big gulp and sighed. "I love this, Mikey," he said. "I love it. A little diesel-ly right here, but…It's going to be a good trip."

As they waited behind the people massed at the door of the bus, Lonnie pointed out a sticker on its side. It was the face of Christ. Beneath it was some lettering.

"What does that mean?"

"'Christ with us'," Mike said. "'Christ with us.'"

"Nice thought, ain't it? 'Christ with us.' Well, they're religious here, anyway - I'll give them that. Their buses, anyway. There was an Inquisition of the Buses here at one time, if I remember my history."

"Is that so?"

"Forced conversions of the native vehicles. Thumbscrews, the rack, the whole Roman shebang. Very few secular buses anymore."

Mike took a closer look at the sticker of the tortured man, his chin tilted up and his eyes raised, a streak of blood dribbling down his forehead from the gnarled crown of spikes on his head.

"Me, I'm like a conquistador myself," Lonnie said.

"Yeah. That's just what I was thinking."

"Well I am, Mikey, despite your sarcasm."

"All you do is go around to different countries and sleep with their women."

"That's what I said. Conquistador."

Mike was agitated by this conversation but was unsure how to object.

"Seventeen," Lonnie said, and he repeated it, as if relishing the number.

A man who seemed to be in charge approached them. "Safer inside," he said in Spanish.

"What's that he's saying?" Lonnie asked.

"We've got to get in."

At the top of the steps Mike paused. Most of the natives had hurried to their places and were already sitting, stiff and impassive, staring forward into space, as if they'd been there, in those exact positions, since the start of time.

Mike led the way down the narrow aisle, sizing up the situation with what he thought was great North American cunning. A couple of *los malos* were seated near the back – one of them young, thin and wiry, the other thick-set, his tattooed forearms crossed, staring ahead with something fierce in his eye. They both exuded the essence of not caring nothing, and Mike would have liked to have gotten behind them for the ride to Jocotenango, but there were no empty seats there.

No Watchers were to be found anywhere. No soldiers.

A woman shifted to a window seat to make room for him, and he smiled at her as he sat. Lonnie took the seat directly across the aisle, next to a teenage boy who was already sleeping, his head propped against the window.

CHAPTER 4

THE DRIVER WHEELED THE bus out of the airport grounds and onto a newly-paved four lane road. The traffic, made up of SUV's, taxis, buses, motorcycles, was thick and fast-moving. The walkways alongside the road, too, were alive. Schoolchildren in identical dark blue and white school uniforms sprang along, passing by old folks with sagging faces. In open doorways men in cowboy hats stood and watched without emotion as the traffic passed. Three cheerful nuns chatted as they walked.

In front of a bus stop a woman stood, straining her neck up the street with an anxious expression. She was tall, with a small waist and firm, square shoulders. Her hair was shoulder-cut, thick and wavy, and a hank of it hung over her right eye. She wore black heels, a tight black skirt that stopped just above her knees and a loose white long sleeve blouse with an oversize bow at the neck. She clutched a shiny black purse across her stomach. Five or six large rings adorned her fingers and from her ears large discs hung, bronzed and shiny like the skin of her legs. She was heavily made up, with bright red lips and thin, blade-like eyebrows, and it was good.

She glanced at him as if his stare was breaking her concentration.

"It is going to be a good trip," Mike said in English, and he looked over at Lonnie, but he was asleep again, slumped down with arms crossed and hair spilling over his eyes.

Mike turned to the woman at his side, who looked to be in her thirties. She ignored him at first, for a few seconds refusing to remove her eyes from the back of the head of the passenger in the seat ahead of her, before she finally looked over at him cautiously and smiled.

"*Hola*," he said.

"*Hola*," she answered.

They introduced themselves. Dunia was her name. She had on a uniform and he asked her about it. She had a job in the airport, cleaning. It was good work. Not too hard. Steady. Every day she took a bus in from her village an hour away. She had one child.

She took a wallet from her bag and flipped it open to a photograph. On the left was a large man with baggy eyes and a friendly, soft smile, on the right Dunia herself in a sun dress, a little younger, a little thinner, a little prettier. Between them a girl – maybe ten years old - looked out at him intently.

"That's Odalys," she said. "She's studying to be a doctor now."

"That's great."

"It's hard, though. Lots of money."

"She's very pretty."

"*Sí.*"

"Like her mother."

"Ahh," she growled, slapping him on the bicep. He flexed.

"And that's your husband?"

"*Sí*. He's a mechanic, and a good mechanic, a good man, but there's no work, in the whole country there's nothing. And he hated to see me work every day, when there was nothing for him. So he tried to get to the United States, but he didn't make it."

"Where is he now?"

"He's back with us."

Mike nodded and looked out the window. The newly-paved surface of the road contrasted with the old buildings abutting it - single and double story shops leaning against each other, with an occasional open lot holding a pyramid of used tires, a pile of rocks, or a smattering of cars in various stages of disrepair. A few of the yards were secured with iron fencing and loops of razor-wire, but most were open to the street. Some of the shops were colorfully painted – orange, blue, red, yellow – and some were the smooth dull gray of old unpainted concrete. The name of the shop or the type of business – *llanteria, carnicero, panaderia* - was scrolled across many of the walls, but graffiti was omnipresent – sloppily done political messages or careful gang-script - nonsense symbols or symbols whose meanings were known only to the initiated, but whose odd bending lines and sharp angles conveyed a demonic malice behind the strange beauty and the precision of execution.

The top floor of some of the buildings had balconies enclosed within plaster railings with lush plants atop them, overflowing with leaves and fronds, each a little oasis in the turmoil. Most of the balconies contained a hammock or a couple of vinyl chairs. In one a man had pulled up a couch and was slouched into it, his feet propped on the rail, his hands folded behind his head.

Dunia asked where Mike was going.

"*Las Palmas*," Mike said, and she looked at him questioningly.

"I know," Mike said. "Wrong direction. We have to go to Jocotenango first, for business." He felt awkward saying it; he was anything but a businessman, and he felt his lack of seriousness. "Just for a day or two," he said. "We have to get some papers signed - he does. My partner there. Lonnie."

He motioned towards the man, slumping over in his chair.

Dunia seemed to accept the explanation, but Mike continued anyway, in a hushed voice, as if confessing something that was weighing on him. "His uncle lives there, in Jocotenango. He has control of Lonnie's money, money he inherited from his parents. They died a long time ago. Car accident. When we were kids."

Mike remembered the day. The door to the third-grade classroom opening, a man with a solemn face entering and whispering to the teacher, the teacher growing serious and beckoning Lonnie. Lonnie rising from his desk and leaving with the man. The teacher announcing that there had been an accident.

Dunia nodded sympathetically.

"They had a lot of money – a lot of money - and Lonnie was so young and…and he was so Lonnie. So they put it in their will that his uncle looks after it all, until he's older - thirty." Mike said. "Every year, he gets some of it. Like an allowance. Except bigger."

Again, Dunia appeared satisfied with the explanation, but again Mike felt compelled to go on.

"He's a monk, Lonnie's uncle, or a brother – whatever they call them. Brother Marco. Every year he has to release the money. But this year he sent for Lonnie, to talk with him before he signs off. That's okay, though - Lonnie likes to travel. He has this goal to go to every country on the planet."

"How many countries are there?"

"Around two hundred."

"That's a lot of countries."

"Yeah, it is. From here he's going to Brazil."

"And you too?"

"Me? No, I can't afford that. I'm just along on this one for the ride. And I speak a little Spanish, so..."

"You speak it well."

"Thanks."

She leaned over to look past Mike, to Lonnie, still sleeping.

"I feel sorry for him," she said.

"Yeah."

He remembered his face as he glanced back at the class just before he disappeared through the doorway. A scared, hollow look, as if he already knew what had happened. He'd barely spoken a word about it since.

"How far away is Belize?" Mike asked.

Dunia shook her head.

The traffic came to a standstill, the two westbound lanes clogged with vehicles, their horns honking to no purpose. The two opposite lanes of traffic were still moving briskly. Beyond them Mike could see down the mouth of an intersecting road – rough and gravelly, sloping downhill for a couple of blocks before winding off to the right, skirting a weedy, trash-speckled hill. The gutters along the side of the road were littered with paper, too, and behind the gutters were the kinds of wretched *casas* he'd seen from the air - crumbling adobe, open windows, wooden plank doors loosely hung. The light down the road was brown, already turning, and in the gloom, on the corner halfway along the road, three boys stood. They looked to be twelve or thirteen years old. Two of them held plastic bags to their mouths.

Mike glanced behind him, towards *los malos*. They were both sleeping now, the thick one with his head tilted back, his mouth open, his bulging arms folded across his chest; even in sleep he was all defiance and aggression.

"We should have stayed in town," Mike said.

A tinny two-stroke motorcycle roared up from behind the bus. It shot through the gap between the lines of traffic and disappeared in the tangle of cars ahead. Its sound awoke Lonnie.

"They crazy here," he said, as if to himself. His closed his eyes again. "They don't care nothing."

CHAPTER 5

ANOTHER FIVE MINUTES PASSED before the bus could work itself free of the traffic. As if he too feared Marco and felt the time passing, the driver raced along the narrow lanes, the bus lilting from side to side as it negotiated the twists in the road. They passed through the ragged outskirts of the city and came to a broad treeless plain. Set off from the road to the left was a prison complex wrapped about with a double row of fencing topped with razor wire. Inside the fence were windowless brick buildings. Lights set on high tapering poles glared down on the empty prison yard, and at each corner was a square brick watch tower with large windows like smoked mirrors.

To the right was a coffee factory rolling gray smoke out of its stack, seeping the area in a rich smell of *cafe*. In the distance an outgrowth of *casas* had crept like fungus up a mountainside, with spores of it beginning to spread out at the edges. At its back was a rusty water tower, its tank marred with black graffiti.

The road began climbing, cutting a wide round turn so that the city was visible in the distance. Dunia pointed toward it.

Mike had to lean close to her to see out the window, and he could smell her body, moist and warm from the day's work.

"There," she said.

At the top of one of the mountains was a white sun-blasted statue of a man, thin and erect, gazing down into the city, his arms spread wide as if he'd just then flung the *casas* across it.

"*Jesu Cristo?*" Mike said.

"*Sí.*" She made the sign of the cross and kissed the back of her thumb.

So she's one of us, thought Mike.

After climbing through a forest of widely-spaced evergreens the way grew steeper and the landscape rockier. In places the road was sliced across the edge of the mountain, leaving a near-vertical rough-cut rock face on one side and on the other a void – the earth fallen away, the facing mountains visible far across the gap. The vehicles carried on with the same reckless speed.

They climbed for nearly half an hour, unevenly, with the driver using the occasional dips in the road to gain momentum for the next rise, letting the bus accelerate to speeds Mike thought wild and dangerous, though as far as he could see none of the other passengers were concerned. Lonnie slept through it all.

Between the steeps they passed pockets of jungle, with small settlements and single *casas* tucked back from the highway. Among the polished green palms Mike caught glimpses of beings like brown ghosts; men reclining in hammocks, women nursing babies, half-naked children running after each other.

A few men on old bikes peddled up the mountain. Twice Mike saw cars pulled over to the side, their drivers relieving themselves on the edge of the precipice, relaxed, seeming to enjoy the scenery.

They finally reached the apex of the mountain range and saw below them a plateau, deep and broad and partly in shadow, walled in on all sides by the blurry blue outlines of yet more mountains in the distance. Lights were already visible on the valley floor below, two saucers of them - a large one directly ahead, a smaller one to the left.

"It's beautiful," Mike said.

"My country is beautiful," Dunia said.

"I hope one of those is Jocotenango."

"There." She pointed to the large one. "Joco."

"Thank God," Mike said. "And that one?"

"Tamalito," she said. "But nobody goes to Tamalito."

"Then I won't, either," thought Mike.

The bus plunged towards the lights, clinging to the road as it scooped around the contours of the mountain, maintaining its speed regardless, so that the centrifugal force, it seemed, must send it tumbling off the side.

Mike was relieved when they finally reached the flats of the plateau and the bus slowed, turning onto a dirt siding at which a number of people waited. The driver winched the door open and a few people got up to exit. Mike glanced behind. *Los malos* gave no indication of budging.

The new passengers climbed into the bus and found their seats. The last one aboard was a blade-thin girl carrying a cardboard box that hung from a cord around her neck. She stood at the front of the bus as it started to move again, bracing herself against a support, staring down at her feet.

Once they were back on the highway she began to move down the aisle silently, darting her eyes left and right at the passengers.

Lonnie had awoken when the bus had stopped, and now he motioned to the girl as she approached. He held a single finger up and the girl took a bag from the box and gave it to him. The bag was of clear plastic and held a dozen or so plantain chips.

"*Diez*," she said without making eye contact.

"You got that change from the newspaper?" Lonnie asked Mike, who took out his wallet to pay the girl.

"And give her a tip, too. How do you say that in Spanish, 'tip'? How do you say that?"

"*Propina.*"

"*Propina.* Make sure you give her a *propina.* Sometimes you get a little cheap with those things." He winked at Mike and turned back to the girl. He pointed at a bottle of sauce nestled in among the bags of chips in her box and the girl handed it to him. Its label had peeled away, leaving only a patch of dirty white backing. The fluid inside looked thin and soupy, watered down with the Lord knew what. Clots of dark crust clung to the rim.

"You're crazy," Mike said.

"*Gracias*," Lonnie said. "But we all crazy here." He widened his eyes and smiled, pouring the sauce into the bag and handing the bottle back to the girl. He took a chip from the bag and held it up at Mike, as if gloating. A thin tentacle of the pinkish sauce slid down it. He put it in his mouth and closed his eyes, pretending to savor it.

They passed a tiny shack with walls of dirty blue tarp shredding at the edges and a corrugated metal roof held in place by rocks stacked in piles atop it. In a flap in the tarp a woman stood, holding a baby, with another sitting in the dirt at her feet, crying. The woman was looking to her right, to a little plot of ground on which a metal hopper stood. It brimmed with garbage, and trash bags were piled against it, many of them broken open and spilling their contents about the ground. Two children were standing on top of the bags, their hands on the edge of the hopper, watching a girl who was standing within it. She had a plastic bag slung over her shoulder and was bent over, digging at the garbage with a stick.

Dunia gave Mike the tiniest of broken-hearted smiles. "*Pobrecitas*," she said.

"You want some of these?" Lonnie held the bag out across the aisle.

"No. You really shouldn't be eating them, either."

"Why not?"

"They'll make you sick."

"Ahh. Who's the world traveler here, huh? Who's the conquistador? Conquistadors never get sick. Iron stomachs." He slapped his abdomen hard, twice, to prove it. "Anyway, it's just chips." He reached into the bag again and extracted another one, dribbling with *salsa*, and put it in his mouth.

The bus stopped at another siding at the entrance to a small town. Dunia rose and Mike stood to let her out. He was surprised when she stretched up to kiss him on the neck, and he watched as she walked to the front of the bus. He sat down and moved over to the window. She appeared outside, easing herself down the last step and then moving to a horse-drawn cart, in which sat the man from the photograph - heavier and a little slacker now, and now without legs – now a stump of a man.

Dunia climbed in beside him and kissed him on the cheek, just as she had Mike, only better. The man smiled back at her and flicked at the horse, and the cart started away. Mike watched for her to glance back at the bus, but she never did.

The chip-girl had exited, too, and now crossed the highway in front of the bus. She took her position on the opposite shoulder, where there was another siding. She looked up the highway, her expression unchanged.

Lonnie slid into the seat beside him.

"Check that out," Mike said. "She's going to catch the next bus back, try to sell some more of those things."

"Hmm mmm."

"She should be in school, for God's sake. I should have given her more money or something."

"You are a little cheap like that. But hey, the poor will always be with us, right? Just hopefully not so close." He held out the bag to Mike, who waved it away. "Relax, Mikey. Look, you could dish out your little *propinas* all day long in this place and it wouldn't change anything. And don't get pissed again."

"She can't be ten years old, Lon. And did you see that other little girl, the one in the garbage hopper?"

"The little picker, you mean? Yeah, I saw her. Come on, take one."

Mike shook his head. "She was probably looking for their next meal," he said. "I can't believe —"

"Sure you can. Of course you can. Did you see how many kids that woman had? They're baby machines, Mikey. If they didn't have so many damn kids, if they had a little self-restraint..." He put a chip into his mouth, and some of the liquid dripped from it onto his finger. He raised the finger to his lips to suck it off. "But don't worry," he said. "It'll be different in *Las Palmas*."

"Hie we to the beach, huh?"

"*Eso.*"

"*Eso?*"

"Yeah, Mike, *eso*. *Eso*. What, do you think you're the only one who can fling the Spanish around?" He took another chip from the bag and held it in the air, turning it around as if admiring the rivulet of sauce creeping down it. "It's coming along, ain't it, my *español*?"

"*Mi español.*"

"Whatever." Lonnie put the chip in his mouth and crunched it.

"I'm just saying, I feel sorry for her."

"Me, too," he said. "I do. I really do. But I don't know what you expected to see in this place. Of course there are kids living like that. Of course they're all poor. It's a poor country. There's nothing we can do about that."

"Some people do something about it."

"Really? Val, you mean? Val and that tightly-wrapped little friend of hers? The heretics? They're going to go build the Church of Whatever in the middle of a garbage dump. What good is that possibly going to do anyone?"

"They're trying."

"They're picking lice out of people's hair, for God's sake. That's all it amounts to. And a week from now, when they jet out of here – Val and Livingstone and the ice-queen, all of them - those people are going to crawl right back onto that garbage dump and those same lice are going to jump right back on them. Look, it's not that I like it. I just recognize it. Nothing they're doing is going to change anything. *Nada*. The same with my uncle."

"I admire your uncle."

"You don't know my uncle."

"I researched his order a little, the brothers. They do a lot of good."

"All right, maybe they do. I hope so. I hope they do good, because he's got a lot to make up for."

"What does that mean?"

Lonnie shook his head and held out the bag of chips again. "Come on. We can't only one of us get sick."

"What do you mean he has a lot to make up for?"

"I haven't told you much about the old uncle, have I?"

"Well, he was in the Army."

"Hmm mmm."

"In Vietnam."

"Yup."

"And after the war, he wandered around a little – in Asia, yeah? - and ended up here, a monk." Mike shook his head. "And oh yeah, he's the executor of your folk's estate, and so you have to suck up to him."

"He wasn't just in the Army, Mikey. He was a Ranger. You know what a Ranger is? It's like a Marine, only worse. They do the real dirty work. I could tell you some stories about him."

"Like what?"

Lonnie took another chip and crunched into it.

"Well, Rangers have this tendency to kill people," he said. "Their job tends to put them in situations where they wind up killing people."

"So Marco killed some people?"

"Not just killed them. I'd say, assassinated them. But don't tell him I said so."

"You sure about that?"

Lonnie shrugged.

"And now he's a monk?"

"And now he's a monk."

"And he controls your money."

"You keep bringing that up."

"And this year he's making you come all the way to this...place, before he signs off. I wonder why he's doing that."

Lonnie tried to laugh it off. "Maybe he's heard some wild rumors or something. You know how people talk. You haven't been talking, have you?"

Mike shook his head. "And I'm supposed to vouch for your character?" he said.

"No, no. Nothing like that. I mean, if you could put in a good word..."

"Well, we'll see exactly how things stand soon, won't we? In the unlikely event that the taxi is still waiting for us."

"It'll be there. If it isn't, we'll get a different one. They seem to be all over the place. And you have the address of the convent in your little notebook there, I would bet."

"It's a mission. A mission. And if there is no taxi?"

"We'll stay on the bus and it'll take us to a terminal, right? There's got to be a terminal. We'll catch a taxi to the convent there."

"And the terminal's probably downtown, and it'll be dark, and remember what your uncle said about downtown at dark."

"Yeah, I know what the uncle said. I know everything he said. How could I not? You keep repeating it. Now stop worrying. There'll be taxis."

"And it's not a convent."

* * *

There were taxis, two of them, waiting at the back of the first Jocotenango bus stop, another meager turnoff on the side of the highway.

"I hope one of those is ours," Mike said as he led Lonnie to the front of the bus, glancing quickly back at *los malos*, making sure they weren't following. The thick one looked back at him blankly, as if it just wasn't worth the time.

The two cabbies were leaning against the hoods of their vehicles, laughing. When he saw Mike and Lonnie, one of them, a round man with a toothpick in his mouth, called to them in English: "You go Brother Marco's, yes?"

"Yes. Who are you?"

"I Rodrigo," the man said. "Driver." He had deep crow's feet and lines across his forehead that added to the friendliness and eagerness of his appearance. "Luke send me," he said.

"Who's Luke?"

"Brother Luke."

"You mean Brother Marco?"

"Him, too."

"What do you think?" Mike asked Lonnie. "Do we go with him?"

Lonnie shrugged. "Either that, or downtown, in the dark."

"You very late," Rodrigo said. "I almost leave."

"Sorry about that," Mike said.

"For wait, charge more."

CHAPTER 6

THE TAXI WAS SCRATCHED and dented and leaned over to the passenger side, having hauled too many large people over too many lousy roads in its too-long life. Inside, it had torn vinyl seats and missing window cranks. A rosary hung from the rearview mirror, which itself dangled from a stem affixed to the windshield, cracked in two places. The passenger side door hung loosely on its hinges, and when Mike tried to close it behind him it thudded against the frame without clicking shut. He swung it open again and pulled it towards him with more force, banging it against the car, but again it failed to lock in.

Rodrigo winced. "Don't slam," he said. "Lift up."

Mike pressed upward on the inside frame of the window with his left palm and shut the door with his right.

"There go," Rodrigo said.

He drove back out onto the highway, up-shifting rapidly to get to speed. The vehicle rattled and swayed. Everything about it felt loose and sloppy and dangerous, and Mike, in the passenger seat, could see the absurd amount of play in the steering wheel.

"You from United States, yes?" Rodrigo asked Mike.

"Yes, we are. You know English?"

"*Sí.*"

"Pretty good, too."

"Yes. Very good." He was pleased at the complement. "I live in there one time. Four year. Virginia." He struggled with the pronunciation of Virginia.

They were moving at a good clip now, and Mike could feel every wrinkle in the road through the collapsed suspension. Still, they accelerated.

"Kind of fast," Mike said.

"*Sí,*" Rodrigo said, as if accepting another complement.

"Does this thing have brakes?"

He laughed but didn't answer.

"You from there? Virginia?" he said.

"No," Mike said. "Michigan."

"I two girls there."

"What's that?"

"Two girls there. Me."

"You have two girlfriends in Virginia?"

"Nah," he growled. "Two little girls."

"Daughters?"

"*Sí. Hijas.* One have three years. One have one."

"So what are you doing in Cortes?"

Rodrigo smirked. "I caught," he said, and smiled over at Mike. "Had two, maybe three drinks okay. And was drive a little fast one time, and caught. But some day, I again," he said. "Maybe you help?"

"What did you do in Virginia?"

"Construction."

"Did you like it there?"

"*Sí. Mucho.* Someday, go back. You help maybe."

They charged up to the bumper of a large, slow-moving truck, and Rodrigo swerved to the left, halfway into the other lane, though it seemed obvious that, with the traffic bearing down on them, there would not be room to pass. But the truck moved to the side and the oncoming vehicles squeezed calmly to the opposite shoulder, the lead car beeping at Rodrigo as he passed between. Rodrigo beeped back, as if to say *hola*.

From the backseat Lonnie laughed. "They don't care nothing," he said.

In another mile they turned off the highway onto a dirt road. It ran for a hundred yards through a weed field before entering the narrow tunnel of a *barrio*, where it deteriorated quickly, with deep gutters at its sides and kettle-sized holes in its surface. Rodrigo moved the taxi slowly along it. Street lights were on but they were weak and widely spaced, and between them long patches of gloom had settled, relieved by light from open doorways of *casas* along the sides, through which Mike strained to see whatever life might be on offer within. Here and there at the edge of the road small trash fires burned with sharp yellow light and rolling gray smoke. An emaciated sow snouted about in the gutter, a litter of half a dozen piglets scrabbling about beneath her, trying to latch on to the black teats dangling from her gut.

People sauntering down the middle of the road made way for them languidly, in no hurry, turning to look as they passed: children, young women with their arms crossed, couples not touching one another. They overtook two young men walking along with the lazy, rolling stride of *los malos*, sinewy arms swaying at their sides. One of them had removed his shirt; his torso was lean and wiry. He glanced with no seeming interest at the taxi.

"A little dangerous here in nighttime," Rodrigo said.

"And in daytime?" Lonnie said.

"Yes. Daytime too a little."

"Well, can't be any more dangerous than your driving, right?" Lonnie clapped him on the shoulder.

Rodrigo laughed and nodded.

They came up to a truck, moving more slowly in the same direction – an ancient industrial-class thing with a five-foot-high metal fence enclosing its bed. Inside the cage were people, children, thin strips of boys and girls crammed inside like cigarettes in a pack. In the headlights Mike could see them pressed against the chain-link at the back end of the truck, staring out towards him with tired eyes.

"What's that all about?" Mike asked Rodrigo.

"*Cafe.*"

"Coffee?"

"They pick it. Go back home now."

For two blocks they followed the truck, unable to pass, until it pulled aside, its right-side tires dipping into the gutter as it crunched to a stop. A man dropped from the cab and went to the back to unlock the cage. Rodrigo beeped and slowly maneuvered the taxi around it as the children began spilling out.

"Awfully young to be working like that, no?" Mike said.

Rodrigo shrugged.

In the taxi's headlights a pack of three emaciated dogs trudged across the road, their heads like skulls, the lines of their ribs showing.

After another six or seven long blocks the *barrio* began to spread out, with more trees and empty overgrown plots of land appearing between some of the casas - more places for *malos* to hide, more places to stash stolen *gringos*.

They seemed to be retreating more and more from what Mike now thought of as civilization – the highway three miles back, jammed with recklessly-driven, broken-down vehicles.

"Is it much longer?" Mike asked.

"No. Is close."

Mike looked back at Lonnie, who shrugged back at him.

Finally the road dipped down to cross a concrete bridge spanning a riverbed sunk in darkness below them. On the other side they climbed a short rise.

"There is," Rodrigo said.

Ahead to the left, illuminated by a string of recessed lights on its eaves, was a long two-story brick building, neat and clean, with rows of white-framed windows along its two floors. In the middle of the first floor was a pair of metal doors and above them a canopy in the shape of an "A" with a large white cross extending from its top, lit by spotlights on either side. Just below the peak was a sign:

Hermanos de le Esperanza
Misión de Jocotenango

A wrought-iron fence with tightly-spaced bars ran the length of the building. In front of the fence, bordering directly on the road, were two large maple trees with three concrete benches in a line beneath them.

Rodrigo brought the taxi to a standstill in front of a gate in the fence.

"*Ya!*" he said.

"*Ya!*" Lonnie said. "*Ya!* What does that mean Mikey?"

"It means already, as in, 'we're already here'."

"*Ya*!" Lonnie said again.

"What think? Nice, yes?"

"*Ya*!" Lonnie said.

They got out and Rodrigo opened the trunk. While Mike and Lonnie lifted their bags out, he walked over to the gate and pressed a button high up on the fence.

"Well, here we go," said Lonnie. "The great Uncle Marco. Let's hope he's not armed, huh? Anyway, better let me do the talking."

Mike had never seen Lonnie so nervous, though he had seen him in plenty of situations where he should have been. Letting him go ahead, Mike paused and looked around. The only people visible in the night were a handful of boys - *malos*, possible *malos* – standing under a streetlamp, far enough away to not pose any immediate threat.

Directly across the road was another line of dilapidated huts. Light glowed from their open doorways, and Mike could hear the weak crying of a baby coming from one of them.

Lonnie called him from the gate, but just as Mike was turning a small shadow appeared in one of the doorways. A little girl, leaning her shoulder against the door frame and picking at it with one hand. She was barefoot and had long scraggly hair. She was chewing on something and staring at him.

"*Hola, chica,*" he called out to her.

She turned her head to look into the house. "He called me '*chica*'," she said and turned back to him without answering.

"I said, *hola*," Mike said. "You can't say *hola*?"

"*Hola*," she finally said, loudly and clearly, as if to prove to this white stranger that she could, indeed, say *hola* when it suited her.

"How are you?" Mike called.

She looked inside the house again. To a question from within that he couldn't hear, she answered in a loud whisper, "*Gringo*," and turned back to him.

"What's your name?" he said.

She didn't respond.

Mike glanced back up the road at *los malos*, standing together under the streetlight, scheming.

"You can't tell me your name?"

The door to the mission unlatched and he looked over. A man had come out and was moving towards the fence. His head was shaven and he wore a long beard and a robe that hung to his ankles. He was of medium height but very strong-looking, stacked up like a weight-lifter, and he waddled a bit as he walked, as if slowed down and stiffened by musculature. He nodded to the visitors, leaned to the right, hiked up his robe to fish out a ring of keys from his pocket, opened the gate, and waited there.

Rodrigo returned to the taxi and Mike paid him and took a card from him with his name and number. "Use if need ride," he said, "and anything else. I do many things. And remember – you promise help me go back."

"I don't remember promising that, but yeah, okay."

As he started away Mike called out to the girl again. "What, is your name some big secret or something?" he said.

She didn't respond.

"Well, mine's a secret, too, then."

The body-builder had opened the gate now and Lonnie called to Mike.

"*Adios*, whoever you are," Mike said.

At the gate, the man in the robe held out his hand.

"Marco?" Mike said.

"No, Luke," he said. "Brother Luke." He squeezed Mike's hand and Mike pretended not to feel it.

The brother locked the gate behind them, and as he led them through the doors into a large atrium, Mike looked over his robe. It was old and faded, like an outworn carpet, and in a dozen places it had been patched with rectangles of different sizes and different shades of gray, roughly stitched into the fabric. It had a large hood hanging like a pouch down the back and baggy, flared sleeves that stopped at the elbows. A braided cord was wrapped around the waist to secure it, and hanging from the cord on his left hip was a large string of beads - a rosary, Mike supposed. From another time it all was, and it struck Mike as odd that anyone should wear such a thing now, in this enlightened age, and he wanted to ask Luke about it, but felt that it would be impolite and probably would embarrass him.

"Belkis," Luke said as they walked. "That little girl's name is Belkis."

The atrium was new-looking and clean, with freshly painted walls and tiled floors. To the left a stairway ascended into shadows, and straight ahead an open walkway led to whatever was at the back of the compound. Luke led them to the right, through open double doors into a well-lit dining room with six aluminum picnic tables. At the far end of the room was a counter that opened to a kitchen beyond. Four stools were pushed up to the counter. Luke had them sit and went into the kitchen, which was large and clean, with stainless steel surfaces and sinks and metal racks hung with stainless steel utensils. He poured three cups from a large coffee maker and set them down on the counter. Mike took a sip from one of them and grimaced.

"They drink it a little sweet here," Luke laughed. "You get used to it." He paused for a moment, looked them over, and leaned across the counter, suddenly serious. "You're late," he said.

"A little," Lonnie said.

"More than a little. You should have stayed in town."

"Yeah, we should have," Mike said.

"That's what Brother Marco told you, correct?"

"That's right," Mike said. "I apologize. We should have stayed there."

"It's different here. You have to be careful. No exceptions."

"They don't care nothing here, huh?" Lonnie said.

"What's that?" There was firmness, even a challenge, in Luke's voice now. Lonnie took no notice of it.

"Just something somebody told us. Yeah, we'll be more careful. Is he here?"

"Is who here?"

"Marco."

"No. Do you understand what I said? No exceptions."

Lonnie nodded. After a moment, Luke nodded back.

"Where is he?" Lonnie said.

"He was called away. He gets called away a lot. Probably be back tomorrow."

"Probably?"

"Yeah, probably."

"I hope so. He has to sign —"

"Probably tomorrow," Luke said, and he checked his watch. "Listen," he said. "I've got to run upstairs. Evening prayer. If you guys can hang here for fifteen minutes, I'll be back to show you your rooms."

Without waiting for a response, he came out from behind the counter and lilted his way to the door, his arms flared away from his sides by the pressure from his lats.

Once he was out of sight, Lonnie chuckled. "Quite a piece of work, huh?"

"Quiet, Lon."

"The Crusher. Brother Luke, Crusher Monk."

CHAPTER 7

MIKE LISTENED TO THE animal sounds that seemed to come directly from beneath the window in his back wall – clucking, crowing, rustling - and watched the light grow on the desktop beneath it. The room was simple and small. Besides the little desk there was a folding chair, a set of shelves, the bed in which he lay, a wastebasket and nothing more. In the corner was a tiny bathroom.

The roof was of corrugated metal laid across metal I-beams, and all but one of the walls was of rough but freshly-painted adobe. The front wall was of steel, the bottom half solid and painted matte black, the top half black mesh shuttered to the outside by a heavy brown curtain.

When he heard the ringing of a bell up front he swung his feet onto the floor, rose, and pulled on the clothes he'd taken off six hours earlier. He yanked the curtain away from the door, unlatched it, and exited. Standing on the tiled walkway – the *pasillo* – he stretched his arms and looked out at the little courtyard that separated the dormitory from the main building. It was clean and trim, with rich black dirt from which sprung neatly-spaced ferns and miniature palms, with a couple of fruit trees, too, in the mix; Mike could smell the citrus. Vines fingered their way up the bricks of the main building beyond the courtyard.

He moved across the *pasillo* and knocked on another of the six bedroom doors, the one at the corner of the building, covered, too, with curtains. There was no response. He banged on it harder, four times, and heard a grunt from within.

"I think it's breakfast time," he said through the curtain.

"You've got to be kidding me."

"I'm going up front."

"All right. Hang on."

In a moment the curtain parted, the door opened, and an unshaven, squinting Lonnie appeared, wearing shorts and an old t-shirt, with nothing on his feet, yawning, his hair disheveled. The two of them made their way along the covered walkway that bordered the courtyard, to the main building, and into the dining room.

At the counter Brother Luke sat beside two other monks, one short and well-built, the other tall and thin, both done up in the medieval code of the place - clean-shaven head, long beard, patched-together gray robe. They each had a plate of food and a coffee in front of them. In the kitchen, facing them from behind the counter, a woman leaned against the stove, her arms crossed, a dish towel hanging from her forearm. She glanced at the visitors a bit skeptically.

Brother Luke stood. "Our travelers - awake, finally," he said. He waved them forward.

"Finally?" Lonnie said. "What is it, like 3:00 AM?"

"After five already," Luke said. He nodded towards the tall brother, who looked to be in his mid-thirties. "This is Brother Greg," he said.

He turned his head twenty degrees and glanced at the newcomers through wire-rimmed glasses, mumbled something that might have been a type of greeting, and swiveled back to his meal.

"And this is Brother Joe, our newest member."

He sprang from his chair and stood before them, his hand thrust forward.

"*Hola*," he said. He shook hands firmly. "What do you think of this place? Cortes, I mean," he asked, and without waiting for an answer hurried on. "I'm still getting used to things myself."

"Well, I haven't seen much of it in the light yet," Mike said.

"There's so much need here, so much poverty. And danger, yeah. But there's so much...blessedness, too. You know what I mean? Like the very first week I was here, a man got stabbed, just a few blocks away, early in the morning, and they brought him here, to Brother Marco - that's what they do here, when there's trouble, they bring them here. And he and Brother Greg – he's a trained nurse - they carried the man into the clinic, and four people from the *barrio* followed him in."

"I'm waiting for the blessedness part," Lonnie said.

Luke looked at Lonnie in an unpleasant way, which Lonnie did not seem to notice.

"We figured they were all his family," Joe continued. "But one of them turned out to be the guy who stabbed him. He was crying, wailing. 'It's okay Paco,' the guy who got stabbed was saying, 'it's okay.' And he was holding a rosary in his hand,

Paco was. Can you believe it? And Brother Marco said to him, he said —"

"These guys must be kind of hungry," Luke said. "Let's let them eat, okay?"

Joe stopped in mid-sentence, looking about as if waiting for someone to give him some encouragement to continue his story, but no one did.

Luke smiled. "Come on and sit down," he said.

Mike sat next to Greg, who, without looking up from his food, said, "We're looking to moderate his enthusiasm."

The woman in the kitchen returned to the counter with two more plates, setting them in front of Mike and Lonnie.

"And this - this is Maria," Brother Luke said. "She does...well, she does everything." He switched to Spanish. "She's awesome," he said.

Maria leaned across the counter and snapped him on the shoulder with the dishcloth. She smiled at the two visitors, wiping her hands on her apron.

"Nice to meet you, Maria," Mike said, to show off his Spanish.

Mike and Lonnie began to eat. After a more or less polite moment Brother Greg pushed his plate away, bowed his head to Maria, folded his hands and closed his eyes for a moment before rising and drifting away from the counter.

"Brother Greg is our resident genius," Luke said. "And so of course you have to cut him some slack. He'll be better in a day or two, once he resolves whatever it is that's bugging him."

"I see," Lonnie said. "You guys eat awfully early."

Luke laughed. "Heck, we've already done morning prayer."

"Of course you have."

Brother Luke smiled at Mike and he smiled back, though in truth he, too, at the words "morning prayer", had felt the heaviness of all things religious.

"Come on," Luke said. "I'll give you the tour."

Besides the dining area, the first floor of the main building was given over to medical facilities, with a couple of examination rooms, a recovery room with two beds, and an immaculate operating room, done up in clinical white. Glass cabinets filled with well-organized supplies and medications lined one of its walls. From its ceiling a metal arm extended, bent at the elbow and wrist, with a large circular light at its end gazing down like the eyeball of a giant at an operating table below. The only non-white thing of any significance was a black wheelchair shunted off to the far corner.

A team of doctors – volunteers - flew in every couple of months, Luke explained, and offered procedures to the people of the *barrio*, fixing hernias, cataracts, cleft palates. "The docs like it here," he said. "They say they can just go about their work, help out some folks, and walk away without a bunch of lawyers stalking them. Between their visits we hold medical and dental clinics. Handle emergencies when we need to —"

"Like Paco," Lonnie said.

"Yeah, for example. Right now, we're having a little outbreak of typhoid fever, and Wednesday morning we're going to be giving out clean water, to try to fight it. We'll have a ton of people coming."

"We're leaving Wednesday," Lonnie said.

"Yeah, that's right," Luke said without taking his eyes off Mike. "*Las Palmas*, right?"

"What exactly is typhoid fever?" Mike asked.

"Typhoid is – well, it's one of the things we fight. We fight a lot of things."

Upstairs were the small, simple bedrooms of the brothers, and in the middle of the floor was a chapel, entered through a pair of heavy wooden doors with small stained-glass windows. Luke opened one of them, put a finger to his lips, and motioned Lonnie and Mike inside. As he entered he dipped his fingertips in a small pearl-colored shell of water attached to the wall and crossed himself.

"Excuse me a minute," he said softly, and he went to the back pew, genuflected, crossed himself again, entered the pew, and knelt.

"Mid-morning prayer, I suppose," Lonnie whispered to Mike. He made a sloppy sign of the cross in the air.

The chapel was dark, with dark wooden walls, thick brown carpeting and four rows of benches running up to a small elevated altar, dimly lit by a half-dozen candles at its sides. In the wall to the left, halfway up, was a door, short and narrow, not looking large enough for a person to pass through. Pinned to the front wall behind the candles was a crucifix with a life-sized statue of Christ in his final throes. His head, crowned with thorns, dropped limply to one side. His mouth hung open, gasping for air. His long skinny arms were stretched backwards and through his mud-colored skin his ribs showed. His side was split open, draining blood.

Mike averted his eyes, looking to a painting propped on a stand behind and to the side of the altar. It was of a woman, hooded, dark-skinned, standing with her hands folded serenely in front of her, looking down calmly to her right. She was clothed in a star-sprinkled blue cloak. A force field of some kind surrounded her, little rays emanating from her, as if she were radioactive.

He'd seen her before, on a decal on a bus windshield in Tinaco, on a little sticker on the dash of Rodrigo's taxi, and a year before, in Mexico, she had been everywhere.

Directly in front of her, in the first pew, a man sat motionless, his unkempt hair silver in the candle glow. He was praying, or meditating, or sleeping. He took no notice of them.

Mike did not know what to do, and was relieved when Luke stood, genuflected, applied the holy water to himself again, and led them out to the hallway.

"We're directly above the operating room here," he said. "When the doctors are working down there, we come up here and pray. Pretty cool, huh?"

"Who was that man?" Mike asked.

"That's Father Zeppi – Giuseppe - our padre. He spends a lot of his mornings in there. He's from Malta."

"He spends the whole morning in there?"

"Sometimes."

He turned as if to lead them to the stairs.

"How about that last door?" Mike asked.

"That's Brother Marco's library," Luke said.

"Can we see it?"

"Afraid not. No one's allowed in there," he said. "Only the man himself. And Brother Greg, of course. He has special dispensation."

"On account of being a genius," Lonnie said.

"That's right. He's probably in there right now, pondering something."

"And he'll be back tomorrow? Marco?" Lonnie asked. "I really need to see him before we go."

Luke shrugged.

They continued the tour, descending the steps and moving through the atrium and along the side of the courtyard, then past Lonnie's and Mike's rooms. Turning left at the far corner of the dorms they came to a brick building containing a pair of small classrooms. Across from this building were the animals that had kept Mike awake for half the night, in pens on the other side of a dirt yard. A pig, a couple goats, some rabbits, a dairy cow. Brother Joe was in the chicken pen, holding a bucket in one hand and tossing feed onto the ground with the other. A dozen hens danced about at his feet, pecking at the food and squabbling. From behind the mesh Joe looked across the yard at them, expectantly, as if poised to continue his Paco story, then glanced at Luke, scooped up another handful of seed and sprayed it over the chickens.

Behind the classrooms was a driveway, just wide enough for two vehicles, though only one was parked there, a small dusty red pick-up. The drive was covered by a tin roof and bordered with short retaining walls on either side, holding back small gardens of miniature palms. At the end of the drive, in the outer wall of the compound, were two large metal doors. Luke unlocked one of these and opened it. He led Lonnie and Mike outside.

A two-rut road ran the length of the mission, and on the other side of it was a soccer field, large, broad, mangy, with two rusty net-less goal frames at each end, leaning toward one another. Seven cows loitered about in the field, digging with their noses at the clipped brown grass growing in patches from the dirt surface. In the far corner of the field a man in a straw hat stood, leaning against a long pole he held out in front of him.

Beyond the field was a growth of trees, and then the outlines of the distant mountains, blue and hazy in the morning air. Suspended between, half a dozen large black birds drifted in the wind, the feathers of their wings spread out like overgrown fingers.

The soccer field was encircled by a chain-link fence, old and sagging in sections, the mesh sliced and bent forward here and there, with a high concrete curb in front of it. A girl, maybe twelve years old, sat on the curb holding a baby that looked half her size. When she saw the door open she rose and with the baby riding on her hip started towards them.

"*Hola*, Cynthia," Brother Luke called to her. She smiled wanly at him. He walked to her and dropped to one knee. Mike couldn't hear their words.

After a moment Luke stood and turned to them. "One minute," he said, and he began leading the girl down the road.

"Listen," Lonnie said once Luke had led the girl out of earshot. "We've got to find a way to get out of here before ten-o'clock-prayer, or ten-fifteen-prayer, or morning-almost-over-and-afternoon-hasn't-quite-started-prayer, or whatever-the-hell's-next-prayer – excuse me, whatever-the-heck's-next."

"What do you suppose is up with that little girl?" Mike said.

"Around here, could be anything."

"You don't suppose that could be her baby?"

"God, I hope not."

"Look at him. I told you they do good things here," Mike said.

"Yeah, but we don't know what they're talking about, do we? Maybe he's late with his child support. Ah, just joking, Mikey. They wouldn't have child support here, would they?" He laughed. "Now don't get pissed, and don't go all monkish on me. We're going to call our cabbie – what's his name? We'll have him take us to the main square – there's always a main square, right? It'll be lively there, I'm thinking. Or deadly. Or something. Anything but brunch prayer."

Brother Luke had led the girl about fifty feet along the side of the building. Now he said one last thing to her and she nodded her head emphatically and continued down the drive, the baby propped on her hip. He turned and came back.

"We have soccer games here with the local kids some days," he said as he opened the door. "You've got to keep an eye out for stuff the cows leave behind, but…"

"Is that little girl all right?" Mike said. "She looked scared."

"Her mother's pretty sick."

"Typhoid?"

Luke shrugged. "I'm going to grab Brother Greg, take a little walk and check it out."

Mike wanted to volunteer, to say he'd go along with them. But he did not know exactly what typhoid was, or how infectious it might be, or what might be the consequences of contracting it in such a place as this, and he hesitated.

"We're thinking about going downtown," Lonnie said.

"If that's all right," Mike said.

"Okay. You're big boys," Luke said. "Aren't you?"

CHAPTER 8

THE TAXI PASSED OVER the bridge and through the wooded rise, back into the bowels of the *barrio*.

The light of day did the place no favors. The *casas* stood stark and hollow, parched white, kilned by the sun, peeling and flaking. The doors and windows that had been points of light in the darkness were now black and empty. The gutters along the road were strewn with trash, and dirty gray smoke struggled up from piles of ash in the gutters, the remnants of the previous night's trash fires.

Yet, as if in defiance of it all, the place teemed with life. Women laughed and gossiped, waving their hands in the air to emphasize a point or to shoo away flies. Teens loitered at the corners, their shirts slung over their shoulders, their hands in their pockets, on the lookout for the next thing. Leathery old men sat under awnings, watching the day go by, and ancient bent women swept dirt from the dirt floors of their *casas* out onto their dirt yards. Two women walked down the street laughing, what looked like dish towels draped on their heads to protect them from the sun. A teenaged boy with a bad complexion, his polished black hair pomaded into a crest on the top of his head, bounced across the road atop an old bicycle, his girl sitting sidesaddle on the frame in front of him, laughing and turning back to smile at him, all youth and beauty on her side, all Cortes against her.

A hen burst from the bushes along the roadside, almost under their wheels, and Rodrigo broke hard to avoid running her over. She strained towards the far side of the road, her neck thrusting forward and recoiling with every panicked step, as if shooting bullets from her head. A motley rooster had after her at once, squawking and cursing. With three sharp flaps of his wings he shot in front of her and landed in her path, turning her and pecking her back to his gutter harem, jealous to ensure she escape neither him nor Jocotenango.

Lonnie laughed. "That's the stuff," he said. "That's us - that rooster's us when we're downtown."

"*Eso.*"

At a corner four *malos* faced each other in a small circle, passing around a hand-rolled smoke.

"Look at there," Lonnie said. "Right in the open. It's like Amsterdam, except, you know..." He turned his head to watch them out the back window. "I bet it would be easy to score some of that stuff."

Mike looked at Rodrigo, who was studiously ignoring them, and he turned back to Lonnie.

"A drug deal in Cortes maybe isn't your sharpest idea, Lon," he said.

"But it's an idea, Mikey. It's an idea. I imagine you could get just about anything around here. No one seems to mind. Cocaine probably runs through this place like typhoid."

"Yeah, so they say. On its way to the states."

THE CHILDREN OF EVE

"Bet it's cheap, then, right? Simple matter of supply and demand."

Rodrigo had seemed to be ignoring their talk, but now he took the toothpick from his mouth and said, "You drugs?"

"No," Mike said. "Me no drugs."

Lonnie scoffed.

"Good," Rodrigo said.

"What's typhoid fever?" Mike asked him.

He shook his head. "Bad," he said.

"Do you die from it?"

"Is possible."

"How do you catch it?"

"Just comes."

Lonnie laughed. "Like babies," he said. "Just comes."

Rodrigo laughed. "Smoke marijuana?" he said.

"Me?" Mike said. "No."

Lonnie scoffed.

"Good."

They took a right onto the highway, toward the city, and in another mile turned onto a one-way street lined with buildings – residences and businesses - all with the same dull, dusted-over look. People strolled along the raised walkways or stood chatting with shop owners, leaning back against the walls or standing in their doorways.

Within a few blocks the traffic thickened and slowed. Cars and motorcycles and delivery trucks were parked along the side, allowing just enough room for the taxi to squeeze through. There was no sight clearance at the corners and traffic signs were limited to an occasional instruction painted on the sides of buildings – "*Alto*" and "*Una Via*" - and even these were ignored, with right-of-way seemingly determined by the timing, length, count and volume of blasts from car horns.

Rodrigo maneuvered through the mess with what seemed to Mike consummate skill.

Scattered along the route, the human wreckage of Jocotenango - people with no legs or one arm, people struggling along on crutches, blind people sitting on the sidewalk, their backs against the buildings, empty cups in front of them. Ghost-people, shadow-people, all but wasted completely away, worn to the edge by want, by hunger, by alcohol, by drugs. By Cortes.

Looking like a pile of rags, an old lady squatted on the walkway with a sleeping child leaning against her side. Propped against her knees was a piece of cardboard with writing on it that Mike couldn't make out. As the taxi passed she looked directly at him, suffering, weariness, hopelessness in her eyes.

"*La plaza*," Rodrigo said. In front of them Mike could see the road T to an end at the edge of an open square crowded with people. They turned right at the T and stopped between the side of a massive church at the head of the plaza and, on the near side of the road, a brightly painted two-story hotel with large letters painted in exuberant cursive over the door, "*Segundo Cielo*".

"I pick you up here, four o'clock, like Brother Luke say. Is safe here daytime."

"Is it?"

"But be together all time. And four o'clock. No to be late."

"No to be late," Lonnie said. "Got it."

Another taxi had crept up behind them and now gave its horn a blast. Rodrigo glanced in his mirror and waved back merrily.

"If you want eat, is good restaurant on other side of church," he said.

Mike handed him some of the blue and red stuff.

"You be care," he said out the window, and pulled away.

CHAPTER 9

THE CATHEDRAL WAS SOFT yellow and had statues of stiff-looking saints tucked into arched nooks hewn into its façade. Its roofline was in the shape of a flattened bell and directly under its peak was another, larger niche with Christ Himself, *Jesu Cristo*, stiffly holding forth his pale yellow arms.

The doors of the church were ajar; within all looked black against the sun-lit yellow.

Lonnie started off.

"Hang on," Mike said. "I'm going to take a look inside first."

"Inside there?"

"Yeah, inside there."

The interior of the church was solemn, dark, cavernous. Candles glowed from sconces along the walls and from half a dozen dull golden stands at the front, partially illuminating an enormous altar that covered the arced front wall.

From somewhere came a cough, dry and muted in the thick air.

Mike walked slowly up the side aisle, trying to cushion the slap of his sandals against the tile. He stopped at a pillar halfway to the front and stood against it as if to hide himself. Lonnie came up beside him, removed his sunglasses and hung them from his collar, as part of being cool.

He made a lazy cross in the air in front of him.

The altar was all of gold and was outrageously ornate, as if growing of its own accord, malignantly, with no plan, no ultimate end in view, no way to stop itself. It had thick mantels running across it and twisting columns climbing up and down, with nooks from which more saints stared, and panels with blackened paintings of figures that could barely be discerned in the gloom. Somewhere in the middle of it, if Mike's memory served, must be a tabernacle housing the Real Presence, or something, but it was lost in the confusion and ruined splendor of the thing.

Beneath the altar, in the first three rows of pews, a group of twenty or so veiled women prayed. Their voices were muted, and Mike could not make out their words, but they, together with the lingering smell of incense, brought on a rush of memories. Midnight Mass in the old church at home. Holding a white candle in front of him, in its glow trying to balance the drop of melted wax that had accumulated atop it, so that it would not fall down the shaft to the white cuff below, while Fr. Kamiński – ancient, white-haired, sour-looking - strode the length of the place, swinging a lamp and making it click against a golden chain, the motion sending rolls of smoke into the air that rose up and lost themselves in a thin band of gray that hung over the parishioners. The old man dipping a cylinder into a silver bucket carried by an altar boy at his side, drawing it out and flicking it at the congregation. Himself standing in the pew, eyes closed, waiting in suspense for the drops to hit. The priest chanting and the congregation responding. Feeling terrified of

Satan, prowling about the earth in search of souls. Hating and fearing him, with all his might denouncing him and all his works.

"Look at all that wood, painted to look like gold," Lonnie said.

"So you're thinking that's all just wood, huh?"

"Probably not the best wood, either. Probably Cortes wood. If it was anything more valuable, it would have been stripped and carted off centuries ago, the day the people who actually built this thing left." He leaned in to whisper: "Because it sure as hell wasn't these folks."

The leader of the prayer group up front coughed again and mumbled something, and her choir responded and fell silent.

"Come on, let's get out of here," Lonnie said. "This place is creeping me out."

Mike paused, feeling that something more was required of him before exiting – a genuflection, a bow of the head, the sign of the cross – a proper one. But he wasn't sure of the protocol anymore, so he simply leaned his head down a fraction of an inch, in such a way that not even Lonnie, standing there at his side, would be likely to notice, and he turned and followed him down the aisle and out the doors.

"Okay then," Lonnie said as they paused at the top of the steps. "We've gotten that out of our systems. But tell me now," he said, spreading his arms out towards the plaza, as if in imitation of the Christ in the wall above him, "Where's your god in all this?"

The plaza boiled with life. Children ran back and forth across the stone floor. Pairs of women strolled under colorful, sun-lit parasols. Young couples sat on benches in the shade of trees planted in small green islands scattered about. Students in blue and white uniforms lugged backpacks on their shoulders. A priest squatted over a wreck of a being propped against a tree trunk, his hand raised in some desperate benediction. A man bent down to kiss the head of his daughter.

"I didn't think so," Lonnie said. "But don't despair, Mikey. *Hombe*. I know just how —"

"*Hombe*?"

"Yeah. *Hombe*. That's how the cool people here say *hombre*."

"And how the hell would you know that?"

"What I was saying was, I know how to compensate for the misery of man in a godless universe. Follow me." He started down the steps and toward a pavilion at the far end of the square. "I get the red one."

"You get the red what?"

"Follow."

A man sat on the top step of the pavilion, stroking a guitar and singing. A small crowd of people stood in front of him. As they approached, Mike spotted them, dressed brightly, one in a clingy red shirt, the other in blue, their jeans winched tight and their hair done up carefully in pony tails. Their long black heels pinned them to the stones like rebar, as if to fix their youth and beauty there forever.

The man was uncanny. The man was a conquistador.

Lonnie traced a shallow arc that offered a better perspective.

"There you go," he said. "Actually, the blue one ain't half bad, either, is she?" He stopped twenty-five feet from the crowd to mull the situation over, staring thoughtfully at the two women. "No, no, red," he said. "Definitely red. Now tell me, what's this guy singing about?"

The man's voice was gravelly and weak with age, and it struggled to stay on key.

"It's a love song," Mike answered. "Something about his heart."

"How do you say that in Spanish, 'heart'?"

"*Corazón*. All their songs have the word '*corazón*' in them. *Corazón*, and *paloma*."

"*Corazón*? *Corazón*. How about 'my *corazón*'? How would you say that?"

"*Mi corazón*."

"*Mi corazón*. And the other word?"

"*Paloma*'. It means…"

"*Paloma. Paloma. Corazón. Mi corazón*."

He started forward again, repeating the words quietly to himself. Acting as if he had no particular destination in mind, he landed nevertheless at the side of the two women. He cocked his legs, folded his arms, and tipped his head, gazing at the singer, who was moaning out his *corazón* song and working his guitar, picking out the bass notes with his long thin thumb and strumming the chords with the backs of his fingers.

The women glanced at Lonnie, looked at each other and laughed. They were nice, all right. And sure enough, the one in red was the prettier of the two, in that slightly drawn-out, hardened and overly-made-up way that Lonnie preferred, when he was on the road.

But she was not to be Mike's, and so he turned his attention to the other one there, the blue one. She was a little short and a little wide, but plenty good-looking, with a *corazón*-shaped face and soft, sleepy eyes. She glanced at Mike with a smile that was pretty and sweet but tinged with something, something sad and hard-bought and profound.

He liked her.

Lonnie turned his head a degree or two towards them without removing his eyes from the musician.

"*Corazón'*," he said, and he tapped his chest three times with the tips of his fingers. "My *corazón'*."

"*Mi corazón'*," Mike said.

"*Mi corazón'*."

The women laughed.

"*Paloma*," Lonnie said.

They looked confused at this, and Lonnie deftly retreated. "*Corazón*," he said again, and he tapped his chest again.

"*Habla español*," the red girl said.

"What's that she's saying, Mike?"

"They think you speak Spanish, God help them."

Lonnie laughed. The one in blue smiled at Mike again, and he turned and looked behind him, his eyes coming to rest on the yellow building, its black rectangular doorway like a portal into another world. He could see now a tree growing from its top, having taken root in some crevice where the masonry had started crumbling ten or fifteen or a thousand years ago. Under it was the yellow Christ, his arms stretched out towards Mike. A pigeon was perched on his right hand, cooing and snapping its head from side to side as if in astonishment at the scene below.

"What the hell's a *paloma* anyway?" Lonnie said.

"It's a dove. A pigeon."

"Why didn't you tell me that? Ask them if we can buy them a drink."

CHAPTER 10

A SHARPLY-DRESSED, WELL-GROOMED man with menus under his arm came to where they sat in the shade of an umbrella at one of the outdoor tables of the restaurant that Rodrigo had recommended. He was unsmiling, detached, professional, though Mike sensed something aloof and disapproving.

They ordered drinks and talked among themselves, Mike interpreting. The women were from Ciudad Tulilla - Tuli, they called it. By all appearances they attributed no great significance to that fact.

But Mike had read about Ciudad Tulilla and had seen the blood in the pages of the papers. The deadliest city in this deadliest of countries. Where women were killed with impunity and children couldn't go outside to play for fear of the gunfire. Where *los malos* ran amuck, murdering even the smallest, humblest of business-owners who refused to be extorted, refused to or simply couldn't pay the war tax the gangs demanded. Where gang members slaughtered each other for control of the drug-routes to *el Norte*, to his own county, to that giant maw that sucked up all the best and all the worst from places like Cortes.

He examined the faces of the two women to see if there might not be some sign of this tumult - in their eyes, maybe, or in worry lines they'd not quite been able to fill with their makeup. But with the red one all was youth, and joy, and the anticipation of more joy and everlasting youth, and the alcohol had even started to loosen some of the sadness off the blue one.

"You like it there, in Ciudad Tulilla?" Mike asked.

The blue one nodded.

"Lots of fun," the red one said. "Clubs...music...dancing..." She held her arms out, snapping her fingers and jiggling her shoulders. It was awesome to behold.

"You like dancing, huh?" Lonnie said. He tried to imitate her movements and they laughed together.

"Waiter!" Lonnie called towards the bar. "Four more."

"Easy there, Lon," Mike said. "Remember how it is with you and alcohol."

"Never mind, Mikey. I can handle my alcohol. Waiter!" he called again, and cursed. "How do you say 'waiter' in Spanish?" he asked. But the man had already appeared at the open front of the restaurant, moving towards them at just the right speed, indicating that he was not at all hurrying for this lout, nor was he going any slower for him, but was moving at exactly the standard velocity, the velocity to be used for everyone. Expressionless, he took Lonnie's order and went back inside the restaurant.

"So, what do you two do in Tulilla?" Mike asked.

"We play," the red one said.

"We work," the blue one said.

"Play," the red one insisted. And she started moving in her seat again.

"Yeah, she likes dancing all right," Lonnie said. "You bet she does. And horizontally, too? Does she dance horizontally? Ask her that, Mikey. Ask her if she'd like to dance in that hotel over there." He pointed towards the *Segundo Cielo* and shook his shoulders. "How do you say hotel?"

"*Hotel*," Mike said. "Pretty much the same."

The woman looked at Mike, laughter in her eyes, awaiting the translation of the question she already seemed to understand. Mike glanced at the blue one. She was still looking down at her drink, but then she, too, lifted her eyes and smiled at him, and she struck Mike now as infinitely sweet and gentle.

He directed the question to the red one. She answered.

"Really?" Mike said.

She nodded once, her eyes staring back at him, still laughing.

"What did she say?" Lonnie said.

"She says she'll dance for a hundred *pesos*."

"A hundred *pesos*? That won't be necessary. Or wait. They're thinking *we* should pay *them*? Are you kidding me?"

"She sees we have money."

"The hell with that. Tell them we have our principles. No, wait – don't tell her that. How much is a hundred *pesos*?"

"Nothing. It's nothing. It's like a tip."

"A *propina*?"

"Yeah, a *propina*." He turned to the blue one. "You too?" he said. She was staring at her feet and didn't respond.

"Well..." he said.

But she was so pretty, and so close, and so sweet, and a hundred *pesos* truly was nothing. A token of appreciation rather than a payment for services rendered. A *propina*.

"Don't be so damn cheap," he said to Lonnie in English.

The blue one put her lips on the straw of her drink, still looking down.

CHAPTER 11

"WELCOME TO THE *SEGUNDO CIELO*," the short, chubby man behind the counter said in stiff, labored English. He put his newspaper down and jumped off his stool. "Can I help you?"

"Yes, I believe you can," Lonnie said.

The paper lay on the counter to Mike's side, turned away from him, but he could make out the photograph on it – a muscular, clean-cut young man, his hands behind his back as if bound, staring at the camera, upside down. Two large masked black figures hung like bats on either side of him.

"We need a room," Lonnie said.

"Two rooms," Mike said.

"One room, two beds," Lonnie said. "Don't be shy, Mikey."

Mike reached out and slid the newspaper towards him, spinning it over so that he could read the headline: "Suspected Assassin of Youth Captured in Tinaco." The criminal, right side up now, stared directly back at him, hard and arrogant and handsome, utterly unrepentant. The batmen behind him sported black ski masks and bullet-proof vests with the word "*POLICIA*" in blood-red letters across their chests. One of them held a rifle up unnaturally, as if straining to ensure the weapon's prominence in the photograph, as a warning to the guilty man's fellow Assassins of Youth that they had best think twice before venturing to Tinaco to retrieve him.

"Okay," the clerk said. "One room. Two beds." He smiled at the women, standing there behind Mike and Lonnie.

"How many nights?" the clerk asked.

"Zero," Lonnie said.

"Don't mind him," Mike said to the clerk. "He's had two drinks already, so he's plastered. Just one night please."

The clerk smiled. "One nights," he said. "Or zero maybe. Hmm mmm."

As if carelessly Mike flipped the newspaper over to see its bottom half. "*Casa Loca* Discovered in Ciudad Tulilla" the headline read. Beneath the words were two more batmen, with their military guns and bullet-proof vests and letters stamped in red. They were standing stiff and upright, staring at the camera through slits in their black ski-masks, their lips swelling from the oval holes below. Behind them was a large rusting shipping container converted into a dwelling of sorts, and on the ground between them lay their prizes - two rows of five evil-looking rifles, a half dozen pistols and four grenades – he guessed they must have been grenades, anyway. In the foreground the trophy - a long black tube with two handles and a strap, flared out at the end – a bazooka, or a rocket launcher, or some such god-awful thing.

"What does that mean, '*casa loca*'?" Mike asked the clerk.

"Ahh," he said. "Tulilla," as if the word explained it all. He waved his hand in the air dismissively, and made another scratch in the register.

"One room, two beds, zero nights," he said, and he slid a key, chained to a little chunk of wood, across the counter. Lonnie picked it up and leaned over to see what Mike was looking at.

"Interesting," he said, and he pushed the paper away. "Never trust a place where it's the good guys that have to wear the ski-masks, huh? Come on."

Mike waited at the bottom of the steps as the others started up the dim, narrow staircase, watching with regret that womanly figure with the tight blue shirt, with the strip of exposed flesh between its hem and the top of the jeans, with the curve of the waist and the round hips swaying in rhythm to the steps, with the dull black shock of hair bobbing from side to side across her back.

He had hoped that it would not get as far as this, as far as him following them up the stairs of a hotel. But why would he have taken a trip with Lonnie if not exactly for this reason?

Halfway up the steps she stumbled and put one hand against the wall, her fingers splaying out against it. She glanced back at Mike with her other hand held limply to her mouth to cover her smile. Little blades of black hair hung sloppily over her gleaming eyes.

He bounded up the five steps to her, turned her so that her back was against the wall, put his hands on the plaster on either side of her and pressed himself against her. She gave a little fake shriek, turned her head away, and pretended to struggle. Lonnie and the red one watched and laughed from the darkness at the top of the stairs. Mike kissed her short but hard, and he looked up at them and laughed. With both hands he grabbed her by her waist and lifted her to the next step. She turned away and hurried up to the landing, Mike right behind her, burning.

At the top he turned her towards him again and pressed her to him. She slid her hands up his biceps. He flexed.

At the door of the bedroom Lonnie was fumbling with the lock.

"Come on," Mike said in English. "Let's go."

"Hang on."

"It's a lock and a key, Lon," he said. "It's just a lock and key." He turned to the girl. "What's your name again?" he said.

"I told you already."

"Yeah, but what is it anyway?"

"I told you."

"Is everyone's name here some big secret?" he said in English. "Do you remember my name?"

"*Sí.*"

"What is it?"

"Miguel."

"Okay, then." He switched to English again. "Come on," he said to Lonnie. "Break it down if it won't open."

"Just a second," Lonnie said, and he cursed.

"Knock the damn thing down, and we'll give the guy some of that worthless blue crap to fix it. He'll be happy to have it. Here," he said, and he took a step back and put his shoulder down, as if he would break it open.

"Man, Mikey. Hang on. It's a Cortes lock – you know that, right? It's not like it's going to work like a real lock."

Mike turned to the woman. She was looking at him uncertainly. He reached up and stroked her cheek. "It's okay," he said.

Finally, the door swung open. Lonnie bowed, stepped aside, and swept his arm inward.

"*Por favor, señoritas,*" he said in perfect Spanish, and for a moment Mike's doubts returned. But the blue one brushed her shoulder against him as she passed, smiling up at him and jabbing him gently in the stomach with her finger, and it was unfair.

He followed. Lonnie locked the door behind them.

The room was small and hot and, with the shades pulled down over the single window, dark like the dusk. There were two small beds next to each other, neatly made up, with a small table between. Against the opposite wall was a single chest-of-drawers. There was no other furniture.

"Don't turn that light on," Lonnie said. "This is perfect."

CHAPTER 12

MIKE LAY ON HIS back listening to the breathing of the woman pressed against his side, feeling her swell and contract. Her body was warm like a little oven, warm and brown, like bread from the oven.

Soft and quiet and gentle, she'd reminded him of what sweetness was, and he tried to put out of his mind the tawdriness of the situation, ignore the presence a couple feet away of two people who couldn't have a clue of what he was feeling.

From outside, muffled by the windows and the curtains, came the buzz of Latino life, proceeding as always; loud, jumpy salsa music playing from some shop close by, voices shouting, taxis honking, motorcycles roaring by. Somewhere far away a jackhammer chewed away at its enemy, the concrete. The bell of the church tolled once.

The woman shifted in her sleep and let out a light moan. Rustling came from the other bed, and then a woman's voice.

"What's that?" Mike heard Lonnie say. "What's she saying, partner?"

Mike asked her to repeat it.

"She wants to know how long we're going to be in town."

"Tell her we have to leave tomorrow."

"We have to leave soon," Mike said to her.

"When?" she said. Mike didn't answer. After a moment of silence, he asked the darkness, "What's a *casa loca?*"

"Where did you hear that?" she said.

"In the paper. They said they discovered a *casa loca*. In Tulilla. Your town."

"I don't know what that is," she said. "When are you leaving?"

"Soon," Mike said.

She shifted and raised herself up to sit on the edge of the bed. She was slim and tapered, with square, athletic shoulders. Mike watched as she swept her hair behind her so that it fell in a black mass down her naked back.

Lonnie reached out a hand to stroke the side of her arm. "Where do you think you're going?" he said.

She moaned. "We have to go. Lupe has to get home."

Lupe – that was what she called herself. He remembered now. Funny name, Lupe.

Mike glanced at her, tucked up under his arm. She slept on, her face slack, her mouth slightly open. He could hear her breath when she exhaled.

"What's the rush?" Mike said.

"Her kids. She needs to get back for them."

Lupe twitched. She moaned and turned over into him, sliding her warm, tacky skin against his, her stomach rubbing against his side, her breasts pressing against his ribs. He tried to ignore the pull of it.

"Hey," he said, and he jostled her.

She opened her eyes and moaned again, laying her hand on his chest, light and soft. She bent her knee, drawing her thigh up so the warm brown bulk of it ran up across the front of his legs, and he could feel the scratch of wiry hair against his hip.

"What time is it?" she asked.

"I don't know," Mike said.

"It's one o'clock," the other girl said. "I told him you have to go home to your kids."

She didn't reply.

"She has two of them," the red one said.

"Shh," Lupe said.

"Two boys."

"Shut up."

"Two," Mike said. "That's great. How old are they?"

In a quiet voice, she told him – six and two.

"And your husband?" he whispered.

She shivered her head no, staring away as if she could not be touched by it all, not by any of it. She said something, but Mike had ceased listening. He was thinking about what that must mean, raising two boys by herself in the city of crazy houses, of grenades and bazookas; he imagined her in three hours, getting home to them, opening the door to a little hut, to her own *casa loca*.

She turned over on to her back. In the gloom he could feel the sadness return to her. He reached over and took a shock of hair from her shoulder and twisted it in his fingers, then stroked her temple, and she smiled half-heartedly.

He bent his head down to her ear and whispered, "I know your name."

"No, you don't."

"Yes, I do."

"What is it then?"

He peeled the sheet off her and drew a figure on her stomach.

"What are you doing?" she laughed.

"That's an 'L'."

"An 'L'?"

"*Sí.*"

Slowly, he drew another letter, a little lower down.

"That's a 'U'," he said.

"U."

"Mmm hmm." He drew a 'P' further down yet, slowly and gently.

"P," she said.

"*Sí.*"

"Do the 'P' again."

"Hey, now. What's going on over there, Mikey?" Lonnie said.

"*Nada*," Mike said. He traced out an 'E', even further down.

"*Hombe*," Lonnie said. "Careful, there. You'll be needing another *propina*."

"Go to sleep," Mike said. He was done with Lonnie. Lonnie was dead to him. He and the red girl were no longer there. Mike would love this one beside him – with her shyness and her sweetness and her sadness. There were only the two of them in the room, only the two of them in all Cortes, in all the world.

"Hey, before we get going again," Lonnie said, "what do you say we swap?"

CHAPTER 13

"NOW THAT'S THE OLD Mikey. That's the Mikey I know. *Eso.*"

The raised walkway was scarcely wide enough for a single person to pass, and Mike followed three feet behind Lonnie as he glided along it, dropping down to the road to clear the way for oncoming foot traffic and leaping back onto it for another five steps before hopping down again. He kept looking back at Mike and smiling, as if not needing to see ahead of him.

"You were a thing in there, Mikey. That was no performance by a monk, I tell you."

For no reason he crossed the street, squeezing between the parked cars bunched together in a line along the road and then through the one-way stream of taxis and motorcycles pushing their way out of Jocotenango.

They came to an intersection at which a crowd waited, mustering up the collective nerve to cross the busy thoroughfare, wildebeests hesitating before an alligator river. Lonnie tapped his feet and cocked his head up and down the road like a *paloma*.

"I was wrong about you, man," he said without looking at Mike. "You were a superhero in there."

"Shut up, Lon."

"All right. All right. I'm just saying, you were a conquistador."

"And I don't like that trading stuff, either."

"Hey, I just wanted to put a little sin back into it, you know? You want to compare notes?"

"No."

He laughed.

"Okay, fair enough, no notes. No notes, no trades, no big deal." He clapped Mike on the shoulder. "Superman!"

They started across the street.

"You have any idea where we're going?" Mike said.

"Mr. BreakTheDamnDoorDown," Lonnie said.

They came to an old ragged man sitting with his back against a building, his legs stretched out across the walkway. Lonnie took some money from his wallet and stuffed it in the cup by the man's side. He stepped over his legs and looked back at Mike.

"There but for the grace of whoever, hey, Mikey?" he said.

He crossed the street at another random spot, halting between two cars and bowing as he let a woman pass in front of him.

"Those girls, hey Mikey, hey Mikey-boy? 'Muchachas' – that's the word, right?" He laughed. "You've got to love a language that has words like 'muchacha' and 'niño' in it, huh?"

"We don't have a lot of time left, Lon. We should probably start heading back pretty quick."

"And just think – that's only their *segundo cielo*." Lonnie clapped his hands together and rubbed them. "That makes eighteen," he said.

"You mean you're counting that one?"

"Am I counting it? Hell yes, I'm counting it."

"But you had to pay for it. I thought the rules were —"

"All the more reason it should count. Besides, it was just a *propina* - you said so yourself. No, that's eighteen. A solid eighteen."

"Eighteen with an asterisk."

"Nineteen, really, but..." he giggled. "I admit, it's not the country I'd have picked for number eighteen – more like two hundred, I'd say, but here we are. The Lord works in mysterious ways."

"Whatever you say, Lon. But we really should get back to the square."

"Soon, Mikey my boy. Mikey my *corazón*."

"*Mi corazón.*"

"*Eso.*"

A young couple came from the other direction, a strong, handsome man maneuvering a wheelbarrow through the street, a woman striding along at his side, both smiling as if having the time of their lives. Taped to the side of the wheelbarrow was a piece of cardboard with words in black marker, carefully written: "*Se Vende*" - "For Sale".

As they passed Mike could see the bottom of the wheelbarrow, covered with containers of brown eggs cooking in the sun.

"Did I ever show you the picture of Maraya, my Brazilian girl?" Lonnie said.

"Oh yeah, I believe I've seen it once or twice."

"She said she's going to treat me like —"

"— like you've never been treated before."

"That's right. But I won't go into the sordid details."

"Thank you."

"She said she has a real surprise for me, though, when I get there."

"I'm thinking she's probably a man."

"Now Mikey - don't be jealous. Here," he said. He stopped and turned to Mike, digging his wallet out of his back pocket and extracting the photo.

Though Lonnie had shown it to him a dozen times already, Mike couldn't resist looking. It showed the top half of a woman, maybe twenty years old - maybe - strong and healthy and tanned, standing in a slight 'S' posture. Her straight, shoulder-cut hair was messy and pushed to one side, as if she had been in the wind. One ear was exposed and a large silver disc dangled from it. She reached her hands above her head, flaring her elbows out, bunching her small round breasts so that they swelled above the cloth of her rainbow-colored string bikini top and stretching out her lean, naked torso, exposing at her flanks faint tracings of the ribcage beneath. A faint ventral line ran down the length of her abdomen to a little silver button plugged into her navel.

Painted tiny on her high cheek was the Brazilian flag, green with a blue circle inside a red diamond.

Maraya.

"And you call that a man, huh?" Lonnie said.

"That's his sister."

"Bah." He tucked the picture back into his wallet, put the wallet away, dropped from the walkway again, dodged around a light pole at its edge, jumped back up.

"Those *muchachas*, hey Mikey? They didn't care nothing, huh?" he said.

"We should get back."

"Plenty of time," Lonnie said. "We have to find some cigars. This is big cigar country, right? Except I'm not seeing any. Ask someone."

Mike approached a man standing in the doorway of a store.

"Five blocks," the man said, gesturing in the direction they'd been going. "Five or six. Then, a right, and then about two more blocks."

"Five or six?"

"*Sí.*"

"A right, and two more blocks?"

"*Sí.*"

"Two or three?"

"*Sí.*"

Mike peeked around him to the interior of the store.

"Is this your place?"

"*Sí.*"

"May I?" Mike said and entered.

From hooks all around the doorframe hats hung – straw cowboy hats, baseball hats, floppy women's hats. Beyond was a hoarder's den, with shelves and counters and the floor itself jammed full of cheap stuff - shoes and shirts, paper and pencils, toys, tools, cooking utensils, useless trinkets. From the ceiling beams hung backpacks and colorful piñatas.

Mike wedged himself around and examined the merchandise, working himself finally to a table shoved up against the back wall, holding a heap of small toys – cars, dolls, sheets of cartoon stickers, balls of assorted sizes.

"What do kids around here like?" he asked the owner, who had been following him about the store.

"Ahh," he answered, and he picked from the pile a palm-sized wooden top.

"*Trompo*," he said.

"*Trompo*, huh?" Mike took it from the man's hand. It was shaped like a tear and painted bright red, with bolts of blue lightening slashed onto its sides. Hammered into its bottom was a blunted nail, on which to spin. A string was wrapped loosely around it.

It was surprisingly heavy.

"How do you work it?" Mike said.

The man took it back from Mike, slipped the string off and began coiling it tightly around the wood, leaving a three-inch piece hanging. A little noose was tied at the end, and the man tried to stuff his chubby finger into it, but quickly gave up and handed it to Mike.

"Okay, I get it," Mike said. "And the kids here like these?"

"*Sí*. Very popular."

"Okay. Give me a couple of them. Girls play with these things?"

The man shook his head severely, as if such a thing were impossible, at least when there were other things to be sold. "Only boys," he said.

"Okay. Well, I'll take them anyway. What do the girls like?"

The man reached into the pile again, taking out a plastic package.

"Ah, jacks," Mike said, taking the package from the man. "What do you call them?"

"*Cantillos*."

"*Cantillos*. All right. I'll take the *cantillos*, too."

"I only have one of them," the man said with regret.

He gathered the things up and moved to the counter, where there was a cash box and a calculator. He started slowly punching numbers into the calculator.

"Anything else?" he said.

"No, that'll do it."

Lonnie's voice came from behind him. "What do you think?"

He was leaning in the doorway, one hand propped against the jamb. In his other fist he held half of some tortilla-wrapped thing; he was chewing open-mouthed on the other half. On his head was a Panama hat.

"Looks pretty sharp on me, doesn't it? I'm thinking Maraya will really dig this look."

"What are you eating?"

"I don't know," he said, looking the thing over as if for the first time. "It's good though. Girl outside was selling them. Bite?"

"No. I have too much to live for."

"Is that so?" He walked to the counter, took the hat off and set it down. "That, too," he said to the store owner, who restarted his calculations with a pleased look.

"What do we have here?" Lonnie said, and he squeezed his way behind the counter to a side wall, where a set of bongo drums hung from a hook.

"Oh yeah," he said. He stuffed the remainder of the tortilla in his mouth and reached for the drums, sunk down on a stool against the wall, placed them on his lap and began banging on them.

The storekeeper nodded at him. "*Bueno*," he said.

He smiled and with his mouth full said, "Get that, Mikey? *'Bueno'*. The man said *'Bueno'*. That doesn't need any interpretation." He swallowed and tipped his head to the man. "You like, huh? *Bueno?*"

"He just wants you to buy them," Mike said.

"So cynical, Mike. So young and so cynical. Don't you think it might be possible that the man just knows innate bongo talent when he hears it?" He rapped away on the thing as if punishing it. "I always knew I'd be good on these things. I'll take them," he said to the man.

"What the hell are you going to do with a set of bongos?" Mike said.

"Play them, of course. I've always wanted to play bongos."

"Since when?"

"Since always. Everyone's always wanted to play bongos."

Mike could not deny this. He glanced at the shop owner, who smiled back at him as if he were part of the conspiracy.

Mike paid the man, who followed them to the door, reluctant to surrender such valuable clients to the uncareful streets of Jocotenango.

"Five blocks that way?" Mike said once they were outside.

The man nodded. "Five or six."

"Is it safe?"

"*Sí*," he said. "But sometimes…" he began tentatively.

"But sometimes what?"

The man shook his head as if to banish the thought, as if, really, it was nothing, not even sometimes.

* * *

They arrived at the cigar shop, two blocks further along than the shopkeeper had said. They had not been good blocks, either, but Joco blocks, hot and close and dangerous-seeming, with sweaty throngs moving along them as if in some strange migration, where schoolgirls in bleached white uniforms walked among tattooed *malos* and emaciated drug addicts led the way for laughing nuns. The narrow walkways were obstructed by street vendors and beggars and others who simply seemed to have nowhere else to go. Unsmiling men with uniforms and shotguns stood guard in front of banks and clothing stores alike - Watchers. Taxis and motorcycles surged along from intersection to intersection, sounding their horns.

The shop was wedged between a miserable hardware store and a miserable shoe shop. Inside it was narrow and dark and miserable, with a couple of small counters containing a sparse collection of smokes. Lonnie picked out two each of three different brands. As he fished around in his wallet the man behind the counter eyed his stash. He pulled out a small wad of bills and held it up.

"Dollars okay?" he said.

The man nodded, and Lonnie handed them over to him. "And that's real money, there, bub," he said, smiling at Mike.

The man, understanding only the money, smiled and nodded and gathered it in. He started slowly writing numbers on a piece of paper.

"Ah hell - keep the change," Lonnie said. "*Propina.*"

The man nodded, beaming. Lonnie stuffed the cigars in the thigh pocket of his shorts. "That's why he was going so slow after all, right?"

They left the store and Lonnie glanced up and down the street, the Panama hat tilted on his head, the bongo drums slung over his shoulder like a slain game animal. Mike drew up alongside him. The sun was lowering and now shined directly down the tunnel of road from the direction of the church, as Mike figured it, and a dusty yellow haze had settled over the place, lending a magical quality to things - to the beaten-up buildings lining the road, to the balls of moss clinging to the sagging wires overhead, to the old woman stooping down to pick up something from the walkway and to the old man at her side, watching her.

There was beauty everywhere, Mike thought. Everywhere. No one was ever safe from it.

"Remember those girls, Mikey? Those *muchachas*? Those Tulis."

"It was half an hour ago, Lon."

"It was, wasn't it? You know, Mikey, that's my calling. That's what I've been called to do."

"What's that?"

He held his finger in the air. "I may not be able to save the world," he said, "but I can give some people a little joy they wouldn't otherwise have," and he let loose with that closed-mouth smile and that dimple wedged into his cheek and that damn gleam in his eye, and Mike loathed him.

"You were Superman in there, Mikey. Superman," he said. "All right then. Get us out of here."

They started off in the direction of the sun.

* * *

The way back looked only sporadically familiar, and Mike was becoming concerned. They passed the front of a building where four young men loitered. Mike ducked his head as they

THE CHILDREN OF EVE

passed and glanced inside, where he saw another dozen standing around four pool tables.

Lonnie smiled and tipped his hat to the *malos*. They glared back at him.

"These pool halls are where it's all happening," Lonnie said. "A guy could pick up a little happiness in one of these things."

Mike was relieved when he finally sighted the top of the church tower hanging over the buildings ahead. When they got to the square, Rodrigo was waiting at the agreed-upon spot, leaning against his taxi, toothpick in his mouth. As they approached he checked his watch and shook his head.

CHAPTER 14

IN THE BACKSEAT OF the cab Lonnie rapped on his bongos, beginning a simple pattern, letting it fizzle away, starting another.

"He not bad," Rodrigo said.

"No," Mike said. "He bad."

He monitored the hour as they made their way through the mess of the city and then the mess of the *barrio*, and was glad when they arrived at the mission just before 4:30 - right on time, nothing for anyone to complain about, nothing for Marco to find fault with. But despite his curiosity about the man, Mike felt himself hoping that he hadn't returned yet from wherever he might have rangered himself into.

He paid Rodrigo and they exited the cab. Lonnie moved directly towards the gate, swinging the drums at his side. Mike stopped there in the road, stretching his arms over his head and standing on his toes. Let bongo-man take the brunt of whatever might come.

It was already starting to darken, and in the gloom the street appeared deserted and inexpressibly lonely; tinny radio music from one of the *casas* across the way only deepened the melancholy. A military helicopter thumped its way overhead, a dull, hollow sound that, too, struck him as remote and sad.

He was relieved when Belkis appeared in the doorway of her *casa*.

"I know what your name is," he called to her.

"Uh uh."

"Yes, I do."

"What is it, then?"

"It's Belkis. Belkis."

She shook her head.

"How old are you, Belkis?"

"Nine."

"Me, too."

"Ahh," she growled. "And I'm not Belkis."

He stooped down, put his backpack on the ground, took the package of jacks from it, and held them in the air a moment. He tore the plastic cover apart and dumped the pieces onto the street – a red ball and ten metal *cantillos* of different colors.

She started to him, slowly at first, then more rapidly as she realized what he had. He picked up one of the jacks and tried to spin it on the hard dirt.

"No," she said, and she dropped to her haunches. "Like this." She picked up the ball and tossed it in front of her. As it dropped she took up one of the *cantillos* with the speed and precision of a chicken pecking up a seed. The ball bounced off the dirt and she turned her hand up and let it land in her palm.

"Two now," she said, and she flipped the ball in the air again, plucking up a pair of jacks this time. "Three," she said, and she picked up three more, as smoothly and effortlessly as she had the others. She put the jacks back on the ground.

"Now you," she said, and she handed the ball to Mike.

He tossed it in the air, picked up a jack, and caught it.

"There you go," he said, and tried to hand the ball and the jack back to her.

She shook her head. "Two now," she said.

"Come on, Mike," Lonnie called from the gate.

"Two, is it?" Mike said. He picked up one of the jacks – a green one - and moved it so that it was nearly on top of another.

Belkis wagged her finger at him and shook her head. "No no no," she said. "*Trampa*. You can't move them." She took the jack and moved it back to its original spot.

"But that's my lucky one," Mike said.

She shook her head once more, looking intently at Mike's hand, the one with the ball in it, as if suspicious of another *trampa*.

"Okay. Fine," Mike said in English. "But you might cut some slack to a beginner."

She looked at him and shrugged her shoulders.

"I really do know your name," he said in Spanish.

She shook her head.

He bounced the ball again, harder, to buy time, but it hit something uneven in the road and sprang to the side, bouncing to a stop fifteen feet away. Without budging, Mike frowned at it as Belkis laughed.

"So what do you think?" he said. "You want to keep these?"

Her eyes widened and she nodded hard.

"Okay, then. They're yours."

She gathered up the jacks and stuffed them in her pocket.

Lonnie called to him again. He started to pick up his backpack from the dirt, and Belkis pointed at it. One of the *trompos* within was visible.

"No no. *Trompos* are for boys, right?" Mike said.

"Girls, too."

"Okay. I believe you, though that's not what they told me. But only one gift at a time, right?"

She pursed her lips. "I had a brother," she said.

"You had a brother?" He was about to ask about the past tense, but caught himself.

"I have a picture of him."

"You do, huh? Maybe I can see it sometime."

"*Sí.*"

Brother Joe had opened the mission door now and was starting towards the gate to unlock it.

"Maybe tomorrow, okay? I have to go now."

She held out her hand. In her palm was the green *cantillo*.

He rubbed the top of her head, took the *cantillo* and put it in his pocket. She started running back to her *casa*, in the door of which her mother had appeared, holding a baby to her breast.

"All right," he called after her. "I can always use a little luck."

* * *

He got it: Marco had not returned. Brother Luke didn't join them for dinner either; he was sequestered, they said, in the chapel, fasting with Padre Zeppi. Fasting appeared a popular recreation in the place. Only Brother Greg and Brother Joe dined with them, the first ignoring them and the second making them wish he would.

"On New Year's Eve they shoot their pistols in the air," he said. "It's some kind of tradition. We try to tell them that once a bullet goes up, it has to come down, but…"

"But they know not what they do, hey, bro?" Lonnie said.

"And they make *pichingos* – that's like scarecrows, and they prop them up in chairs and stuff firecrackers in their pockets – bottle rockets and stuff - and at midnight they light them on fire. There's one on every block, pretty much. It's wild. But the rockets go wherever they want to, of course, and people get hurt – burned - and Brother Greg has to patch him up."

"I want to help you guys tomorrow," Mike said. "With the water. I can help pour or something, right? Something nice and low-skill."

Lonnie frowned over at him.

"That'd be great," Joe said.

Greg adjusted his glasses.

* * *

After dinner Mike showered quickly and carried his newspaper, together with Trent York, Private Eye, out to the *pasillo*, pulling out one of the vinyl chairs placed against the dormitory wall and moving it under an unshielded bulb that hung from the awning. He sat, glanced over the paper, dropped it on the tile, and opened the book:

> *She looked at me and I averted my eyes and I don't avert my eyes for much.*
>
> *"It's just a job," I said, looking straight ahead at the brick wall of the tavern.*

But the words failed to distract him from the thoughts of the afternoon. He peeled open one of the cigars Lonnie had given him and lit it.

> *...looking straight ahead at the brick wall of the tavern. At the top of the wall a neon blue sign flashed "Terminal Bar", except that the last two letters had gone dark.*
>
> *"Some job." She opened the door, swung her naked legs out and lifted herself from the car, slamming the door shut...*

Finally, the man himself came from his bedroom door, his hair wet and pasted to his brow, his new hat riding atop his head, his sunglasses on - even though it was already turning dark. He, too, had a cigar in his hand, and had already burned his way through half of it. Without a word he pulled up one of the vinyl chairs, set it beside Mike, and sat, removing his glasses and hanging them from the front of his shirt.

"What do you think of that cigar?" he said.

"A little dry, but it'll do."

"Agreed."

They sat puffing for a moment, Lonnie tapping his feet and glancing about. He slapped at his thigh and cursed. "Damn mosquitoes," he said.

"You've been taking your malaria pills, right?"

"Ahh, malaria," he said disdainfully. "Damn malaria."

"Malaria's nothing to mess with."

"Ahh."

He stood, walked down the *pasillo* twenty feet, stopped, removed his hat, brushed his hair back from his forehead and put it back on. He turned and walked back to Mike.

"Those girls, hey Mikey?" he said, though it lacked the conviction of the afternoon.

"Yeah," Mike said. "Those girls." He looked down at the book again.

"Those girls."

Lonnie passed behind his chair, walked another twenty feet the other way, and stopped, frowning out over the courtyard.

"They didn't care nothing."

"No, they didn't."

"Nothing." He slapped at his arm and cursed. "But you know, they lacked the true *barrio* touch, didn't they?"

"What do you mean?"

"The essence of the whole thing I mean. They didn't really have it. They lacked…authenticity."

"Authenticity?"

"Yeah, authenticity. I mean, I like to really experience the culture of the places I go. I'm a multiculturist, really, maybe the only real one. And those girls, they weren't really *of* this place, you know what I mean? They were city girls, like any other city girls anywhere, really."

Mike thought of the blue one again – she had never really left his mind. Her sad, soft, heart-shaped face. The way she'd turned to him on the stairs and hidden her smile with the tips of her fingers, with her hair hanging in strands over her pretty black drooping eyes.

"And of course, they were whores."

"I wouldn't say that."

THE CHILDREN OF EVE

Lonnie shrugged. "Well, opportunists, then. But me, I want to submerge myself in the real guts of this place, you know what I mean?"

"You want to sleep with a *barrio* woman?"

"I'm a multiculturalist, Mikey."

"Well, you've got to be a little careful around here."

"A little careful, huh? A little careful."

He walked back to his chair and sat. He tapped his feet.

"Ah, it won't matter anyway," he said. "Once I get that signature, bang! We're out of here. Hie we to *Las Palmas*. See what the culture there has to offer, right?"

"If you say so."

"I say so. Hey, you're not reading your paper." He picked it up and opened it to an inside page.

"I read as much as I had stomach for."

"Hmm mmm. Hmm mmm. What's going on here?"

Mike leaned over to read.

"Some kid went at his father with an iron bar, it seems."

"With what?"

"With an iron bar."

"Nice."

"Over a woman."

"Hmm mmm." He flipped the paper over. "And what would this word mean?"

Mike leaned over to see. "'*Mara'*," he said. "That would be a gang."

"I see. And this one?"

"*Decapitado?* That means...well, that means, head cut off, I guess."

"Yeah, thought so. Well, there you go, more useful Spanish words."

He dropped the paper back onto the tile, took another puff on his cigar and blew out the exhaust in a tight little circle that floated up, expanded, grew wobbly, and dissipated in the black air.

"Are you really going to help with that water thing tomorrow?"

"Yup," Mike said.

"All right, then. The water thing."

He rose and started toward his room, leaving the empty chair at Mike's side. "*Buenas noches*," he said just before he drew the curtain.

After a moment Mike heard the bongos start up again.

He picked up his book:

> "*Some job.*" *She opened the door,*
> *swung her gorgeous, naked legs out*
> *and lifted herself from the car,*
> *slamming the door shut, like she had*
> *something to be ticked off about.*
>   "*Easy there, girl*" *I said.* "*This is*
> *a —*"
>   "*A classic, yeah, so you told me.*"

He closed the book, feeling a little dirty. He was about to rise to go into his room when Brother Greg appeared from the main building, walking toward him.

"*Hola*," Mike said.

"We're going to have to moderate that," Greg said, tipping his head towards Lonnie's room.

"The bongos? Yeah, agreed. I'll talk to him."

"You read?" he said, as if surprised. "What is it?"

He walked to the side of Mike's chair. Mike closed the book and surreptitiously slid his hand over its cover.

"Nothing," he said.

Greg bent down and craned his neck to see, and Mike had no choice but to expose it.

"You're right, it's nothing."

"Well…" Mike said.

"But I suppose it qualifies as reading, in some sense."

"In some sense," Mike said. "To tell you the truth, it doesn't do much for me either. I read a lot, actually, but I'm not sure why."

"Maybe if you had something a little more…worthwhile."

"I'm open to suggestions."

"We have a little library here."

"So I've heard. Off limits to non-geniuses, though."

"Perhaps you could borrow something. We don't have a lot of smutty crime fiction, but…"

This appeared to be an attempt at humor, though the monk hadn't smiled when he'd said it.

He turned and began walking in the direction he'd come. Just before entering the main building he looked back, surprised to see that Mike hadn't followed.

CHAPTER 15

THE LIBRARY WAS SMALL and square and with its ceiling-high shelves covering every wall seemed to be constructed of books. There were lines of ten or fifteen volumes held in place by horizontal stacks, and others in small piles, their corners out of sync, like playing cards that had just been dealt. More lay haphazardly at the foot of the shelves, as if they had been bullied off by the other books.

In the near left corner of the room was a very old desk that was too large for the place, positioned so that a person sitting behind it would look out into the room. Stuffed in the opposite corner was a small recliner with a lamp at its side. On the floor by the chair was a pile of four or five more books, and a notepad with a pen atop it. A newspaper was draped over its arm.

Greg went to the shelves to the left, pulled, as it were, to them, and he carefully slid out a volume and flipped it open. Under its enchantment he seemed to immediately forget Mike's presence.

Mike surveyed the contents of the desktop. On one of the corners was a thin wooden crucifix on a pedestal, and at another a small nondescript desk lamp; under it was a neat stack of type-written documents. In the middle of the desk was a chess set - a wooden board an inch thick with black and white pieces that looked to be of ivory, well-worn; pagodas for the rooks, elephants for the knights, tall thin figures wearing saucer hats for the bishops. A few of the pieces had been taken out of the game and waited with oriental patience at the side of the board. The others were scattered about the squares.

Mike had played some chess in high school; like most things he'd tried, he was fanatical about it for half a year or so before dropping it entirely, but in his mind, he was a grandmaster. He pretended to size up the situation.

"It's about even, huh?" he said.

Without lifting his eyes from the book Greg said, "No, it's not."

"Who do you think is winning?"

"Me. Black. I've already won. Marco just doesn't see it yet. You won't see it either."

"Who's move?"

"Mine. Bishop to e6."

"Bishop to e6, huh?"

Mike imagined the black bishop moving to the designated square. "You sure about that?" he said.

"Hmm mmm."

"You're just throwing your queen away, then."

"Oh, really," Greg said in a dismissive tone, his eyes still on the book in his hands. "I'll have to take a look at that."

"Hey, I'm just trying to help you." Bishop to e6. Madness.

Mike shook his head and transferred his attention to the crucifix. It was roughly carved, as if by a child: a dark wooden cross with a deformed man pinned to it, his extremities without articulation, his features smudged as if he had been beaten until his face had swollen. Presumably the statue had value for Marco beyond its artistic one.

Wound in coils around the base of the crucifix was a rosary with cream-colored beads carved in the form of skulls, small ones for the many Hail Marys, larger ones for the Our Fathers sprinkled among them. A brown stranded cord ran into the tops of their skulls and exited at the bottoms, where the spinal cord should have been. Their faces were twisted every which way, some gazing directly down into the wood of the desk, others looking away from Mike as if purposely ignoring him. The *Padre Nuestro* closest to Mike, however, was staring directly at him from huge black eye-sockets, hollow, as if the eyeballs had sunk into the abyss within. It had a triangular nose cavity and cheek bones that arched back from its jaw. Cracks were traced into the top of its cranium like black lightening strokes. It bared its teeth at Mike like a chimpanzee baiting him.

He looked at the top sheet of the stack of papers. Some kind of poem it was, written in a small, neat hand. Mike leaned down to read. "The Clinic and the Temple" was its title:

> *One soul slipped out the clinic door*
> *In a temple for two an hour before*
> *The other lies broken in its own blood and gore*
> *Four hundred, six hundred, eight hundred more*
> *As two more souls pace the killing floor.*

"Some poem," he said. "Did he write that?"

"So you're a critic, now, too?" Greg replied, again without looking up from his book. "Get away from the desk please."

"The Clinic and the Temple," Mike whispered to himself. He shook his head and sauntered over to the other side of the room, towards the reading chair.

He glanced at the paper. There was another full-color picture, with another assassin and another cop – unmasked this time, as if caught off guard, but hiding her face under the brim of her hat - and he looked away. In the shelves behind the chair were more books, and more books, and almost lost amidst them a photograph in a small wooden frame. He picked it up. It was old and a bit out of focus and had the overbearing color of old photographs. It showed a pretty, smiling oriental woman, her long black hair falling over her left shoulder and spilling over the white smock she wore. At her side was an athletic-looking man with a two-day growth of beard, wearing loose-fitting clothes and looking as if he had just woken up. He was staring at the woman and smiling at her, his arm draped around her shoulder, powerful, loose, and comfortable.

They were standing in the middle of some street, the busyness and messiness of which reminded Mike of those in downtown Joco, except that the signs on the buildings behind them were in some oriental script.

He thought to ask Brother Greg if the man was Marco, and if so, who the woman was, but when he looked over he saw him, his glasses pushed down along the bridge of his nose, frowning down at the book in his hand with a monkish intensity that to disrupt would have been sacrilegious.

He leaned closer in to study the picture, to see if there was any hint of the future monk in the man, but if there was, it was lost on Mike.

He replaced the picture and tilted his head to read the titles from the spines of the upright books at its side. They were in English and Spanish and the Oriental Something. He picked out a small one in his native language, opened it, and read the first few sentences, and reread them, and reread them again until he could stand it no longer. "Get this," he said to Brother Greg, and he read aloud:

> *What is the self? The self is a relation*
> *which relates itself to its own self, or*
> *it is that in the relation that relates*
> *itself to its own self; the self is not the*
> *relation but that in the relation that*
> *relates itself to its own self...*

Greg looked over at him as if startled to see another human being there in the room. He marched over to Mike, took the book from his hands, and slapped it shut.

"We won't start with that one," he said.

"All right. Hard to tear yourself away, though, isn't it? Is that Marco in that picture?"

Greg ignored the question. "I'll find a better one for you."

"Who's the woman?"

Without answering Greg replaced the offending book on the shelf. He went back to his position at the far wall and started scanning the shelves again, but almost immediately picked out another book, opened it, and lost himself.

A large volume caught Mike's eye. It had gold oriental lettering impressed into his spine. Its cover was worn smooth and its back was broken by the years, and as Mike lifted it it felt impossibly heavy with depth and age.

On the shelf behind it he noticed something shiny, and he reached in and extracted it carefully, holding it by the handle so that the barrel pointed to the ground.

He looked over at Greg, now finally searching the shelves for something easy and innocuous enough for the beginner.

Mike cleared his throat. "Well, this is interesting," he said.

"Where did you get that?" Greg said sharply.

"It was behind this book. Must be Marco's."

"Put it back."

"It's not loaded, is it?"

"Just put it back."

"All right. All right." Mike set it on the shelf, slid it back in place, and set the book in front of it. "It's his though, right? He was a Ranger, Lonnie said."

"I don't know. He doesn't talk about that."

"He was though."

"I don't talk about it either."

"All right. It's interesting, though, isn't it? He's interesting."

"Here," Greg said, holding out a book to him. It was an old library volume: handwritten horizontally across the bottom of its loose spine was its ID with its Dewey Decimal coding - 194.9, P27. Its title was printed in tiny black letters across the top of its spine and in a little box outlined on its dark gray cover, which hung limply from it by some interior mesh cloth. The edges of the cover had worn away, exposing its compressed paper core. Despite its size, it was thick and heavy.

"It's not really a whole book," Greg said. "He didn't live to complete it. It's notes for a book."

Mike flipped it open. Glued to the inside of its cover was a vanilla-colored pouch for the check-out card, and page numbers scribbled in pencil, light gray and fading away. He opened it carefully to a random spot and read aloud:

> *Unity joined to infinity adds nothing to it, no more than one foot to an infinite measure. The finite is annihilated in the presence of the infinite, and becomes a pure nothing. So our spirit before God...*

"Are you sure I can't just have the one about the self relating itself to itself?"

"Concentrate on the underlined parts."

"Okay, underlined parts." He read:

> *Between us and heaven or hell there is only life, which is the frailest thing in the world.*

"All right, then," he said.

CHAPTER 16

OUTSIDE THE FENCE THE next morning, Mike stood with Lonnie, dispensing water from a five-gallon jug suspended in a wire frame. In front of them was a table where people received their water, and behind in the shade of a tree were rows of more jugs, the full ones arranged neatly in rows, the empties strewn about. It didn't seem to Mike that there was water enough for everyone in the line, which stretched along the road to their right, down to the river, across the bridge and half-way up the facing hill.

"What'll you suppose they'll do when we run out?" Mike said.

Lonnie drew his finger across his throat. "*Decapitado*?" he said.

In his pockets Mike had pieces of candy Luke had given him for the children. The bag with the rest of the candy was in his backpack, propped against the tree, and he wondered as well if they would last.

The line was lively but surprisingly well-ordered, with the people patiently waiting their turn, as only those too accustomed to waiting can. They carried small water bottles, gallon milk jugs, cooking pots - anything that could hold liquid. Mothers held babies in one arm and containers in the other, with one or two other children clinging to their skirts, each of them holding a container as well, while clusters of older kids played, ran, and kicked soccer balls all along the length of the line. When their turn for water came, the women would shuffle up to the table smiling, watch as their water was poured, say "thank you" softly, and move on.

The cage holding the water jug had a lever that tilted the bottle over to pour. Mike pressed down on the lever too fast and the water gushed out and spilled over the side of the pitcher he was filling, splashing on his feet. The people in line laughed as at the funniest thing in the world.

"Everyone's so damn happy," Lonnie said. "What do they have to be so damn happy about?"

Brothers Luke and Joe worked the line, the first chatting to the people in his hesitant, broken, unembarrassed Spanish, the other moving about more quickly, speaking with a stiff English accent. They inquired of the poor wretches how they were, how their families were, if they had anyone sick at home. They came to the table to fill plastic cups and carried them back to the elderly and the children waiting in line. The very frail they escorted to the front.

"Some of these people have got to be double-dipping," Lonnie said, and he poured himself another cup. "Take this next woman. She looks familiar, doesn't she?"

"No, she doesn't."

"They all look familiar, I say. Well, I ain't planning to be at this all day, I tell you that." He took a gulp of water and slapped at his arm. "Where the hell is the uncle anyway?"

Mike had at first attempted to detect signs of typhoid fever as each person approached the table, whatever those signs might be. But here in the third hour he had come to terms with the notion that any affliction these poor creatures had was bound to have already leaped or crawled or been coughed into him, with all the consequences to follow. Resigned thus to his fate, he found the work easier and he loosened up, determined to suck whatever enjoyment he could from these, his last days on earth.

"Clothes today?" a woman asked as she approached the table.

"Just water today," Mike said. The woman nodded and held out her container.

A little girl was tucked behind the woman's dress, her arm reaching around to hold her finger. "*Hola,*" Mike said to her. One lovely black eye peeked around the woman's hip for a second and disappeared.

Mike walked around to the front of the table and squatted, but the girl shifted around to the other side of her mother to stay out of sight of this strange *gringo*. She peeked out again.

"What's your name?" Mike said.

She disappeared again.

"Dariela," the mother said to her, "tell the man your name."

"Ah, Darela, is it?" Mike said. "Beautiful name."

"Dariela," her mother corrected him.

"Dariela. More beautiful yet. How old are you, Dariela?"

The eye appeared from around the dress again, and almost whispering the girl responded, "Five."

"Me, too," Mike said, but the girl didn't laugh.

He took one of the pieces of candy from his pocket and held it out to her. The eye locked onto it. He stretched his arm to move the candy closer to her, and after a moment she came halfway out from behind the dress and moved one bare foot towards him. Mike could see now why she was hiding; she was in an advanced stage of typhoid fever, or something, her nose exuding a germ-laced liquid that ran in a slimy slab from her nostrils down to her upper lip and thence into her mouth.

She reached out to take the candy.

It wouldn't do now for Mike to turn and run, though his entire being insisted on it. It wouldn't look good. And so he remained there, squatting, even by some perverse impulse leaning in closer to hear her tiny voice after her mother admonished her, "Dariela, say thank you to the man."

She raised her head and lifted her stunning black eyes to meet his. She opened her mouth as if to talk, and Mike nodded to encourage her. But instead of words she let go a cough of surprising violence and content that hit Mike hard and full in the face.

She wiped her forearm across her nose. "Thank you," she whispered.

"Thank you," Mike answered. He stood. "Well..." he said and nodded goodbye. He moved back behind the table.

"So how was that?" Lonnie laughed.

Mike ignored him.

"Looked to me like you caught a little dengue cough there."

"Just pour," Mike said.

"Just pour. Pour and pour and pour. But there's no end to it, is there? It's like picking lice."

Luke walked back towards the table, leading a woman with a small girl on either side of her, each carrying an empty milk jug. The woman was cradling a third child, a sleeping baby, in her arm. In her other hand she held aloft a bright red and yellow parasol.

"Fill these folks up," he said to Lonnie and Mike, and he went back into the mission, returning quickly with Brother Greg, carrying a duffle bag, and the old priest, Padre Zeppi. He was dressed in priest's black and a collar, and he had untended hair, silver with ashen streaks, and bushy white eyelashes that curled down and threatened to inundate his eyes. His face was weathered and fallen, but there was a gleam in his eye; his entire being, in fact, seemed to shine somehow. As a young man he would have been good-looking, Mike thought.

"There's a sick boy in this woman's house," Luke said. "Brother Greg and I are going to check it out. Brother Joe and the padre can take over pouring the water, and you two can take a break," he said, addressing Lonnie and Mike. The two brothers turned and started down the road with the woman and her children, Greg with the duffle strapped to his shoulder and Luke with a full water jug in each hand.

When they were out of earshot, Lonnie blew out his breath. "About time," he said. And he headed back towards the mission. "*Siesta*," he said to Mike.

"I'm going to stay out here," Mike said.

"Suit yourself. Don't let anything exciting happen while I'm gone."

CHAPTER 17

MIKE STROLLED ALONG THE road beside the line of *cortezeños* awaiting their turn at the water. They smiled and nodded politely as he passed. Feeling uncomfortable, he picked up a pebble from the road and began tossing it in the air and catching it, so that it might look as if he were concentrating on something important.

About halfway to the bridge he heard footsteps behind him and turned to see Belkis, her head down, her hair flying from shoulder to shoulder behind her head, her skinny brown arms flailing at her sides. She was wearing a tattered, dirty pink shirt and a red skirt. She slowed as she approached and took three final skipping steps to light at his side. She took hold of his hand and began walking with him.

"Hola, Belkis," Mike said.

"Not my name."

"What do you have there?"

She opened her hand to show him the little red ball from the set of jacks.

Mike reached into his pocket where he'd been keeping the lucky *cantillo*, mixed in with the candies. He showed it to her. She put her hand out, but Mike drew it back.

"Uh uh. It's my lucky one, remember?"

The bridge was broad but lacked rails or curbs to guard its edges. They stopped about halfway across it and Mike squatted down at its lip. The riverbed below was wide and strewn with chalky white boulders through which the shrunken river picked its way, running from one pool to the next. In one of them, a hundred feet upstream, two women washed their clothes. A little further up a gaggle of naked children splashed about, their shouts and laughter clear and fine in the morning air.

A women's voice called Belkis' name, and she stood, shielded her eyes with her hand and squinted up the road. She suddenly brightened, shouted "Pilar", and took off across the bridge, running halfway up the facing rise, to the end of the line. She came to rest in the outstretched arms of a young woman who had stooped down to catch her. The woman looked to be of interest, and Mike let the stone roll off his hand and drop to the water below. It was a nice touch, he thought, the kind of thing Trent York might have done, if Trent York had been mad enough to take a case in Cortes, and he hoped she had seen it. He stood and started off towards them, assuming a slow, rolling gait that, as he thought, was jaunty and full of the carelessness of those who could afford to be careless. He slipped his hands into his pockets and rolled the lucky *cantillo* around. He looked about at the people in line, trying to glance ahead only occasionally, and as if at Belkis.

Pilar was watching and listening intently and with barely controlled delight as Belkis spoke. Her hair was drawn back

THE CHILDREN OF EVE

tightly behind her head and pulled away from her face, which was perfect. Belkis turned to point at Mike, and she smiled at him, and, though he was still thirty feet away, Mike flexed. Pilar stood, laid her hand on Belkis' head and looked over at another young woman standing at her side, who Mike had only half-noticed. They both glanced at him, and the other woman leaned towards Pilar's ear and said something, and they laughed.

When he finally reached her - which, with his relaxed, cool pace seemed to be hours later - she looked down shyly and shifted her eyes over to her friend. They both giggled again.

"This kid bothering you?" Mike asked as cool as could be, and he shoved his hip into Belkis' shoulder. The little girl bounced away, staggering a couple steps to the side before recovering her balance. With both arms extended she ran at him and pushed him with surprising force that he pretended not to feel.

"No," said the friend. She beamed at Mike, her huge teeth flashing in the sun. She was six inches taller than Pilar, wearing tight blue jeans and a white, frilly shirt with wide strips of lace fringing the collar and cuffs; the backs of her hands were half covered in it. The shirt was a size or two too big for her, and her body shifted about in it like an animal trapped in a bag. She had a high, smooth brow and long legs, and was not without her own beauty, and it was unfair to judge her against the being at her side. But he did.

"Yes," said Pilar. "She is."

"Yeah, she bugs everybody," he said. "Her name is Belkis."

"No it's not," Belkis said.

"I'm Mike." He held out his hand.

"I'm Sara," the friend intervened, grabbing Mike's hand and shaking it. "And this is Pilar."

"She's my cousin," Belkis said proudly.

"I'm sorry," Mike said to Pilar, and as Belkis shoved him again he took Pilar's hand to shake it. It felt limp and warm, the skin of her fingers rough and dry and cracked.

"Are you waiting for water?" Mike said.

"Of course they're waiting for water," Belkis said.

"Well, this is the right line, then," Mike said.

"Are you from the United States?" Sara asked.

"*Sí.* From Michigan."

"From the United States?"

"*Sí.* Michigan is part of the United States."

"New York?"

"Michigan."

"Okay" Sara said, but she couldn't hide her disappointment that he wasn't from New York, whatever New York was.

"Where do you two live?" Mike said.

"Cortes, of course," Belkis said.

"Yeah, Cortes. But where?"

"Over there," she said with a measure of disgust in her voice, as if Mike should have known such a simple thing, and she waved her hand in the direction of the rise behind them. "*Los Ángeles.*"

"*Los Ángeles?*"

"The next *barrio*," Sara said.

"Is it far?"

Belkis exhaled loudly. "No," she said.

"Okay. Well…" Mike said. "I suppose I should get back to work," but he didn't move.

"My neighbor," Pilar said.

"What about your neighbor?"

Her smile was gone now. "He's sick," she said.

"He is?"

She nodded. "Can Brother Marco come see him?"

"You know Brother Marco?"

"*Sí.*"

"Well, he isn't here today, I'm afraid. I'm not sure where he is."

Pilar frowned.

"But Padre Zeppi's here. And Brother Joe."

"Mmmmm," she said.

"Is he very sick?"

She nodded.

"Maybe you should come with me."

They started off towards the table, Mike trying to appear serious, trying not to smile, trying to pretend that everything was still as it had been. But the trick was impossible when even the people in line seemed to realize and appreciate the situation, and looked upon him now with more respect and admiration as he floated there alongside Pilar. Even the *barrio* dog that slanted across the road in front of them – a rib cage stuck atop four sticks - swung its skull back towards him with a knowing grin, as if to say, "¡*Hombe*!".

Oh, he was Trent York, all right. He was all of Trent York. And she - she was the perfect weapon.

Putting his hands in his pockets, to appear more nonchalant, he felt the spikes against his finger and laughed. He took the *cantillo* from his pocket, gazed at it a moment in appreciation, and handed it to Belkis; he wouldn't be needing it anymore. Already the thing had done its magic; it had been one of the fast working ones.

In perfect Spanish Padre Zeppi asked Pilar about her neighbor's condition. He had a fever – it seemed very high to Pilar's touch. Headache, no appetite, diarrhea.

"And now he's going...you know," Pilar said.

"*Loco,*" Sara said. Only now did Mike realize she had followed them.

"*Sí,*" Pilar said. "Last night, he was shouting in the street in front of his house."

"I see."

"With only his boots on and a machete."

"No clothes," Sara said, and she laughed.

"Sounds pretty bad," the padre said to Joe, who frowned and looked up the road in the direction in which the other brothers had disappeared fifteen minutes earlier.

Mike was finally tuning into the gravity of the discussion and becoming aware of the possibility that something other than raw admiration for Pilar might be required of him, when the door of the mission clanked open, and his spirits fell. He'd forgotten the conquistador.

He held his hat in his hands, turning it by the brim as he approached the group. He cast a leer at Pilar. "So, what's going on here?" he said. "I thought I told you not to let anything exciting —"

"It's nothing," Mike said.

"I should go see him," Joe said to the padre, who nodded his consent.

"Go see who?" Lonnie said.

"These women have a neighbor who's sick."

"Typhoid fever?"

"Maybe."

"*Enfermo*?" Lonnie said to Pilar. Mike wondered how he had managed to pick up that Spanish word just in time to use it like that on the most beautiful woman in the world. In his lamblike innocence, had Mike taught him it?

Pilar nodded.

"I'll go with you, bro," Lonnie said to Joe, in the tone of someone sacrificing something.

Mike scoffed audibly, but seeing that the brother was relieved at the offer and seemed poised to accept it, he jumped in. "That's all right, I'll go," he said.

"Okay," Lonnie said. "We can both go. How far is it?"

"Four, five miles," Mike said.

"No," Brother Joe said. "Not that far. Just over the hill a little ways, in *Los Ángeles*."

"I love Los Angeles," Lonnie said.

"I need one of you to stay here," Padre said, looking at Mike.

"But I saw her first," Mike was about to say, but it struck him as a bit childish, even for him, and he realized that he had been outmaneuvered.

"It's okay, Mikey," Lonnie whispered as he passed. "I'll take care of everything. *Cálmate.*"

What, had he taught him that, too?

"Come on, bro," he said to Joe.

"Please don't call me that," Joe said.

"Oh, okay. I just thought brother, bro, you know."

"Still…" Joe said.

"Okay."

Belkis started off with them, eager like the others to abandon Mike. But Pilar told her that she would have to ask her mother, and Belkis slumped over and turned back. With her head down, she went to the tree behind the table and started stripping pieces of bark from it, tossing them disdainfully to the ground.

"Come over here," Mike said to her. "You can handle the line for us. That's the most important job anyway. Tell people to come up when it's their turn. One family at a time."

"I know how to do it," she said.

She rose and walked to the table. With the peculiar Latino downward flick of her hand – a gesture that looked to Mike more like a shooing away - she waved forward the next woman, taking the container from her in a firm and businesslike manner and without so much as a glance at Mike handing it back to him to be filled.

As Mike poured, he watched the four traitors walking away: the little brother carrying the two jugs, talking without stop; the cheetah figure of Pilar, her arms crossed in front of her; Sara surging along to her left; Lonnie, broad-shouldered and athletic, the ridiculous hat on his head, slobbering forward at their side. They disappeared down the dip in the road.

"So," the padre said to Mike. "What do you think of our country so far?"

"What's that?" he said.

"What do you think of Cortes?"

"Cortes? So far? Well, I suppose a man could fall in love with Cortes."

Padre laughed and poured himself a cup from the pitcher on the table, took a sip and smacked his lips, seeming to enjoy it with his entire, formidable being.

"They're all *mestizos*, you know," he said.

"Who's that?"

"Our friends here. Mixed blood. Mongrels, like us all, I suppose. When the Spanish arrived, they found the native women attractive."

"Imagine that," Mike said.

"Yeah. Imagine that."

He finished off the water, smacking his lips again and grunting with pleasure.

"How about you?" he said. "Do you?"

"Do I what?"

"Find them attractive."

"Yeah, I suppose I do."

Padre nodded, and after a moment said, "But you know, you have to be careful here, with these ones. For one thing, it's more than a little dangerous."

"Okay."

"And it's not really fair to them, is it?"

Mike had been watching for the deserters to reappear on the bridge, and had not heard what the old man had said.

"How's that?" he said.

Zeppi stopped talking until Mike looked at him.

"Sorry, Padre," he said. "What did you say? Not fair?"

"They live in poverty and want, in the midst of violence, where life is cheap. But they want to live, just like you do. They want to leave this place, some of them, even if only for an hour. And they're liable to read too much into whatever attention you give them, and it would be easy to take advantage of them, then, wouldn't it?"

"I suppose it would, yeah."

"But when you leave, they'll still be here, won't they?"

Mike nodded. Finally, they appeared on the bridge and started up the rise.

"And they'll have to clean up the mess by themselves, alone."

"Yeah," Mike said. "I understand."

"Good."

He watched as the foursome crested the hill and was gone, on its way to some magical place called *Los Ángeles,* where they reared children that grew into Pilars.

Only Mike was left behind.

Belkis shooed forward the next family.

CHAPTER 18

THE BROTHERS RAY AND Greg returned an hour later. They were subdued, and only when he saw Belkis managing the waterline with great seriousness did Luke smile. When Padre told him where Joe and Lonnie had gone, he grew somber again. "I'll go pick them up in the truck," he said.

"I know where she lives," Belkis said, and she waved her hand. "In "Los Ángeles.""

"I'll go with you, too" Mike said.

But just then they appeared at the top of the hill, two figures with remarkably similar physiques, one in an asinine hat, the other, like a miniature of the first but sporting a beard and draped in a long gray robe. In the building heat they descended the hill, crossed the bridge and climbed up to the mission.

Brother Joe was talking quickly, his hands moving in the air for emphasize.

"It's not even a question of sacrifice, really," he was saying to Lonnie. "There was a saint - I can't remember which one. But this saint, she said this, she said, 'All the way to heaven is heaven'. Beautiful, isn't it? 'All the way to heaven is heaven'. And you know, it's true."

"I do not well understand that," Lonnie said.

"What I mean is, well, take where we just were. It was poor, sure, but —"

"Yup, it was poor all right. Poor and dirty. Kind of scary, really."

"Yeah, okay, but didn't you also feel —"

"Depressing, really, bro."

"Don't call him that again," Luke said.

"All right," Lonnie shrugged.

Luke took Joe by the shoulder, leading him further along the road, out of earshot. He listened intently as Joe spoke, holding his head down and stroking his beard.

Lonnie, sweating streams, poured himself a cup of water and dropped onto the ground under the canopy of one of the trees.

"I just figured brother, bro…"

Mike left the table and sat beside him. Belkis frowned back at them.

"Just a little break," he said to her, and turned to Lonnie. "So?" he said.

"So what?"

"So how was it?"

"Well, the term 'not very far' apparently has a different meaning here," Lonnie said.

"I told you —"

"But it wasn't five miles. No, that was a lie." He laughed. "Anyway, as they say, 'all the way to heaven is heaven'. And that girl, she is heaven, ain't she? There's like a voodoo thing about her."

"I think voodoo's from the Caribbean, Lon."

"No, no. That's voodoo. There's no other explanation. Anyway, I got a little tour of her house. I tell you, if we wanted authenticity…"

"It was you that wanted authenticity."

"Well, it was all that, anyway."

"Pretty bad?"

"Pretty rustic. Dirt floors. No sink or anything, just some kind of well in the front yard, and a kitchen with a trough they fill up. They don't even have electricity, just a car battery that they run a jumper cable from, and a light bulb, and a little radio. God knows what they do for a bathroom."

"They're poor, Lon."

"And Pilar's room," he said. "She has this rotting mattress in this little…closet she shares with her sister and - get this - she keeps a box of chickens next to it."

Belkis looked back at Mike from the table sternly.

"One more minute, Belk," Mike said. "Chickens?"

"Little ones. Chicks. I guess they treat them like pets until they grow enough meat on them, then – pffft – *decapitado*, and bingo, they're soup. One of them escaped from the box and got himself crushed by a dog or something, I don't know – there're animals all over. And Naila – that's Pilar's little sister - she picks it up by one leg and slings it back in the box, like it was an old sock or something, except they don't have socks."

"They're poor."

"I know they're poor, Mike. I know they're poor. I'm just saying. Poor or not though, I want."

"You want?"

"I want." He looked over at Mike and slapped him on the knee. "And yours, she was there the whole time, too."

"Mine? Sara, you mean?"

"*Eso*. Sara. She actually ain't a bad little piece in her own right."

"So she's mine, huh? You've decided to give her to me?"

"You don't have to thank me. It's what I do. It's my calling. Some people are called to...well, you know."

He looked up and down the string of people still waiting for water. "Damn," he said. "This line is as long as when I left. Have you guys been working at all?"

"Yeah Lonnie. We've been working."

"Well, it doesn't look like it."

"How about the neighbor, the sick guy?"

"He's not real good, I gather. I don't know though, I was at Pilar's most of the time. I saw another interesting guy there, though. Mean-looking cuss. He walked by the road when we were sitting in front of her house, and he slowed down and looked in – glared in, I would say. He wasn't too happy, and he didn't appear to like me much, if you can imagine that. I said '*hola*', but he ignored me. Ah, well." He looked up the line again. "I tell you, some of these people have got to be double-dipping."

"You've got to be careful, Lon. This isn't —"

"Yeah I know. I know."

Brother Luke had finished his conversation with Joe, and now beckoned to the padre and Greg to join them. After a minute or two they came to some agreement and broke the huddle. Greg and the padre went into the mission and Luke and Joe started working the line again.

Five minutes later the red pick-up came out along the side road of the mission, Greg at the wheel. He turned right onto the main road. The line shifted aside lethargically as he drove slowly along it.

In another hour the crowd had begun to dwindle, and Luke told Mike and Lonnie they could go. He asked them what their plans were for the afternoon.

"Depends. Is Marco coming?" Lonnie said.

"Probably not today."

"All right. Okay. Well, we were thinking we'd go downtown for a little while, then. Maybe pick up some more souvenirs," Lonnie said.

* * *

Back in his room Mike took an envelope from under his mattress and counted the money within. The trip – which had seemed like such a good idea three months ago – was going to bust him good. Something would have to be done when he got back home. Decisions would have to be made.

He peeled out four twenties and slipped the remaining stack – alarmingly thin already – back into the envelope.

CHAPTER 19

RODRIGO PICKED THEM UP behind the mission, and as they passed to the side of it on their way out, Mike glanced over to see Brother Luke and the padre at the table, still pouring water for the remnant left waiting in line. He felt some satisfaction, some odd kind of calmness even, at what they'd done.

As they crossed the bridge Mike looked down at the stream, but there was no one to be seen. The washing had been done and the women had taken their children home and were resting, now, Mike imagined, taking their *siestas* in the gloom of their dirt-floor hovels, lying on their thin, musty mattresses, sleeping through the clucking coming from the boxes beneath them.

He twisted around to look at Lonnie sitting in the middle of the back seat. "That was a good thing to do, wasn't it?" he said.

"Sure," Lonnie said. "Sure it was. I'd say we've earned some fun."

A mile or so later, as they approached an intersection, Lonnie tapped Rodrigo on the shoulder and told him to turn left. Rodrigo stopped the car and gazed down the road.

"Downtown straight," he said.

"Yeah, I know, downtown straight. Just humor me."

"What's up, Lon?" Mike said.

"This is *Los Ángeles*. Those two girls live down there. I'll show you where."

"Are you okay going in there?" Mike asked Rodrigo.

"I don't know this *barrio*."

"It doesn't look any worse than what we've just driven through," Mike said.

"But is," Rodrigo said.

"You know what you're doing?" Mike asked Lonnie.

"Sure. It's just a couple blocks."

Mike nodded to Rodrigo.

"Okay, but charge more," Rodrigo said.

"Fair enough."

"Fair enough," Rodrigo said. He liked the phrase, and repeated it twice to burn it into his memory. He cranked on the wheel.

The road sloped slightly but steadily downward. Its surface was rocky and crowned in the middle, crumbling away at the sides to gutters that were empty now of everything except the trash that had been tossed there by the *barrio* residents or dragged there by the water from the last rainy season, months ago, and the chickens that pecked about in it for a living. Rodrigo slowed to ease into and out of the crevices that had been washed into the road and never filled. He squeezed around a manhole that was poking up from the center of the road four or five inches, its top left exposed when the rain that had carved away the surrounding dirt disappeared. In two or three places, home-made speed bumps – thin strings of small sharp rocks sticking up on end - lay across the way.

Only a handful of people moved along the road – two women with bundles in their arms, a tiny old man with a machete in his belt, a trio of boys in school uniforms. They made room for the taxi to pass but avoided eye contact.

"Taxis no go here very good," Rodrigo said. "Here people say, taxi …" and he rubbed his fingers together.

"They think they'd be carrying cash, huh?" Mike said.

"*Sí*. Cash. Like ATM. And sometime…" and he pointed his index finger at his head.

"I suppose," Mike said.

"For danger, charge extra." Rodrigo removed the toothpick from his mouth. "Fair enough."

They had gone three blocks into the *barrio* now, and the place had grown more oppressive, more threatening, with every turn of the wheel.

"Exactly where is this place, Lon?" Mike said.

"Just up ahead. One of these side streets," Lonnie said. "To the right."

Rodrigo slowed to a crawl at each of the intersecting roads, staring down them with a look that grew more and more anxious. The roads were even worse than the one they were driving along, narrow and rough, some mere two rut paths that twisted away between barbed wire fences and the tattooed cinder block husks of abandoned or never-completed *casas*, with brush growing from their dirt floors and out through their open windows and roofless tops.

"Bet you got to be care *here* at night, huh?" Lonnie laughed nervously.

Mike felt again, and more intensely, what he had first experienced from the air, looking down upon the ghetto *casas* of Tinaco - the absolute otherness of the place. As if casually, like a mildly interested tourist, he scanned the side streets and the spaces between the *casas* for threats, but all seemed asleep and indifferent to two clueless *gringos* passing along in the dust. Even the street corners were bereft of the usual *malos,* and in the emptiness Mike missed even their presence.

"Turn around," he told Rodrigo.

"No, hang on, Mikey. It's that one," Lonnie said. He pointed to the next intersection. There was a half-built husk of a *casa* on one corner and on another a barred-up neighborhood store – the word "*Pulperia*" was painted on its wall.

Rodrigo stopped the taxi. He looked at Mike.

"You sure?" Mike said to Lonnie.

"Yeah. Just take a right. If that's not it, we'll go back."

They turned the corner and Lonnie had them stop in the middle of the block, in front of a fence made of rough, weathered boards hung vertically and leaning away from the road. There was an opening in the middle of it with a gate made of strands of barbed-wire strung between two broken-off tree branches. The gate was swung ajar and sagged against the boards of the fence.

"Yup, this is it," Lonnie said.

Within the fence Mike could see a packed-dirt yard – tidy and swept smooth, almost polished - that extended back thirty feet to a peeling adobe hut. To the right of the hut was a path that disappeared along the side and to the left a large cistern on a cement pad, shaded by two palm trees. In the doorway stood a girl with a halo of curly black hair, looking out at them. Mike rolled down his window and called to her. "*Niña*, does Pilar live here?"

She frowned at them, but when Lonnie opened the rear door of the taxi and got out, she smiled in recognition, waved at him and dipped into the house.

"That's Naila," Lonnie said. "Her sister. She likes me."

She returned in an instant. Behind her was Pilar in all her *barrio* glory. She was stroking the head of a salt-and-pepper cat cradled in the crook of her arm. She said something to the little girl, and they both started forward.

As Mike opened his door, Rodrigo grabbed his arm. "If I need wait here, cost more," he smiled. "Fair enough?"

"Yeah, okay. Fair enough."

"For the danger." He turned on the radio and began bopping his head along to the music, assuming an air of unconcern. He kept the engine idling.

When Pilar arrived at the gate Lonnie reached out to hug her. She succumbed to his embrace all right, Mike thought, but not without hesitation, and with the cat safely tucked between them. She immediately turned to him.

"*Hola*, Miquel," she said.

"*Hola*, Pilar. How are you?"

"This is my cat, *Orejas*."

"*Orejas*?" he said. "In English, that's 'Ears'."

She tried to say the English word but it was a difficult sound for her and she gave up.

"'*Orejas*' because they're so big, no?" She said, and flicked at the cat's ear. It shook its head and she laughed and looked at Mike to make sure he thought it funny as well. She leaned towards him and twisted her shoulders so he could more easily pet it. When he reached to scratch its mangy little head, it hunched backward and bristled at him.

Pilar laughed and let it drop to the ground. It lit softly and shot back inside the fence, disappearing along the path that led to the back of the *casa*.

"He doesn't like you," she said.

"I think you're right."

It was impossible to keep his eyes off her.

"Ask her if she wants to come downtown with us," Lonnie said.

"What?"

"Ask her if she wants to come with us."

Pilar looked up at Mike for the translation.

"I don't know, Lon."

"I do. I know. I know enough for both of us. Trust me. It'll be good. Ask her."

She was staring up at him, smiling a bit, her mouth slightly open, her eyes wide and questioning.

"How would you like to go downtown with me?" he said.

"Me?" she said. "With you?"

"*Sí*. Downtown."

"I have to ask." Pilar turned to run back into the yard, but already waddling out from the *casa* was a large woman with a kindly round face. She held a towel in her hand and was flicking it back and forth to fan herself and keep the flies away.

"That's Ana, the *madre*," Lonnie said to Mike. "She likes me, too. And lookie over there – another one."

From further up the road, striding towards them with her long legs, smiling broadly, her eyes open wide, was Sara.

"It's almost like she was waiting for us," Lonnie said.

She walked directly up to them and parked herself next to Mike, looking at him expectantly.

"Ask her," Lonnie said.

"Ask her, huh?" Mike said. "All right, I'll ask her."

She accepted, nodding hard and rapidly, with great enthusiasm, biting her lower lip as if to suppress a cry of joy.

"Do you have to ask your mother?" Mike said to her.

She shook her head, and he was sorry for having asked.

Halfway across the yard Pilar and Ana were talking, Pilar pleading, Ana frowning, her hand to her chin and her eyes on the ground. She glanced back at Mike and Lonnie and looked to her daughter again.

Finally, she started towards them, walking slowly and stiffly, as if her every movement took great effort and caused much discomfort. Pilar trailed behind her.

She nodded hello to Lonnie and introduced herself to Mike.

"You want Pilar to go with you?" she said.

"If it's okay. Just for a couple of hours."

"And you're staying with Brother Marco, too?"

"*Sí.*"

"Is he your uncle, too?"

"No. I'm just a friend of Lonnie's."

She nodded as if all this was important information to be seriously considered in her evaluation, and as she pondered, Mike asked Pilar how old she was.

"Eighteen," she said. She turned to Ana. "Please, *mamá.*"

"There's a nice restaurant there," Mike said. "We're just going to eat and then maybe she can show us around downtown a little bit."

They laughed.

"She's never been downtown," Ana said.

"Never been downtown?"

"She's never eaten in a restaurant."

"What's she saying, Mike?" Lonnie asked.

"Hang on."

"Please *mamá*."

Ana looked at her daughter, narrowing her eyes and tilting her face away, and now Mike saw the resemblance. Pilar raised her eyebrows and gave her the sweetest smile Mike had ever seen, a spellbinding, bewitching smile, a smile that could make a person do whatever was asked. A voodoo smile.

Mike was surprised Ana could resist so long.

"And you're going with them?" she finally said, directing the question at Sara.

"*Sí*," Sara said. "*Sí*."

Ana looked at her daughter again, smiled skeptically, and slowly nodded her head.

"Thank you, *mamá*," Pilar said, and she ran back across the yard and into the *casa*, Naila skipping after her.

"But you'll take care of her?" Ana said to Mike.

"I won't let anything happen to her," Mike said. "I promise."

"What are you guys talking about?" Lonnie said.

"Do you want some coffee?" Ana said.

"No thanks. We're kind of in a hurry."

"Pilar picked it," she said proudly.

"She picks coffee?"

"*Sí*. Up in the mountains. But there was only one truck today, and there were enough men, so…Naila, too, when she's not in school."

"Pilar doesn't go to school?"

Ana shook her head. "Next year. This year, because of the money, but next year…"

Pilar came out of the *casa* wearing a different shirt, just as old as the other, and holding Naila's hand. "No, baby," she said to her. "You can't go this time." Naila slouched and went to Ana, coming to rest, pouting, under her arm. Pilar walked quickly to the cistern. She bent over and with both hands splashed water onto her face, drying her cheeks by rubbing them with her palms. She glanced over at them, shy, self-conscious.

"Wow," Lonnie said.

"I'm not so sure about all this, Lon."

"I am," he answered. "I'm sure. More sure than ever now. Come on. You said you wanted authenticity."

"No, you said you wanted authenticity."

"I think we agreed on it."

Just as Pilar joined them at the gate, Sara said her name and motioned up the street with a tic of her head.

A man was approaching, rolling along the road. A *malo* - wiry and athletic, wearing a baseball cap tilted over to one side, baggy but too-short trousers tugged down low and a shred of a tank top that exposed long, sinewy arms, traced with tattoos from the shoulders to the wrists.

"That's him," Lonnie whispered.

Pilar stopped, straightened up, and crossed her arms. She fixed her eyes straight in front of her, over Sara's shoulder toward her neighbor's *casa*. Her smile had vanished.

The man passed by without looking at them.

"Who's that?" Mike asked her.

Pilar shook her head once without moving her eyes or changing her expression.

"Not a good guy," Sara said.

The man walked to the street corner and stopped, leaning his shoulder against the wall of the *pulperia*, his back to them.

Ana came from behind and put her hand on Pilar's shoulder and Pilar turned into her and hugged her, still not smiling.

"Be careful," Ana said.

"*Mamá*," she whispered, "don't worry."

"You promised," Ana said to Mike.

They packed into the cab, Mike in front, Lonnie and the two women in back, exactly as Lonnie himself would have drawn it up. Rodrigo drove to the next corner, the corner from which Sara had emerged, turned to the left, and stopped to put the car in reverse.

"That's my house," Sara said proudly, pointing to another tiny hut a hundred feet further along the miserable scratch of road.

"That's nice, Sara," Mike said. "Maybe we can visit it sometime."

"When?" she said.

"Sometime later."

"Promise?"

"Sure. Promise."

Rodrigo wheeled the car around and started back along Pilar's road, but as they passed her house she asked him to stop.

"I forgot," she said, and she exited the car, went into her *casa*, came out with a milk jug and carried it over to her neighbor's house. Lonnie held the door open for her when she returned.

"How's he doing?" Lonnie asked.

"Better, I think," Pilar said.

"Did he have his clothes on?" Sara laughed.

The not-good guy was still standing there on the corner, his back to them. As they passed, he turned and glared into the cab with an empty, hard, pitiless look, a look from the front pages of the local newspapers, a look Mike was getting used to, but not really. Pilar stared forward with the same rigid, determined expression.

CHAPTER 20

MIKE SCANNED THE SQUARE quickly but could see no sign of the Tuli women.

"First, food," Lonnie said, and he started across the front of the cathedral towards the restaurant. They sat at the same table as the day before and the same waiter served them with the same air of insulted dignity. Pretending not to recognize them, he asked what they'd like to drink.

"*Vino*," Lonnie said. "A bottle of wine, hey Mikey? Four glasses." He held up four fingers.

"No, Lon," Mike said. "No wine for them."

"Why not?"

"I'm not bringing them home drunk."

"Then we'll leave them here drunk." He laughed. "Nah. Just kidding. A little drink is all, to loosen things up."

"Three lemonades, and a glass of wine for him," Mike said to the waiter, who executed a quarter of a bow and retreated.

"Did you say lemonade?" Lonnie said. He removed his hat, gathered his hair off his forehead and leaned sideways in his chair. "You're starting to worry me a little bit. This is vacation, remember."

"Is it ever not vacation with you?"

"Mikey, Mikey. Where did that come from?"

"Look, just no drinks right now, all right?"

"Okay, okay. No drinks. I'm just worried about you, that's all."

The waiter brought the drinks and a basket of bread and stood by the table ready for their orders. Pilar, who had been alternately gazing at the people in the plaza behind her and looking through the menu, pointed at an item on it and looked at Mike.

"Anything you want," he said.

The waiter wrote it down, took the orders of the others, and went back inside the restaurant.

"Usually people warm up to me as they get to know me," Lonnie said. "But this guy…"

Two rag dolls had been watching them from the shade of some trees off at the side of the plaza, and now they started cautiously towards them, the girl leading the boy, little more than half her size, by the hand. She looked warily into the restaurant as she approached, stopping ten feet from the table and staring at their bread basket. The boy stayed a step behind her.

"This is a little awkward," Lonnie said. "It's kind of like one of those horror movies."

The little girl's eyes met Mike's for a moment, and then dropped towards her feet. He looked at Pilar, who pointed at the basket, then at the children. Mike nodded. She stood, took two slices and carried them over to the girl, who glanced up into the restaurant again before taking them. She gave one slice to the boy and he immediately took a bite. They started away and Pilar returned to the table.

"I used to be like that," she said. She was still watching the children as they crossed the front of the church.

"You did?" Mike asked.

"*Sí*."

She stood again and picked up the basket.

"Hey, hold on a minute." Lonnie half-rose from his chair and reached out as if to grab another slice, but at the last moment thought better of it. "Ah, never mind," he said, and sat back down.

Pilar started from the table, walking quickly, then breaking into a run and quickly disappearing behind the side of the church where the children had gone.

"What did she mean, she used to be like that?" Mike asked Sara.

"When she was little, when her father died, her mother used to go to the market, the little one in the *barrio*, to sell food. Pilar would go with her."

"And beg?"

"They were very poor."

"I see," Mike said. "Well...So who was that guy, the one in the *barrio* that she was afraid of?"

"She's not afraid of him. She just wants him to leave her alone. He bothers her. He tells people she's his girlfriend."

"But she's not?"

"With him, if he says you are..."

"Is he dangerous?"

She shrugged.

"Has he ever done anything to her?"

"Not yet," she said.

Mike was keeping his eye on the corner behind which Pilar had disappeared, and she finally turned back around it, walking towards him with that easy grace of hers, lean, athletic, like a lioness. The basket, empty now, swung in her hand.

"How did her father die?"

Sara shrugged.

Pilar returned to the table. Lonnie rose to hold her chair.

"That was a good thing you just did there," he said.

She appeared to understand, and she smiled sweetly and said "*Gracias*." He placed his hand on her shoulder and rubbed it, and let it linger there. It was for that he'd said it in the first place, Mike thought, and for lack of anything better to do he chugged down his glass of lemonade without enjoyment.

Lonnie inched his chair closer to Pilar, his legs crossed figure-four style so that his knee almost touched her forearm, resting on the arm of her chair. He was glancing between his plate of food and her, wearing his ingratiating smile.

"How long are you staying here?" Sara asked Mike.

"A couple days. Then we're going to *Las Palmas*, where the beaches are. *La playa.* We don't get much *playa* weather where we're from."

"Is it cold where you live?

"Very cold, in the winter. Lots of snow."

"Really?" Sara seemed troubled by this, and thought hard about it for a moment. "Do you like snow?" she said.

"Snow is like magic, Sara. It's these little frozen flakes that fall from the sky, and they're like nothing at all. They melt right away in your hand. But they keep falling and falling, and pretty soon they cover the ground in white, up to your knees even. And sometimes it's like feathers - you can walk right through it. And it covers the pine branches like sugar."

"Does it taste like sugar?"

"No, it doesn't taste like anything."

She frowned again. "Is it real?" she said.

"Sure it's real."

Mike checked Lonnie again. He was trying to communicate with Pilar using gestures and facial expressions, complemented by the handful of Spanish words that Mike had been gull-witted enough to teach him.

"What does it feel like to ride in an airplane?" Sara said.

"It's horrible."

Over Sara's laughter Mike heard the word "*corazón*" and he looked over to see Lonnie point at his chest, and then at Pilar's, almost touching her breast. He nodded at her to see if she understood. She looked down at her plate and didn't respond.

"What are you trying to say to her, Lon?"

"Just talking, Mikey, practicing *mi español*. You just pay attention to Sara there. She'll be a handful for you."

"You don't like flying?"

"No. Nobody likes flying, Sara. Only crazy people like flying."

"Why?"

"Because it's terrible. They pack you inside this little tube, and then they shoot you into space, and then the thing starts shaking —"

"It sounds like fun."

"Fun? You're locked inside, scrunched up with a bunch of other people, you're 30,000 feet above the ground and if anything happens…And then they all try to tell you how safe it is."

"Is it?"

"Is it what?"

"Is it safe?"

"How can it be safe? You're hurtling through the air, the thing is jerking around like a…And now, they have columns of ice. Columns of ice! You probably haven't heard about those."

She shook her head, but her eyes were gleaming with delight at the thought.

"So it's not safe?" she said.

"Well, statistically, I suppose it's safe. But it doesn't *feel* safe. I mean, columns of ice!"

Sara frowned, and as Mike was thinking of how to explain it, he heard the word *"hotel"*, and turned to look at Lonnie again. He was reaching for Pilar's hand.

"Stop it," Mike said.

"Don't worry, we'll do separate rooms."

"We won't do any rooms, because we're not going to the hotel."

"*Hotel*?" Sara said.

"No," Mike said. "No *hotel*." He turned back to Lonnie and repeated it to him.

"What the hell, Mike?"

"We're not doing that today."

Lonnie leaned back in his chair, blew out a column of air and swept his hand up over his forehead. His hair filtered back through his fingers and immediately dropped back down over his brow. "We're not doing that today? What's so special about today? What the hell happened to Superman? What happened to 'break the damn door down'?"

"I promised her mother."

"Really, Mike? You promised? Well then, if you promised…All right, fine. Then just tell me what we're going to do for the next two hours?'

* * *

Pilar had eaten only one of her pieces of chicken, wrapping the other in a napkin - for her mother, she said - and now she carried it along with her as she followed Lonnie along the narrow walkways, with Sara and Mike trailing behind them. At their side the traffic moved in fifteen-foot increments, like some segmented creature groping blindly through the gritty Joco streets.

At an intersection a pack of twenty school children passed, watched over by two women in gray habits. Strutting along twenty feet behind the sisters and as if in rebuke of them came two women in high heels, tight jeans, and loud blouses. Metal flashed from their fingers and their earlobes. Their makeup was overdone to just that perfect degree.

Lonnie glanced at Mike. "Tulis," he said. He removed his hat and bowed as the women passed in front of them, smiling, amused, flattered, interested, and as they walked away they looked back and laughed in a certain way. Mike said something to Lonnie in English and the two of them laughed, too. Pilar seemed to catch the gist of it and she looked down at her feet.

"I don't have all that," she said.

Mike was at a loss for words, so he pretended he hadn't heard.

They entered an indoor market, and it was like climbing into the catacombs; all was hot and tight and labyrinthine. The booths, separated by hanging sheets of cloth, were crammed full of cheap merchandise - shoes, clothes, toys, school supplies. In places the stuff spilled out into the aisle; a fallen stack of hats, a heap of cloth, a dozen shoes, frozen in the act of running away to freedom.

The proprietors sat on stools at the sides of their *tiendas*, looking up hopefully as the potential marks walked by. "Dresses," they said softly. "Notebooks." Pilar and Sara looked on all in wonder.

The air was thick with the smell of cooking, and soon they came to a food court of sorts, a small clearing at the intersection of two aisles. In the clearing were four rough-hewn picnic tables surrounded by six food stalls.

"Time for a little desert," Lonnie said. "Desert is allowed by your order, isn't it?"

"I don't like the looks of that food, Lon," Mike said.

"Nonsense." He ordered something at one of the booths and carried it to a table.

There were two old men seated at an adjacent table. One of them made eye contact with Mike. *"Americanos?"* he said.

"Sí."

"Where from?" the man said in English.

"Michigan."

The man shook his head as if that wasn't the correct answer. "I live Carolina one time," he said. "Twelve year. Three children there. All born. Legal as you."

"Probably more," Lonnie said, "if you knew us."

The man asked Mike what they were doing there, and then, with no change of expression on his wrinkled, shiny brown face, he said, "It safe here," answering a question that no one had put to him. "Safe in this market."

His partner, a tiny, toothless, gummy man, looked over at him with what Mike interpreted as skepticism. The first man noticed it and amended his declaration. "But sometime people grab purse...swoosh," he said. He made a grabbing motion with his hand, and laughed.

"Swoosh," Lonnie said, imitating the man's motion and laughing. "Purse, huh? Well, we got no purse."

"Thanks, thanks for that," Mike said to the man. He rose and walked to the far edge of the food court, where there was some kind of shrine, an old wooden table draped with a white cloth atop which stood an ancient statue of a man, his robes brightly painted and his head crowned with real hair, or something hair-like – long, black, frizzy and dry - topped by a hoop of gold-colored metal suspended from the back of his skull by a tiny brass rod. A thick orange porcelain flame flared from the crown of his head. He had a staff in one arm and with the other he held over his chest a large round plaque with the profile of *Jesu Cristo* in bas-relief within.

Propped up against the side of the altar were four sets of old wooden crutches and a pair of walking canes. On each side of the statue was a candle in a small dull bronze holder. One of the candles was lit, and its flame flickered uncertainly; the other was cold and melted down to the nub. Scattered around the tabletop was a myriad of odd things, tokens to the dead, or the healed, or whatever: flower petals; an empty liquor bottle; a pack of cigarettes, a quarter full; three little blue buttons with indistinct images on them; an old carved wooden toy. Among the junk were a dozen slips of paper, folded-over with their top flaps sprung open 45 degrees so that they looked like a bed of square white clams.

Such simple people they were, of such a funny religion, even if it was in some way his.

He leaned over to examine the statue more closely. He could see now that its head had been broken off once, and there was a line around its neck where it had been glued back on. White chalk spots showed where it had chipped when it fell. It had led an active, hard, Cortesian life, right down to the *decapitado*.

Mike looked around; no one was watching. He picked up one of the pieces of paper and unfolded it as quietly as he could, holding it close to his chest. It was written on in a sloppy, unskilled hand, with words run together, uninterrupted by the courtesy of punctuation:

pleaseseñorthatmysonmakeshisjourneysafelyandthatsomedayweseehi magain

He folded it back up, looked around, picked up another:

blessyouseñorthankyouforcuringmyhusbandofhisthirstforotherwome nandlettinghimdieinpeace

"Are you supposed to be reading those?" Lonnie had crept up behind him, the two women following. He was still chewing, his mouth half open.

Mike refolded the paper and let it drop to the table.

"Didn't think so. And who is this chap exactly?"

Mike read from a small plastic plaque leaning against the front of the statue's base. "Saint Jude, apparently."

"Nice hair. What's his story?"

"The Saint of Lost Causes, it says."

Lonnie laughed. "Well, that's only perfect," he said.

* * *

They sat on the steps at the side of the cathedral waiting for Rodrigo. Lonnie held his hat in his hands, turning it in circles by the brim, gazing longingly at the doors of the *Segundo Cielo*. Pilar stared down at her hands, holding the napkin containing Ana's piece of chicken. Sara looked about, her eyes wide and full of glee, still hungry to take it all in. A half dozen pigeons patrolled the walkway in front of them, pecking up invisible tidbits from the dusty stone, flapping upwards and away from passing taxis, returning immediately.

"It's time we get out of here," Lonnie said. "Time to get to the beach."

"Hie we to the beach, huh?"

"There's nothing more here for a couple guys like us. I mean, once upon a time there were these two, but…"

"What about Brother Marco, the signature?"

Lonnie cursed. "Maybe I'll just leave the damn papers at the convent, pick them up on the way out."

"That a good idea, you think?"

"Hell, I don't know. Probably not." He cursed again.

The bell from the church struck, giving off a loud, tinny, shallow, cheap sound that sent the pigeons spraying into the air again and made Pilar and Sara jump. They leaned into each other, laughing, their forearms touching. Lonnie smiled at them.

"Are you sure about this, Mikey?" he said.

CHAPTER 21

THEY ENTERED THE DINING area just as the three brothers were sitting down for supper. Maria brought them their plates, each with a mound of sweet potatoes, a piece of chicken, a couple disks of pineapple.

When Luke began leading them in grace, Lonnie set his chicken down and stopped chewing. He bowed his head, glancing at Mike with the Lonnie-twinkle in his eye. Mike folded his hands on his lap and tried to remember the words as Luke invoked them. At "Amen" they began digging in as one, all except Mike, who wasn't hungry, had had his fill of chicken, and didn't like sweet potatoes anyway. He patted at them with his spoon.

"No Marco yet?" he asked.

Luke, gnawing on his chicken bone, shook his head.

"And Padre?"

"Fasting," Brother Luke mumbled.

"Why?" Lonnie said.

"Purify the soul," Luke said. He let the bone drop to his plate, licked his fingers, and took up a spoonful of potatoes.

"Penitential suffering. Showing solidarity with the poor. Shall I go on?" There was a note of challenge in his voice.

Lonnie looked as though he were about to say something in response, but surprised Mike by holding his tongue.

"We think what we do with our bodies doesn't affect our souls," Luke said. "We've forgotten what we are."

"What are we?" Mike asked.

"See – that's what I mean."

Mike paused for a moment, nodded as if finally remembering what he was, and took a bite of pineapple. It was sweet and sharp and juicy, the best he'd ever eaten.

"Did you guys hear what happened in *Los Ángeles*?" Brother Joe said.

"That's where we were, right bro?" Lonnie said. "Brother Joe, I mean."

"They caught a thief there last night, and they took him and they cut off his hands."

"What?"

"Machete. The people of the *barrio*. He'd stolen a lot of things," Joe said, as if in justification of his *cortezeños'* actions.

"Brother Joe," Luke said. "Let's talk about something else while we're eating, shall we?"

Joe took a bite of his chicken and restrained himself for all of seven seconds.

"That's what they do here, they take things into their own hands. Once they caught a member of one of the *maras* – do you know what a *mara* is?"

"A gang."

"And they shot him in the leg, then they pointed the gun at his other leg and started counting to three, until he told them the name of his partners, and they went out and caught them, too, and —"

"Okay, Brother Joe. That'll do," Luke said.

"It's because they can't trust the police," Joe slipped in quickly.

Luke stopped chewing and gave Joe a look that might have shut another man down cold, but only caused Joe to change subjects.

"Over five hundred families today," he said.

"For the water, you mean?" Mike said. "That's a lot, isn't it?"

"Yeah, I think it is. Isn't it?" He looked at Brother Luke, who, satisfied with the new topic, smiled at him affectionately and nodded.

"Good," Mike said. "How's that little boy you went to see?"

"Brother Greg says he'll be okay."

When they'd finished dinner, Maria brought out a tray with five glass tumblers, little bigger than shot-glasses, and an oddly-shaped, ancient-looking bottle. Luke unstopped the bottle and poured each glass half fill. He passed them down the table. "*Salud*," he said, and they clinked glasses and drank.

The stuff was strong and tasted of licorice; Mike had to force himself to sip at it.

Luke smacked his lips. "So how was downtown?" he asked. "What did you guys do?"

"Nothing," Lonnie answered.

"Went to an indoor market – that was interesting," Mike said. He felt complicit in some wrong for not telling Luke about the women they'd spent the day with, and he continued. "And we had lunch. We were —"

"Restaurant right next to the big church," Lonnie interrupted.

"Cathedral," Luke said.

"Church...cathedral..."

"There's a difference."

"Okay."

"And what did you think of it?"

"It was nice, good food. But the waiter carried this attitude around with him —"

"What did you think of the cathedral?"

"Ah, the cathedral." Lonnie nodded his approval. "Needs some work, though," he said.

"It's Cortes." Luke spread his arms to indicate the Cortesness of it. "Maybe not quite as spectacular as the French cathedrals —"

Lonnie blew out audibly and shook his head, as if the comparison was absurd.

"But still pretty impressive," Luke said. He turned to Lonnie. "You've seen the French cathedrals?"

Again the note of defiance in his voice, which Lonnie seemed to miss. "A couple of them," he said.

"Whole different kind of architecture, isn't it?" Mike said.

"And what did you think of them?" Luke was staring at Lonnie, who was focused on digging up another scoop of potatoes.

"Incredible buildings, of course. But they would be, right? They took hundreds of years to build, some of them. That and a graveyard or two of peasants."

"And you don't think it was worth the effort?"

He shrugged. "Do you?"

Luke looked as if he were winding up to something, but while they'd been speaking a phone had rung from somewhere within, and Maria had hurried across the room and out the door to answer it. Now she appeared in the doorway and called to him.

As he rose he clapped Lonnie on the shoulder harder than was necessary. "We'll continue this little chat later," he said, and got up to follow Maria out to wherever the phone was.

When Luke had gone, Lonnie muttered, "He sure feels strongly about his French cathedrals, doesn't he?"

Though he had said it for Mike's ears, Brother Greg responded without looking up from his food. "He believes there's more to life than utility. But you wouldn't understand."

"I might," Mike said.

"They didn't build them based on some cost/benefit analysis. They loved God and wanted to express it, wanted to build something that pointed to him, that reached up towards him, that tried to touch him."

Lonnie smiled at Mike and surreptitiously rolled his eyes.

"They didn't calculate the cost," Greg continued. "But people who've lost their faith wouldn't get that."

"I haven't lost my faith," Mike said. "Just because I don't —"

"You let people take it away from you, people you don't even know. And in exchange for what?" He still had not looked up from his plate.

"It's not that simple."

"In exchange for nothing. I mean literally, nothing…No, no. I get it," he said, as if he sensed Mike was about to object. "It's a common thing."

"I didn't lose my faith," Mike said.

Greg shrugged and took another bite. They ate in silence until Luke came tilting back into the room. "That was our good sisters," he announced. "They got word that the road up is okay after all, so we're on again for tomorrow. Padre and I will go. You two can make the rounds," he said to the two other brothers. "Be sure you bring some water to the Chévez house, and spend a little time with them, all right? Check on Mercedes especially; she seemed to be a little unwell. Evening prayer in ten minutes."

He turned to Mike. "So you guys will be on your own tomorrow. I can trust you right? No parties in here, huh?" he laughed.

"We're big boys," Lonnie said, and he smiled at Luke just right.

"Big boys," Luke said, and he picked up his plate, brought it into the kitchen and left the room. Greg followed, leaving Joe with Mike and Lonnie.

As soon as they were out of earshot, Joe started in.

"They didn't know if the guy would make it," he said.

"What guy?"

"The robber. The one who got his hands cut off."

"He's still alive?"

"He was, but now, I don't know."

"Couldn't they have just taken one off?" Mike said.

Joe shrugged.

"You should have been here last month. Some prisoners, they take this other guy – member of a different gang - they kill him, they put his head in a bag and play *fútbol* with it. They played *fútbol* with his head, right in the prison yard. And the guards, they just watched it, let them do it until —"

"What sisters was Luke talking about?" Mike said.

"Take your pick," Lonnie said. "Plenty to choose from."

"The Missionaries of Charity," Brother Joe responded. "Mother Teresa's order. They have an *asilo* – a shelter - a couple miles from here, for old folks and orphans, girls. HIV-positive girls. Once a month they bring medicine and clothes up to the mountains. It's even poorer up there. We go along and give them a hand. "

"Girls with AIDS?" Mike said.

"Well, HIV-positive. There's quite a problem with that here."

"Of course there is," Lonnie said.

"Yeah," Joe said. "This place is a little…troubled. Like what happened in Ochao, the bad alcohol. Did you hear about that? They brewed up some homemade stuff - moonshine, basically. Four men died from it, and like twenty more went blind."

"Is there any problem this country doesn't have?" Lonnie said.

"No better place for us, then."

CHAPTER 22

MIKE HAD MANAGED TO down his glass of liqueur, strong and sharp, and Maria had offered him another, which tasted better, and another, even better, and now, sitting in the *pasillo*, he began to appreciate the warm cozy buzz of it. The evening had softened, and a firm cool breeze was working its way into the compound, sweeping at the leaves of the little palms scattered in front of him. The stars had come out with a fury.

He read from the old book on his lap:

> *Now, what harm will befall you in taking this side, in acting as a believer? You will be faithful, humble, grateful, generous, a sincere friend, truthful. Certainly you will not have those poisonous pleasures, glory and luxury; but will you not have others?*

He heard the latch to Lonnie's door open, and he rushed to finish the paragraph:

> *I will tell you that you will thereby gain in this life, and that, at each step you take on this road, you will see so great certainty of gain, so much nothingness in what you risk, that you will at last recognize that you have wagered for something certain and infinite, for which you have given nothing.*

He closed the book and put it on the tile beside his chair.

Lonnie emerged from his room, an unlit cigar stub in his mouth.

"Dozed off there for a minute," he said.

He pulled up a chair beside Mike and casually picked up the book from the tile.

"This isn't that trash you were reading before," he said.

"Nah, it's just a book Greg gave me."

"Oh boy, I bet it's really exciting then." He flipped it open and read aloud:

> *The difference between the mathematical and the intuitive mind: In the one, the principles are palpable, but removed from ordinary use; so that for want of habit —*

"Only the underlined parts," Mike said.

Lonnie turned to another page:

> *Man is full of wants: he loves only*
> *those who can satisfy them all.*

"Well, he's onto something there."

"Is that an underlined part?" Mike said.

Lonnie held the book up a moment to show him, flipped the pages, and read again:

> *You must wager. It is not optional.*
> *You are embarked.*

"We are embarked, huh? Embarked. This is monk stuff," he said. He flipped the pages one more time:

> *"I would soon have renounced*
> *pleasure," say they, "had I faith."*
> *For my part I tell you, "You would*
> *soon have faith, if you renounced*
> *pleasure."*

He closed the book and shook his head. "Nope. No, Mike. It's gloomy. Too gloomy. You like it because you're gloomy right now, too. Even after the Tulis you're gloomy, and I don't know why."

He dropped the book onto the tile, took a lighter from his pocket and lit the cigar stub, drawing in and blowing out a cloud of smoke that wafted forward, was caught in the breeze, shredded apart, and carried away. He leaned back to balance

THE CHILDREN OF EVE

on the two hind legs of his chair, putting his hands behind his head, the black butt of his cigar sticking out from between his fingers.

"You kind of crossed me up there at the restaurant, Mikey," he said. "I was doing all right, too. I was doing okay. She let me have her hand there for a second – you saw that, right? "

"I promised her mother we'd take care of her."

"Oh, we'd have taken care of her, all right. Besides, a promise to a mother is not a promise at all – you know that. It's a first principle. But look, I'm not an idiot. I get what's really going on here. You've got a little thing going for her."

Mike scoffed.

"No, I don't blame you. Powerful voodoo, she have. But look, Mike, you've got Sara. We agreed on that."

"No, we didn't."

"You love Sara."

"And I didn't like the looks of that tattoo guy."

"The guy at her house? The stalker? There's a million of those little pricks around here."

"Yeah, that's the problem."

Mike felt as though there was more to say, more he should say, something in the monkish line, but he wasn't sure exactly what, speaking as he was, as someone as compromised as Lonnie.

"Well, we've got to be careful, that's all I'm saying. We have to be careful around those women.

"No, no. I can't, Mikey, I can't do it, I can't renounce pleasure. It's too…pleasurable."

"I'm not saying —"

"And you know, you're not monk material, either, no matter how many of those books you read."

"If you say so, Lon."

"No, really. 'Brother Miquel'. Nah. 'Brother Tear-the-door-down-so-I-can-have-at-this-girl'. That doesn't really work either, does it?"

"Shut up."

"All right. Okay. I'll shut up now."

A giant toad had appeared from behind a bush to their right and was now crossing the courtyard in fits and starts fifteen feet in front of them. It took two quick hops and stopped dead still.

"Man, they've got some toads around here," Lonnie said.

"*Sapos*," Mike said, using the Spanish word.

"*Sapo. Sapo* huh?" He puffed on the cigar again. "*Sapo*." He spit out into the courtyard. "I wish the uncle would get back here so we could get out of this place. Where the hell is he, anyway?"

"I don't believe he ever killed people."

"You don't, huh?"

"He's a monk."

"He's a monk now, but...I'll tell you a story that we always heard about Uncle Marky when we were kids. You want to hear it?"

"No."

"It seems there were two bad guys – yellow guys, you know - guarding a tiny hut in the middle of the jungle."

"Vietnam?"

"'Nam," Lonnie said melodramatically. "Inside the hut was a good guy, tied to a chair. He was hurt from having been shot out of a plane, and pretty soon another bad guy was going to come, and he was going to hurt the man some more.

"But what none of them knew was that there were a couple other good guys hanging around, too, and they had high-powered rifles. They were very far away, but not far away enough. They'd been lying in a swamp for five hours, because that's where they could get the clearest shots. Every god-awful insect and reptile in the jungle had set up house inside their clothing. But they didn't care, and they didn't budge, because they were the good guys.

"They waited and waited for the bad guy who was going to hurt the man in the chair, until finally he appeared. But still, they waited, until they had the best possible shots, and then – bang!"

"Bang?"

"Bang."

"And that was Marco?"

"One of the good guys, yeah. That's what they'd say around the Thanksgiving table, anyway, when he wasn't there. If he was there, you couldn't talk about it – he didn't like that. He didn't like when you asked him about any of that stuff. By the way, you shouldn't ask him about it, either."

"Yeah, that's what Greg said."

"You talked to Greg about it?" Lonnie said, and cursed. "I suppose I'll hear about that."

The toad took two more quick hops and stopped. "Stupid *sapo*," he said, and he tossed the butt end of his cigar at it, missing by three feet. The creature didn't budge.

"Did he get the pilot back?" Mike said.

"Yeah, of course. He's Uncle Marco."

"And the bad guys?"

"Right in the noggin, Mikey, all three of them. The story has a happy ending."

"And you think that was a bad thing?"

"Well, it's a different thing, isn't it? Different then what he's doing now."

Mike thought of the pistol behind the books but didn't mention it to Lonnie, who rose from his chair, yawned loudly, and stretched his arms above his head.

"I'm going to hit the rack," he said. "Dream of Pilar." He laughed and slapped Mike on the shoulder. "Powerful voodoo, she."

* * *

Mike was half an hour alone in the *pasillo*, struggling with the Brother Greg book, reading from it, closing it, shutting his eyes, reading again, before Luke came from the front and sat in the chair Lonnie had vacated.

"What's up?" he said.

"*Nada*," Mike answered. "Just sitting here thinking."

"About what?"

"I was just thinking that the self is a relation that relates itself to its own self —"

"What?"

"Something I saw in Marco's library. Brother Greg let me in."

"He did? That's quite an honor."

"He let me borrow a book."

"And out of all the books in there, he gave you that one?"

"No, not that one. I just glanced in it. Still, hard to get a thing like that out of your head, isn't it, once you've read it? He gave me this." Mike turned it over so Luke could see the title on its spine.

Luke nodded his approval. "What do you think of it?"

"So far so good. I just started it though. I'm concentrating on the underlined parts. They're a little less abstract."

"Where's your partner?"

"Sleeping. He's like a dog: When there's nothing to do, he sleeps."

"Too bad. I wanted to talk to him about cathedrals."

Mike shook his head and laughed.

"Some god-awful big toads here, huh?" Luke said.

"Yeah. *Sapos*. It was good what we did today, wasn't it? Giving out water like that?"

"Yeah, it was good."

"The people appreciated it."

"They always do."

"It's hard to see how poor they are though, isn't it?"

"Yup."

"And they're even poorer up in the mountains?"

"They are."

"I was wondering - suppose there's any chance I could go there with you tomorrow?"

Luke looked at him with surprise.

"I think there's a chance, sure. We leave early, though – 5:30. And we're gone most of the day."

"Is it safe?"

"As safe as it is here, more or less."

"Which is it – more, or less?"

"Less, actually. But you'll be fine. And him?"

"I would guess he wouldn't be interested," Mike said. "He won't want to miss Marco, if he gets here."

"He's anxious to get to the beach, I suppose."

"Yeah, he wants to hie we to the beach."

"You too?"

"Not so sure anymore, actually, now that you ask. When do you think he'll be back?"

"Marco? I don't know."

"But he will be back, right? I mean, the guy does exist?"

"Oh, yeah. He exists."

"In time and space?"

"In time and space."

"He's an interesting man, isn't he?"

"Hmm mmm."

"For example, he was an Army Ranger, right?"

"He doesn't like to talk about that."

"In the library I saw the picture of him with a woman, a Vietnamese woman, maybe."

"He doesn't like to talk about that, either."

"And now, here he is in our *barrio*."

"You see a little incongruity there?"

"I wish I could meet him. I think I do, anyway."

"He's working on something pretty important. Otherwise, he wouldn't miss a trip with the sisters; he has a special spot in his heart for them. They saved him, he says."

"How did they do that?"

Luke look at Mike, sizing him up, as if wondering if he could be trusted, and after a moment began to speak.

"After the war, when they let Americans back in, he went there looking for her, for that woman in the photo. He searched for months, until they told him she was dead, killed because she'd been with an American, with him. They'd starved her. And he ended up wandering Asia, dead broke, lost, searching. Finally he found himself in Calcutta, like he was drawn to it, he says. He was walking in some slum there one day, and he came upon a little bundle on the edge of the sidewalk. He saw it move, so he went to it. It was a baby with a little piece of cloth over it, and it was just kicking one leg in the air, slowly, just moving that one leg. The thing was weak to the point where it couldn't even cry. All it could do was kick that one leg like that, there on the street, in broad daylight, with everyone walking by as if it were nothing.

"He asked the people whose it was, but no one knew or would say, or seemed to care; it was just another discarded human being; the place traffics in them. So he picked it up. He didn't know what he was going to do with it, he just knew he wasn't going to leave it there to die. He started walking again, not knowing where he was going.

"He walked for an hour, through the filth and the beggars and the dying people. And the only thing that came to matter to him was that baby. If the baby didn't die, then something would remain, something would survive. Hope would survive. That baby was hope.

"But he bought some milk in a market, and the baby wouldn't drink. He noticed that it had stopped kicking, and he tried to move its leg, but it wouldn't respond any more.

"As it was turning dark he found himself in front of a building with a sign over the door, 'House for the Sick and Dying', and he knocked, and a sister opened it. She let him in and gave the baby to a helper, who took it away to feed it. But as they were talking the helper returned and whispered something in the sister's ear."

He stopped, as if the story was finished.

"And then?" Mike said.

"I guess he broke down. He felt he was at the end, but he was actually at the beginning, as they say. The sisters let him stay there for a while, and he started to work with them and in a few months decided to become a brother, one of us."

"And here he is."

"And here he is. And that's why we work with the sisters, because he loves them. And of course because they're awesome."

CHAPTER 23

IT WAS STILL DARK as they made their way through the *barrio*, with Padre driving and Brother Luke in the passenger seat. Mike was sitting backwards in the bed of the truck, his back resting against the rear window. The shocks of the vehicle were worn, and he felt every bump the miserable road served up. The chilly morning seeped through the denim work shirt he wore. But it was thrilling to ride in the open in the dawn, with the *barrio* just coming to life around him.

Lights showed in a few of the *casas* and he peered into them as they went by, but could see only shadows moving within. They passed the entrance to *Los Ángeles* as if there were no significance to it; the road climbing down to her *casa* was dark and empty.

A few miles further along and a few confusing turns later they came to a concrete wall that enclosed an entire block. It was high and without windows, with razor wire coiled neatly atop it, and Mike thought it must be a prison wall, and wondered to himself about the horrors within. But they stopped halfway down the block, in front of a large steel door in the wall lit by a single bulb in a tin cone stuck overhead, with the name of the place painted on the metal of the door:

Misioneras de la Caridad
Asilo de Cortes

Luke got out of the truck and pressed a button fixed high up on the wall. He answered a question from inside, and in a moment the door swung open, exposing a short concrete drive, ending in a blank cinder block building. An SUV was parked on the drive. A slump-shouldered boy sat on its open tailgate, watching the newcomers through slightly crossed eyes, his mouth hanging open. At the side of the vehicle a woman stood with her arms crossed.

Mike hopped down from the truck and walked inside.

"*Hola*," the boy on the tailgate said to them. "*Hola*."

"*Hola*," Mike answered.

"*Hola*." The boy stood up and shuffled over to him, his fat hand extended.

Mike shook it. It was soft and wet. He let go, but the boy didn't. "*Hola*," he said.

"*Hola*," Mike answered.

"*Hola*."

"Oscar," the woman said to him. She came up and put her hand on the boy's shoulder, but he persisted. "*Hola*," he said again.

"*Hola*," Mike said. He pulled his hand away.

"*Hola*."

Along the walkway at the side of the building two women came, clad in nun's habits, white with soft blue trim. One was extremely tall and thin, with deep black skin and fine features.

She held herself upright, as if to emphasize her height, and seemed to glide as she walked. The other was tiny behind her, with olive skin and a large nose. She wore a gentle smile.

"This is Mike," Padre said. "Mike, this is Sister Rosario." He indicated the smaller woman.

"*Hola*," Mike said.

"*Hola*," Oscar said.

The sister smiled and stepped up to Mike, taking his hand in both of hers. "Welcome, welcome," she said in sing-song English. "It is so nice to have you. And you are coming up with us?"

"If I can help," Mike said.

"Of course. We are happy to have you. Thank you."

"And this is Sister Ibekwe," Padre said, indicating the tall woman. She smiled at him pleasantly and bowed. There was something impressively dignified about her, and Mike bowed back, more deeply.

"And this is Suyapa," Sister Rosario said, indicating a girl who Mike had not noticed, and who had stopped at the corner of the building and now stood leaning against it, her head slightly lowered and her eyes raised. "She is coming with us, too."

She was small and thin, unhealthily thin, Mike thought, with her skinny arms crossed over her narrow torso and her skinny legs sticking down from her knee-length skirt. Her hair was parted in the middle and pulled back behind her ears sloppily. Her nose was strong and a little flattened, and her mouth was small, her lips pressed together. But it was her eyes that struck Mike - huge, black, almond-shaped, spread wide apart - and as he watched they shifted to him, and it seemed as if there were some purpose to her look, as if she were asking him some important, uncomfortable, unanswerable question. Finally, a shadow of a smile appeared at the edge of her mouth.

"*Hola,*" she whispered.

"*Hola,*" Oscar said.

"Kritza," Sister Rosario said to the woman watching Oscar. "Perhaps you can take him to the kitchen and give him a cookie?"

Oscar looked at Sister Rosario, clutched his hands together and nodded twice. "Cookie," he said. He turned to Mike. "Cookie."

"Cookie," Mike said.

"*Hola,*" Oscar said. Kritza took him by the hand and guided him away by the elbow.

Rosario tipped her head down. "Oscar is Kritza's son. He is..."

"He likes cookies," Mike said.

"Yes. He likes cookies."

"And he likes to say hello."

"Yes."

Another sister – Candelaria – joined them as they packed the backs of the vehicles with stuff taken from a room in the cinderblock building - boxes of medicine, hygiene supplies, garbage bags full of clothes. When all was loaded, the padre pulled a small plastic bottle from his pocket and walked around the SUV, sprinkling water onto it and whispering some incantation. He did the same to the pickup, still parked on the road, and then turned the water on the group, waiting with bowed heads and hands folded together. As the drops hit them they crossed themselves, so Mike did, too.

"All right," Sister Rosario said, clapping her hands together. "Brother Luke, if you will drive our car, the sisters and Suyapa will go with you. Padre, you and Mike in the truck, yes?"

* * *

They followed the SUV for four or five blocks until the dirt road intersected with a boulevard. Things were starting to jump now, and they had to wait for taxi and motorcycle traffic before turning onto the pavement. A few miles later the boulevard came to a T against the main highway that passed Jocotenango at its southern edge. They turned left on it and followed as it curved around the fringe of the city, the traffic ever heavier, ever crazier, until at last they reached its outside edge. They made a left onto a worn and pocked asphalt road and saw the blue bulk of the mountains waiting for them ahead, the sun striking them from the side and lighting up their peaks and ridges.

"It's really a beautiful place," Mike said.

"Yes," Padre said. "It is."

In a few more miles, the country opened up, and they found themselves driving between orderly green crop fields, fenced in with new chain link. Here and there a paved drive stretched from the road, through a field, to a small, well-kept farm house, so different from the thrown-together huts of the *barrio* or the pinched-in *casas* of the city. Occasionally they passed a young man pedaling a bike or an older one walking, heading to work on one of the farms, machetes in hand. Already a couple had set up a rickety wooden stand with a palm-leave roof and stacked a neat, four-foot-high pyramid of melons within it; they were seated in vinyl chairs facing the road, ready for customers.

They came to the outskirts of a village and slowed to negotiate a speed bump - a *túmulo,* as the padre called it. Strung across two light poles at the entrance of the town was a banner adorned with colorful cut-out flowers and butterflies, with the words *"Feria Patronal a San Jose".*

"A fair?" Mike said.

"This is San Jose," Zeppe explained. "The feast of their patron saint is this week."

"All week?"

"They take their patron saints seriously here."

The highway narrowed to squeeze through the town, with *túmulos* every forty feet or so. The doors of the *casas* and *pulperias* along the way opened onto narrow, single-file walkways that in turn stepped down a foot, directly onto the surface of the road. All along the route people were out and about, leaning against the walls or standing with one foot on the asphalt and one on the stoop, chatting and watching the traffic pass. They loitered in twos and threes at the mouths of the little unpaved side roads that ran away from the asphalt and back into the guts of the town; looking up into them, Mike could see the same dirt and dust and meanness of the brother's own *barrio,* of what he thought of now as his own *barrio.*

The fair itself was set up along a road that intersected the main street and bordered the central plaza of the town. Two rows of neat white tents straddled this road, and from cables strung over them unlit paper lanterns hung like white bee's nests. Mike caught a glimpse of circus rides beyond the tents, and over everything arched the top of a Ferris wheel, motionless now, awaiting the night. A few forlorn-looking people moved about the grounds.

The plaza was the equivalent of four blocks and was raised up two high steps from the level of the street. It was clean and new and unCortesian. Scattered about it were some fifty trees, about ten feet tall - half of them palms and the others some kind of elm or maple, with bright, sparse leaves that cast a greenish light on the space below. There were ornate iron lampposts every fifteen feet or so, each holding in the air an array of four frosted round globes. At the far side of the plaza a handful of people sat on a retaining wall that held back a small grove of lavish ferns and short but lush palm trees. In front of the wall was a pavilion, on the steps of which three more people sat.

As they passed, Mike caught a view through the trees of an ancient-looking brown church at the back of the square.

Beyond San Jose the road continued narrow and straight over the plain before it began working its way along the edge of the mountains to the south and east. A sign at an intersection read "Tamalito, 11 km" with an arrow pointing straight and beneath it, "Curillo, 9 km", with another arrow pointing to the right, down the narrow intersecting road. They turned onto this road and immediately it began rising and twisting. The surface quickly worsened and soon the pavement disappeared, and on gravel and dirt they continued, struggling up switchbacks in what was now jungle. Mike peered into the foliage; in spots the sunlight found its way through the canopy to ignite the palm leaves in emerald. Occasionally he could see, hiding in the foliage, a *casa* of mud brick.

"By the way, it's a little more lawless up here," the padre said, "and a little cooler," as if these two things were equivalent.

"More lawless?"

"And cooler."

"More lawless than Joco?"

"And cooler. It's not that bad, though. Just be aware."

"Oh, I'm aware, Padre. More and more am I aware."

"Personal quarrels sometimes don't end up well here. So...don't get in any."

"Okay."

The trees cleared for a moment, and Mike caught a view of the valley below, and was amazed at how high they'd already climbed. He could see what must be Jocotenango in the distance, huddled up against another bulwark of mountains, with all its messy details erased by the distance.

"And there's drug-trafficking you don't want to interrupt. Your well-being won't be of particular interest to those engaged in it."

"How much you think your life is, huh?"

"How's that?"

"Nothing. Something someone said in the airport."

"Anyway, it's unlikely we'll run into anything like that, but if we do...well...don't."

They entered Curillo, a small village squeezed onto a shelf in the mountains. *Casas* baked in the mid-morning sun. An emaciated weathered old man watched a trash fire from a chair set on the bank of the road as if he were in front of a television. Four chickens stood under a pick-up truck, and a wretchedly thin, mangy *barrio* dog pressed itself against the side of a building to take advantage of the small strip of shade there. It looked like a mere sticker of a dog someone had pasted on to the adobe, and when it turned its head to look at them, Mike could see that it was missing an eye; the socket where it should have been was black and sunken.

They stopped at a *pulperia* with a bright yellow front. A woman stared at them from the doorway for a moment before retreating into the dark interior. While the others headed towards the store, Mike sauntered across the road in the direction of a little church. It was stark and uninviting, and looked almost more like a mausoleum than a church, with no windows in its front wall. Its door was held ajar with rocks. It looked dark and lifeless within.

A path led around its side, and Mike followed it. At the back the mountain resumed its plunge. Mike walked to its edge. The tops of trees rooted on the slope below were almost within his reach. He took another step and peered down. The bottom of the chasm was lost far below, hidden beneath a ledge, thirty feet down. A narrow pathway followed the ledge. On it, almost directly below him, a burro stood. It was tied to a bush and its head was hung low, almost to the ground. Mike could see no one to whom it might belong. Like the pigs and the chickens of the *barrio*, it seemed just another potentially useful animal unclaimed or abandoned in this land of want.

He heard someone approaching from behind and turned to see Suyapa, cradling something in her arms and picking her way along the path.

She was sticks; it was almost nothing coming towards him. Mike's heart rushed out to her. She came to his side and in the sunlight, now, Mike could see, impressed on her right cheek, an inch-long scar, stained darker brown then the surrounding skin and shaped like a crescent moon with its tips pointed upward.

In her arms were two small bags of clear liquid. Without a word she gave one to Mike. It was cold and wet and felt good in his hand. He pressed it against his forehead and felt the shock of the cold as it spread across the top of his head. Drops of condensation ran into his eyes, and he sighed.

Suyapa frowned. "No no no. To drink," she said, and she made a drinking motion with the other bag.

"*Sí*, but first..." He reached out to hold it against her forehead, but she jumped back quickly.

"It's all right," he said. "It feels good."

She smiled at him with her mouth closed and set at an angle. An odd smile, Mike thought, the kind that, if examined too closely, might reveal itself to be not a smile at all. He put the bag of water against his neck and looked back at the facing mountainside, far away, outlined against the pure blue sky and flooded in sunlight.

"It's beautiful, isn't it?" he said.

"*Sí*. My country is beautiful."

He noticed on the facing mountain, on what seemed an impossibly steep slope, a little brown mark, like a bug, shift to one side. There were others like it, he saw now, four or five of them, and as he watched he saw another move in the same fashion.

"Those aren't people up there, are they?" he said.

"*Sí*."

"What are they doing?"

"Picking coffee."

"But it looks so steep."

"*Sí*. It's very steep."

"Hard work."

"*Sí*, very hard," Suyapa said. "Dangerous. And even little children —"

"Yeah, I know."

He watched as another of the little marks shifted position.

"Well..." he said. "So how exactly do I drink this?"

Suyapa held her bag out and tore a little triangle off the corner, pinching it closed, and then put it to her lips and tilted her head, loosening her fingers to let the water stream into her mouth. Mike tried to do the same with his bag, but clipped too much off of it, and held it too tightly, and an arc of water jumped out and splashed against his face and neck. Suyapa stepped back to avoid getting wet and laughed.

Mike pinched off the flow. Suyapa held her hand over her mouth and shook her head, her black eyes sparkling with glee. She could laugh after all.

Mike tried again, bringing the bag up to his lips, tilting his head and releasing a stream of liquid into his mouth. As he savored the coldness and the wetness of it, Suyapa began to sing, her voice high and soft, as if she were singing to herself:

Adentro de ti lo sabes
Adentro de mí lo sé

She tipped the bag in her hands so that its opening pointed at Mike, and she smiled at him.

"No, you don't want to do that," Mike said.

She nodded her head and sang again:

Es que Él nos pone adentro
Amor, esperanza y fe.

"No, Suyapa. I'm not joking," Mike said.

She let her fingers go, squeezing the bag so that the water shot from it. Mike turned and the water splashed against his back, cold and shocking. She turned and began to run, and he started after her. She screamed, high and light, and bounded down the path, lithe and skinny, like a fawn just getting its legs, almost running into the arms of the padre as he turned the far corner of the chapel. She dodged lightly around him and disappeared.

The old priest watched her go and turned to Mike, shaking his head. "We're all ready to go over there," he said.

CHAPTER 24

THEY TWISTED UP THE face of the mountain for another hour, the jungle around them growing tighter and wilder as they climbed. People began appearing, walking uphill in the same direction as the vehicles, leapfrogging them as the road worsened and the vehicles slowed. The road ended in a circular clearing twenty-five yards in diameter. The banks of the mountain rose up steeply on three sides of the clearing and on the forth lay an arc of huge white boulders, somehow carried there to the edge of the level ground. Beyond the boulders the earth fell away sharply again, leaving a view of the distant facing mountains. At one edge of the boulders a rocky path led steeply upwards, disappearing far above them.

A hundred or so people – mostly women and children - waited there, perched on the rocks or sitting under the foliage at the clearing's edge.

The vehicles hooked around in the middle of the circle and came to rest. Women gathered to form a line behind them and children ran up to greet the arrivals. The twenty or so men kept their positions along the edges, unmoving, in the shadows, as if they did not want to be discovered.

Others – the people they'd passed – were still entering the clearing from the road.

Luke exited the truck, let the sisters out, and lowered the tailgates. In the back of the SUV the sisters and Suyapa arranged the medical supplies, and in the bed of the truck the clothes, stacking them by size. Ibekwe and Candelaria organized the line, backing it up ten feet from the SUV to provide some level of privacy, and doing what they could to form a single file. When everything was ready, Rosario went out towards the middle of the clearing and began to speak in Spanish, in a voice louder and stronger than Mike would have thought she could command.

"We thank God," she said, "for letting us be together again today, and we ask his help in our need. We know he is a loving God and looks down upon us all, and he knows when we are suffering, he knows what is needed to cure us, to cure our bodies, to cure our souls. Let us trust in him and pray to him. Let us allow him to guide us in all..."

And so on, to "Amen".

She motioned for the first woman in line, who was carrying a small baby, chubby and healthy-looking but sobbing, with tears smeared on its cheeks. Rosario spoke quietly with the mother, who lifted up the baby's sweatshirt to expose its stomach, dotted over with some kind of rash. The sister examined it, without hesitation touched it – something that struck Mike as utterly reckless - nodded, and pulled the sweatshirt down. She said something to Candelaria, who retrieved from the back of the SUV a small bottle of medicine and a baggie, knotted closed, a third full of white cream.

Rosario told the woman how to use the stuff and then pointed to the truck where Mike was, leaning back against its side and watching. Suyapa was seated on the tailgate. As the woman came toward them she slid to the ground.

"Pants," the woman said quietly to Suyapa.

"For the *niño*?"

"*Sí.*"

She picked out a tiny pair of blue jeans and held them up to the baby, nodding and handing them to the woman, who thanked her and started away.

Suyapa jumped back onto the tailgate.

"There's really nothing for me to do here, is there?" Mike said.

She shook her head. "Useless," she said.

Mike shoved her, and it was like blowing a feather. She leaned to the side, bounced upright and poked him in the shoulder.

"What's Padre doing over there?" Mike asked.

The old man had taken two vinyl chairs from the bed of the truck and positioned them in front of the boulders, and now was sitting face to face with a short, fat woman. She was speaking to him with urgency, her hands working the air. He listened intently, his chin in his hand, his elbow on his knee. A line of a dozen more women waited their turn, a decent distance behind the woman.

"Confessions," Suyapa said. "Don't you know about confession?"

"Yes, I know about confession."

"Then you should go."

"Me? No thanks."

"You should go, *Mojado.*"

"*Mojado?*"

"*Sí. Mojado.*"

"Nice."

"You have no sins?"

Mike scoffed. "Oh, I'm a sinner, all right," he said. "A great sinner."

She laughed; even at her age she could see through his bluster. He was no great sinner, but a petty one. His were paltry sins, done not from the will, but from the lack of it, from cowardice and lust and a love of the easy way. An embarrassment it would be to confess such things.

"Now you've gone and hurt my feelings," he said. "A man likes to be known as a great sinner."

"*Estupido,*" she said.

"*Estupido,*" he repeated. "That's me. *Estupido.*"

"But you must go, *Mojado*. It's important."

"I'll think about it," he lied, and he gave her another shove and started away, to the mouth of the road, where Luke was kicking a soccer ball with a circle of skinny, shirtless, shoeless kids. Mike joined them for a moment, playing half-heartedly, then left them and started walking along the edge of the clearing.

The men hanging in the shadows of the mountainside were brown and worn. They wore old clothes and high plastic boots and held machetes at their sides. They ignored Mike as he passed. Joyless men, he thought, grim men. Only the very old ones seemed capable of smiling, knowing as they did that they would not have to endure any of it much longer.

None of them joined Rosario's line, though no doubt many of them needed what the sisters were offering. None of them joined Padre's line.

"*Hola*," Mike heard as he passed what he'd thought was a deserted part of the mountainside, and he turned to see a little boy, blended into the green and brown. It must have been him, the boy, who'd greeted him, but he was looking away, out towards the open side of the clearing beyond Padre and the boulders, out into the sky.

"*Hola*," Mike said, but the boy didn't respond. Mike waited a moment before walking on. After ten steps he heard a rustling behind him and then the crunch of footsteps, and he turned to see the boy following him. He'd stopped walking when Mike had and was looking over Mike's head, to the mountainside beyond.

Mike took another five steps, stopped and turned. The boy halted again.

He had tousled hair and a smudged face. He was barefoot and wore a threadbare hand-me-down shirt that he would not fit into for another few years, if ever, and a pair of red pants that he'd grown out of long ago.

"You're following me then?" Mike said.

He was silent.

"Yeah, you're following me. What's your name?"

The boy ignored the question.

"A secret, I suppose. Well…"

"Alejandro," the boy said, still not making eye contact. "Alejandro Cristiano Saurez de la…"

"No no. Only one name," Mike said. "I know how you people are. You wear names out." Then more loudly, as if to tell all the children in Cortes: "From now on, everyone gets only one name."

Over the boy's shoulder he saw Suyapa coming toward them, frowning at what he'd said and holding a plastic bag.

Two children followed closely behind her, then three, then five, and eight and twelve.

"*Mojado*," she said as she came up to him. She held out the bag. It was full of hard candy. "For the *niños*."

He took a piece from the bag and held it up. "Alejandro," he said. With the other sixteen children the boy rushed to him, and as he began to hand out the candy more appeared, from between the boulders, from the mountainside, from out of the very dirt, it seemed, and they poured towards him and engulfed him, their dirty, cracked hands held out, their voices filling the air. He could feel the power of their combined mass, like the strength of a river's current; they could wash him away if they wanted to, they could tear him apart and carry him off in bits like ants with a grasshopper. A sea of brown faces and glistening black eyes, ragged hair and runny noses. What *did* they have to be so happy about? What did he have to be so happy about?

Suyapa saved him, making the children form and keep a line, ragged as it was, and ejecting a dozen or so who tried to return for seconds and several adults who attempted to join in, too. When they'd run out of children the two of them sat on one of the boulders, a handful of filthy ones arrayed in a semicircle in front of them, sucking on their candy and looking up at them, expecting more fun or more sweets or more something.

"*Pobrecitos*," Suyapa said.

Back at the center of the clearing a pregnant young girl was talking to Sister Ibekwe, fear in her eyes. Taking her by the elbow, the sister began guiding her toward the padre, still sitting in the vinyl chair, listening, but the girl broke away, shaking her head, and with her arms crossed marched across the clearing to the mountainside and sat by herself.

"What do you want to be when you grow up?" Mike asked Suyapa, in order to say something. But he immediately realized how clumsy and stupid a question it was. He was talking to a poor girl in Cortes, a poor HIV-positive girl. She would not grow up to be anything. She would be nothing. She was nothing.

"I'm going to be a sister," she said without hesitation. "Like them. I always wanted to be like them."

He looked at her with pity.

"You never wanted to have a family?" That question, too, sounded absurd as soon as he'd mouthed it.

"For a sister," she said, "all the world is family."

Luke had wrapped up his ball game, and now came toward them with Candelaria and a short, leathery, bow-legged man.

"This man says there's a woman farther up," he told Mike, motioning toward the trail. "Too sick to come down, so we're going to her. Care to come along?"

CHAPTER 25

MIKE HAD THOUGHT HIMSELF in decent shape, but already, on the trail's third switchback, his breathing was short, the tops of his thighs and the backs of his shins were burning and he struggled to keep up with the others who, ten unbridgeable feet ahead, seemed to be having no trouble at all. Sister Candelaria moved along like a creature in a place of no gravity, swinging a long tree branch she was using as a walking stick. Brother Luke was on one side of her and the stick figure of Suyapa on the other, her arm linked to the sisters. Slightly ahead of them and to the side moved the bow-legged guide, whose name, apparently, was Hector.

The trail folded over itself again and headed in the opposite direction, still climbing. He was fifteen feet behind now and losing ground. Luke was absorbed in conservation with Candelaria and hadn't noticed his struggles. Only Suyapa glanced back occasionally, smiling at him with a touch of skepticism and waving him forward.

Candelaria's stick was a couple feet taller than she was, and the end of it moved back and forth above her head as she walked, like an upside-down pendulum. Mike counted its swings until she reached the next corner and turned again out of sight.

He stopped in the shade at the inside edge of the trail, stood on one foot and removed his sandal to shake out a sharp little rock that had been poking at his sole; he'd worn the wrong choice of footwear for climbing a mountain. He took his water bottle from his back pocket and allowed himself a small sip, and wondered how far the trek was; he had not taken enough water. His sandals were wrong. He had not taken enough water. The air was too thin. He was not in the shape he'd thought he'd been in. Turning back was the only rational thing to do, and he'd all but convinced himself that he must do it when he heard Suyapa's voice from over his head. Looking up he saw her leaning over the edge of the bank above, surrounded by scrub pine trees.

"*Mojado!*" she said. "Careful with that water!" She waved him along with the back of her hand and waited as he turned the corner and trudged his way up to her side. She pointed down the mountainside to the clearing, already far below, with people like little brown fingers stuck on the rocks and others in a line leading to a pair of toy-like vehicles, where two figures shone white in the sun, one thin as a wick and towering over the other.

"Come on," Suyapa said.

"I need a break. Air's awful thin up here."

"*Rapido*," she said.

"That's why. Because of the air."

"I see," she said, and laughed.

She took his hand and tugged at it, and they started forward again. They walked together for seven steps before she let go and ran forward to the group, waiting at the next corner.

They climbed for another half hour, Mike struggling and falling back, looking ahead at the group gliding along ahead of him, watching the end of Candelaria's stick ticking in the air steadily, reminding him that the hour was late, that decisions would have to be made. Suyapa goading him on. The others stopping at last and waiting for him, generously pretending to be taking a break. Him falling behind again.

At one point, the group came upon a burro grazing in the shade alongside the road. It started after them half-heartedly, stopped and swung its head around to look at Mike, thirty feet behind. Mike swerved to the side to give it leeway, not being certain how aggressive a burro could be. But the animal let him pass and followed behind lethargically for ten paces before stopping in the middle of the trail and with one eye watching him climb gasping away.

The group stopped again to wait for him at what he thought must be the top of the world, but which turned out to be just another mocking turn in the road, with the trail beyond continuing its demonic climb. Somewhere along the way they'd picked up a ragged little boy who waited with the others, eyeballing Mike, shifting a baseball-sized rock from hand to hand in a way that struck him as threatening.

"Are you going to make it?" Luke asked.

"I might. It's possible. Any idea how much further?"

"Hector says it's not too far."

"That right, Hector?" Mike asked the old man.

The hard little piece of wire named Hector gave Mike a smile that took over his entire face, deepening the creases in his polished brown skin, squinting his eyes almost closed and revealing a gap where his front teeth had been, back beyond the memory of men.

"I think he's playing a trick on us," Mike said in English. "Look at him. Do you trust this guy? And that kid – what's he going to do with that rock?"

"We'll take a break," Luke said. He led Mike off to the side of the trail and sat with him on the bank. Candelaria propped her walking stick on the gravel, leaned against it and looked up the trail as if longing to continue.

"Just for a minute," Luke said to her, and he turned to Mike. "So what do you think of our country?"

Mike nodded his head so as not to have to expend the effort to speak.

"Yeah," Luke said. "Me, too." He picked up a pebble and flipped it into the middle of the road. "I hear you went to Mexico with him, too," he said.

"With Lonnie? Did Marco tell you that?"

"To Mexico City, for Holy Week, of all things. And not one of the resorts?"

"Well, we went to Mazatlán, too, of course. I mean… But Lonnie likes to go places other than tourist spots. He calls it 'being authentic'."

"Hmm mmm. And then last year, to Spain. What did you do there?"

"Running of the bulls." Mike said softly.

"You ran with the bulls?"

"I didn't say that. I purposely avoided a complete sentence."

"You watched the running of the bulls."

"Yeah. A little different flavor when you say it like that. And we went to a bullfight."

"So you're a bullfighting fan?"

"Not really. Not since I've seen one, no."

"So you went halfway around the world to see a bullfight, but you're not a bullfighting fan."

"Yeah, I guess so."

"And you went to a Holy Week celebration, but you're not Catholic."

"I am Catholic."

"Well..."

"I am. I'm just —"

"And you're not rich, like him?"

"No, not rich. The opposite of rich."

"I'm a little confused."

"Yeah, me too."

"Why do you do those things?"

"I don't know. So I can say I did them?"

"And to whom would you say that?"

"I don't know. To you, I guess. No one else seems quite so interested."

"And you would say it to impress me?"

"I didn't bring it up, you did."

"I was just wondering why you'd do that, go to those places. Why you'd come here. I understand your partner coming – that's strictly for the money. But you...I don't get it."

"I don't know, Luke. I don't think so deeply into it." He laughed and looked at the brother. "Don't you get it? I don't think so deeply into anything."

"I see. Just a minute, sister," he said, and turned to Mike again. "And you guys don't work?"

"Sure, we work. Well, right now I'm between jobs. Or between a job and something, anyway. I'm signed up for college next semester, but I'm not exactly sure…I may or may not go." Decisions would have to be made. "And you know Lonnie's story, right? He doesn't have to work."

"Not as long as Marco keeps signing the papers."

"He will, though, won't he?"

Luke shrugged.

"Lonnie's got this idea of visiting every country in the world."

"In lieu of working."

"I suppose."

"And hence Spain. Hence Mexico."

"Yeah, hence. When he leaves here, he's going to Brazil."

"But not you?"

"No, not me."

"Because he didn't invite you?"

"I don't have the money for it."

"But it would have been nice to have been asked."

Mike shrugged.

"They speak Portuguese there, I believe, not Spanish."

"That's right. Portuguese." He turned to face Luke. "Look, if you're saying he's using me for my awesome Spanish skills – well, I know. I'm aware of that. But I enjoy his company, and I go to places I wouldn't otherwise go. I do things I wouldn't otherwise get a chance to do."

"Like go to bull fights you don't like?"

"Yeah, for example. Something like that."

"Lovely," Luke said, and he began to rise. "Lovely. We better get going."

"What's a *casa loca*?" Mike said.

"*Casa loca*? 'Crazy house', it means. I would think someone with your awesome Spanish skills —"

"I know the translation, but what does it mean? Here, in this country, in Cortes."

"It's a place where they take people and torture them to death."

"Yeah. I was afraid it might be something like that."

* * *

The trail narrowed and shot up a ten foot rise that Mike had to clamber up on all fours. It seemed like the last straw to him, again, and he wondered what he would do if the trail kept rising, wondered if he could go on, but at the top he was relieved to see the way flatten out for fifty yards, running through the baked-hard yard of a white adobe hovel. Bushes bordering the yard were hung with pieces of clothing drying in the sun, like some strange colorful fruit. Behind them stood trees with clumps of small green bananas growing upside down from their branches.

They slipped past the side of the hut and around three dogs lying in the sun, sleeping, utterly uninterested in the troop passing by.

The place appeared abandoned, but at the far end of the clearing Mike looked back and glimpsed a girl peering out from the corner of the *casa*. She ducked behind the wall again for a moment before peeking out once more. He walked half way back across the yard towards her, took a piece of candy from his pocket and held it up. She began walking towards him tentatively.

She was bare-footed and wore a ragged print dress a few sizes too big for her, and her right forearm had a twenty-degree bend in its middle, as if it had been broken and not set. Utterly alone in the world, she seemed, tiny and lean and hollow. An elf, a mountain elf. A hunger elf. A starvation elf.

Mike sunk to his haunches and held out the candy. The girl came to within five feet of him and stopped. One of the dogs behind her lifted up its skull to look, was unimpressed, and laid it back down.

"How old are you?" Mike said.

The girl shrugged.

"Me too. Go ahead. It's yours."

She looked up at him and smiled, a deep dimple appearing in her cheek. He nodded and she shifted forward another step, took the candy and backed up two paces. Through the dirt on her face he could see her honey skin.

"But it costs a lot," Mike said.

The girl stepped back and furrowed her brow.

"Costs one hug."

He heard movement behind him and turned to see Brother Luke at the edge of the jungle, watching him.

He kissed the girl on top of her head and let her out of his arms.

CHAPTER 26

THE PATH DROPPED DOWN a fifteen-foot pitch, so steep that Mike could use one hand to balance against the mountainside as he descended. It landed on a shelf that stuck out some thirty feet, filled along its entire length by an adobe *casa*, its back wall – windowless, blackening, peeling - almost touching the steep dirt bank, as if it, too, would use the mountain for support. The path squeezed along between the side of the *casa* and a line of palm trees that bordered the lip of the shelf. The group followed it in single file. Over the edge Mike could see, twenty-five feet below, the trail winding back on itself and disappearing into jungle.

They turned the corner onto a narrow strip of dirt that ran across the front of the building, and from an open doorway an elderly woman watched them – slight, gray-haired, leather-skinned and wrinkled, frail; filled, it seemed to Mike, with hard years. She greeted them with a stretched and toothless smile. Without a word she turned and went inside.

Hector sat down on the ground beside the doorway, his back against the wall, and smiled up at the others as they stepped over his outstretched legs. They followed the old lady into the *casa*, Mike bringing up the rear. The silent little boy with the rock had disappeared.

The old woman was standing with two others in the middle of the darkened room, and they started speaking with Luke and Candelaria, slowly, quietly, as at a funeral. Suyapa stood beside the sister, holding her hand. Mike stayed just inside the doorway and surveyed the place.

The floor was dirt, hard packed, uneven, crumbly, like cement badly poured. Along the walls were three wood-framed beds with thin mattresses, sloppily made up. From the low roof two hammocks sagged. Stuffed up in the ancient black rafters were bundles of stuff netted together – pots and pans, clothes, and God knew what else - with more junk bunched together in nets hanging from spikes hammered into the walls. Dirty light slanted into the room from a narrow doorway in the far wall.

In the gloom Mike looked over the women, wondering which of them was ill. They were speaking very quietly, and he took two steps towards them.

A shuffling noise came from behind him, and a soft moan, and he turned. There was another bed in the darkness behind the door, with a body in it. Mike retreated a step and looked over at the others; they had heard it too, and they came up to the bed as Mike moved aside, Suyapa still holding Candelaria's hand. The sister bent over and talked softly to the body, which whispered some response that Mike also couldn't hear. She uncovered its upper half and gently pressed on the naked torso. The body moaned again. Candelaria covered it back up and stroked its cheek with her hand.

"She wants to be turned over," she said.

Luke and the women stepped up to the bed. Mike paused long enough so that there was no room for him.

"There is a disease that makes the body hard," Candelaria said.

Mike took another step back.

"It is this that she has."

As they turned the woman over, she moaned more loudly, more pitifully, with the last scrap of life she had left, it seemed to Mike. He looked away, and his eyes came to rest on a small crooked table leaning against the opposite wall, draped with a white cloth fringed in yellow and blue. On either side of the table was a vase of palm fronds and a lit candle in a small, ornate medal stand. Behind them stood a statue of the radioactive woman, her hands folded in prayer, her face calm, her eyes gazing down and to the side, ignoring the death happening to her left. Consistently, strangely indifferent to suffering, she was.

He heard another moan from the bed – sharper and more urgent still, shocking in the quiet of the room.

"She should see a priest," Candelaria said.

The older woman shook her head and one of the other, younger ones waved her arm in the air to indicate the impossibility of it.

"It's too bad our padre couldn't come with us. But he is old, and he could not make the climb. Nonetheless," she said, without specifying nonetheless what.

Two small solemn brown faces had appeared in the doorway in the far wall, staring cautiously at the goings-on. They ducked away as Mike stepped carefully around the huddle and started moving towards them.

The doorway did not lead outside, as he'd thought, but into a narrow room lit by three rough windows cut through the newly painted white walls. Beneath them, running along one of the walls and rough-molded of the same plastic-looking stuff was a low counter with round edges. On it were a variety of kitchen things - old tin pans, plastic bowls, eating utensils. At a corner of the shelf was an oven – a small igloo-like adobe mound with a trough cut into it for feeding wood and extracting ashes. A metal coffee pot sat on top of a grid placed over the trough, and along its sides smoke rose from the cinders beneath. Crooked black sticks lay bound in a bundle on the counter alongside.

There were gaps between the top of the wall and the cross beams that supported the corrugated tin roof, which was sprayed with a dozen tiny pinholes that must have been hell in the rain. On spikes hung an empty gallon milk jug and a fraying wooden basket.

The two girls had retreated to the corner of the kitchen, and they stared at the white man, the younger one peeking out over the shoulder of the older. They had broad noses, high cheekbones, and enormous eyes. Their hair was long and ratty. They wore identical white dresses, as if their mother had dressed them in their finest for the occasion. The dresses were too small for the larger girl and too large for the smaller. They held their fingers in their mouths and looked up at Mike warily.

He smiled at them, said *hola*, and sunk to his haunches. As he reached into his pocket, he heard chanting behind him, and he stretched his head back through the doorway to see the group crowded around the bed, their heads bowed. Suyapa stood at the side of Candelaria with her wand of an arm extended across the nun's waist.

Mike turned again to the girls. "How are you?" he said.

Their expressions did not change.

"Do you live here?" he asked. They were silent.

At the other end of the room was a narrow doorway leading outside, its door ajar. Mike placed two pieces of candy on the ground, stood, picked his way around the stuff on the floor – a clay coffee cup, an empty plastic bag, a length of metal beam – and went outside.

There was a strip of cleared ground bordered on the far edge by a line of trees, just beyond which the mountain fell away. In the intervening space, spread atop a stiff-looking white tarp, lay a circle of small brown oval pellets, spread out in the sun in a single layer. The smell of coffee soaked the air.

Mike stooped down to pick up one of the beans and held it to his nose. He rubbed it between his fingers and put it in his mouth. He loosened a sandal to release another rock, examining the sun-burnt pattern that the sandal had left on his foot. As he reached for another bean he heard rustling to his right.

In the shadows at the inside edge of the clearing a man sat on a makeshift bench, his back towards the black bank of the mountain. Resting horizontally on his lap was a long wooden pole.

Mike put the bean down and stood. "I'm sorry," he said. "They smell so good. They taste so good."

The man stood and walked forward, scooping up a fistful of the beans. He held them out to Mike without a word.

"Thank you," Mike said. He put them in his pocket.

"That's my wife inside," the man said. "The dead one."

* * *

When the group returned to the clearing the vehicles were already packed. The shade had grown to cover half the ground, and under it the padre and the two sisters stood talking with a group of ten or so mountain folks.

"Many people today," Sister Rosario said as they walked toward the vehicles. "We were able to see many people. How much God loves us."

CHAPTER 27

THE VEHICLES JOSTLED ALONG the road, squeezing past clumps of people working their way down from the clearing, carrying the booty they'd received from the sisters.

"They really are worse off up here, aren't they?" Mike said.

"Some pretty hard lives," the padre said. He seemed distracted and tired.

"You heard a lot of confessions."

"Yes. They don't get many chances to see a priest. I didn't get to hear yours, though, did I?"

"Ah, Padre. You wouldn't want to hear my sins."

"It's okay. It's in my job description."

"Yeah, I suppose. I guess I should say, I wouldn't want to hear them."

"Forgiveness, mercy – these are great things," the padre said. "Or maybe it all seems like nonsense to you?"

"I'm not much of a judge of what's nonsense." He took a coffee bean from his pocket and put it in his mouth. "I don't know, Padre. I don't feel ready for it, I guess."

"Well, if you change your mind..." Even his voice sounded weary, and Mike turned to look at him as he drove. All the gleam in him was extinguished, and his eyes had a heavy look.

"Terrible things, you hear," he said, as if to himself.

"What kind of things?"

The padre looked at him and smiled sadly.

"You can't say, I suppose."

"No, I can't."

They rode in silence for a mile, steadily downhill.

"It's the women and children who suffer most," the padre said.

"Yeah, I suppose. A lot of violence up here, I imagine?" Mike said.

"Yes, much violence."

"Husbands abusing their wives?"

He nodded.

"Aren't there any police?"

"No."

"So if someone gets killed?"

"Revenge, maybe. Maybe nothing."

After a moment he went on. "The girls here," he said, "some of them, they get pregnant at a very young age - fourteen or fifteen, even younger. And they go down to the city by themselves..." His voice faded.

"I suppose they feel trapped, like they have no choice," Mike said.

"And the men, the boys, nothing matters to them. Nothing is expected of them. It all lands on the girls."

Mike looked out the window.

"It's a terrible thing," the padre said. "Violence preying upon violence."

They passed three boys, lean and gangly, loping down the road with big steps, their arms swinging freely. They made way for the car and as it passed turned to look through its windows at Mike, laughing as if one of them had told a joke.

"Worse things, too," the padre continued. "To the children."

"What about the children?"

"The worst you can imagine."

Mike looked away and tried not to imagine at all.

"You know, Padre," he said after a moment. "I've heard people say that coming to places like this helps them find God. Deepens their faith, or something. I've got to say, though, it seems to me that it'd be more likely to make you give up on the idea of God altogether."

"And yet that's not the effect it's having on you."

Mike said nothing, and after a moment, the padre continued. "If there were no God," he said, "it would mean these little ones have been completely abandoned. And that cannot be."

"Are you sure about that, Padre?"

He looked at Mike with the sadness collected in his face. "Yes," he said. "I am."

* * *

They stopped again at the corner store in Curillo, and as the others entered it Mike sauntered across the road towards the little chapel. Everything was still. He saw only two people - an old woman watching him without interest from her doorway and an ancient man in a straw sombrero sitting motionless on a stoop. It appeared to be a town of no children.

An old *barrio* dog lay in the middle of the road. It opened an eye and tracked Mike as he walked to the doorway of the church.

The interior was weakly illuminated by the sunlight from the doorway and the two barred windows at its side. It had a white and black checkered tile floor and five rows of ancient wooden pews that staggered up to a bare wooden altar. Pinned to the wall behind the altar was a large rough cross on which hung a statue of Christ, his thorned, bleeding head leaning to one side, his eyes open and his face placid and curious, as if contemplating this oddity, the arrival of this white man at his door, interrupting his suffering.

He became aware of someone behind him, turned, and saw Suyapa. She gave him the slightest of smiles before dropping her head and moving past him. She walked slowly forward, her hands folded in front of her, like a pious little skeleton, and she side-stepped into one of the middle pews, knelt, crossed herself, and bowed her head.

After a moment's indecision, Mike followed. She sidled over on her knees to make room for him. He knelt beside her, feeling awkward. She looked at him out of the corner of her eye, then slowly raised the tips of her fingers to her forehead, holding them there for a moment. When Mike did nothing, she lowered her hand, paused, and brought it up to touch her forehead again. He did the same. She smiled and put her hand to her sternum, and he copied her. To her left shoulder, to her right shoulder, Mike following along. She kissed the back of her thumb, and Mike did that, too, and felt very *latino* about it. She smiled at him again and turned back towards the altar, bowed her head and closed her eyes.

A wisp of smoke kneeling there beside him. Barely there now, soon gone forever.

Mike wanted to save her. He wanted to wrap himself around her and protect her like a shell protects its egg.

He looked up again at the tortured body on the cross. "Oh Lord," he said silently, for that, he knew, was how all prayers began. "Oh Lord." And he thought of the woman hardening to death up in the mountains, and the gravel elf with the permanently broken arm, and the pregnant fourteen-year-olds, and children to whom even worse things were done, and most of all he thought of the innocent girl there beside him, so alive and so doomed. "Leave her alone," he prayed. "Leave them all alone and do it to me instead."

* * *

When they came out of the church the rest of the group was standing by the cars holding bottles of Coke and bags of water. Suyapa ran ahead to where Sister Rosario was standing with Luke. The sister engulfed her in her arms, and they hugged as if they hadn't seen each other in years.

Mike walked to them and the brother handed him a bag of water. He tore the corner off carefully, watching Suyapa watching him. He brought the bag to his mouth and squeezed it so that the water arced cleanly out of it and into his mouth. He looked at Suyapa proudly.

"*Mojado*," she said. She let go of Rosario and ran to hug Candelaria, standing at the open trunk of the SUV, rearranging the stuff inside.

"There's nothing to her," Mike said to Rosario.

"She has been very sick. She was in the hospital for a while. But she is getting better. She was born in mountains like these. She was poor like this. And she likes to come up with us when she can, so I could not say no."

"Why was she in the hospital?"

"She had a…" and she paused for a movement and gave him a small, shy smile, stuck up her little finger and wiggled it. "You understand?"

"No."

"In the stomach."

"In the stomach what?"

"A parasite. A worm."

"I see," he said. "Well…" He took another drink of water. He wanted to ask her about her condition, about the HIV, but didn't think it the right time, so asked instead if she was an orphan.

"No. She has a family, but…"

"But what?"

"It is not good. Her father drinks. And he was not good to her mother. And I think to Suyapa, too, he was not good." She looked over at Mike to gauge his reaction.

"He hit them?" he asked.

"I think so, yes."

"Go on."

"A month ago, she left us, and went back to them."

"Why?"

"It is her family. She wants to be a sister, yes, but she wants her family, too. She is just a little girl, after all. She packed up a paper bag and left without telling anyone. She just left a note."

"What did it say?"

"I cannot tell you."

"Where does her family live?"

"In a *barrio* in Tamalito. It is a dangerous place. How much courage she had to go there."

"What happened?"

She hesitated again for a moment.

"When she got to the house, her father became angry with her. He told her that they did not have to feed her, and why should they? He said that they had never wanted her, that she was a problem for them since the day she was born – before, even, since the day her mother became pregnant with her, and all she had ever done was to cost them money, and never brought them home any money. And then he said something horrible to her."

"More horrible than that?"

"He said that he had never wanted to have her at all, and that they had gone all the way into town with the money, but the bitch would not do it - that's the word he used for her mother. She would not go through with it."

"He told Suyapa that?"

"*Sí.* So she came back to us. And then, the parasite."

"But she's okay now?"

Before she could answer, Brother Luke clapped his hands. "Let's do it," he said. They returned to their vehicles and continued down the mountain.

* * *

It was dusk by the time they reached San Jose, and the place had turned magical, lit by the glow of the streetlamps and the lanterns of the fair. Children ran around the square and couples moved arm and arm about the white tent village. Fireworks sprayed out in the sky and cracked overhead. The Ferris wheel, trimmed with blue, red, and green lights, turned rapidly in the air.

In front of the pavilion, at the corner of the square, couples danced to music coming from speakers set atop its step. Under its roof, the DJ's – two sharp-looking boys with gelled hair - stood around a small bank of electronics.

From the window of the SUV in front of them a thin brown arm stuck out and a finger pointed.

CHAPTER 28

IT WAS DARK WHEN they arrived back at the mission. The other brothers and Lonnie had already eaten, but Maria had kept plates warm for the travelers. As they ate Mike tried to keep the conversation going to block out the occasional muted beats of a bongo drum coming from the back, but he wasn't entirely successful, and he noticed significant looks pass between Luke and the padre.

"He is getting a little better," Mike said. Damn him.

The brothers didn't respond.

Mike excused himself and retreated to the dorm. Lonnie was sitting in front of his bedroom door with his hat on, a cigar in his mouth and the drums between his knees, looking smug. When he saw Mike coming he beat out a drum roll.

"Ah," Lonnie said. "Brother Miguel. Miguel the Pious. Great sinner and holy man." He blew out a smoke ring.

"Funny," Mike said. He pulled up a chair and sat. "You have another one of those?"

"Still allowed to smoke, are we?"

"Just give me one."

Lonnie extracted a cigar from his shirt pocket and put it with a book of matches on the arm of Mike's chair. "But don't touch me," he said. "You may be sacred now, but you're all sweaty, and God only knows what you picked up out there."

Mike unwrapped the cigar, lit it, and took a big draw. He sighed deeply.

"How was your day?" he said.

"It was all right," Lonnie said in a self-satisfied way.

"Did you see Pilar?"

"Right away to Pilar, is it? Well, yeah, I must confess I got a little bored with Brother Joe's stories about the moral depravity of this place he loves so much - did you know they kidnap people here to sell their organs? - and I gave Rodrigo a call," Lonnie said. "He took me there, to Pilar's. She wasn't home, though. Off picking coffee or some damn thing. So I went with him to one of those *palenque*s."

"You went where?"

"A *palenque*. A cock-fight. You've seen the signs around, right? And let me tell you, it was an edifying experience. Saw a man making love to his chicken – what was left of his chicken, that is."

"You mean he —"

"No, not like that. Making love in the old fashion sense. You're a sick man, you are. No, this was a platonic love, as far as I could see. But that man loved that chicken, Mikey. The scraggly little thing had lost, though, and when a chicken loses one of those things, it really loses. Kind of like a bullfight. Well, the guy runs into the ring and picks up the bloody corpse and cradles it in his arms like it was his baby, rocking it and kissing it on the beak – making love to it. He tried to stick its wing back on, but...you know."

"He kissed it?"

"That man loved that chicken, Mikey. He shook it a couple of times, like to wake it up, and it twitched a little, but nothing doing."

"So you didn't see Pilar."

"Probably making soup out of it now. Kind of a stringy thing, though."

"Did you see her?"

"Yeah, sure I saw her, after the *palenque*. I got back to her house just as she was coming from work, and I tell you, she may be the finest woman in the world – which, of course, she is - but picking coffee's apparently no stroll in the park. Renders one a little gamey, it seems."

"You wanted authenticity."

"Yeah, I wonder about that, though. Anyway, we sat there for a little while, until it became obvious that Ana wasn't going to let us be. And with the little sister running around —"

"Naila."

"Yeah, her. I tell you, she's another one in the making, isn't she?"

"What do you mean?"

"Even the way she walks. Take a look at her next time."

"She's like eight years old, Lon."

"She's eleven. But I know, I know. I'm just saying. There'll come a time though...And don't tell me you haven't thought the same thing. I know you, I know who you really are. You're Superman. But it was nice. Ana would ask me something in Spanish, and I'd pretend to understand her, then I'd answer her something in English, and she'd pretend to understand me, and so on, for about half an hour. She gave me some coffee and some kind of taco thing."

"And you ate it?"

"Yeah. It was good. Anyway, things weren't going anywhere, so I came home. And don't look so smug about it. If I didn't know better, I could almost think you were wishing me bad luck with that girl. But we straightened all that out, remember? Pilar – me. Friend of Pilar – you."

"Sara."

"Her, yeah. She asked about you, by the way."

"Pilar?"

"No, Mike - Sara. Well, Pilar, too, actually, but I told her you weren't interested in her. Pity she couldn't understand me."

He sucked on his cigar and blew another ring into the air.

"Ana wouldn't even let her walk back with me, not even part way."

"You walked back?"

"Had to. Rodrigo wouldn't stick around. I'd call him a chicken, but after what I just saw of chickens...Besides, it's not that far."

"You walked by yourself?"

"Sara walked me part of the way, to the main street. She knows a few English words, so..."

"Did you see the tattoo guy?"

"The stalker, you mean? Yeah, I saw him, holding up his usual corner. He lacks gainful employment, that lad does. He sure hasn't warmed up to me much."

"Why do you say that?"

"Well, I was all nice to him. I nodded and said 'hola', all neighborly-like. But he didn't seem to take it in the spirit in which it was offered. He just kind of glared at me, and then he said something."

"He said something?"

"He said *'otra dia'*."

"*Otra dia*? Do you know what that means?"

Lonnie nodded sheepishly, or mock-sheepishly.

"'Another day', Lon. That's what it means – 'another day'. You like that translation?"

"I knew that's what it meant."

"You have to be more careful."

"I've got to tell you, Mikey, he just doesn't scare me."

"Well, he should. A guy like that will kill you for nothing here, man. Look at the newspapers."

"I know, I know. *Decapitado. Descuartizado.*"

"It's not funny."

"Ahh, don't worry Mikey. I be care. My idea of a good death isn't bleeding out somewhere in the slums of Joco…Joco…Joco wherever the hell we are. Besides, we'll be out of here soon, right? Hie we to the *playa*, where we belong, and we'll forget them all. This stuff is getting old, this waiting for Marco. I mean, if he thinks leaving me hanging here in this hellhole – if he thinks it's going to change my attitude about anything, then he don't know me, do he? Anyway, enough about me. How were the peoples of the mountain?"

There was a touch of sarcasm in his voice, and Mike didn't respond. After a moment, Lonnie went on in a more sympathetic tone. "Joe says they're even worse off up there."

Mike nodded.

"Though I suppose once you've achieved a certain level of poverty, it becomes academic."

"No, not really."

"Pregnant fourteen-years-olds, I suppose? Don't look at me like that - I saw them here, too. They're all over. The babies just come, like typhoid fever. And all the good sisters telling them they must go ahead and deliver their little brown bundles of joy, their little *niños*. Because God knows, what this country needs is more mouths to feed."

"The sisters are good people," Mike said.

"No doubt. I don't question that. I'm just saying —"

"I'm going to a fair with one of them tomorrow night."

"You have a date with a nun? Maybe I'm wrong about you."

"I'm taking her and some of her kids. It's in San Jose - a little place on the way to the mountains."

"You mean, unless we get our papers signed you're going. If we get our papers signed, then, of course...But all right, count me in. Sounds better than another night here, anyway."

He played a flourish on the bongos and set them down. He slid forward in his chair, stretched his legs out and crossed his hands on his gut, the smoldering cigar sticking out from between his fingers as if he were smoking it from his navel. He gave the appearance of being deep in thought about something.

"So how old do you suppose she is?"

"Pilar? She says she's eighteen."

"No, her mother."

"Ana? No idea. Fifty. Fifty-five?"

"Lower."

"Forty?"

"Thirty-four."

"Really?"

"Really. She was another one, in her day, I suppose. But they don't seem to wear particularly well around here."

He stood, blowing out one final smoke ring that struggled in the air before succumbing to the wind, and he flicked the smoking end of the cigar onto the dirt of the courtyard, picked up his bongos and walked toward his room.

"All that picking coffee, I suppose."

CHAPTER 29

"MIGUEL? MIKE? ARE YOU awake?"

"Am now, Padre. What's up?"

"We could use a little help up front."

"Yeah, sure. What's going on?" There was no response, and all Mike could hear was the slap of sandals receding down the *pasillo*.

He lifted himself from his bed, took the clothes from the back of the chair where he'd hung them a few hours before, and pulled them on. He left his room and walked towards the front, noticing that the light in Marco's library was on. As he approached the atrium the commotion increased, and he could see children dragging duffle bags and carrying boxes from the front door into the dining room.

Out from the jumble of people Greg appeared, walking down the hallway towards Mike. With him was Maria and, between them, a boy of about ten. He stopped at the first examination room, opening the door and holding it as Maria and the boy entered. He nodded at Mike as he passed.

In the dining room there were another thirty or so kids, ranging in age from about five years up to the early teens. The older ones were busy along the walls arranging bedding, while the younger ones ran about the room playing. The tables had been pushed to one side and in the middle of the room was a pile of stuff – blankets, pillows, clothes, stuffed animals, toys, books. More kids were rummaging through the pile.

Mike walked around them and went to the counter where the padre, Brother Joe, and Brother Luke were standing. They were a solemn lot; even Joe was subdued and sleepy-looking.

"Kind of lively here this morning," Mike said. "What's going on?"

"We're going to have some guests for a couple of days," Brother Luke said.

"I see. And who are they?"

"They're from an orphanage out east."

"To what do we owe their presence?"

"I'll have to explain it later."

"Did Marco bring them?"

"Yes."

"And he's here now?"

"Yes."

"Upstairs?"

"Yes."

"Is he going to come down?"

"I don't know."

"All right. Well, what do we need to do?"

"We're going to finish unloading their things, and then feed them a little bit and get them to bed."

"Sounds good." Mike started moving towards the door but Padre stopped him.

"Be careful what you talk about with them," he said. "If they try to tell you about where they came from or why they're here, just change the subject, get them on to something else."

* * *

In another hour and a half the bus the orphans had arrived in was unloaded, the bedding was laid out around the walls of the dining room, and the children were fed. Some of the younger ones were asleep, but most of the children were bunched in around Mike at a table he had pulled back to the center of the room. They were crammed into the benches and standing three and four deep on all sides, watching as he put a piece of candy under one of three Styrofoam cups and shuffled the cups around on the tabletop. The children at the back stood on their toes to see.

Every ten minutes or so throughout the night, Greg and Maria had entered the dining room, picked out another of the children, and escorted him or her out toward the medical rooms.

Joe had gone to bed an hour before, explaining that he had been up for thirty hours straight.

Marco had not come down.

The girl sitting at Mike's right – tall and thin and darker-skinned than the others - planted her forearm on Mike's shoulder and leaned on him, watching the moving cups intensely while absentmindedly stroking the hair on Mike's forearm with the backs of her fingers.

Mike stopped shuffling, and looked around at the kids. "So," he said, "which one?"

They all pointed to the cups.

"One at a time," Mike said. "What's your name?" he asked one of the boys.

"Juan Carlos...Juan Carlos Suazo Jimi..."

"Juan Carlos. All right, Juan Carlos. "Take your chances."

The boy looked up at him with slightly oriental-looking eyes.

"That means pick one," Mike said.

The kids around them pointed at the cups again. Juan Carlos knocked some of their arms away and frowned down on the cups, as if he could think himself to the solution. Finally, he pointed to the one in the middle.

"Are you sure?" Mike said.

Without removing his eyes from the cup the boy nodded. Mike pried it up slowly, but there was nothing beneath. The restlessness of the children increased. The girl leaning on his shoulder snapped her wrists in the air.

Juan Carlos pointed at the one to the right, but Mike shook his head. "One try per customer. Who's next?"

A thicket of scrawny brown arms shot up into the air, and a chorus of voices cried out.

"What's your name?" Mike said.

"Anthony David Garc —"

"Anthony. What do you think, Anthony? Take your chances."

He pointed at one of the remaining cups, but the candy wasn't under it either.

All the arms shot up again, and all the voices begged him. Mike looked around at the faces, eager, excited, some concentrating on the remaining cup, others looking up at him with bright eyes and bright smiles, and it came to him again, the feeling that had come upon him in the mountain clearing, when the kids had engulfed him, the feeling of being lifted up and swept away.

"Hang on, hang on. Everybody gets a chance."

The girl leaning on him snapped her wrists and tapped him on the shoulder. "Me," she said. Mike tilted his head to look at her. She had delicate features and a mass of frizzy black hair. Her eyes were huge and beautiful and stood out sharply from her black skin.

"What's your name?" he said.

"Wendy Milagro Venegas…"

"Wendy," Mike said.

"*La negra*," Juan Carlos said.

Wendy reached across the table and punched him sharp on the shoulder, her hair jumping to life as she moved, and Juan Carlos leaned away from her and rubbed where she'd hit him.

"*Chino*," she said to him.

"Who's that?" one of the boys said.

Mike turned, and there in the doorway was Lonnie, rumpled, slouching, half-asleep, squinting into the room with his brow furrowed. Looking confused, he nodded at Mike, swept his hair out of his face, turned back towards the dormitory and shuffled away.

"Nobody," he said. "That's nobody." He turned to Wendy. "Come on. Take your chances."

She smiled triumphantly and pried up the rim of the last cup, but under it, too, there was nothing.

A moment's stunned silence followed, and then the table exploded, kids pointing, shouting, arguing with each other as to whether it had been magic or just cheating.

Juan Carlos believed the latter. "*Trampa!*" he cried. "*Trampa!*"

Wendy snapped both her wrists in the air three times.

"I don't get it," Mike said. "What happened?"

"Ah," Juan Carlos growled. "*Trampa.*"

"Oh, wait a minute, here it is." He held the candy up in his palm. They all stuck out their hands.

He gave the candy to Wendy and took two more pieces from his pocket, handing them to Juan Carlos and Anthony.

"Okay. Again. Everybody gets their turn. And no more *trampas.* He reloaded the cups and began shuffling them. "Who's next?" he said.

He glanced over to the counter where Brother Luke and Padre Zeppi stood, drinking coffee and smiling over at him. At that moment, Greg appeared in the doorway, alone this time, and entered the dining room.

"Where's Mr. Aquirre?" Wendy asked Mike as he shuffled the cups, watching as Greg walked to the counter.

"Where's who?"

"Mr. Aquirre."

Greg leaned in toward Luke and said something to him. Luke lowered his eyes and nodded.

"I don't know. Was he with you guys on the bus?" Mike said.

"I told you," Juan Carlos said to Wendy. "The police took him."

Wendy pursed her lips and shook her head twice sharply, her mane of black hair trailing the movement of her head like some restless, shiny animal.

Juan Carlos nodded at her emphatically. "*Negra,*" he mumbled.

"*Chino,*" she said, and she punched him again.

Luke said something to Greg, who turned and walked out of the room.

"Never mind about Mr. Aquirre," Mike said. "Come on. Take your chances. And no more of your *trampas*."

Off to the side of the table, twenty feet from the crowd, a little girl stood alone, her head down, the fingers of one hand in her mouth, the other hand tucked behind her. She had light brown hair and a small pointed nose, courtesy of some careless, passing gringo, Mike supposed.

"What's your name?" he called to her.

She leaned backward and dropped her head an inch.

"That's Jesi," Juan Carlos said.

"Jesi," Mike said to her. "That's a beautiful name, Jesi." He motioned to her to come, but she didn't move. He slid out from the table and started towards her, but she retreated two steps and pivoted a quarter turn away. Mike stopped.

"Okay, Jesi" he said. "Okay." He stooped down. "How about a piece of candy?"

She stared over at his hand but didn't move.

Wendy rose, took the candy from him and brought it to her. She took it and put her hand behind her back again.

"It's okay, Mike," Padre said. He had come up behind him and now put his hand on his shoulder. "Let's let her be for now."

"Is she okay?"

"She's shy," Wendy said.

"Yes, she's shy," Padre said.

* * *

With the kids safely sleeping along the sides of the room, Mike sat at the counter sipping coffee with Luke, the padre, and Greg, who had returned after being gone for about an hour after consulting with them.

"So, tell me, Padre," Mike said, "is this a typical night in this place? People coming and going at all hours?"

"You never know."

"And these kids, they're all orphans?"

"Most of them. Without parents one way or the other – passed away, or in prison, or just gone," Padre said. He wore again that weary, burdened look that he'd had on the way down the mountain, a look that Mike hated.

"So why are they here?"

"Their orphanage burned down, so they needed somewhere to stay for a day or two, until we can find another place for them."

"Did they all get out okay?"

"Yes."

"Well, that's good anyway. And Greg, you were taking them out to check up on them?"

"That's right."

"But then you didn't come back."

"I had to take one of them to the hospital."

"I see. I see. A boy or a girl?"

"One of the boys."

"And is he all right?"

"I think so, yes. They're going to keep him for a couple days."

"I see. And that's where Marco's been this whole time, taking care of all this?"

"Yes."

234

"Do you think he'll come down?"

"He's probably in bed by now. He hasn't had much sleep the last few days."

"I see. Well, tomorrow then."

"Tomorrow." The padre got up to leave. "Some of these guys will be up early, so…"

"Who's this Aquirre guy?" Mike said. "Why did the police take him?"

The padre sat back down.

"You talked to the kids?" Luke said.

"They asked me about him, that's all. I changed the subject."

Luke looked down at his coffee cup.

"It's not good, is it?"

"No, it's not." Luke said. "Aguirre was the head of the orphanage."

"And the police took him away?"

"He's the one who burned it down."

"He burned it himself? What, on purpose?"

"Yeah. On purpose."

"Why would he do that?"

Luke looked at the padre.

"He thought he could get rid of the evidence," the old man said, "after one of the little girls killed herself."

"What?"

"An eight-year-old," Luke said. "Hung herself."

"An eight-year-old? Why would an eight-year-old —"

"She was being abused."

"Abused? You mean sexually abused? By him? By Aquirre?"

"And not just her."

Mike stood. "You mean, some of these kids, too? He went after some of them?"

"Or all of them," Luke said.

"What?"

"He taped it."

"He taped what? He taped himself, with them?"

Mike cursed, turned and paced ten feet towards the door, pivoted and marched back. He picked up his coffee cup and lifted his arm as if to throw it, but everywhere he looked the little mummies lay, swaddled in blankets, sleeping.

"What kind of animal —"

"Only one kind," Luke said. "Only one kind of animal."

"Yeah, the Cortes one. Who are these people, anyway? What kind of country —"

"He was from the United States," Luke said. "Your Mr. Aquirre, he was an American."

Mike dropped to the seat and hung his head for a moment before looking beseechingly at Luke.

"These kids," Luke said, "they're our victims. They're just like the children getting shot by the *maras*, right down the street here. They're all paying for the monster appetites of our own country."

"They should just shoot him. Marco is a Ranger. Why didn't he just —"

"What? Kill him?"

"He's got a gun."

Luke looked at Brother Greg.

"He was in the library, and he saw it," Brother Greg said. "My mistake."

Luke frowned, took another drink of coffee, and without taking his eyes from his cup spoke.

"You ever take drugs, Mike?" he said. "I have. And I liked them. I liked them a lot. What kind of drugs have you done? Marijuana, I suppose?"

Mike nodded.

"And now?"

"Very little."

"But you still do?"

Mike nodded.

"And cocaine?"

"No," he said. "Maybe once a year."

"Maybe? And no damage done, right? No harm? Well, take a look around; here's the damage."

"Yeah but you can't really blame —"

"It's putting your momentary pleasure ahead of other people's lives. It's saying that you don't care about the consequences for anyone else, that you just want. Just like our Mr. Aquirre. It's denying the fact that we're all brothers. It's denying the connectedness of all people."

Mike rotated his coffee cup on the table top.

"What was he doing down here?" he asked finally. "Aquirre? Why the hell was he down here in the first place?"

"He was with some mission group," the padre answered. "The church of himself almighty, or something. They built the orphanage, and they left him in charge. I'm sure they thought of him as a pious, kindly older gentleman who loved kids. Maybe he thought of himself that way - at first, anyway. Maybe he still does."

He rose. "We should get some sleep," he said.

Mike stood and went towards the door. The shrouded bodies lined the edges of the room like victims of war, quiet and still. Beside Wendy the minuscule figure of Jesi lay, her eyes closed, an old threadbare quilt pulled up to her waist. In her arms she cradled a stuffed doll with a twisted cloth mouth and a single eye. He knelt beside her. Almost imperceptibly her shoulder rose and fell as she breathed, taking in and letting out tiny gulps of air that didn't seem enough to sustain even a life as small and circumscribed as hers. He pulled the cover up over the knob of her shoulder and reached out to brush the wisps of hair from her face, but stopped before touching her.

Walking along the *pasillo*, on his way back to his bedroom, Mike looked back to see the window of Marco's library was still lit.

CHAPTER 30

CHILDREN'S VOICES WOKE HIM, coming through his back window, rapid and urgent. They were trying to keep it to a whisper, but their enthusiasm was too much for them to contain.

Mike lay on his back and listened. They stopped for a moment, as if waiting for someone to pass by, and then started in together all at once, their words unintelligible in the muddle. It grew quiet for a moment again until one small voice whispered loudly, "*gringo*", and another reprimanded it. Mike swung his feet off the bed and sat up.

"What are you little hoodlums doing?" he said.

Another voice called his name at half-volume. "Miguel!"

He reached over to hold away the curtain. Light pushed into the room. A pair of oriental eyes peeked over the ledge.

"Juan Carlos," Mike said. "And here I was hoping I was just having a nightmare."

"Ahh," the boy growled.

"No, really."

"Time to wake up. Time for *fútbol*."

"*Fútbol*," another voice said, and Mike saw a forehead appear beside Juan Carlos. Behind it, the crowns of other children bobbed in and out of view as they jumped up to catch a glimpse into the room, their black hair flipping about in the air.

"What time is it?"

"It's late," Juan Carlos said. "He wouldn't let us wake you up."

"Who wouldn't let you? Brother Marco?"

"The padre."

"The padre is a wise man."

Juan Carlos growled again and lifted an old dirty soccer ball up to the window, as if the sight of it would be impossible for Mike to resist.

"I have to eat," Mike said.

"Breakfast is over," Juan Carlos said. "You promised *fútbol*."

"Did I?"

"*Sí*." They all seemed to say it at once. "Last night."

"I must have been crazy."

"You promised."

"Well, if I promised..."

Mike dressed, splashed water on his face, and went out. The gaggle of kids had run around the building and was waiting for him at his door. Juan Carlos had the ball wedged under his arm and one of the girls held a jump rope. Another girl had a stack of plastic cups in her hand. She wore a black eye patch.

"This is going to be a circus, isn't it?" Mike said.

"*Sí*," Juan Carlos said. "I hope so."

They followed him to the dining room, Wendy taking his left hand, the girl with the plastic cups his right.

"So you guys had breakfast already?" Mike said.

"*Sí*. Pancakes."

"I love pancakes."

"We ate them all," Juan Carlos said.

There was no one else in the room, not even Maria, and the kids dispersed throughout it as Mike went into the kitchen and poured a bowl of cereal. He sat at one of the tables and the group re-formed around him, the girl with the eye patch sitting directly across from him and very carefully spreading the cups out on the tabletop, shifting them a centimeter here and there to line them up just so. The cups were clear, and under the middle one a little black rock was visible.

"Take your chances," the girl said to Mike in a squeak of a voice.

All the children pointed at the middle cup.

"Take my chances, huh?" Mike laughed. "Hmmm."

The padre entered the room, a book in his hands. The children made way for him and he sat next to the girl with the eyepatch, rubbed his hands together, and pointed at the cup on the right. The girl smiled at Mike as if to ask his permission. He nodded, and the girl lifted it up.

"Again!" the padre said. "She's been beating me at this all morning."

He placed the book on the table and set his hand atop it.

"Apparently last night I promised these guys I'd play some soccer with them. *Fútbol*," Mike said. "I must have been punch-drunk."

"Nevertheless, a promise is a promise. It'll have to be in the road out front, though. The farmers have their cows in the back in the morning."

"Got it. And then tonight I told the sisters I'd take their girls to the fair in San Jose."

THE CHILDREN OF EVE

"You've been making a lot of promises."

"Yeah, I guess I have. But I don't know now, with these guys here…"

"Oh, I think we might be able to get by for one evening without your special brand of magic."

"My special brand of magic, huh? All right. But I have to say, I never thought I'd wind up taking a nun to a fair in Cortes," Mike laughed.

"Mysterious ways," the padre said.

Mike had been casting glances at the book without the padre seeming to notice, and finally he asked about it. The old man lifted his hand and looked down at it. "I found it in here this morning," he said. "Over on the counter."

"It's mine," Mike said. "I mean, it's the one I borrowed from the library. I couldn't sleep last night after everything settled down. Too much coffee, I guess. I came back here for a while. To read."

"To read, huh?"

"I guess I left it here."

"Do you like it?" he said.

"The book? Yeah, I think I do. A little different from Trent York, Private Eye, but…Is Marco up yet?"

"Oh yeah, up and gone."

"Gone?"

"Off to find a permanent home for these guys."

Padre slid the book across the table to him. A strip of orange paper stuck up from its pages.

Mike stuffed the book in the thigh pocket of his pants.

* * *

The morning was turning hot by the time they were let out through the front gate of the mission. The street was in midday condition already, dusty and deserted. The only person Mike could see was an old woman further up the road in a loose flower-print dress, sweeping her yard. No one was visible in Belkis' house, though from it music played – a jumpy, happy song shot through with percussion, as if the musicians had taken up whatever lay at hand and started in to beating on it.

Four of the girls stopped in front of the concrete benches and began jumping rope. The rest of the children kicked the ball into the road and immediately began playing, as if resuming a game that had been interrupted, with no need for the specification of teams or the delineation of goal markers.

Only Jesi stood to one side, watching. Mike smiled at her but she didn't respond.

In the dirt of the road Arnold dominated the game. He was smooth and quick, able to stick the ball from foot to foot while keeping his eyes forward, watching, evaluating. He kicked the ball hard past everyone and down the road, raising his arms to indicate a goal. Everyone seemed to agree.

"Come on," Juan Carlos called to Mike from the middle of the scrum, flicking his hand down.

For ten minutes he lumbered about in the middle of the mob as it swarmed up and down the road. He managed to touch the ball once or twice, by accident and to no effect; each time it was quickly stolen by one of the darting, skilled, starving little people. Finally, the game left him altogether, the kids flying away quickly in a wavering mass, like a flock of songbirds, leaving Mike panting in the middle of the road, bent over with his hands on his thighs. Only Wendy - who had been running along at the fringes without ever becoming a proper part of the game – only Wendy stayed behind with him, putting her hand on his shoulder to comfort him.

"It's because it's hot," Mike said in English. "Besides, that ain't football." Then in Spanish: "These guys don't know nothing about '*fútbol*'."

A leather strap of a man stroked past on a dilapidated bicycle, a machete tucked through his belt, swinging to the cadence of his pedaling. A rickety taxi came by and the soccer kids made way for it. Further along a three-legged *barrio* dog rocked across the road, a resentful look on his face.

Belkis had appeared in her doorway now, watching the goings-on with a neutral expression. She was holding something rectangular up against her chest, with her arms crossed over it.

Mike shouted to her, asking if she wanted to play. She shook her head.

Arnold had stolen the ball again. He kicked it and it shot past the other players and towards three *malos* who had appeared on the road, walking towards them.

Mike called the kids back. Arnold ran to retrieve the ball - just fifteen feet or so from the advancing gangsters – and turned and loped towards Mike.

They were young, lean, unkempt. The two on the sides rolled forward in the smooth *malo* gait, their eyes fixed firmly ahead of them. The one in the middle, smaller and younger, glanced from side to side with glassy eyes, smiling crookedly, excited and eager, with a little spring in his step, as if this whole *malo* thing – this *decapitado* thing, this *descuartizado* thing - was yet new to him, fresh and invigorating, sweet and lovely.

Mike looked behind to the girls at the side of the road. Two of them swung the rope in a long, slow arc while the other two hopped over it as it swung under them. Jesi lingered at the side, two steps off the road, watching with her hollow, pitiful look, one hand drawn behind her back.

The soccer players had come back to Mike and given him the ball, and now stood around him at the edge of the road. Mike started talking, pretending to coach them.

"Do you know what we call *fútbol* in the United Sates?" he said. "We call it soccer. And what we call football is something completely different."

The kids all looked at him, puzzled, but he continued talking until *los malos* finally reached them. As they drew close, Mike glanced over his shoulder at them and nodded.

"Good morning," he said, not unfriendly but in his deepest voice. He flexed.

The two taller ones ignored him. The younger one looked at him with liquidy, unfocused eyes.

"Good night," he said, and he smirked at his companions. Mike turned back to the soccer children. He stood motionless, his ears tuned backward, waiting, until he finally heard the footsteps of *los malos* on his other side. He turned to watch as they sauntered away and sunk out of sight down the dip in the road.

"*Bolos*," said Wendy, shaking her head.

"Good night," Juan Carlos said, slurring his speech and taking three staggering steps, his arms swinging about limply at his sides. He smiled at Mike, who looked down the road again to see *los malos* crossing the bridge. They turned off the road towards the trees lining the river. The youngest shot a last look back at Mike, and they all disappeared into the foliage.

A *barrio* dog came tapping across the road in front of them, and before Mike could stop him one of the orphans flung a rock at it. It thudded against the dog's flank, making a dull, hollow sound. The dog yipped and jumped forward, looking back to see who'd done it, and if they were going to do it again.

After another half hour of *fútbol* the mission gate opened and Lonnie strolled out, slinging his bongo drums at his side, squinting under the brim of his Panama hat and looking up and down the road. He took his sunglasses from where they hung from the collar of his shirt and put them on, leaning back against the fence to watch the girls jumping rope.

Mike went to him. Wendy followed.

"What's up?" Mike said.

"Apparently they don't have any taste in bongo music in there," Lonnie said.

"That so?"

From Mike's side Wendy reached out and tapped the drumhead. It gave out a tight, hollow, jungle note.

Lonnie smiled at her and shifted the drums to his other hand.

"He got yelled at this morning," she said to Mike.

"He did?" Mike said.

"*Sí.*"

"She says you got yelled at."

"Oh she does, does she?"

"By Marco?" Mike said.

"I wouldn't say yelled at," Lonnie said. "But it appears he's not too big on our staying out past curfew."

"That's it?"

"Yeah, that's about it. He seems to take it pretty seriously, though. Just as well he doesn't know about your other shenanigans – don't worry, I didn't rat you out."

Wendy shifted around behind Mike and tapped the drum again. Lonnie frowned and moved it back to his other hip.

"I'm thinking this would be a good time for us to check out of here, get to the beach."

"*La playa.*"

"Yeah, *la playa.*"

"He signed your papers then?"

"Well not quite. He says we have to talk a little more when he gets back. He's gone again you know."

"Yeah, the padre told me."

"Off to find somewhere to stick these little glue-sniffers."

"I'll never meet the guy."

"Consider yourself lucky."

"He really lit you up, didn't he?"

"Ah," Lonnie scoffed.

"Is he going to sign?"

"He'll sign."

"Did he say that?"

"He'll sign."

"You're on probation, aren't you?"

"If he doesn't sign, I'll get a damn lawyer when I'm back in the States. He won't stand a chance. But enough of this waiting, huh? What do you say? Let's go to the beach. Or hell, maybe even get out of this country altogether. Change our flights. I mean, eighteen's in the bag anyway."

"Eighteen with an asterisk."

"All right, fine. If it makes you feel better, with an asterisk. But really, what's left here for two guys like us Mikey? Really. Heat and dust and...chickens and...garbage bags filled with —"

"Authenticity."

"*Eso.* Hey, we could go to Belize."

"Actually, I've been thinking I might stay here."

"What? Stay here you mean? Here with the bros, in the convent?"

"The mission. Yeah, if they let me."

"Are you nuts? No, we'll go to the *playa, Las Palmas.* We'll hie us is what we'll do. To the sand and the sun and the number eighteen without an asterisk."

Wendy had worked her way around Mike's back again and again popped the bongo.

"Okay, enough," Lonnie said, and he hoisted the drums up on to his shoulder. "This isn't about that Pilar girl, is it? Because if it is —"

"No, it's not about Pilar."

"Good. That's good. But Mike, we have obligations there, at the beach. We can't just slough off our obligations."

"We have a reservation. A reservation isn't an obligation. We just call them and cancel."

"They won't refund the money."

"You're on probation for an hour, and you're already starting to obsess about money. Look, you go. Nothing's preventing you from going. You should go."

"It *is* about Pilar. No, I get it. You're trying to clear me out. I get it." He turned and started towards the gate. "You're a tricky one," he said. "But I'll just stick around here too, I think. Keep an eye on you."

Belkis was still watching from her doorway, and as Lonnie went inside the mission she started towards Mike, still hugging the rectangular object against her chest. Without a word she gave it to him. It was a photograph in a metal frame.

"Your brother?" Mike said.

"Sí."

In the lower left corner was a young girl with Belkis' distinctive features, but younger and tinier, like a cartoon of Belkis. She was holding the hand of a boy, a man, and looking up at him with admiration and pride. The man-child was not looking back at her. He was staring straight at the photographer with that hard, grim, threatening glare that just three or four days ago Mike would have written off as adolescent bluster but now knew to be associated with assassinry of youth.

"Chucho," Belkis said.

"And was Chucho a good boy?"

Belkis shrugged.

CHAPTER 31

"SO LET ME SEE if I got this: A fair for some saint or other, with a bunch of young girls and a nun? That about it?"

"Yeah, Lon. That's about it."

Rodrigo was guiding the taxi through the barrio, with Mike on his right and Lonnie in the middle of the back seat, leaning forward.

"You know, I was afraid this country would be priest-ridden, but it's actually nun-ridden, isn't it?"

"Do you have any idea what sisters do, Lon?"

"I don't know. Walk around and eat? Ah, I'm just pulling your leg. I'm sure it's all good work, all good work."

"You didn't have to come. I don't remember inviting you."

"No, no, don't get me wrong. I'm looking forward to it. Bound to be quite a show."

As they approached the intersection with the road into *Los Ángeles*, Lonnie leaned forward from the back seat and stuck his head between Rodrigo and Mike. "What do we have here?" he said.

THE CHILDREN OF EVE

Two young women stood at the corner with their arms folded, looking towards the taxi.

"I'll be damned if that's not them," Lonnie said. "The women-folk. Pull over there, Rodrigo. We'll have to say *hola*."

When they stopped Lonnie leaped out of the taxi and bowed to the women, sweeping his hand with the Panama hat in it towards the open door of the taxi. They started forward as if to get in.

"What are you doing, Lonnie?" Mike had exited the cab now and was standing at his door with his eyes fixed on Pilar.

"Looks to me like they want to come along."

"Are you out of your mind? We can't take them with us."

"Well of course we can."

"We'd have to talk to Ana."

"*Ya!*" Lonnie said. "I've already talked to her. *Ya!* She trusts us, simple peasant soul that she is."

"How could you —"

"Sara has a cell phone. I know – crazy, huh? She doesn't have a pot to piss in, but she goes out and gets herself a phone, a track phone. If you're nice, I'll give you her number."

"But you can't speak Spanish."

"I'm a little hurt that you could say that, Mikey. But okay, I'll confess: I had a little help. From Rodrigo."

"This Rodrigo?"

"*Cheque.*"

"*Cheque*?"

"Yeah, *cheque*. He taught me that, too, right Roderigo? *Cheque*?"

The *taxista* had lifted himself out of the vehicle now, too, and stood looking at Mike with his stupid, open smile, a toothpick hanging from the corner of his mouth.

"Cheque," he said.

"Rodrigo's a surprising guy. Aren't you, Rodrigo?"

"Does your mother know about this, Pilar?" Mike said.

She nodded. He turned again to Lonnie.

"Aren't you on probation?"

"Bah."

"But the sisters aren't expecting anyone but us."

"Relax, Mike. It'll be fine. They'll love to have them. In case you haven't noticed, these are the most hospitable people in the world – the ones who don't chop you up and put you in a garbage bag, I mean. Besides, if we're really going to stick around here this entire trip with that monk thing you've got going on, we've got to find some way to amuse ourselves."

"You know we won't be back until late, Pilar, right? Until after dark? Does your mother know that?"

"Sí," Sara said. Pilar nodded.

"Don't sweat it, Mikey," Lonnie said. "We'll be with a nun, for God's sake. We're sure not to have any fun."

Mike glanced down the road that fell away into *Los Ángeles.* Smoke rolled into the air from the gutters. Balls of Spanish moss clung to tangled wires. Strings of black graffiti challenged, defied.

The strangeness of the place struck him again. Unknowable, incommensurable, laced with a quiet danger.

"All right," he said. "Let's get the hell out of here."

"There you go," Lonnie said, and he motioned for the women to enter the cab. "There's the old Mikey."

Rodrigo put it in gear.

"You know," Mike said to Lonnie, "I've never met anyone so full of bad ideas."

"Gracias."

* * *

In front of the doors to the sister's place a bus was idling. Rosario stood next to it with a child in her arms and a dozen or so girls of various ages around her, talking amongst themselves. One of the older girls stood behind one of the younger, braiding her hair. All of them wore identical get-ups - brown knee-length pleated skirts, white socks that ascended halfway up the calve, white blouses buttoned to the top.

Mike's eyes went to Suyapa, who gave him her vague smile. She was holding a tiny kitten and some of the other girls were petting at it.

When Rosario saw Lonnie, Pilar, and Sara, she was kind enough to act pleased. Mike apologized in English.

"I didn't know they were coming," he said. He nodded towards Lonnie to blame him.

"It is fine," the sister said. "They are welcome. Except the bus is very small."

"I see," Mike said. "One minute." He returned to the cab to speak with Rodrigo as Pilar and Sara went over to the girls. When he returned Pilar was crouched down and holding the kitten while Suyapa stroked its back. It looked up at Mike and hissed. Pilar laughed.

"Rodrigo will take us," Mike said to the sister. "We'll follow you."

Rosario nodded and called the girls. Suyapa took Pilar's hand and began pulling her towards the bus. Pilar looked at Mike.

"Looks like they want you," Mike said. He asked Rosario if there was room for the women, and she smiled and nodded.

"And you're paying Rodrigo the extra mileage," he said to Lonnie. "I don't care how broke you're going to be soon."

CHAPTER 32

THE BUS PULLED OFF the highway and came to a stop at the head of the fair, bustling now with people. As the taxi drew up behind it, its door swung open and Rosario exited, descending to the pavement and taking a step backward. The young child she had been holding clung to her habit with one hand and held the other above her head, fingers spread open, silently begging to be picked up again. The girls spilled out onto the road in front of Rosario, looking about in wonder, glancing at each other, laughing, the older ones holding the hands of the younger.

"You wouldn't know they were sick by looking at them, would you?" Lonnie said. "I mean, they're skinny enough all right - most of them - but, heck, everything's kind of skinny here."

"You've got a real gift with words, Lon," Mike said.

"*Gracias.*"

Suyapa stepped from the bus, followed by Pilar, then Sara and another girl, all as enthralled as the others at the scene in front of them. Rosario took the kitten from Pilar's arms and put it back on the bus. The little girl, her arms extended, followed her every move without making a sound.

Mike arranged a rendezvous time with Rodrigo, leaving his backpack in the taxi. The two vehicles pulled away.

Suyapa took Pilar's hand and they started with the others toward the fair.

In the tents closest to the road women were calling out the strange names of the foods they were peddling – *pupusas, baleadas, tostones*. The busy walkway between them led away to an arcade of a dozen or so stalls. Beyond the arcade the huge wheel arced into the sky, turning slowly, its frame outlined with colored lights. It was empty.

The girls were eager to go to it, but Rosario insisted that they eat first.

"What should we have, then?" Mike asked her. "*Nacatamales*, whatever those are? *Elotes* – is that how you say that? Those *catrachita* things look interesting."

"Chicken," Rosario said.

"Chicken?"

"*Sí.*"

"Just chicken?"

"And French fries."

"All right. I was kind of hoping for authenticity, but…"

They ate at picnic tables set up between two of the booths. Mike was starved but he waited for the girls to begin eating. For such gaunt, needy creatures, they took their time getting to their first mouthfuls, first delicately arranging their plates and napkins and plastic utensils in front of them. Attempting to ignore the smell of the chicken ascending from the dish in front of him, Mike looked around at them as they sat, their hands on their laps, waiting silently for Rosario to say grace. Were there some signs of the progress of the disease that he could detect? Was the sweet, confident, teen-aged girl next to him – her name was Luz - was she not just a little too thin? And were there not bags under the eyes of the one next to her, a heavier, native-looking girl with straight black bangs and a small straight mouth? And who had coughed at the other table?

He smiled and they smiled back, sitting there in their old-fashioned, modest school-girl outfits, uniforms of the doomed.

Suyapa, seated with Pilar across the table, seemed to have guessed what he was thinking, and looked at him disapprovingly.

When the prayer was finished, the girls finally began eating, with great delicacy. Mike waited three more seconds, for the politeness of it, and dove in. The chicken was juicy and salty and perfect, and the fries crisp and greasy and perfect, and though he tried to eat slowly he finished well before the girls. He wiped his mouth contentedly and leaned backwards in his chair.

The older girls pretended to not notice his gluttony; the younger ones gawked and smiled.

"We should save some for Marisol," one of the younger girls said.

"I'm afraid she wouldn't be able to eat it," Rosario said.

The girl nodded. "She would like it here."

"*Sí.*"

"She liked chicken."

"*Sí.*"

After a moment's pause, for Marisol, Luz pointed at Mike's plate. Mike shrugged. She advanced her finger so it almost touched one of the bones lying there. He leaned forward to examine it more closely, noticing a wisp of meat left strung along it.

"Thank you," he said, and he picked up the bone with both hands and with his incisors clipped off the thread of chicken, smacking his lips just as if there had been enough substance there to taste. He took a gulp of water and wiped his mouth with his fingers. The girls laughed, and Luz whispered something. Mike looked at her. She was chewing lightly, with her lips closed, and focusing her eyes on the plate in front of her, pretending not to have said anything, though she wore a tiny grin.

"What did you just say?" Mike asked.

She shook her head.

"*Mojado*," Suyapa said from across the table.

Luz lifted her eyes to Suyapa and held her hand to her mouth.

When they were done they stood and Pilar picked up her piece of chicken – half eaten - and wrapped it in a napkin.

From a booth at the side of the tables a young woman had been calling out in a high feminine voice, "*Ponche*! *Ponche*!" In front of her on a propane burner was a large dented silver pot which she stirred with a wooden spoon, twirling its long thin handle between her palms. "*Ponche*," she cried.

Inside the pot was a white froth.

"Look at there, Mike." Lonnie motioned to an unlabeled bottle of clear liquid, stopped with a cork, sitting on the table beside the burner. "One might think that was alcohol."

The woman smiled and nodded. "*Alcol*," she said.

"And it goes in the *ponche*? I think it goes in the *ponche*, Mikey. Well there you go."

He turned to the woman. "I'll take one," he said. "With *alcol.*"

"Sure about that?" Mike said. "Remember the probation."

"Bah. Screw the probation, I say. *Dos,*" he said to the woman, holding up two fingers. "In honor of the patron saint of this place, Saint Josie...or whoever. *Dos ponche* with *alcol.* You're going to have one with me, Mikey. Sister?"

Rosario shook her head.

"Is it okay if we have one?" Mike asked.

She smiled and nodded pleasantly.

Lonnie glanced at Pilar, and they both looked at Mike, who shook his head.

With a long metal dipper the woman filled two Styrofoam cups. She uncorked the bottle, topped off the cups and handed them to the men.

They were steaming. Lonnie blew at his, sipped it, blew, and took a drink. He smacked his lips. "I love *ponche,*" he said. "I knew I would." And to the woman: "Keep stirring. We'll be back."

They walked quickly through the arcade, past the mess of people talking and laughing, throwing baseballs, tossing darts, shooting toy rifles at little plastic figures arranged on shelves, trying to win the stuffed animals hanging on the walls of the tents. They hurried towards the Ferris wheel.

It had stopped moving now, however, and its lights were extinguished. High up in its webbing a good-looking young man clung, his feet on a strut, one hand grasping a bar and the other reaching inside. A cigarette dangled from his lips.

An older man on the ground below shouted something up to him, and the young man looked down, spotted the girls and smiled. Assured now that they were all looking at him, he released his grip and let himself fall backwards, slowly at first, then with increasing momentum, his feet still planted on the strut. The girls gasped and a couple of them turned away, but at the last moment the man caught himself with one hand, laughed, pulled himself back up and began working again, a self-satisfied smile on his face.

"If their life mean so little to them," Lonnie said. "He don't care nothing, huh?"

On the other side of the wheel was a small roller coaster with plastic cars, yellow with green spots. The lead car was molded into the head of a wide-eyed, grinning dragon. Two small children sat in it as it crawled along the track, suspended a few feet in the air.

Rosario gave money to the girls for tickets. Sara looked at Mike.

"You don't want to go on this?" Mike said.

"*Sí.*"

"But it's for little kids."

"*Sí.*"

"Pilar? You too?"

* * *

He stood with Lonnie and Sister Rosario - the little girl still clinging to her – and watched as the others climbed into the dragon, talking and laughing, two to a car. Pilar climbed into the last car with Suyapa and Sara sat in front of them with another girl; to fit her long legs in she had to bend her knees so they came almost to her chin.

"*Ridículo,*" Lonnie said, and he started back towards the tents. "I'm going to need another *ponche* for this."

The dragon began to move. Pilar opened her mouth wide in surprise and looked down at Suyapa, tiny beside her, leaning forward with her hands gripping the plastic of the car tightly, concentrating fiercely, as if she were steering.

"She looks okay, though, doesn't she? Suyapa, I mean," Mike said.

"*Sí*," Rosario said.

"A little sad, but that's just her, right?"

The sister nodded.

"How did she get that scar on her cheek?"

"I am not sure. They cook on open fires here, the poor ones. And children sometimes fall. Maybe this is what happened." She shook her head. "Think of how they must suffer."

They were silent for a moment, Mike feeling obligated to ponder the suffering, until Rosario started again.

"Once she came from school with a little bird she'd found on the ground. It was yellow and black, tiny, and it could not fly. She carried it with her hands cupped around it so she would not drop it. She said she would keep it until it could fly again, and then it would just stay here, with us, she said. She was so sure it would get better, and would want to stay with us. She tried to feed it crumbs, but it would not eat. She caught flies for it, but it did not want them, either. It was going to die; it moved no more, and its eyes were half shut. But it meant so much to her. The next day while she was at school, I took it from her room. I was going to tell her it flew away, so she could believe it was still alive, but I did not know what to do with it. I could not just leave it out for a cat or a snake to get it, or a cruel boy to find. And I could not kill it myself. So when she got home that day, I was there, holding it, waiting for her.

"She took it from me and went into the chapel, and she stayed there all night. And when I came to get her in the morning, she was still sitting there with the bird in her hand."

The girl at her feet was grunting now, holding both hands in the air, reaching up to her. Rosario bent down and gathered her in her arms.

"She is our newest girl," she explained. "She'll get better."

The dragon made another loop, and Suyapa glanced at Mike and raised one hand to wave at him before quickly putting it back on the plastic, making sure the thing didn't get away from her.

"How long, do you think?" Mike said. "I mean, how long do you suppose she has left?"

"How long does she have left for what?"

"You know what I mean, Sister. How long will she live?"

"I do not know. Why do you ask this?"

"Well, the disease, right? The HIV. Eventually she's going to...right?"

"Is that what you think?" she said. "You think Suyapa is sick that way? No, no, it is not like that at all."

"What do you mean?"

"She is not sick, not like that."

"But she lives with you. She's one of your girls."

"No. Yes. Yes, she stays with us, but she is not sick that way. She came to us in the spring. She is thinking about becoming a sister, one of us, so..."

"She's not sick?"

"Not like that, no.

Mike looked over again at the little figure sitting with Pilar, guiding the dragon along the rails. So small and so thin she was - there was nothing to her; the breeze could blow her away.

And she was sad, no doubt. And the little scar on her cheek - how much she must have suffered. And there she sat, among the forsaken, wearing the uniform of the forsaken. But she wasn't sick, not like that, anyway.

"What about the others?" Mike said.

"As God desires."

"As God desires. As God desires. But Suyapa - she's okay?"

"Yes, she is fine." But there was something hesitant in the sister's tone, and Mike gave her an interrogatory look.

"Something else," she said.

Yes. Of course. Something else. Always something else. It was the land of something else.

"Tell me."

"When she was in the hospital, her mother left," Rosario said, "trying to get to the United States."

"I see," Mike said.

"It is very dangerous. Walking. Riding on top of trains. Through Guatemala, through Mexico. Many try. Even little children try, so they don't have to join the *maras*. But it is dangerous. Many fall from the trains, and lose arms and legs, or they die. And the gangs, they prey on those poor people. And for a woman, it is…you can imagine what it is."

"Did she make it?"

"It was just a week ago she left, so…Suyapa did not even know she had gone until he came for her, when she was still in the hospital."

"Until who came for her?"

She let the girl down, and she immediately grabbed hold of her habit again with one hand and raised the other.

"She is our newest one."

"Until who came for her, Sister?" Mike said. "Not her father?"

She nodded. "He made Suyapa read the note her mother had left when she went away," she said. "And when she did, he became angry, and said she was lying like the rest of them, and then he tried to take her away."

"Why would he do that? He didn't want her - you said he didn't want her. He told her that he'd never wanted her."

Rosario shrugged and looked away again to the dragon.

"Oh, I get it. Now that his wife's gone he needs someone to take care of him. Cook for him. Clean up after him. Beat up on when he's drunk."

"She tried to go with him. She could barely stand, she was so sick, but she got out of bed and tried. The guards had to stop her."

The happy dragon rounded the curve and there she was again, steering intently, strands of her hair shifting in the breeze, sheltered under the arm of Pilar, who held the greasy napkin in her hand.

"And then, two days ago, he came to our house. Suyapa was not there, thank God, she was in the market with me, or who knows what would have happened? He wanted to talk to his daughter, he said - he had the right to talk to his daughter. When they would not unlock the door, he started to curse at them, to threaten them. He said the most vile things."

"Did you call the police?"

"If we called them, he would tell them that she was his daughter, and she would say she wanted to go with him – she would think she had to. And then what would happen? We were afraid of what would happen."

She picked up the little girl again.

"Is she safe now?" Mike said. "With her father out here somewhere, do you think she's safe?"

"He was drunk. And when men are drunk..."

"But he's always drunk, isn't he?"

From behind, Lonnie approached them, carrying two cups. "*Ponche infernal*," he said, and he held one of them out to Mike.

"*Ponche* what?"

"*Infernal. Ponche infernal.* It means —"

"I know what it means."

"From over there. Stronger, the woman said. I think that's what she said. She put more *alcol* in it, that's for sure. I knocked back a quick one at the booth," - he took another sip - "while I flirted with her. So that makes you one behind."

CHAPTER 33

THE FERRIS WHEEL WAS turning now, slowly, its benches still empty. The young man and the older one were on the loading platform, analyzing the situation, discussing the odds of the thing holding together for a turn or two more, long enough, anyway, to choke out a couple more rides, another dozen *pesos* or so from each of the suckers waiting there at its steps, before the inevitable catastrophe brought it down.

As the group hurried towards it they came upon a young girl selling flowers from a cart. Lonnie picked out a yellow one and handed her a wad of blues and reds.

"Pretty big tip you're giving her there, Lon," Mike said.

"*Propina*," Lonnie said. "On account of her being so damn cute." He twisted off the top of the flower quickly and smoothly, without watching, as if he did it for a living.

"Remember, you're going to be poor soon."

He scoffed, but then appeared to consider for a moment, twirling the flower in his hand. "How big?" he said. "The *propina*. How big?"

"Big."

He thought for another second. "Bah," he said. He turned to Pilar and with both hands pinned the flower behind her ear. He tilted back his head and looked at her. "Amazing," he said. "Pure voodoo."

A happy, toothless old man who had been standing at the side watching them now limped up to Lonnie and nudged him. "*Una rosa por otra cosa,*" he said, as if in secret, and he smiled at Pilar and walked off.

"What was that guy saying?" Lonnie asked.

Mike repeated it.

"What does that mean?"

"*Una rosa* is a rose. *Por otra cosa*...for another thing, for something else."

"A rose for another thing, huh? A rose in exchange for another thing. Ha ha. I get it. And we all know what that other thing is, don't we? The old pervert." He looked over at the old man limping away, as if he would run and shake his hand.

Mike turned and started towards the Ferris wheel.

"You should really buy one for Sara," Lonnie said. "*Una rosa.*"

He didn't answer. He hated all flowers now, now and for all time forward. He hated the cute girl, too, for selling them, and he hated Lonnie for buying one, hated him for putting it in Pilar's hair and hated her for allowing him to, for wearing it so brazenly like that, with that innocent-seeming smile and that little glance toward him. Hated her for being so beautiful with it. Hated her for *otras cosas.*

"Don't be so damn cheap," Lonnie said. "I know we had some unexpected Tuli expenses back there, but hell, we're on vacation. Remember those *muchachas* though?"

At the wheel the young man had begun letting the holy innocents on. Pilar held Suyapa's hand as they climbed the steps to the loading platform. Mike thought to stay with Rosario, safe on the ground, but Sara reached for his hand and led him up the stairs.

Lonnie looked on from below, shaking his head. "*Loco*," he said. "*Ridículo*." He turned and strolled away.

Mike had a fleeting notion to somehow maneuver himself to sit with Pilar, but Sara clung to him, and with Pilar and Suyapa already so damn chummy, there was no escaping her short of pushing her back down the steps. They sat and the young man with the cigarette sticking from his mouth, the young man who didn't care nothing, swung the guard bar down on them.

The benches were arranged in pairs facing each other, and it was a blessing, anyway, that Pilar was in the seat directly behind his, her back to him, so that he would at least be spared the sight of her, of the wonderful her and her yellow flower.

Directly across from him was Luz – calm and confident - sitting beside the chubby girl with the straight bangs, pensive-looking now and staring blankly through Mike's chest.

The operator pulled a lever and the machine gave a jerk. Mike's seat was swept slowly backwards and up, giving him a closer look at the innards of the contraption on which his life now hung. He looked away.

From behind him came a female voice, half screaming, half laughing, and he thanked God again that she was back there behind him, out of sight. But as he was carried higher and began to be pulled inward again, her chair slid into view from over his head, a development he had not calculated. At the top of the wheel, when she was directly across from him, it jerked to a stop. The benches swayed dangerously. Mike gripped the safety bar.

The man with the cigarette hadn't done his job, for all his showing off. He'd Cortesed it, damn him, hadn't fixed the thing well enough to make more than half a turn, leaving them swaying fifty feet in the air.

Sara tipped back and forth to rock the chair.

"What are you doing?" Mike said.

She laughed with a careless air, as if she were on a park bench enjoying a sunny afternoon, rather than dangling here in the black Cortesian night, held aloft by nothing.

"I knew the damn thing would break again. We'll never get down from here now."

She shook her head and pointed to the platform, directly below them, where the operator was loading more riders in a desperate attempt to maintain the delicate balance of the thing.

She laughed and rocked the bench again.

"Stop it," Mike said.

There was more laughter coming from the seat in front of them, in the direction his eyes had been avoiding. Now he looked. They were hitting it off spectacularly, Pilar and Suyapa. Bunched up against each other, Pilar's arm draped across the younger girl's scrawny shoulders, Suyapa gripping the bar in front of her with both hands, ready to take control again whenever the wheel lurched awake.

Pilar turned her head to look at Suyapa, and the yellow demon flower flashed at him.

He turned away.

Darkness had started to sink in and the street lights had come on throughout the town, strung along in lines that marked the progress of the dirt lanes beyond the square. Mike's eyes followed them from the far end of the carnival to the shadows beyond. In the distance a sparse string of lights hung in the air like magic, tracing out the route of a road as it scaled the invisible mountains. He thought for a moment of the hardening woman suffering somewhere up there, and he hoped...he hoped...he didn't know what he hoped. That she was still alive, still battling up there, in spite of it all? But why? Why prolong it? That a priest had made it to her in time? To what purpose? That the disease would disappear and she would live again to sort coffee beans, to mash *maiz* and flatten tortillas, to give the coffee-picker in the shadows half a dozen more mouths that he had no way to feed, to bequeath to them all the gifts of that same miserable, debased life? No, what he hoped was that the process had run its course, that the great work had been accomplished, and that the woman, now, finally, had hardened to rock, was at last at peace as only the rocks were.

The first firework of the evening cracked in the sky above the square, in the direction of the church. Suyapa pointed it out to Pilar, who smiled back at her and turned her head to look at Mike, showing off the accursed flower.

Sara shifted closer to him so that the entire length of her thigh pressed against his. It was heavy and warm and alive, better than the *ponche,* better even than the *ponche infernal.* He looked over at Pilar again, but she was ignoring him in an obviously willful way, looking off towards another firework flaring out against the dark.

The wheel lunged back into motion, the seats began swaying again and the riders screamed. Mike's bench crested the peak and started downward, Pilar slipping below him and out of sight. From over his head appeared Luz and the nervous girl, who was holding her head down now, frozen.

They disappeared below him, were replaced by Pilar and Suyapa, then Luz and the nervous girl again. Faster they went, and faster. Pilar, Luz, Suyapa, the nervous girl, faster and faster, as if *diablo* himself had taken dominion of the thing. Mike could feel it shudder beneath him and had a vision of the frame collapsing and the wheel careening away, flinging bodies into the air and rolling over unsuspecting innocents on the ground; in his sulk he half-welcomed the coming carnage.

Faster and faster yet. Pilar, her head back, laughing. Luz, still smiling her confident little smile. Suyapa, workmanlike, her hands on the bar, steering with great concentration. The nervous girl with the terror in her eyes. Pilar, Luz, Suyapa, the scared one, and then Pilar again, in all her glory. Pilar, *Ángel de Los Ángeles*, with her bright white teeth and the sharp line of her cheek and her caramel skin and her night-black hair and the yellow flower above her ear and he loved her and why wouldn't the damn thing fall out, anyway? What voodoo was holding it there?

She disappeared and Luz dropped into view as if from the heavens. Tears were running down the cheeks of the nervous girl.

He put his arm around Sara for a moment, but it was awkward and wrong and he quickly withdrew it.

"I'll buy you a flower if we get back on the ground," he said to her as Pilar appeared again, but he said it in English.

CHAPTER 34

AT THE SIDE OF the Ferris wheel the girls huddled, talking excitedly among themselves and glancing back up at the wheel looping above them, as if they could not believe they had ever been atop such a thing. In the middle of them was the nervous girl, her head lowered, tears running freely down her cheeks. Suyapa and two other girls tried to calm her.

"An emotional experience," Lonnie whispered to Mike.

"Shut up, Lon."

"No, I don't blame her. Look at that thing. I'd be crying too." He took a sip of *infernal* and smacked his lips.

A firework whistled up into the black sky and cracked softly overhead, spraying out a fan of sparks.

"Pitiful," Lonnie said. "Just pitiful."

From the church at the back of the plaza a noise arose, a cheap, tinny clanging, rapid and urgent, as if people were hammering out a warning on pieces of scrap metal.

"What the hell?"

"It is time for Mass," Rosario said.

"Those are bells?"

"Sí."

"Are we going to go?" Mike asked.

"Uh uh," Lonnie said.

The sister smiled. "Maybe we can take a quick look inside?" She started away toward the church, holding the hand of the new girl, begging to be picked up.

* * *

The church was smaller, less ornate and even more age-beaten than the Joco cathedral had been, but still imposing and dignified. The two floodlights at its base, slanting their lights up toward the cross at its peak, gave it a ghostly look. On each side was a tower through the arched windows of which Mike could see the dull glint of the swinging bells.

On the broad porch of the church and on the steps leading to it a crowd of people had assembled, waiting for more fireworks and watching the people mingling and passing by on the plaza below. On five columns evenly spaced along the front of the porch stood five angels, identical, four feet tall, their wings curving gracefully out from their backs. They surveyed the goings on below them with the tranquil, passive gaze that even divine beings in Cortes wore, though, Mike noticed, each of them had her right hand extended as if to ward off a blow.

The doors of the church were ajar and yellow light seeped out. Rosario led the girls through the crowd. Mike and the others followed. At the entrance he stopped Lonnie.

"You can't take that in with you," he said.

Lonnie looked at the cup in his hand as if surprised to see it there.

"No, I suppose not," he said. He paused for a moment as if to brace himself, then brought the cup to his mouth and downed its contents in a gulp. He grimaced, crunched up the cup and jammed it into his back pocket. *"Infernal,"* he said.

"And take that hat off."

"All right. Ready then. Lead on, Christian soldier."

They entered. The smell of incense hit Mike again and he battled back the old memories, battled against the return of the Polish priest with his golden lamp and his silver bucket and his stern demeanor.

Rosario and the girls filed into a row of benches at the back, knelt and made the sign of the cross, kissing their thumbs. Pilar looked at Mike as if waiting to see what he would do. She was still holding the napkin with the piece of chicken against her thigh.

A door opened in the wall, halfway up the front, and a woman clad in black as if in mourning shuffled through it and out into the aisle. She went to a pew, knelt and crossed herself as another woman entered the little closet and shut the door behind her.

"Bless me Padre, for I have sinned," Lonnie whispered to Mike.

"Quiet," Mike said.

"My last confession was...well, let's just say *mucho*."

"Enough," Mike said.

"These are my sins: I abused *ponche*, Padre, and shamelessly did I abuseth it. And then of course there was the incident with the Tulis."

"Damn it, Lonnie."

"But I never cursed in church – I never did that. But all right, I'll be quiet."

The sister and the girls finished their prayers. They crossed themselves again, stood and started shuffling out to the aisle, genuflecting towards the altar. Mike and the others followed them through the doors and paused amidst the crowd on the porch. The square was charged with life, and joy and excitement and goodwill surrounded them – or the *ponche* made it seem so.

"But I can't really say I'm sorry, Padre," Lonnie said. "Not heartfully sorry, anyway. No, not heartfully."

"Stop it, now," Mike said angrily.

Sister Rosario looked over at them. Lonnie held his mitts in the air as if pleading innocence.

"I don't like it when you do that," Mike said.

"Do what?"

"Poke fun at it like that. Some of us might still believe, you know."

"Like you, you mean? Compared to me, you believe?"

"Just leave it alone."

"Hell, Mikey. I'm the opposite of an unbeliever. I believe in him so much, I blame him. All right, though, enough of that. Let's find some *ponche*."

CHAPTER 35

MUSIC WAS COMING FROM the pavilion at the far corner of the square, where the two DJ's with the gelled-back hair held court. A dozen couples were dancing on the floor of the plaza below. The group started towards them, crossing the square in the frosty glow of the streetlamps. Lonnie seemed suddenly subdued by Lonnie standards, and Mike's spirits rose when he patted his gut and made an exaggerated, showy grimace.

"You all right there?" Mike said. "Not getting sick, I hope."

"I'm fine."

"You sure? Maybe you should lighten up on that *ponche* stuff."

"Don't go blaming the *ponche*, Mikey. Everyone's always blaming the *ponche*."

"Maybe you're right, maybe it's not the *ponche*. Maybe it's all that street food you've been slopping down like a *barrio* sow."

"I'm fine."

"If you say so."

A girl came running hard in their direction, swinging a glowing blue toy in her hand. She was looking backwards and nearly plowed into Luz before slowing down to weave her way through the group. Twenty feet behind her a boy came on, chugging his arms and bobbing his head. He slalomed through the group deftly. Pilar reached out for him, but he shifted his body sideways, slipped past her and continued after the girl, nearly catching her before she came to a stop where a woman was standing in the middle of the square. She hid behind the woman, grabbing her sleeve and peeking out at the boy, holding up the little toy to taunt him.

The boy slowed to a crawl, his hands on his hips. He said something to the girl and she shook her head, waving the toy at him. The boy suddenly grabbed it from her hand and was off.

"*Mami*," cried the girl, and started after him. The boy adjusted his speed to stay just out of her reach, looking back and laughing at her.

Pilar had been watching it all with profound concern and now broke from the group and had after the boy. Seeing her his eyes widened and he started running in earnest towards the crowd on the porch of the church, hoping there to lose her. But Pilar was on him before he'd gotten across the gap, grabbing his shirttail and dragging him to a stop. He turned to face her with a guilty smile and held out the toy as the girl caught up to them. She took it from his hand, turned, and skipped back across the plaza, waving it in the air. Pilar let the boy go and walked back to rejoin the group.

As she approached she glanced at Mike, wagging her head.

"*Malo*," she said, and she tried to frown, but couldn't pull it off. Her eyes glittered at him and she smiled.

This would have been a perfect time to tell her something, but instead he nodded at her stupidly.

"You're pretty quick, there, Pilar," he said.

She looked down, smiling, as if recognizing his dissembling.

They took their places in the arc of people watching the dancers. In defiance of Mike's hopes, Lonnie seemed to have recovered, and as he watched the dancers moving to the slick, rapid Latin music, he started swaying his hips, shifting his hands, palms downward, in front of him and shuffling his feet from side to side and back and forth, in imitation of them.

He wasn't at all bad.

He held his hand out to Pilar. "What do you think, *mi ponchita*? Shall we dance?" he said. "No? Sara?"

Sara shook her head, too, but without conviction, and he took her hand and led her forward. They began dancing, Lonnie confident and utterly unselfconscious, Sara hesitant and not knowing exactly what to do. Lonnie snapped off a pirouette, holding his *ponche* away from his body – where had he gotten another cup of *ponche*? - and letting out a whoop. He took Sara's hand and spun her around clockwise, paused for a beat, and spun her the other way. She turned about awkwardly, glancing back at the group, delight in her eyes. Lonnie, too, looked over to see what impression he was making. All signs of the malady seemed forgotten. Except, except...There was something there after all, if Mike wasn't mistaken - some little hesitation, unLonnie-like in its uncertainty.

At the end of the song, on the very last note, Lonnie struck a pose, curling his right hand above his head as if to pour his *ponche* over his hat, curving his other hand over his stomach, rising onto his toes and jerking his chin up and to the side. He shouted into the night, "*Eso!*"

All that was missing was the flower between his teeth, and he'd left that in Pilar's hair, where it would hurt even more.

The girls laughed among themselves and Rosario, too, seemed to enjoy it. Pilar looked on passively until, feeling Mike's eyes on her, she turned to him and smiled weakly.

"*Estupido,*" Mike said.

She smiled.

"*Idiota,*" he said.

She laughed. "*Zonzo,*" she said.

He put his arm around her shoulder.

"*Tonto.*"

This would have been a good time, too, and he turned his head to look at her.

"Hey," Lonnie said as he returned to the group. "Take your hands off my *ponchita…mi ponchita.*"

But Mike could see now, after the flourish, that the man was hurting, and he asked again, with increased hope, how he felt.

"Eh, a little shaky, actually," he responded. "I know, I know - you couldn't tell it by the dancing. But I'm thinking maybe I could sit for a minute – just a minute. Over there maybe."

He and Mike started towards the retaining wall on the other side of the pavilion. Sitting atop the wall a smattering of people watched the goings-on - young couples, women holding bags, an old man in a straw hat.

"No more *ponche,*" Mike said.

Lonnie looked down at the cup in his hand wistfully. "I guess not," he said. He handed the cup to Mike. "Hey, is it getting darker out? I think it's getting darker."

"I don't think so."

"Then I'm going blind, Mikey. It's the alcohol. Everything's going dark."

"Really?"

"No, not really." He tried to laugh. "But just in case, sit me over there, by those two, so I can get one last glimpse of it." He angled off to where two young women sat smiling at them, their teeth gleaming in the dusk.

"My Lord they have beautiful women here, don't they?" he said. "Before they wear out, I mean. *Hola, ponchitas,*" he called to them, forcing out a Lonnie smile, diluted a bit by his suffering but still charming as hell.

The women laughed.

"Don't mind him, he's sick," Mike told them. "He's going to sit here for a while, if that's all right. Over here. But watch out for him. He can't be trusted."

"What did you tell them, Mikey?"

"That you were going to sit down."

"Hell of a lot of words just to say that."

"Over here."

"Okay, but just make sure no one steals me, all right?" he said. "Unless it's these two." He leered over at them.

* * *

"He'll be all right," Mike said to Rosario as he rejoined the group. "Just overdid it a little. All that street food."

"All that *ponche,*" Sara said.

"Yeah, maybe a little of that too. It's kind of strong, isn't it?"

"*Infernal.*"

"Yeah, *infernal.*"

"*Bolo,*" he heard Sara whisper to Luz, and they both laughed.

Another firework blew up overhead. Mike turned to see the spray of sparks fan slowly out over the church. Beyond, the lights of the Ferris wheel rolled over in the black air and the pinpricks of white ascended the mountain. The angels in front of the church reached out to him from their columns, offering him their blessing. All this, and Lonnie sick.

It was a slow song now, a *corazón* song, thick and weepy, with a bongo popping along beneath it, redeeming its melancholy. The dancers had slowed their pace and pressed themselves up against each other.

As he listened Mike became conscious of singing coming from his right, high and clear, perfectly on pitch. He leaned toward Sara to listen.

"My God, that's beautiful, Sara," he said. "You sing like a bird."

She beamed and looked over at Pilar to see if she had heard.

"Pilar, can you sing, too?" Mike said.

She shook her head.

"She sounds like a *sapo*," Sara said.

"Shut up," Pilar said.

"A *sapo* doesn't make any noise, does it?" Mike said to Sara.

"If you step on it," she laughed.

As if she had seen it all and understood, Suyapa broke from the girls at Rosario's side and came to Pilar, who leaned down to hear her whisper something. Pilar nodded, and Suyapa took one of her hands and one of Mike's and began pulling them forward, towards the dancers.

"Come on, *Mojado*," she said.

She took the piece of chicken from Pilar, who looked up at Mike as Suyapa turned and started back to the sidelines.

"For *mamá*," Mike said.

"*Si.*"

"You're a good daughter, Pilar."

"*Gracias.*"

"I think we're supposed to dance now."

"*Si.* But I don't know how."

"It's easy."

He took her left hand and put it on his shoulder, took her right hand with his left and laced his fingers into hers, and set his other hand lightly against her back. He started to lead her slowly, keeping her body at a safe distance. They danced for a few turns in silence, until Pilar whispered something that Mike couldn't hear. He asked her to repeat it. She refused. He asked her again.

"*Tonto,*" she said.

"Me?"

She shook her head.

"Oh, him," Mike said. "*Si. Tonto.* I have to spin you now."

"What?"

"I'm going to turn you around."

"No. No. I don't know how."

He raised her hand and guided her so that she revolved under it.

"See, that wasn't hard, was it?"

"No."

"Again."

"No."

He spun her again, and she came to rest back in his arms, looking up at him so that he could no longer resist, and he stopped dancing and pulled her into him. "Mmmmm," she purred.

He looked over at the group. Rosario was watching them with her pretty, restrained little smile, Suyapa with a smug but skeptical look. Luz was beside her, swaying in place, shuffling her feet, holding the side of her dress out with the tips of her fingers and swishing it gently back and forth, smiling down at the waves of cloth rippling against her thigh.

She looked up and their eyes met. Her face lit up, and she looked away again, smiling.

He glanced over to where Lonnie was sitting, his hands together, his head down and half turned in the direction of the two girls on the wall, one of whom was gleaming back at him.

"Listen," Mike said. "You have to be careful with him, Pilar. You can't be fooled by him, all right?"

"By who?"

"Lonnie. I mean, don't think he's going to be around. This is a trip for him, just a trip. And he does lots of trips. Do you know what I mean?"

"No."

"He's a *tiburon*, Pilar."

"He's a fish?"

"It's a saying. A *tiburon* is a guy who…who's not a good guy, with women. In English, it's 'shark'. It's a better word."

"Chark?"

"Shark."

"Chark?"

"Yeah, chark. Anyway, I just don't want you to think…Do you know what I mean?"

"I think so."

Another firework flared into the sky, but just for them, now. The music changed and they started dancing again.

"He thinks I'm trying to steal you from him."

"What?"

"Lonnie. He thinks I'm trying to steal you."

"I see," she said.

He glanced at Luz again. Without interrupting her perfect little dance, she nodded at him, then looked down at her feet as if to ensure they wouldn't get away from her.

Forever – she should have been able to dance like that forever.

"Are you?" Pilar said.

"Am I what?"

"Are you stealing me?"

"Yeah. I suppose I am."

"It's okay though," she said. "Spin me."

She turned around slowly in front of him, paused, looking up at him, and stepped back into his arms, laying her forehead lightly against his chest so that the top of her head was under his chin; her bristly hair made him itch.

He drew her closer, pressing his hand against her back. Another firework went off, this one directly above their heads. She jumped in his arms at the explosion.

"You know I'll be leaving, too, though, Pilar. You know that, right? I mean, I can't warn you off one shark, and on to another one."

"Another chark?"

"Si."

"You're a chark, too?"

"Yeah, I suppose I am."

"I don't think you're a chark."

Mike crooked his head back to look at her, but she was turned away. She stopped dancing, unlocked her hand from his and wiped her eye with her palm.

"I wish…" he said.

She put her hands on his biceps, and he flexed. She tugged him down towards her, holding her lips – light and dry - on his cheek for a moment. She took a step back.

With both hands he picked the flower from her hair and stuffed it into his pocket.

He walked her back to the group and then went to Lonnie, who was hunched over now, his elbows on his knees, his hat in his hands. The two gleaming girls were nowhere to be seen.

"You all right, there, conquistador?" Mike said.

He didn't reply.

"Come on. Time to go."

He grunted.

"You ought to hear Sara sing," Mike said. "She has a voice like a bell."

"Yeah, a Cortes bell."

"No, a real bell. Come on. Let's go."

Lonnie mumbled something about *ponche*.

"You've had too much of that stuff already," Mike said.

"No. I said you should stay away from my *ponche*, my *ponchita*," he said. "Stop taking advantage of a stricken man."

"Look, Lon —"

"No, no. Why go on when you can't even trust your best friend."

"I'm not your best friend."

"Not anymore, you're not."

"I'm not your best friend, and Pilar's not your *ponche*."

"We'll see," he said, and he brushed away Mike's hand, braced himself on the concrete bench, and slowly rose.

CHAPTER 36

THE GIRLS BEGGED PILAR and Sara to ride with them on the bus back to the sister's place, and so they did. Rodrigo followed in his cab, Mike in the front seat, Lonnie - suffering nicely - in the back. When they stopped at the sister's place, Lonnie stayed in the car while Mike got out to collect the women. Suyapa asked him to wait and disappeared inside, leaving Mike in the road with the other girls. He looked them over, one by one.

Such bright, open faces they had. Smiling, full of life, the joy of the evening in their eyes. Even the nervous one who had cried because of the Ferris wheel was now looking back at him eagerly, like the others, lined up in front of him in their uniforms as if waiting to be counted.

Well..." he said. "Did you like the fair?"

"*Sí*," they responded.

"Good, good. Me, too. I liked the rides."

"*Sí*."

"*Sí*. And the music - the music was good."

They nodded as one.

"The dancing," said Luz, and she let go a little flurry of perfect dance steps that made Mike smile, made him yearn.

"Yeah, the dancing," he said. He glanced at Pilar, standing at the side with Sara and Rosario. The little girl had fallen asleep and was lying limp now in the sister's arms.

"And the *ponche*," one of the girls said, and the others laughed.

"Okay. The *ponche*."

There was another moment of silence.

"It was a nice church."

The girls agreed.

He looked to the side of the road opposite the *asilo*. It was lined by the same run-together jumble of makeshift *casas* that carpeted Cortes - old wood planks and cement block, plastic and tin and cardboard, open doors leading into the mysteries of *barrio* life.

"Your country is beautiful," he said.

They agreed.

"Beautiful," he repeated. He looked at them again. Waiting for something, expecting something, needing something - something he did not have.

"I'm sorry," he said, in English, so they would not understand, and they nodded at him. "I'm sorry for Marisol, too."

At the mention of Marisol, the smiles of the girls disappeared and something else replaced them.

Mike turned away and looked back at the *casas*. An emaciated old woman had come from within one of them and now stood uncertainly in the doorway, looking out towards him without seeming to see him.

"I should..." he started to say. "Maybe I should..."

But before he could figure out what it was he should maybe do, the door to the *asilo* opened and Suyapa appeared, carrying some papers that she distributed, one page each to him, Pilar, and Sara.

In the dim light of the road he looked his over. It was a page torn from a coloring book, crayoned in with yellows and blues and reds. A cartoon rabbit standing on his haunches and smiling back at him.

Suyapa had something else in her hand, and she offered it to Mike. It was a photograph of herself in full graduation regalia, sitting on a stool and looking out at the camera. Mike examined it a moment, smiled to show his appreciation, and put it in his wallet.

They said their goodbyes. Each of the girls came up to him and gave him a hug, and one by one they disappeared through the doorway, still looking disturbed at the mention of Marisol.

Suyapa came up and hugged him around the waist. "I love you, *Mojado*," she said. The words took him aback, but she didn't seem to expect any response, and turned quickly and followed the others inside.

At the car, Mike slid the drawing into his backpack. Pilar and Sara asked if he would carry theirs, too, and he asked Pilar if she wanted him to take the chicken for her as well. She thought for a moment before agreeing.

The women got in the rear seat of the taxi with Lonnie, who woke up long enough to greet them with a grunt before immediately falling back asleep.

* * *

It was dark and ghostly along the road into *Los Ángeles*. Loose groups of teens hung about the ill-lit corners, eyeing the taxi as it passed. In the gutters a few fires threw yellow into the air. Rodrigo drove as fast as he could, but the bumps and changes of speed as he maneuvered along the scars in the road woke Lonnie.

"Where?" he moaned.

"Los Ángeles."

"Los Angeles..." he murmured, as if surprised. He shut his eyes again.

They turned onto Pilar's street to see a crowd of thirty or so people scattered about the road between her *casa* and that of her neighbor.

"Mmmmm," Pilar purred. She strained to see forward out the windshield. Rodrigo stopped the taxi at the edge of the crowd and she got out quickly and ran towards her neighbor's *casa*, dodging through the mob. Sara followed more slowly, and Mike began to open his door.

"Stay in," Rodrigo said in a tone he hadn't used before. He got out himself, quickly closed the door that Pilar had left open, got back in and started the cab forward. The mob parted reluctantly. He drove to the next corner, Sara's corner, executed a rushed three-point turn and headed back through the crowd. As they passed the gate of the neighbor's house Mike spotted Sara talking to three other women. He could not see Pilar; she must have gone into the *casa*.

At the far edge of the crowd Mike spotted the tattooed *malo* standing a bit off the road, his arm resting against a fence post, his eyes tracking the taxi. He looked injured, seething.

"When a crowd around here this time night," Rodrigo said. "Better no stop."

* * *

The road in front of the mission was empty and quiet, peaceful-looking. Nonetheless, Mike was relieved when Brother Joe opened the door and came to the front gate to unlock it, as if he had been waiting just inside for their arrival.

"Look," Mike said to Rodrigo as he paid him, "we don't have to tell anyone about those women, right?"

"I tell nobody. I good at telling nobody."

Mike opened the door for Lonnie and led him to the gate.

"Is he drunk?" Joe asked.

"No, just sick. He's been eating street food."

"He looks drunk."

"Just a couple *ponches*," Lonnie said, his face slack, his speech a little slurred. *"Ponchi."*

"Ponche, huh? Well, there's *ponche* and there's *ponche."*

"Infernal," Lonnie said, as if boasting. *"Ponche infernal."*

"I see."

"Is Marco here?" Mike asked.

"No."

"Good," Mike thought. He led Lonnie past the empty dining room, past the medical rooms and out along the *pasillo* towards the dorm, where he deposited him in his bedroom before entering his own.

He took Suyapa's graduation photograph out of his wallet and examined it. She was dressed in red from head to toe – gown, square cap, tassel. On her lap she held a carefully rolled diploma, and superimposed at the bottom was a ribbon with the words *"Belén de la Meseta; El Campo Barrio; Tamalito"*.

She looked out at him with that same expectant, questioning, unsettling look.

He remembered that he still had her coloring pages in his backpack, and he took them out and looked them over. One showed a smiling bird gliding along in front of a puffy cloud. Another was of a gleeful pig in overalls, leaning against a wooden fence with a straw bending from the corner of his mouth, wearing a Lonnie-style hat – though not as well as Lonnie did. And then there was Mike's rabbit. He wore a purple vest, and was propped up on his haunches, holding a multi-colored bouquet. He looked even happier here in the better light of the room. At the top of the page was a little banner in which appeared the words, in English, "God Loves You", each letter filled in with a different color. At the bottom of the page she'd printed her name in tiny letters, like an artist signing her work.

CHAPTER 37

MIKE ROSE, DRESSED, AND left his room, feeling a bit unsettled from the previous night's *ponche*. He passed by Lonnie's door, shrouded with the heavy brown curtain, and walked along the *pasillo* towards the front. The chatter of children's voices became louder and clearer, and he found himself quickening his pace. When he entered the dining room the entire mob came running towards him, some calling his name, some demanding *fútbol*. At one side the little girl with the eye patch stood gazing at him with her one eye. In her hand were the three plastic cups.

"*Fútbol* today," Juan Carlos said. "You promised."

"I promised?"

"*Sí*," they all shouted to him.

"I think you guys are scamming me. But okay, maybe this afternoon."

As they complained, Mike maneuvered through them towards the counter, where the brothers were sitting with their coffee.

"Looks like you've picked up a few fans," Brother Luke said.

"It appears so."

"And your partner?"

"Lonnie? Still in his room, I guess. He's a little under the weather."

"All that *ponche?*"

"Yeah, he did have a couple. Personally, though, I think it's all the street food he's been eating."

Luke looking at him skeptically, and Mike tried not to notice.

"Is there a plan for these guys today?" Mike asked. "They say I promised them *fútbol* again, but they're lying. I think."

"It'll have to be later. One of our sisters is on her way here; she's going to give them some classes while we do our chores."

"Maybe I can give you a hand," Mike said.

Brother Luke was surprised. "Ever milk a cow?" he said.

"Maybe I can give you a hand with something else."

"Ah, it's easy. It'll be good penance for you. It'll be a penance cow."

"A penance cow?"

"Yeah, you need a penance cow, don't you?"

The bell up front rang.

"That'll be Ibekwe," Luke said.

Brother Joe rose.

"She might need some help with supplies."

* * *

The sister was at the front gate, holding a large cardboard box. Beside her, with another box in his hands and a duffle slung over his shoulder, was a short well-built Cortesian man in a neat light-brown suit. His shirt was buttoned all the way to the collar and he wore a black string tie and a cream-colored cowboy hat, its brim neatly flared up at the sides. He leaned to the right under the weight of the duffle.

The sister called hello in a deep penetrating voice.

They opened the gate. Joe took the man's duffle, hiked it up on his shoulders and turned towards the door. Mike held his arms out to Ibekwe; she smiled gently at him and put the box in his arms. It was filled with loose school supplies – pencils, crayons, notebooks – and was surprisingly heavy. As he turned to follow the others inside, he heard someone call his name quietly, as if to ensure that only he could hear. Belkis was peeking out from behind one of the maple trees. She waved him over with a downward motion of her hand, but Mike shook his head and shifted the box up to indicate that he was busy. She looked behind her and Pilar glanced out from over her shoulder.

"Brother Joe," Mike said. "I'll be right in."

He walked to where Pilar was hiding, and he could see she'd been crying. He asked her what was wrong, and she turned away.

"*Señor* Ruiz," Belkis said.

"Your neighbor?" he said to Pilar.

"*Sí*," Belkis said. "He died."

"I'm sorry."

He was still holding the box in both his hands, and Belkis stepped up and peered inside it.

"Is there anything I can do?" he asked Pilar.

"She wants her drawing," Belkis said. She reached into the box, fished around a bit, and extracted a blue pen. She held it up to Mike with a questioning look.

"It's not mine," Mike said. "I can't give it to you. What drawing?"

"Please?"

Mike shook his head, and Belkis sighed, reached into the box to put the pen back, and again started fishing around.

"The drawing from Suyapa," she said.

"Oh, yeah. The drawing. It's inside. If you can wait here."

"And the chicken," Belkis said.

"The chicken?"

Pilar nodded.

"Oh, yeah. The chicken. For your *mamá*. I'll have to…let me check."

Mike left them at the tree and went inside, where Brother Joe was waiting for him. He handed him the box.

"I have to get something," he said, and he shuffled past him and went to his room, noting with satisfaction that Lonnie's curtain was still closed. He took Pilar's and Suyapa's drawings from the shelf and dug out the chicken from the trashcan, still wrapped in napkin. He carried them back through the compound, passing again as inconspicuously as possible by the dining room, where Ibekwe was already at work getting the children organized, her thick voice calling out commands in African-accented Spanish.

He returned to Pilar and gave her the drawings and the chicken.

Belkis asked to see the drawings. She examined them and shrugged, unimpressed.

"Go, now," Pilar said to her. Belkis protested but Pilar pushed her away, smiling as she watched her slowly cross the street and take up her position against the tree in front of her *casa*.

As if remembering herself, Pilar backed up to the tree again and looked down at the ground, her arms folded. Mike stepped toward her and rubbed her on the shoulder for a moment – it was firm, muscular.

"You were close to him, weren't you?" he said.

"*Sí.*" Tears started from her eyes. "He helped us when *papá* died. He gave..." she said, but she was fighting back sobs and had to stop. Mike glanced away towards Belkis, who was picking bark from the tree and watching them.

"He gave us money for food," Pilar spoke again. "But he didn't have any himself." She held her palms up imploringly, as if pleading to understand how such a thing could be.

"Do you want to sit, Pilar?" Mike said, pointing to one of the concrete benches. "Come on. Let's sit down."

She shook her head and pressed the water out of her eyes with her palm. They stood there silent for a full minute, Mike not knowing what to say, Pilar seeming unable to speak.

"I have to go back," she finally said, and she straightened up and raised her eyes to Mike.

"I'll see you later?" he said.

She nodded and started away.

"We're going to play *fútbol* this afternoon," Mike said to her. "Out back here, if you want to come."

Her saw her head nod, but she kept walking. He watched as she sunk down below the hill and waited for what seemed another five minutes until she finally appeared on the bridge, crossed it and climbed the other side. Almost at the top, she finally glanced around to look at him, raising her hand to wave just before she disappeared towards *Los Ángeles*.

When he turned to go back inside, Belkis, still standing by the tree across the road, smiled as if she'd been waiting for him to look at her. She drew a pink pen from her pocket, held it up for a moment, laughed, and ran inside.

* * *

Mike had determined to check on Lonnie before returning to his room, and fought to maintain his resolve as he made his way back inside, through the atrium, past the dining room – empty now – and along the *pasillo*. But on seeing the curtain still drawn over the door, he felt a faint revulsion, as if from the *ponche* of the night before, and he pivoted on the tiles, returning through the atrium and bounding up the stairs to the mysterious second floor. As carefully and as quietly as he could he opened the chapel door and slid inside. Padre was standing at the front, beneath the crucifix, a book in his hands. The brothers were all in the front pew, facing him.

"Oh God, come to our assistance," the padre intoned.

In response, the brothers chanted: "Lord, make haste to help me."

Mike went to the back pew and sat.

CHAPTER 38

MIKE HELD THE DOOR open for the others as they went out of the chapel, and walked with Brother Luke at the back of the pack, towards the stairs.

"So, what did you think of that?" the brother asked him.

Mike nodded. "Maybe I can join you in the mornings for that."

"I thought you guys were moving on."

"About that. I wonder how you'd feel if I stayed here instead. Maybe I can help out a little with the kids."

Luke leaned away and squinted over at him. "You want to stay?"

"If I can help with the kids."

"And your partner?"

"Who knows? Who cares? He won't be happy, I imagine."

"I imagine," Luke said.

They were quiet as they started down the steps. At the landing Luke stopped. "It's not because of her that you want to stay, is it?" he said. "That girl out front? She's not something I have to worry about, is she?"

"Pilar? No."

"Good. Because she looks like she might be."

"Her neighbor died," Mike said as if in explanation. "She came to tell me about it."

"*Señor* Ruiz, yes. I heard. Padre is going over there this morning. Did you know him?"

"No. I had to give Pilar something, though. Something that belonged to her."

"What would that be?"

"A drawing...and a piece of chicken."

"A drawing of a piece of chicken?"

"No, a drawing, and a piece of chicken."

"You had a piece of chicken that belonged to her?"

"And a drawing. It's a long story."

They started walking again, out the main building, towards the back. Luke said nothing; he seemed to be waiting for the long story.

Mike stopped near his own bedroom door and turned to him. "She went with us last night," he finally said. "To the fair. Pilar and her friend Sara."

"Yeah, I know," Luke said. "It's a small *barrio*. So you guys had yourself a little date?"

"To call it a date would be glorifying it. We just went to the fair with Sister Rosario and her girls. I didn't even know we were going to pick the women up."

"You didn't?"

Mike paused, thinking how far to go. "No, I didn't. And they went downtown with us, too, on Monday. But I suppose you knew that already, too."

Luke didn't respond.

"It's not like we arranged it beforehand," Mike said. "At least, I don't think we did. Lonnie was just going to show me where they live, because he'd gone there with Brother Joe – remember? And somehow they ended up coming with us."

"Somehow."

"We didn't...We just had lunch and walked around a little. We talked to Pilar's mother. She was okay with it. And nothing happened, Luke."

"You didn't sleep with them then?"

"No." Mike tried to put a drop of indignation into his denial, to pretend to be offended at the impertinence of the question, but in light of the Tuli girls, it was too much to ask. "It was nothing, really," he said.

"No, no. Whatever it was, it wasn't nothing. Not to them."

"Yeah, I know."

They walked on, turning the corner of the dorm buildings and seeing the pens across the yard. The smell of animals, always faint at the front of the compound, here was strong and rich.

"Yeah, you can stay here," Luke said. "And look, I know you're not monks. No one would mistake you guys for monks, would they? But you're staying with monks – well, with brothers. It won't do to have you two living with us but acting like you do in Spain, or Mexico, or wherever the hell your little adventures take you next."

"Understood. I was wondering about the boy Greg took to the hospital. How's he doing?"

"He's okay," Luke said, then thought a bit. "We'll see."

Mike walked with him across the yard to the cages, looking at the animals milling about in their pens and wondering what he was getting into. A small black and white pig grunted about in some muck thoughtfully slopped into its pen. A couple of goats chewed straw with strange, thoughtful, severe looks on their faces. A wooden palette had been modified - some of its crosspieces yanked out - and it was leaning against the wall of the chicken coop, serving as a perch. The top couple rows of it were lined with birds, staring forward, waiting there for Mike like a jury of his peers.

Tied to a rope at the end of the pens was the cow, and as Mike was looking it over, wondering how it might be approached, Padre came from around the corner, heading for the pick-up truck parked on the drive. Mike asked Luke if he could go talk to him, and the brother consented.

He helped the padre open the exterior doors. He was happy to see that he had his gleam back.

"You're going to Ruiz's?" Mike said.

"I am."

"Could you check on Pilar for me? She was upset by it, by his death. You know who she is?"

He nodded. They walked to the pickup.

"Was he a young guy, Ruiz?"

The padre shook his head. "*Señor* Ruiz had a long, full life, believe me. It'll be more a celebration over there than anything. And Pilar – she'll be fine."

Mike opened the door of the truck for him and he climbed in.

"I'm going to stay here," Mike said. "I mean, for the rest of our trip."

The padre turned and looked at him, head tilted, eyebrow raised. Mike was relieved to see that he didn't seem upset at the prospect.

"I'd go with you now, but I have to milk a cow, or something."

"Ah, a penance cow, huh? Well, when I get back, I'm hearing confession for Maria and the brothers. If you —"

"We'll see, Padre."

He closed the doors behind the truck and joined the brothers, mustering at the shed. He looked over to where the cow stood, staring stupidly at the ground, its udder like a basketball stuffed between its hind legs.

"I'm supposed to get milk out of that thing?"

"It's not so bad," Luke said. "And when you're done, there's some penance manure that needs to be shoveled."

CHAPTER 39

TWO HOURS LATER MIKE started back to his room, hot and miserable and tired and proud. On the way he heard the thick voice of Sister Ibekwe coming from one of the classrooms. He peeked in. The sister stood behind a long table on which were laid an assortment of odd things - figurines, a paper mache model of a city, little priests garments of different colors hanging on small stick frames. She was holding aloft two small dolls with beards, and she was speaking slowly in Spanish to the orphans fanned out in front of her, sitting on the tile.

Juan Carlos was near the back of the group, fidgeting, glancing about, looking generally uncomfortable without a soccer ball in his hands. He spotted Mike and made as if to get up, but Mike motioned for him to stay. Wendy, sitting just behind him in the back row, caught the boy's movements and looked back with a jerk, her hair sparking about around her head. She smiled at Mike and shifted over to make room for him on the floor, waving him forward with a downward swipe of her hand. Sister Ibekwe frowned. Mike turned away and started back towards his room.

He rounded the corner of the dorm and saw that Lonnie's room was still shuddered; a blessed thing. He went to his own room, carefully opening and closing the latch on his door. He took a quick, frigid shower, laid down and quickly fell asleep, waking an hour later, hungry and happy. He dressed, went out, and stood before the sick man's room.

All was dead quiet within, and Mike pondered a moment before coming to a decision.

"You alive in there?" he finally said.

There was no answer. He called again, a bit more loudly, and finally heard a grunt from inside.

"How're you feeling?"

"Like a dozen Cortesians beat me with an iron bar."

"All right, I'll leave you be, then."

"No. Come in here. I need to talk to you."

Mike swept the curtain aside and entered the gloom. Lonnie was sprawled out on his bed, uncovered, with just a pair of shorts on.

"Pretty provocative, there," Mike said.

"Don't try to make nice to me. Don't try to capitalize on my good nature."

"Why not?"

"Because you tried to steal my *ponche*, that's why not."

"What are you talking about?"

"Ah, don't give me that. I remember."

"Actually, you're not provocative at all. You look like hell."

Lonnie slowly swung his legs to the floor, sat up, and with his claw brushed his hair, disheveled and greasy, from his forehead. He swayed slightly until he found his balance.

"I bring you on a fun-packed Cortes vacation," he said, "but that's not good enough. I all but hand you a wild Tuli adventure on a platter, but that ain't enough, either."

"The brothers say you probably don't have typhoid. Damn shame."

"And Sara! Happy, welcoming, willing Sara!"

"You're saying you gave me Sara?"

"But even that's not enough for Mr. BreakDownTheDoor. *Señor* TearDownThisWall. You had to have my *ponche*, too. No, no. I saw it. I saw the whole thing. No use denying it."

"They said it's probably just all the crap you've been eating."

Lonnie eyeballed Mike with his accustomed, sarcastic smile.

"Well, then," Mike finally said. "I just came by to see if you needed anything, but you have yourself, so…"

"I could use a friend who won't steal my *ponche*."

"I danced with her one time, Lon. They wanted us to dance together."

"Oh, I see - they forced her on you. There was nothing you could do. And they forced you to take my flower out of her hair, too, I suppose? Oh yeah, I saw that too. You deflowered her. Right in front of me you deflowered her." He waved his hand at Mike dismissively and looked away. "Aw, that's all right," he said. "That's all right. Part of the game, huh? You saw your chance, and you took it. You had your own *ponche*, but your *ponche* wasn't good enough, though it was pretty damn good *ponche*. But I understand."

"Pilar's not your *ponche*."

"Pilar is my *ponche*, Mikey. *Mi ponchita*. I love that girl, Mikey."

"Bah."

"I love her like Romeo loved Juliet, man. I love her like that guy loved his chicken – all right, maybe that's going too far. But I like her a lot. I want her. And you can't deny her to me. You can't deny her to me. After all, I can't be sick forever," he said, waving a finger in the air. "I don't think so, anyway. And she liked that flower, didn't she? Until you took it from her, anyway, she liked it."

"I suppose she did."

"There you go. Now give me my bongos."

Mike took them from the desk where Lonnie had put them and handed them to him. He tapped them a couple of times with his fingertips, and then held them out in front of him, looking at them with disgust. He let them drop to the floor. "I ain't got it today," he said, and he lay back down.

CHAPTER 40

BROTHER DOUG OPENED THE back door of the mission and the
orphan hoard rushed out, booting the soccer ball in front of
them. Joe, Luke, Ibekwe and Mike followed. The boys and
some of the girls began playing soccer in the field, and
immediately the children of the *barrio* began appearing,
sprouting up as if from the surrounding shrubs. Soon they
were moving in a roiling mass from end to end of the field in
some uncertain alliance of individuals, all of them trying to
keep up with the handful of players who dominated the game,
the foremost of whom was Arnold, playing with the same grace
and ease he'd shown in the street out front.

It wasn't clear to which team Mike belonged, if any, nor did
it seem to matter: He jogged about without purpose between
the rusting, net-less goals, stabbing at the ball when it came near
him, dodging as best he could the pillows of cow dung
decomposing on the turf – leather-brown, flattened by gravity,
buzzed about by microscopic black flies. A half an hour of it
winded him and he deserted the scrum and set off towards the
low cinder block wall that ran along the far end of the field,

separating it from the scrub brush beyond. A handful of boys left the melee and followed him, and some of the girls who had been playing along the fence at the side of the field came running to him, too, among them Wendy, who rushed up to take one of his hands. Another girl whom Mike had not seen before took hold of the other.

When they realized where he was heading they let go and with the others ran ahead to claim a seat on top of the wall, nudging each other to clear spaces for themselves and for Mike. He sat between Wendy and a boy who had been waiting there the entire time, unable to join in because of an injured arm that hung from a hand-made sling around his neck. The arm was wrapped in a hank of dirty white linen stained with a brown blotch.

The other kids shifted around to get as close as they could to Mike, with the overflow sitting in the grass in an arc at his feet. They looked up at him like students awaiting a lesson from some great wise man.

"Well..." he said in English.

This did not seem to satisfy them, so Mike continued: "How is everybody?"

"*Bien*," they called in unison, and fell silent, awaiting his next words of wisdom.

"Well..." Mike repeated.

Beyond the heads of the kids the mob chased the ball, with Joe and Luke laboring in their wake, the skirts of their robes and the beads of their rosary-belts swinging about as they ran.

In the middle of it all was the long, lean, splendid figure of Ibekwe, standing like a black and white buoy in the midst of heaving, muddy waves. Her huge white teeth gleamed out of her black skin. She revolved to watch the turmoil around her and took a tentative step in the direction of the action. Three little girls clung to her like shipwrecks.

"She ain't much for soccer," Mike said. "But she'd kill those guys in basketball."

"*Basquetbol, sí,*" said the injured boy beside him. "Very tall."

Mike asked the boy what had happened to his arm. He made a cutting motion in the air over the stain. "*Machete,*" he said.

"Accident?"

The kid shrugged.

"Does it hurt?"

He nodded.

"Yeah, it looks like it would. Have you seen a doctor?"

He shrugged again.

"All right. Let's see what we can do about that. You guys save my seat, okay?"

He rose and led the boy towards Brother Greg, who had appeared from the mission and was watching the goings-on from the fence, scanning the field with a furrowed, disapproving brow.

"This little guy hurt his arm," Mike told him. "Machete."

Greg nodded, pushed his glasses down the bridge of his nose, and bent over to look at the blood-stained bandage. "Does it hurt to touch it?" he said.

The boy nodded. Greg reached out towards the arm, but the boy drew it back and let out a little gasp.

"All right. I won't," Greg said. "How long ago did you hurt it?"

"Two days," the boy said.

"Was it an accident?"

The boy shrugged again.

"Come with me," Greg said, and took five steps toward the mission doors before stopping to wait for the boy, who had not moved but had remained with Mike, and was looking up at him.

"It's okay," Mike said. "He's going to help you."

Greg led him into the compound, and Mike returned to the wall and sat in the gap Wendy had guarded for him. He glanced back to the corner of the mission. Still no Pilar.

"That was very good," Wendy said, "what you did."

"You approve, then?" Mike laughed.

Belkis came sprinting toward them from the corner of the building, wearing the same dirty pink top and red skirt that she'd worn when she'd helped out in the water line. As she ran she searched the crowd playing soccer and the groups of girls skipping rope along the sideline. When she spotted Mike, she slowed down and started skipping towards him.

Mike made room for her and she sat next to him, where the little boy with the injured arm had been.

"How's your mother?" he asked her.

"*Bien*," Belkis said.

"And the baby?"

"*Bien*."

He dug into his pocket and pulled out a pen and the little pad of paper, opening it to the first empty page. As the kids crowded around closer, he sketched a stick figure at the bottom of the page, a girl, with two little hooks of hair at the side of the little oval that represented her head and a horizontal line – the hem of her skirt – extending from knee to knee. He wrote beneath it in tiny letters, "Belkis".

"That's not my name," she said.

"Well, I have to write something."

Near the top he drew a slightly larger version of the same figure.

"What's your mother's name?" he asked her. "Or is that a secret, too?"

"Mirian," she said.

Mike asked how it was spelled and wrote it under the second figure, connecting it to Belkis with an arrow. Belkis nodded her approval.

He drew an even smaller figure alongside Belkis, lying on its back, its arms and legs sticking up in the air.

"Alejandro," Belkis said.

"*Sí*. The baby."

She looked up at him, beaming.

"And Chucho," she said.

Ah, Chucho. The former future assassin of youth. Most likely to commit mayhem. Mike drew him, giving him the smiley face he'd probably never had occasion to wear in life. Belkis approved.

"Lucero," she said.

"Lucero?"

"My dog."

"Okay. Your dog. All right." He drew a stick dog. He added a couple small strokes along its flank to represent ribs, but they seemed to confuse Belkis.

"And Blanco – Chucho's dog. He's bigger."

"Okay, but we're going to draw the line at chickens," he said in English, rubbing the top of her head. "No chickens," he said in Spanish. Mike drew Blanco, adorning him with the same smile as Chucho.

"And Pilar?" he said. "We have to have Pilar." Here he glanced towards the corner again. "She's your cousin, right? She has to be in the picture."

"*Sí.*" Belkis pointed to an unused corner of the page. "I have lots of cousins."

"We'll just do Pilar, though. She's our favorite, right?"

Mike looked at her; she was smiling up at him with her she-devil grin. He elbowed her and she elbowed him back. He started to draw Pilar, carefully, painstakingly, but when he came to her face he realized he could not do it justice. He drew a tiny eye, but it wasn't a Pilar eye, not by any stretch. He tried harder with the second eye, but it wasn't any better. It lacked the voodoo.

"She's kind of sad today, isn't she?" he said.

"*Sí.* Because of *Señor* Ruiz."

"Well I'm not going to make her sad," Mike said. He gave her an inadequate smile and held up the notepad so Belkis could see. "So, there's your family," he announced.

"And my grandmother," she said. "Renata."

"No room for Renata, Belk. We'll have to leave it at that."

She nodded and took the tablet from Mike's hand, putting it on her thigh and turning to a blank page. She reached into her pocket to take out the pink pen she'd stolen from Ibekwe, smiled at Mike and began to write, concentrating intensely, turning away and raising her shoulder to hide what she was doing.

A couple of the boys sitting in front of Mike yanked from the ground some of the scrub grass surrounding them and leaned over to sprinkle it on his knees.

"Hey," he shouted. The boys backed away, laughing.

"There," Belkis said. She tore out the sheet, folded it in quarters and put it down on the wall between them, covering it with the notepad. She put the pen back in the pocket of her skirt and sprang up and away, cutting across the soccer field to join the other girls jumping rope near the fence.

More players had deserted the game, including Sister Ibekwe, who was loping away like a black and white giraffe, moving toward the girls at the side of the field. Luke, too, had given it up and was bobbing along towards Mike, a handful of kids schooling around him like remora.

Mike stuffed the paper into his pocket.

The kids reshuffled along the wall, making room for Luke, and reformed the arc at their feet; it was now three and four deep.

"Brutal game," Luke said.

"Yeah. Brutal sun. I'm not used to the heat."

"You never really get used to it."

"Lot of kids," Mike said.

"Lots of kids."

Ibekwe had started a game with a dozen girls, tossing a ball around in a circle, faster and faster.

"They seem so poor to have so many," Mike said in English.

"Oh yeah? They'd be richer if they had fewer?" Luke said.

"Wouldn't they?"

"I don't know. I don't think of them like accounting entries."

"I didn't mean that. It just seems they'd have more of a chance if there weren't so many of them."

"More of a chance?"

"Yeah. To be happy, you know."

"Happy like you, you mean?" Luke said. "No offense, but when I look at you, happiness isn't the thing that jumps out at me."

"Okay. Maybe I'm not the best example."

One of the girls in Ibekwe's circle had dropped the ball and the sister and the other girls began clapping. The one who'd made the error slumped over a moment, then marched to the middle of the circle and began dancing, moving her feet rhythmically and swaying her arms, her hands waist-high. She looked away, above the girls around her, a determined look on her face.

Mike glanced at the corner of the mission again.

"So, tell me," Luke said. "Which ones will have to go?"

"What's that?"

"You say we need fewer of them. Which ones do you want to get rid of?"

"I didn't mean —"

"What about Santiago there – the rough-looking kid."

"They all look —"

"The tallest one out there, see him? Right there. Santiago was one of the first kids I got to know here. He was always headstrong, even back then. And now, I'm afraid for him now. Maybe he's destined to do bad things in life. Maybe he's already done some, I don't know. But on the other hand, there's something about him. He's really sharp for one thing. Clever. A couple of months ago I was making the rounds, walking the *barrio*, and he came up to me, and he said, 'Padre' – he always calls me Padre, no matter how many times I correct him. 'Padre,' he says, 'if we pray for a sunny day so we can play football, and God gives us a sunny day, what about all the farmers who prayed for rain for their corn?'"

"What did you tell him?"

"I said pray for the farmer, and the rain, and the grace to endure a day without football."

"Did he buy it?"

"Santiago? Nah, he's *terco* - stubborn. He said that if he did that every day, they'd never get to play football, and the crops would be flooded. I had to concede the point."

He brushed away the blades of grass that the boys had put on his robe. "So, what do you think – expendable, Santiago?"

"No."

"For the economics of it, I mean. So that the remainder will be happy, like you."

"I'm not saying that."

"All right, maybe we'll let Santiago alone, for now anyway. How about that poor soul over there?" He motioned towards a boy at the far corner of the fence, by himself, his fingers laced through the chain link. He had distorted features and a wild head of hair.

"He's deaf," Luke said. "And he's got some other problems. He's up against the fence like that because he can't really stand. He pushes himself along with his hands in that cart there at his side – not so easy on these *barrio* roads. Never been to school a day in his life. Don't see him out much – his mother usually hides him in their little *casa*.

"What utility can we possibly expect of him? And yet, who can say? I don't really know him. Then again, we don't really know anyone, do we? Not even ourselves. But still, we're so damn quick to...And then there's Jesi over there." He motioned to where she sat, at the very end of the wall, curled up inside herself, viewing the world with hard-earned suspicion. "Hell, she doesn't even talk, does she? I'm not even sure she can talk.

I mean, if talking is part of the criteria. I don't know – no one ever seems to define the criteria."

"I don't mean anyone specific, Luke."

"No, no," he said. "You have to be specific. It's too easy to pretend that we're just discussing numbers, theoretical beings. It's the most specific thing in the world to our victims, though, isn't it? Whether they have a voice to tell you that or not. But I guess if it's just random, why not Juan Carlos or Wendy? Or Belkis. She'd be as good as any, I suppose."

"I don't mean anyone already here."

The three culprits on the ground at their feet leaned over to drop more grass on Brother Luke, on his robe where it was draped between his knees. "That's it," Luke said and he feigned getting up to go after them. The boys jumped up and ran three steps, hoping to be chased, halting when they saw they weren't going to be, and taking their seats again.

"See what I mean?" he said.

"I'm not talking about anyone like that."

Luke brushed his robe clean. "Because once we know them," he said, "there's some cost that goes along with losing them, isn't there? Whereas, for those we've never met, all the cost lies on them, doesn't it? We can just wash our hands of it and walk away. I wonder if they'd think about it in the same way, though.

"Let me ask you something: Where do you suppose you would be right now if you'd been born here, like these kids?"

"Same place, I imagine."

"Me too. No doubt. But I'd still want to be alive. How about you?"

"Yeah, I'd want to be alive."

"Would you have wanted to have been born in the first place, though, regardless?"

"I would have wanted to be born."

"Would you have wanted someone else to make that decision for you?"

"No."

"Well, there you go. We can't lose any of them, then, can we? And we have to treat them like what they are - brothers and sisters. Because they're just like you and me - there's a soul in them. He's in them."

"Who's in them?"

"You can feel him."

"You can feel who?"

Luke pulled some grass from the patches of green at his feet and flung it at the boys.

"I guess I just wish there was something I could do for them," Mike said.

"You are doing something for them."

"Yeah, what's that? Kicking a ball with them for half an hour? Giving them some candy? Drawing stickmen? It's so damn little, Luke. It's nothing."

"Ask them if it's nothing."

He looked around at the kids again. They all had their faces turned up to him, waiting, hanging on his any word, his any movement, his anything.

At his side, a little boy who had squeezed in between him and Wendy was rubbing his fingers lightly over the hair on his forearm, with Wendy watching him intently. She looked up at Mike, glowing.

Out in front of them the games raged on. Arnold had notched another goal and now ran in a graceful arc across the goal mouth, his head down, his arms extended out to his sides. Ibekwe was in the middle of the circle of girls, smiling, swaying like a reed in the breeze, dancing as she must have danced as a girl in the Nigerian sun, lithe and languid, cobra-like.

The three little boys were pulling up more grass.

"If you don't want to ask them," Luke said, "just read your note."

"What note?"

"The one in your pocket there. The one Belkis gave you."

"Oh, you saw that, huh?" He took it out sheepishly, unfolded it and straightened it on his knee. There were no spaces between the words, and no capitalization or punctuation, and every third word was misspelled, but when he'd finally parsed it out he couldn't lift his head for ten seconds.

Luke stood and brushed grass from his robe. "Little rug-rats," he said, and he turned to Mike. "It's okay, you know," he said.

"What's that?"

"To love them. It's all right to love them like you do; that's how they love you."

He started away.

"You know," Mike said, "that wasn't really my idea, anyway, the too-many-kids thing. That wasn't mine."

"No, didn't sound like you."

CHAPTER 41

THE ORPHANS WERE PUT to bed soon after dinner. The spare rooms in the main building had been set up for the girls, and the boys had been moved to the other rooms of the dorm where Lonnie and Mike were, as best they could be fitted. Mike had been careful not to disturb them when he went to his own room, and now lay quietly on his bed. After half an hour he rose and slipped back outside, the old gray book in his hands. All day he'd been carrying the thing in his thigh pocket, where its weight and its stiffness and the sharpness of its corners continually reminded him of its presence, and of the presence of Padre's orange bookmark. But he'd held back from taking it out and opening it, like one holds back a desert. He'd waited for just this moment, when everyone else was in bed and he could give it the attention he thought it must deserve, here in the stillness, here in the dim light of the *pasillo*. Even the thunder sounding in the distance seemed the perfect accompaniment to the words that must change his life.

He pulled a chair up to the edge of the tile, took out the book and opened it to the bookmark, reading and rereading the underlined words.

He put the book down on the tile beside him, closed his eyes, and let his head drop backwards.

The day had cooled off nicely, even to the point where he felt a faint, welcome chill. He crossed his arms and concentrated on the silence of the compound, and after a moment he could hear the night noises of the *barrio* beyond – the random barking of a half dozen dogs, the occasional crow of a confused rooster, the muffled, angry-seeming voices of people in minor conflict, some faint music, a sudden shout, the cracking of fireworks (if that was what it was) – all punctuated by the boom of thunder. From within the curtained rooms behind him came an occasional moan or the shuffle of a child shifting beneath covers.

He opened the book again, reread the words that Padre had marked for him, then flipped to a random page:

> *The eternal silence of these infinite*
> *spaces frightens me.*

The thunder banged again, more loudly, and the air suddenly jumped to life, the breeze sweeping down into the courtyard to rustle the palm leaves; they made a sifting, tropical sound.

The light was on in the library again, next to the red glow from the chapel window. Brother Greg, no doubt, standing at a bookshelf, boning up on how the self relates itself to its own self, or sitting in Marco's chair, the throne he seemed to have relinquished, leering over the chessboard, savoring the hellish tangle of it. Wondering why he hadn't listened to Mike and saved his queen.

And yet, perhaps it was Marco up there after all, reading, thinking, praying, writing poems. Perhaps he'd come in silently, like a Ranger in the night. It would be just like him, maybe. And the more Mike thought of it the more he became convinced that indeed it must be him, and twice he rose to go there before sitting back down, and now had made up his mind on a third try when he detected a movement alongside him. A *sapo* – large and fat and stupid – had hopped up from somewhere behind, stopping six inches from the edge of the tile, a yard or so from where Mike sat. It stared out towards the courtyard, motionless and quiet, as if to help Mike think through the heavy things that were on his mind.

He read again:

> *The eternal silence of these infinite*
> *spaces frightens me.*

"What do you think?" he said in English to the *sapo*. "You get anything out of that?"

As if in response the miserable little creature lunged forward with its round bulb of a body, keeping its feet stuck onto the tile and flicking out its thick pink tongue to pick a large beetle off the edge of the *pasillo*. The bug's spiky legs stuck out of the *sapo*'s beak, kicking in panic, until finally the *sapo* gulped once, twice, three times, his chubby body shuddering as the insect finally went down. Mike's stomach turned. It would be like him swallowing whole, alive, a large turtle or an armadillo.

"Why, you're nothing but a little carnivore after all, aren't you?" Mike said.

"He's talking to the *sapos*," a voice whispered from behind.

Mike turned to see two shadows standing between the curtain and the grill of the boy's room next to his own.

"Is that you, Juan Carlos?" he said. "You're asleep, remember?"

"The thunder," he said. "I can't sleep."

"No, me neither."

"Do the *sapos* ever talk back to you?" the other boy said, and Mike heard laughter from behind the curtain. Juan Carlos opened the door and they came out, four of them, wearing just their pants, no shirts, no shoes. They gathered their scrawny bodies around Mike's chair and sat on the tile, scaring the *sapo* so that it turned to the side with a little hop, jumped three more times along the edge of the *pasillo* and flung itself out onto the black dirt of the courtyard, landing with a light thud, its momentum tipping it forward onto its chin before it righted itself.

"No, they never do." In English he added, "They're as silent as the infinite spaces."

The boys looked at each other and shrugged.

Mike laid the book down beside him.

"So tell me," he said. "What do you guys think of this place?"

"We like it," Juan Carlos said.

"Yeah, me too."

"Is Mr. Acquire going to come here?" the smallest boy said.

Juan Carlos elbowed him.

"No," Mike said. "He's not."

"Where is he?" the boy said.

"Hey, you know what? Wait here. I've got something."

He went to his room and returned with the two *trompos*. When the boys saw them, they jumped up and ran for them, taking them from him and twisting the strings around them with great concentration.

"You have to take turns," Mike said. "I'll get you more later."

Juan Carlos wound up to let his go on the tile of the *pasillo* until Mike stopped him.

"On the dirt," he told them. "Too noisy on the tile. We don't want to wake up the sleeping children - you know, the ones who aren't completely *loco*."

Juan Carlos nodded as if he'd made a legitimate and necessary point, and he led the others onto the surface of the courtyard where they started flinging the toys at the dirt. One of them had the delightful Cortesian notion to take aim at the *sapo*, barely missing it with a fierce toss; the little wooden weapon whizzed past the animal's snout and started spinning a foot in front of it. It turned away and did what *sapos* in panic apparently did – blinked, took two small, slow hops in a random direction and stopped, since things were bound to be safe at such a distance. The boy with the other *trompo* prepared to try his own luck against the creature, until Mike stopped him and called them all to him.

They squatted on the ground beneath him, and he looked around at their faces, all turned to him expectantly.

"Listen, guys," he said. "No matter what happens - no matter what." He checked their faces to see if they understood. "You know what I mean?" he said.

Juan Carlos nodded in a way one might to someone known to talk to *sapos*.

The thunder had been increasing in volume, and now it came again, hard and close, and in another moment the rain started, tentatively at first, with a few heavy drops that were full of foreboding. Then the explosion, water driving vertically down so that the air seemed white with it, splattering on the hard black dirt of the courtyard and slapping against the metal awning of the *pasillo*, raising a din that drowned out everything, mercifully rendering further talk impossible. The boys jumped up under the awning. Pools quickly formed and spread in the dirt in front of them, reaching out over to the *sapo*, who blinked as the rain hit his eyes, but otherwise did not move.

A curtain of water hung from the awning in front of them, and at the corner of the *pasillo*, where the awning met the roof of the walkway running towards the front, a thick column poured as if from a hydrant. Juan Carlos went to it and stuck the flat of his hand out. The water splashed from his palm, leaping in all directions, the power of it driving his hand downward. He stepped onto the dirt directly under the water, holding back his head so that it struck his brow, splashing into the air and streaming down his face and his back. The other kids ran to him and pushed one another to get under the spout.

They called for Mike and he stood and walked slowly to them, shaking his head. He hesitated for a moment and breathed in deeply before stepping into the water.

It was joltingly cold, but he let the water cover him, sopping his t-shirt, his shorts, his sandals. He spread his hands out and tilted his head up like Juan Carlos had, feeling the power of the water as it drove against his forehead. Laughing, he fell back to sit on the edge of the *pasillo*, leaving his feet in the torrent.

As quickly as it had begun the rain stopped, and the flow of water from the roof slowed to a dribble. Juan Carlos cupped his hands under it until they were half full, drank from them, and threw the rest of the water at the other kids.

"Little criminals," a voice came from behind them. Mike turned to see Lonnie, disheveled, yawning, shuffling barefoot along the *pasillo* from his room.

"Good lord, it's alive," Mike said.

Lonnie grunted and lumbered past them, going directly to Mike's chair and plopping himself into it. "Riff-raff," he groaned. He picked up the book from where Mike had left it, face-down on the tile and wedged open to the page over which he'd been pondering.

"All right, you guys – bedtime," Mike said. "Let's go."

They complained but finally headed back to their rooms.

"Make sure you dry off before you lay down," he said.

He went to his own room, changed into dry clothes and came back out, taking another chair from against the dorm wall and pulling it up beside Lonnie. Already the pools of water in the courtyard were starting to disappear, soaking into the earth.

"This book again, huh?" Lonnie said. He held it up to the light and read aloud:

> *The eternal silence of these infinite*
> *spaces frightens me.*

He let the arm holding the book drop down to his side. "Now what the hell, Mikey?" he said. "What the hell?"

"You wouldn't get it."

"No, I wouldn't. I admit it. And you do?'

Mike shrugged.

Voices came from the boy's room.

"Go to sleep," Mike called from his chair, and the voices ceased.

"You've really got something for these little strays, don't you?" Lonnie said.

"They do get into your blood."

"That's what I'd be worried about."

"Yeah, well, who's the sick one here?"

"Feeling better now, though. May just pull through."

"That'd be a shame," Mike said.

"Now don't hold grudges, Mikey. Not over a woman. It's bad form. It's un-Christian. You're supposed to turn the other cheek, that sort of thing. Besides, that whole thing was, what? A year ago? Back when you tried to steal my *ponche*, I mean? I've been sleeping at least that long, right?" With the book still in his hand, he held his arms out and stretched, to prove that he had been sleeping for a year, and brushed his hair back. "Let bygones be bygones, I say."

The air was fresh, scrubbed clean by the deluge. The lightening was still flashing in the sky to the East, and water was dripping from the palm fronds, greener now, more alive, polished and bright against the black dirt. To the west the clouds were separating, and stars had begun to show.

They sat in silence for a moment before Lonnie spoke again. "It's kind of a beautiful country, though, isn't it?" he said.

"Kind of, yeah."

"I mean, it has its issues, but everyplace does, right? We have too much traffic, they've got a problem with people leaving garbage bags lying around. Anyway, what do you say we take another stab at it, tomorrow?"

"Another stab at what?"

"At them. At the girls."

"What girls?"

"What girls? Pilar, and the other one, her friend. If I could just shake loose that mother of hers for fifteen minutes or so, I think I could —"

"I said we're not going after those girls."

"I'm thinking – I've had a lot of time to think – I'm thinking you could create a little diversion. Take Pilar's mother and her friend there on a nice slow walk to one of those pulpers, buy them some ice cream or something."

"You're not listening to me."

"Yeah, I'm listening. I'm just not believing. I've got to get you out of here. This whole convent thing is getting to you. I tell you, man, you wouldn't make a good monk."

"Brother."

"That either." He changed to a comic, low tone. 'Tear the door down'," he said, chuckling and clapping Mike on the shoulder. "Remember that? Remember those girls? 'Break the damn door down.'" He laughed and changed his tone again. "Brother Miguel," he said disdainfully. "And this thing – this thing ain't helping."

"Give me that." Mike reached for the book, but Lonnie held it out away from him.

"No, no. It's putting ideas in your head."

"Yeah, you don't want to be getting ideas from books."

"No, no you don't. Not ideas like this…" He held the book up closer to the light and read:

Faith is different from proof; the one
is human; the other is a gift of God.

"Really, Mikey. No wonder you're all turned around."

"It's an interesting book, actually."

"Mmm hmm." He flipped to another page:

Man is a thinking reed.

"Well, okay. He's half right there."

"You know why he's interesting?"

"I have no idea," Lonnie said, still perusing the text and frowning, making as if he wasn't listening to Mike at all. "Enlighten me."

"He believes life should be lived like there's something at stake, if you can imagine that." And then, more softly, "We are embarked."

"We're embarked, huh? We're embarked." Lonnie let the book down again and turned to face Mike with a serious look, devoid for once of the smile or the smirk, absent the accustomed patina of irony.

"There's nothing at stake, Mikey," he said. "The only thing at stake is what you make up for yourself."

"I don't believe that."

"Look. Maybe faith is a great and marvelous thing. I don't know, probably it is. Probably people who have it live a meaningful life, in some way I can't imagine. But even if you believe that, it doesn't mean you get to have it."

"Is that not a thing to say sadly, as the saddest thing in the world?"

"That's from this book again, isn't it? Sounds just like him. Come on. Enough books. Enough bookish...stuff. We have something serious to talk about."

"So you don't think there's a right way to act?"

"You mean like some standard?"

"That's right."

"Some standard we'll be held to, in the end?"

"Yeah."

"In the great by and by."

"Whatever."

"By God, you mean?"

"Yeah. By God. That's what I mean."

"And what standard could he possibly hold us to that he hasn't violated himself a billion times."

"What are you talking about?"

"I mean the things he lets happen, that's what I mean."

"Oh, I see. While we were just standing there, innocent?"

"Well, tell me - how guilty can a third-grader be?"

Mike was taken aback by the words, disarmed by them. He looked away, his eyes drawn to the glowing window of the chapel and to the other, curtained window at its side, that of Marco's library. Someone still at it up there, thinking and praying, praying and thinking, doing the two simultaneously, maybe. Maybe the two things were the same for him, whoever it was. Maybe things had gotten that far out of hand.

"You're the one who said you had so much faith that you blamed him."

"Did I? Did I say that? So I did. So I did. Ah, but enough of this." He handed the book back to Mike. "Enough of this book talk, this not-vacation talk. We're going to put all that away now. And tomorrow – tomorrow's going to be big for us."

"We're not going to —"

"Don't worry. I got it. No Pilar, no what's her name, no little diversion while I...you know. It's a life-long dream of mine, but okay. I renounce it. Only the silence of these infinite spaces, and downtown, of course. We can still go downtown, right? Yes? I'm going to be healthy, and you're going to put that book away and not be so damn gloomy. Think of it, a whole city crawling with thinking reeds, and half of them of the female variety, your very best kind of thinking reed, just waiting for a couple guys like us to come along and sing them a *corazón* song."

"All right," Mike heard himself say.

"That a boy, Mikey. That's the Mikey I know. I better get some sleep though. I've only had about twenty-three hours today." He rose. "But tomorrow, *muchachas*", he said. He pointed at the book. "And you be careful with that thing."

Halfway to his room he looked back. "*Muchacha*," he said, shaking his head. "*Muchacha*."

He disappeared behind the curtain.

Mike picked the book up from where Lonnie had dropped it and opened it to Padre's mark. Twice he reread the words, then clapped the book shut and looked back to the library window, but the light was out now.

Behind him came a sharp, gravelly chirp. Halfway up the wall near his bedroom door a gecko clung to the adobe, its fingers and toes splayed wide, its tail curved like a sickle behind it. It hung there for fifteen seconds, utterly motionless, like a green stain, then ran another twelve inches up towards the roofline before freezing again. Or at least it must have run, but with a motion so rapid that it seemed rather to have transported itself magically to its new spot, without having to traverse the intervening space. It chirped again.

Strange, strange creature, thought Mike, shifting about in the night like this, unnoted, invisible, as if it were God's little secret, as if it had no existence apart from these twenty seconds when it carelessly exposed itself to him, to a human, to a being even stranger yet. One of a hundred thousand, a hundred million.

There was no denying it: The eternal silence of these infinite spaces was utterly terrifying.

The gecko turned its head, sharply, instantaneously, and as if spotting the danger out of the top of its eye disappeared.

A whisper came from behind him. "Miguel," it said.

"Go to sleep, Juan Carlos."

CHAPTER 42

MIKE STRUGGLED TO SLEEP, and for what seemed to him three quarters of the night lay in limbo, in a kind of half-sleep that had little of rest in it. In the dark, he considered the coming day. Lonnie would expect it all to be just like their first trip downtown, with the plaza, the music, the drinks, the hotel, and he would do everything in his power, work every charm in his formidable repertoire to ensure that it was. And Mike? Mike would allow himself to be dragged along in its wake. And why not? Why not take advantage of the opportunity? Perhaps she would be in the square again, the blue one, Lupe. "I was hoping to find you," he would say to her. "I know how to spell your name."

How she had smiled at him. How a single, weak drink had made her sparkle and how she'd looked at him then. Sipping at the drink and glancing up at him. Stumbling and laughing down at him from the staircase, strands of hair falling over her eyes. The heat of her skin. The gentleness of her. The smell of her. Even the way she had taken the measly wad of money from him, as if embarrassed by it, as if, were it up to her, she would never have considered such a thing.

No sooner had real, deep slumber finally come – as it seemed to him – than the grill of his room clanged opened and Lonnie appeared, shouldering aside the curtain. In one of his huge hands he held two Styrofoam cups with their lids on, balanced one on top of the other.

"Come on," he mumbled, his hat on his head, cocked to one side, and his lips clamped around the unlit stub of an old exhausted cigar, plugged in there for the show of it. "It's nine o'clock already. How much sleep does a guy need, anyway?" He giggled.

"Nine o'clock?"

"*Ya!*"

"Damn," Mike said.

"No morning prayer for you," Lonnie giggled. "Yeah, I've heard about your conversion. But no monkish things today."

With his free hand he shut the door and made fast the little latch that locked it from the inside.

"Don't do that. Don't lock that door," Mike said, bunching his pillow up behind his head. "And stay right there. I'm not your Maraya."

"I'll say you're not."

"I have less body hair than he does."

"Jealousy is an ugly, ugly thing, Mike."

"But not as ugly as Maraya."

"Do I have to show you the picture again?"

"The picture of his sister? No, no thanks."

"Mikey, Mikey," Lonnie said. He went to the table and hooked his foot around the leg of the chair, dragging it out and turning it so that it faced the bed. He placed the top cup on the table and handed the other to Mike, who took it, scootching himself up to prop his back against the wall. He sipped at it.

"I made a new pot without all that sugar," Lonnie said proudly. "I had to stand guard though. The good brothers kept coming in to try to pour some into it."

Mike took another slurp. "Looks like you're feeling all better today," he said.

Lonnie spread his arms out triumphantly and smiled. "Can't keep a conquistador down," he said. "Plus I had a little medicine to help me."

"Medicine?"

He picked up the second cup from the table, and Mike could see now that it was not full of coffee, that in fact it was empty, and that there were actually three cups nested together. He carefully separated them and put them top-down on the table.

"What's this?" Mike said.

Lonnie looked at him with devilish glee.

"You know, I've got to tell you, I was kind of liking the old, sick Lonnie better."

"Why do you say such things? They're hurtful things. And after I spent all morning coming up with a plan just for you."

"A plan for me? Just for me?"

"Yup. Rodrigo's going to take you to the square."

"He is?"

"I already arranged it."

"Just me?"

"Unless you want company. Which you do. We're going to eat at our lucky restaurant and then…see what develops."

"See what develops? That's your plan? See what develops? You spent your whole morning on 'see what develops'?"

"There's a secret part of the plan, too."

"You're so full of it, Lonnie."

"No, it's true. Watch carefully." He extracted something from his shirt pocket and slid it under one of the cups, hiding it from Mike. He shuffled the cups around on the tabletop.

"All right," he said, "Take your chances!" With a smirk he leaned back in his chair and crossed his arms. "Learned this trick this morning - one of your little rag-pickers out there showed it to me. She uses a rock, though. Mine's better. Come on. Choose."

Mike looked up at Lonnie and shook his head.

"*Hombe*. You must choose," Lonnie said. "You must wager. You are embarked."

Mike pointed at the rightmost cup. "Uh uh," Lonnie said, and he jogged his head to indicate the cup on the left. Mike pointed at it.

"Bingo," Lonnie said. "Bingo bongo." He slowly lifted the cup, exposing a white piece of paper folded into a small, neat rectangular packet, like a little pillow.

"Tell me that's not what I think it is," Mike said.

"*Eso!*" He giggled again and pulled out a little brown wallet from his pocket. Mike had seen this wallet before. It contained a small mirror and a single-edged razor blade. He took them out and carefully set them on the table. Delicately with his massive hands he unfolded the little envelope, tapping white powder from it onto the mirror.

"You're kidding me, right? You made a drug deal in Cortes? You can't even speak the language, but you go out and buy coke?"

"*Cocaína*, Mikey. *Cocaína*. All you need is that word and a little real American cash. And some help from Rodrigo of course."

"Our *taxista*?"

"The man's ambitious," Lonnie said. "Who'd have thunk it, hey? I mean, I wouldn't call him a dealer, exactly, but he can hook a guy up all right, he can take care of a guy. You've just got to take care of him a little bit in return. He's a *cortezeño*, take him for all in all. So while we're waiting for Pilar to get home from work the other day – the day you went up to the mountains - he takes me to one of those pool halls. I was right about those things, Mikey – they're awesome. Met a man there they call '*El Pececito*'."

"The little fish?"

"I thought that's what that meant. I tell you, if that's the little fish, I'd hate to see the big one."

"You bought drugs from the Little Fish?"

"Not too intimating, is it, Little Fish?"

"You're nuts."

As he chopped at the white stuff with the blade, Lonnie smiled and shuffled his shoulders back and forth in delight, as if this was the exact thing he'd wanted to hear.

"*Gracias*," he said.

"And all this time you've been holding out on me."

"I was afraid you wouldn't approve." He'd taken a twenty-dollar bill from a flap inside the wallet and was rolling it up.

"I don't approve."

"Then I was right." He handed Mike the bill, twisted into a tight hard tube.

Mike stared at the two thick, fuzzy lines of powder lying there on the mirror, like two white caterpillars admiring themselves.

"I haven't done this in like a year."

"Yeah, me neither. Come on now. You're up. And then, hie we downtown!"

"Pretty big lines there, Lon. Do we know how strong this stuff is?"

"It's fine."

"You first then."

"*Ya!*"

"You've already done some?"

"*Ya!*" He giggled.

"All right."

Mike took the rolled-up bill from Lonnie, brought it to his nostril, and bent towards the mirror. He was about to inhale when he heard the slap of sandals along the tile outside. He stopped and looked up at Lonnie, who let his mouth drop open and spread his eyes wide in mock-horror. Slowly though, he took the bill from Mike's hand and stuffed it into his pocket. He removed his hat and set it over the mirror. He restacked the three cups.

Mike stopped breathing. Lonnie raised his eyes at him, grinning. The footsteps approached the door and seemed to slow before finally passing by and fading down the *pasillo*. Lonnie withdrew the hat and slipped it back on his head. He took out the twenty, tightened it back up and handed it to Mike.

"Okay then," he said. "Fire one."

"You know what Luke says about drugs?" Mike whispered.

"Let me guess - he doesn't approve either. Come on, bottoms up."

"Not so loud," Mike said and paused for another five seconds, listening. "He says people here die because we do stuff like this, we Americans."

Lonnie scoffed. "He's a monk. What's he going to say? Come on."

"He says to use drugs is to deny the connectedness of all people."

"I do deny it. I do. Hell, Mike, this is the only time I do feel — what did you call it?"

"Connectedness."

"*Eso*. This, and, you know, with Tulis. And with Maraya, of course. No matter what slanders you spread about her."

"Him."

"Besides, connectedness – that isn't even a word."

"Yes it is."

"Maybe in Spanish it is."

"And he has a point, too, if you think about it."

"Then let's don't think about it. Look, Mikey, they have narco-saints down here. Let that sink in for a minute. Narco-saints. How're you going to redeem that? I mean, you could be one or the other, it seems to me - a narco, or a saint. But you'd have to choose. Hell, the reality is, in a place like this nothing we could do is going to hurt them and nothing is going to help them. You can pick lice out of their hair, or you can buy a little fun from them, and it won't make a lick of difference, not in a place with narco-saints."

"And us?"

"What about us?"

"What'll it do to us?"

"That's monkish! That's monkish! You promised," he said, though Mike had done nothing of the kind. "Where is it? Where's that book? You can't be trusted with it." He looked around the room.

"I hid it."

"Good. Now come on. Let's have at it. I don't want to take any of this stuff to Brazil with me."

Mike eyeballed the powdery white lines for a moment, bent over them, put the tube to his nostril, and snorted. It was strong; it burned. He held his head back and sniffed in again.

"Wow," he said, pinching his nostrils together.

Lonnie giggled.

"Yeah, wow. Just wait a second, you'll see wow. And don't hand that thing back to me. You have one more there," he said. He clapped his hands and rubbed them together, shifting his shoulders back and forth. "Haha. That's the Mikey I know," he said. "Come on. Let's get connected."

CHAPTER 43

"WE'VE GOT TO LEAVE word with someone," Mike said, and he started towards the back, from where voices could be heard.

"We do?" Lonnie said. "I thought we were big boys. Even what's-his-name said that, remember?" He chuckled.

Mike glanced at him, bopping along at his side in all his glory, almost dancing, with the cigar butt stuck in his mouth and atop his head the silly hat.

"You're crazy, you know," he said, and there was laughter in his voice.

"*Gracias,*" Lonnie said with great sincerity, almost with humility. "*Gracias.*"

It was good to be with him.

"*Hombe,*" Mike said.

"Yeah, that's it. That's right, Mikey. *Hombe.*"

"Come on."

"Okay, but *rapido,* huh?"

Ibekwe was busy in the classroom, standing at the front reading aloud from a large picture book, holding it in front of her to show the orphans the drawings. At the pens, only the dumb animals remained, the pig slopping around in its filth, the jury of chickens arrayed on their pallet, staring ahead dispassionately, as if they had reached a verdict. The penitential cow, roped to a stake with its rear-end facing them, turned its head and looked at Mike. It lowed: "Youuuuuuu," it said, with a deep bovine accent.

"That stuff's pretty good," Mike said.

"I told you, Mikey. I told you it was good."

They turned toward the front. The medical rooms, the atrium, the dining room, the kitchen – all were empty.

"See? That's a break right there," Lonnie said. "That's a break right there. Now if only that front door is unlocked, we'll slip out of here without anyone weighing us down with a lecture on words that don't exist, or inviting us to whatever-time-it-is-prayer. Hey, maybe those Tulis will be back in the square, huh? Remember those Tulis?"

"Yeah, Lon, I remember them."

"In which case we're going to need money for the *propina*, won't we? Ahh, you're laughing. Don't try to hide it – you're laughing. That's the Mikey I know." Then he suddenly grew serious. "No more of that sharing stuff, though," he said, and he broke into laughter again.

"I should go upstairs and see if any of the brothers are there."

"No, Mike. No bros. We're big boys, remember?"

"Okay, but we should leave a note, at least," Mike said, trying to hold back laughter at just how big of boys they were.

"All right. But *rapido!*"

He tore a page from his notepad, scribbled on it and left it on top of one of the tables. As they were leaving the dining area he turned back. The little white clam looked lonely and lost in the vast, unlit gloom of the place.

"You think that's enough?" he said.

"That's plenty. Come on now. Time's a-wasting. How're you feeling?"

"*Ridículo*," Mike said.

"Good, good. Me, too. *Ridículo*. I've got more of that stuff, when you need it."

"You're not bringing any of it along with us, are you? You're not carrying it with you right now?"

"No."

"Because that would be just the kind of thing —"

"I know. I know. I'm not an idiot."

"*Idiota*."

"I'm not an *idiota*."

"But I mean it, Lon."

"No. I said no."

"Good. I don't think I'll be needing any more of it anyway." Lonnie chuckled.

"I think I'm a big enough boy for now."

He chuckled again.

When they reached the door, he stopped to face Mike. He smirked, unplugged the cigar butt from his mouth and flicked it over the retaining wall into the miniature palms beyond. "Here we go," he said. He took the latch in his hand and paused dramatically before raising it. It clicked.

"Bingo," he said, and he looked at Mike expectantly.

"Bongo," Mike said.

"Bingo bongo. And lookie there, you're smiling again."

And indeed, he couldn't stop smiling, though he wasn't sure why. All he knew was that he was on some higher plane, now, and that something big was about to happen, and that it would be tragic if he were to miss out on it, and even more tragic if it were to miss out on him.

The infinite spaces might indeed be silent – who could say? - but they had no power over him anymore.

"*Una rosa?*" Lonnie said.

"*Por otra cosa,*" Mike said.

"There you go! There you go! That's the Mikey I love."

Slowly he began swinging the door to. When it was a quarter way open, he triumphantly pushed it the rest of the way, looked toward the road, and cursed.

There in front of them were Luke and Joe, standing outside the gate at the side of the road, palavering with a handful of natives. Across the way another group of twenty was congregated, including Belkis and Mirian, holding her baby to her breast. They were all gazing in the direction of the river.

They walked over to the brothers and looked up the road.

A parade of some kind was heading slowly towards them, people marching four and five abreast. The head of it was invisible, hidden in the dip of the river, and the tail extended nearly to the top of the rise on the other side. Marching along at the end was a band, eight or ten men playing horns and drums, a song slow, weepy, and wavering.

A respectful distance behind, Rodrigo's cab crept forward.

"What's going on?" Mike asked the brothers.

"Funeral," Luke said.

"Oh yeah?" He strained to see up the road.

"You guys going somewhere?"

"We were thinking about downtown, if that's all right. Just Lonnie and me. We left a note, but…Who's funeral?"

"The man from *Los Ángeles*. Ruiz."

"Oh really?" Already the big thing was happening. Mike scanned the back of the parade again, with more attention now, but she wasn't there. He focused on the lip of the rise, waiting for the head of it to lift out of the road.

"What are you going to do downtown?"

"I don't know."

A black horse with a long dry mane ascended from the road, dragging behind it a flatbed wagon. The driver was slumped on the bench and held the reigns slackly. In the middle of the bed of the wagon, looking tiny and insignificant, was the coffin of *Señor* Ruiz.

In line on each side of the wagon three young men walked, good-looking and sharply-dressed, with healthy faces and slicked-back hair. All but one seemed to be between twenty and twenty-five years old – Mike's age; the sixth was significantly younger. The older all wore serious faces, stoic, stone faces that showed only determination, no trace of grief, but the young one was visibly trying to suppress his tears, gulping down his sobs as he walked. At his heels was an even younger girl, slight and homely, wearing a light-colored dress and a wide-brimmed hat that looked festive and out of place. She was carrying a spray of dark purple flowers and she, too, was trying to battle back tears, but with less success. Walking along on the far side of the wagon was a small loosely-dressed man with disheveled hair holding a handkerchief to his mouth with one hand and with the other reaching out between the pallbearers to touch the edge of the wagon bed.

The coffin was plain, lacquered black, with three evenly-spaced handles along the side and a square window in the top panel where the head would be, though Mike could not see into it from where he stood.

"What, does everyone get a procession?" Lonnie said. "He was just some poor guy, wasn't he?"

Luke ignored him.

From up close the horse looked old and tired, and its head dipped wearily at each step of its hairy legs, its hooves with their dull black shells clopping against the dirt. As it drew even with them, it blew the air out of its lungs, shook its head, and set its huge black eye - some dark gummy substance draining from it – directly on Mike, and through it he read its mind: "I am what life is," it was thinking, "and behind me is what it all comes to."

Mike watched in amazement as it smiled at him, and winked.

For the first time he recognized that the drug had taken him beyond where he wanted to go, and he was starting to be afraid of it.

He stuck a coffee bean in his mouth.

"What are you going to do downtown?" Luke asked again.

"Oh, just have lunch. Look around," Lonnie said. "Buy a souvenir."

Big boys, they were.

Luke nodded and looked him up and down. "Nice hat," he said.

"*Gracias*."

The crowd behind the wagon was moving slowly forward like some monster millipede, shuffling along silently to the slow beat of the music.

Mike, trying to fight it back now, fixed his eyes on the edge of the rise again, focusing on each head as it appeared from out of the dirt, examining it just long enough to verify who it wasn't.

Finally a mound of black hair rose from the road, bobbing back and forth ahead of the rhythm of the music, as if trying to push it forward, and he knew immediately that it was Sara, and then her eyes and her nose and her mouth, and then beside her a little dome of dark wire, somehow prettier, that he knew must belong to Pilar, and then Pilar herself – sprouting from the ground, clad in black - her head down, her shoulders hunched as if she were collapsing into herself, her arms folded over her breast and a bunch of flowers in her hand.

Ana, her head bowed, had one arm draped around her. At Ana's other side was Naila. As she passed, Pilar lifted her eyes from the ground to glance up at Mike, and quickly looked down again.

"I'm going with them," Mike said to Luke. "Would that be okay if I went with them?"

"What about downtown?" the brother said.

"Yeah," Lonnie said, "what about downtown?"

"It's all right if I go with them, isn't it Luke? I'd like to see it."

"I guess it'd be all right. You have to stay with the crowd though."

"Sure."

"Mikey…"

"You can go with Rodrigo," Mike said.

"I'm not going downtown alone."

"Then you can wait here until I get back."

"But we had a plan."

"Here," Mike said. "Pay him out of this." He drew out a stack of bills from his wallet, gave it to Lonnie and started after Pilar.

When he caught up to her she smiled through her tears and the sight of it almost made him forget his rising sense of anxiety. They walked together in silence for ten steps before he felt a tiny hand slip into his and he looked down to see Belkis. Without looking at him she glanced over at Pilar to see if she was okay.

"Does your mom know you're coming?" Mike asked.

She nodded.

"You sure about that?"

He looked back to saw Mirian hurrying along the side of the procession, fifty feet back but gaining quickly, waving a rag in the air, her baby shifting back and forth in her arms as she ran. Trotting up behind her was Lonnie.

"Someone's coming for you," Mike said to Belkis.

She looked back. "*Aye*," she said. She let go of his hand and stepped to the side, out of the way of the marchers, her arms folded, an angry look on her face. When Mirian caught up to her, she whipped her once across the rear with the rag and started leading her home.

Lonnie jogged up to the other side of Sara.

"Well, how'd it go with Rodrigo?" Mike asked him.

"I'm not talking to you."

"Sure you are. There's no one else for you to talk to, and we all know you aren't going to shut up."

Lonnie pressed his lips together and shook his head.

"Especially not after whatever that rat poison was we just snorted. Is that stuff ever going to let up?"

Lonnie refused to acknowledge him.

"Okay," Mike said. "Have it your way."

They took six more steps.

"He took it like a man," Lonnie said. "Rodrigo. Once I gave him the money."

"You didn't give him the whole thing, did you?"

Lonnie smiled back at him. Mike cursed.

"I don't have a lot more money, Lon."

"Had to give the man a *propina*, didn't I?" He let go half a giggle but stopped himself, out of respect for the dead.

They crept along the road, the band squeezing out the same dirge-like noise - the big bass drum strapped across the drummer's shoulder booming out the funeral beat, the tuba oomping along with it, the trumpet bleating, two trombones weeping from note to note. A woman was palming a tambourine, holding her head down and wagging it along to the music.

Mike's breathing was harder now, heavier, and he tried to calm himself, tried to stay on top of it.

"So how far is this stuff going to go?" he asked Lonnie.

"It's pretty good, huh?"

"I'd be okay if it didn't get any better."

"Yeah," Lonnie shook his head. "I can't believe you took so much of it."

Mike turned to Pilar to distract himself. "Lots of people," he said. "He must have had lots of friends."

"He had a big family. Many children. All those boys with him are his sons."

"His sons? But they look like they're all the same age."

"*Sí.* And they're all just like him," she said. "Charks." She glanced up at Mike and let go a tiny smile, and it relieved some of his distress. He wanted to put his arm around her, and it felt like the perfect thing to do, though it was a funeral procession, for God's sake, and he refrained. Hell, even Sara had dialed it back a click or two, in observance of the solemnity of the occasion.

Lonnie asked Mike what he and Pilar had been talking about, and giggled when Mike told him. "Ten children from a thousand different mothers," he said.

More people came from the intersecting streets to join the parade, and along the sides, parallel with the procession, a mob of onlookers formed, mostly children who ran and skipped along the roadside for a block or two before stopping and being replaced by others of the same general description, as if they were handing the thing off, block by block.

They took a route different from that which led to the highway, and soon came to a paved boulevard that seemed to mark the boundary of the *barrio*. There were well over two hundred of them now, Mike reckoned. Without a pause, oblivious to the traffic, they started across the four lanes, vehicles stacking up at their sides without complaint as they passed. On the other side of the boulevard the road, paved long ago but pot-holed now and crumbling back to dirt, continued along between the white stucco wall of the cemetary and an empty lot. The road was lined on both sides by parked vehicles and between them the procession constricted and stretched out.

The lot was pierced in the middle by a dead, pale-white tree, a witch's tree. In its gnarled branches seven black vultures perched, sizing up the mourners as they passed. One of them nudged another, leaned over and whispered something about Mike. The other one chuckled and shook its head.

"I swear to God, Lonnie, if this stuff doesn't back off pretty soon…"

"*Tranquilo*, Mikey."

"*Tranquilo*?"

"Just trust me. Go with it."

The road worked its way another fifty feet or so to the cemetery entrance, a wide portal with two wrought iron gates held open with boulders. At the threshold more people waited, watching with bowed heads as the casket passed.

The driver of the carriage yanked the horse to a stop, and the charks slid the coffin to the back of the wagon, lifted it and began carrying it to the gate. The crowd followed. A neat unpaved road led into the cemetary, and set off on its right side, just inside the walls, was a small dome-shaped chapel with brilliant white cement walls on three sides and its front open to the air. Six rows of white vinyl chairs were set around it in an arc; they were already nearly filled with people. Just under the shade of the dome, facing the crowd from in front of a concrete altar, stood Father Zeppi.

CHAPTER 44

THE PADRE WAS LISTENING to a short, thin *cortezeño* who was standing beside him at the altar, holding a straw hat behind his back with two hands, squinting up at the priest and jabbering. Zeppi glanced towards the entrance just as Mike and Lonnie came through, almost as if he had been expecting them.

The pallbearers carried the coffin down the aisle between the chairs and placed it atop two saw-horses set up directly in front of the altar, so that the deceased's feet pointed at the priest. When they had let the coffin down, they looked at each other, nodded, and went to sit on chairs that had been reserved for them in the front row. All the remaining seats were filled now with old men and women and mothers with babies; the rest of the crowd stood in a semicircle in the grass behind them. Some of the men drifted back to the far side of the road and took positions leaning against palm trees or sitting in the shade, as if not wanting to be too closely associated with the proceedings. Mike and Pilar and the others landed at the edge of the crowd behind the chairs.

Padre dismissed the talking man, walked behind the altar and awkwardly, almost shyly, nodded at the crowd. After a moment they quieted down and he began to talk. From where Mike stood he could make out only part of what he said. He quoted the Bible some, consoled the audience, made references to the deceased's life in this present world - some of which caused the women in the vinyl seats to laugh mutedly and shake their heads - and hopes for the next, which some present seemed to find questionable.

By the time the padre finished, Mike's buzz had settled in, and he was no longer quite so afraid of it. His breathing was lighter, almost normal, and the feeling of anxiety had been replaced with a moderated euphoria, an uncertain sense that the big thing – while still possibly about to happen – might not be quite so big after all, but not quite so dangerous, either.

The pallbearers rose as a man, stepped to the edge of the raised platform on which the altar stood, and turned to face the crowd. The mourners rose and formed two lines that began walking slowly on either side of the casket. As they passed it, they leaned over to look through the little window in its top, some putting the tips of their fingers on the glass as if to touch the dead man's face, some shaking their heads in sorrow, some crossing themselves with their rosaries and kissing their thumbs. Mike followed Pilar near the back of the line, with Ana holding Naila's hand just ahead of them. When they reached the coffin Naila stood on tiptoes to try to see into it, but it was too tall for her. Mike picked her up by the waist and held her over the little window. She looked in wonder through it, and Mike glanced inside, too. The old man wore a neat white shirt buttoned all the way up and fastened with a white string tie. His hands were pinned up towards his neck, holding the rim of a cowboy hat that was laid over his chest. His face was thin and withered and dead, his skin stretched over his skull like cellophane.

No more, old man, no more. No more dancing, no more women, no more children. No more of that.

Naila nodded, and Mike let her down. Pilar walked past the pallbearers with her head lowered. Each of them - true sons of Ruiz - glanced at her as she passed.

"Why did he have to die?" she said when they'd returned to the crowd in back.

"He was a very old man, Pilar, no?"

"*Sí,*" she said in a questioning tone, as if she did not see how the one was related to the other.

When the last person had paid their respects, the pallbearers lifted the coffin and carried it up the aisle to the road. They turned right and started forward into the cemetery. As the little weeping girl in the holiday dress passed, Pilar whispered loudly to her, "Erica!" A look of recognition and joy flitted across her face before the sorrow and confusion returned.

The procession reformed and followed the casket into the depths of the cemetery. Mike walked at the side of Pilar, with Ana and Naila up ahead; Lonnie and Sara were lost somewhere in the throng.

The cemetery was well cared for, laid out in a grid with above-ground tombs and white mausoleums set back in the grass, four feet off the road, with humbler graves fitted in amongst them, marked by simple rectangular stones engraved with names and dates. Lush palm trees and ferns were scattered about, spraying their shade over the places of burial, and pots of flowers stood on the edge of many of the tombs and in the nooks of the mausoleums. Some of the graves were tiled over in bright colors, with inlays depicting angels, or Christ, or other, more ambiguous biblical-looking figures. From some, the enigmatic, dispassionate, radioactive women looked out.

It was indeed a restful place, Mike thought, where a man could sleep well after a hard Cortesian life. Even the birds appeared to have taken refuge inside its walls; the trees shimmered with them.

As they walked, he stole glances at Pilar, though she said nothing to him and seemed to be barely aware of his presence. When they reached the first intersecting road, she turned and without a word began walking down it, away from the crowd. Naila saw her go and tried to follow, but Ana grabbed her arm. She looked at Mike.

"Should I follow her?" he whispered, and she nodded.

He tried to tread as quietly as he could, though he had the feeling she knew he was behind her. She walked quickly for fifty feet or so, still holding the flowers, then she slowed, and slowed again, as if to creep up on something. Mike altered his pace to stay well behind her. Finally, she stopped and turned her head to look at him before ducking off the road behind a pair of palm trees.

Mike walked to the trees and saw her standing in front of a small gravestone tucked away between two mausoleums. She had her back to him and her head down. Her shoulders shuddered.

He walked to her, still trying to be as quiet as he could, though he didn't know why.

"Are you okay, Pilar?" He put his hand on her shoulder. She leaned sideways against him, both hands holding the flowers against her breast. He let her slip under his arm, and for a good minute they stood together in silence until Pilar finally spoke.

"*Papá*," she said.

She released one hand from the flowers and put her arm across his back.

"Pilar," he said. She turned into him and he took her in his arms. She turned her head so that her temple rested on his chest; he felt the wetness of her tears through his t-shirt and the shudder of her sobs against his body.

"I'm sorry, Pilar," he said. He felt her head nod twice.

A half a minute passed before she spoke again. "Suyapa said something funny last night."

"She did?"

"*Sí.*"

He waited but she didn't go on. "What did she say?" he finally asked.

"She said we could be a family, you, and me, and her." She put her fist, clenching the flowers, on Mike's chest. "Father," she said. She held them against her own breast. "Mother." She put them out to her side. "Daughter."

"Pilar," Mike said.

"What do you think? Do you think it's funny, too?"

"Pilar."

"*Sí?*"

"You know I'm leaving."

"*Sí.*"

"In a few days I have to leave."

"*Sí.*"

He drew one of the flowers from the bouquet, broke off its stem, and slipped it into the wiry hair above her ear.

"Purple is even prettier on you," he said.

She looked up at him.

"*Una rosa,*" he heard the voice from behind, and he turned to see the man standing on the road with Sara, his legs cocked, his arms folded. He shook his head and started forward. "*Una rosa por otra cosa.*"

Pilar took a step away from Mike and wiped at her eyes with the palm of her hand.

"You show up at all the wrong times," Mike said.

"Just in time, I'd say. Exactly what's going on here?"

"This is where her father's buried."

"All right," Lonnie said. "I get it. Are you okay, Pilar?"

She looked cautiously between Lonnie and Mike and turned and walked to the head of the tomb, where she laid the flowers in front of the stone, taking the one from her hair, too, and laying it beside the others.

* * *

The burial had ended, and groups of mourners began to appear, some seeking out the graves of their lost, others making their way in small groups towards the gate. Ana and Naila came and paid their respects to *papá*, standing silently at the foot of the grave with Pilar. Lonnie was anxious and jumpy, and Mike could see his relief when Ana finally turned and started leading them away.

When they were a quarter of the way back to the mission, Padre pulled up alongside them in his truck, rolled down the window and offered them a ride. Lonnie started to climb into the truck bed.

"Go ahead," Mike told him. "I'll walk."

"We've got to get going, though," Lonnie said. "Downtown. There's still time. We can see these folks later."

"You go ahead," Mike said. "We'll be there in a while."

Lonnie dropped back onto the road and waved Padre on. He sulked as they continued along.

In front of the mission Mike asked Pilar if he could walk with her the rest of the way to her house. She shook her head.

"Tomorrow then?" he said.

"*Sí*. Tomorrow."

Mike watched as she walked away, lean and solid, sheltered under the arm of her mother and hanging onto Naila's hand, her oval head of black hair and her square shoulders moving smoothly and neatly and efficiently, without the profligate disturbance of God's universe that was Sara, sparking along at her side. Pilar glanced back once at Mike; Sara, seeing it, looked back, too.

"I'm trying not to have impure thoughts right now, what with the probation and all," Lonnie said.

"Try harder."

They went to the gate and rang the bell.

"How you feeling?" Lonnie said.

"All right," Mike said. "Pretty good, actually. Once that stuff settles down, it's okay."

"There you go. You got to trust me, Mikey. You've got to learn to trust me." He chuckled. Mike almost chuckled back.

Maria came out and unlocked the gate.

"He's waiting in the dining room," she said.

"Marco?" Mike said.

"The padre."

"Oh, great," Lonnie said, and he started away with Mike.

"No, just you," Maria said.

"Just Mike? Just you? Well," Lonnie said, "looks like your turn in the fire," and he giggled. "When you're done, come get me in my room, what's left of you, and hie we downtown! And hey - good luck in there." He pointed his index finger at Mike and pulled the trigger.

In the dining room Padre sat at one of the picnic tables, his head bent over a coffee cup. He was still dressed in black from the funeral, with the little white priest's tab in the middle of his collar. When he finally looked up there was something sad and tired and frightening in his face.

"I have something to tell you," he said.

"All right," Mike said.

"We got a call from Sister Rosario."

"What is it?"

"It's Suyapa."

CHAPTER 45

"WHAT DOES THAT MEAN, she's gone?" Mike said.

"She left the sister's place. She went with her father."

"Her father? She left with her father? He kidnapped her, you mean."

"No, that's not what I mean. She packed a bag and left."

"And no one stopped her?"

The padre shrugged. "There was only one other girl with her, and she couldn't do anything."

"He kidnapped her."

"No, he didn't."

Mike walked five steps towards the door, stopped, turned, and walked back to the table.

"Do the police know he took her?"

"The sisters talked to them."

"And?"

"What can they do?"

"Oh, I don't know. They could go get her. I know where she'd be."

"How do you know that?"

"I know the school she graduated from. It was just half a year ago. He must still live around there." He took the photograph from his wallet and showed the padre.

"That's a bad *barrio*," he said.

"Are there any good ones?"

"So we call the police, and they go there, and then what?"

"They arrest him."

"For what? For being her father?"

"He's no more her father than I am. He's a savage."

"There's no law against that."

"No, because if there was, this whole damn country would have bars around it."

He turned, walked towards the door again, stopped and walked back. "What are we going to do? We have to do something," he said.

Padre stared down at his coffee cup without speaking.

"Or is that it? Nothing? We're going to do nothing? We're going to pretend she's just another disposable kid. Damn it. Damn it. Doesn't anyone in this place ever get tired of throwing kids away? You guys have been in this country too long."

Mike turned around again, as if searching for some place to go, paused for a moment, and then sat. He sighed deeply.

"I'm sorry, Padre," he said. "It's just that this is the worst thing that can happen to her. You know that, right? He didn't suddenly start wanting her out of fatherly love. He just wanted her so she could be his little slave. And then she'll end up just another of those women in a shack with five kids, starving."

"She wanted to go with him," the padre said softly.

"She felt obligated to go with him. She thought she could have a father for once in her life. But she can't, can she? She can never have a father. She can never be anyone's daughter."

"She's God's daughter."

"Well he's not doing a very good job then. Do you know what he told her? He told her that he'd never wanted her, that he wanted to kill her before she was born. That was back when he would have to feed her. Now that things are reversed, now that he needs her to feed him..." He ran his hand through his hair. "She'll never be at peace while that bastard is alive. Does Brother Luke know about this?"

Padre nodded.

"And what does he say?"

"We have to pray," he said.

"Pray, pray, pray. It's not enough to pray."

"Sometimes it's all we have."

"I don't buy that. We have to go look for her."

"And if we find her? What do we do if we find her? We'd be the ones doing the kidnapping."

Mike rose again and just as he turned towards the doorway he saw Lonnie come around the corner and stop. He had combed his hair back under his Panama hat and had changed into a ridiculously bright yellow Hawaiian shirt with dozens of identical blue sailboats scattered about it every which way - right side up, upside down, sideways - as if some great yellow storm had descended upon a peaceful blue regatta to visit the wrath of God upon it.

"Well," he said cheerfully, "ready when you are."

"Ready for what?" Mike said.

"For downtown. We're going to hie us there, remember?"

"I'm not going downtown."

"Yes, of course you are."

"No, I'm not." He turned back to the priest. "Padre," he said.

"We'll talk about this later, with Marco," the priest said. "He'll have some ideas."

"He's here?"

"No. He'll be back tomorrow."

"Tomorrow's too late."

"Maybe later today, but – "

"Where is he?

"A town called Valera. He found a place for the orphans to live."

"Is that nearby?"

"No."

Mike cursed. "So they're leaving then, the kids. When?"

"In a couple of days."

"Where are they now?"

"With Ibekwe, out back."

Mike started towards the door, Lonnie following. When they were in the atrium, Lonnie said, "He'll have some ideas about what?"

"What?"

"He said Marco will have some ideas. Ideas about what?"

"Nothing," Mike said. He started down the *pasillo* towards the dorm rooms.

"Tell me what's going on," Lonnie asked.

"Nothing."

"All right. A secret. Great. I like secrets. But Rodrigo's on his way, Mike."

"I'm not going downtown."

"We can't just leave him hanging again."

"We'll pay him." He started reaching for his wallet. "He doesn't give a damn what we do as long as he gets our money."

Lonnie grabbed his bicep in one of his meaty hands and squeezed. "No, we can't just pay him again. Look. Whatever's going on, it sounds like there's nothing we can do about it until tomorrow, right? And I'll help you, I swear. Whatever it is, I'll help you. But in the meantime..."

Mike stopped in front of the dorm building and thought for a minute.

"You want to go downtown?" he said.

"That's what we agreed on."

"All right."

"All right?"

"Yeah, all right. We'll go."

"Good. Now you're talking. That's the old —"

"I need ten minutes."

"You got it. Ten minutes. I'll be right in there," he said, pointing to his door.

Mike entered his room. He sat down on the edge of the bed, staring at the ground. He stayed there for a full minute before rising and going to the shower, turning on the water and sticking his head under the freezing stream. He dried his hair quickly and put a few things in his backpack. He took the gray book from his desktop and quietly left the room, heading for the back.

He heard the voices of the children, followed them to the classroom, and peeked inside. They were seated, backs to him, watching Ibekwe at the front of the room writing the names of the months in English on the backboard. He picked out the close-shaved, round head of Juan Carlos, the slicked black matt of Arnold, and the brownish locks of Jesi, combed out and straightened now, neat and clean. Beside Jesi sat the one who'd done the combing and the straightening and the cleaning, with her own explosion of black sparkling curls.

He returned along the back of the dorm to avoid running into Lonnie, reentering the main building through a door in the side of the atrium, away from the dining room. Padre was in the kitchen with his back turned, putting away his coffee cup. He didn't see Mike as he passed by and started up the steps.

He put his ear to the door of Marco's library but heard nothing. He gently tried to turn the knob but it was locked. He tapped lightly, putting his ear to the wood again, but still heard nothing. He tried the knob again.

"What are you doing?" a voice, hard and stern, from down the hall. He turned to see Brother Greg marching towards him.

"I just wanted to return the book." He held it up as proof.

Greg took it.

"You finished it?" he said.

"The underlined parts. It was good," he said. "I liked it."

The brother stood in front of the door, waiting for Mike to leave.

"There was another one I wanted to borrow," he said.

Greg pondered a moment. "I can get it for you," he said. "What's it called?"

"I'm not sure, but I'll be able to pick it out."

The brother hitched up his robe, pulled out a key ring, stopped and eyed him for a moment. Finally, out of respect for books and those who read them, he began to unlock the door.

"The orphans are leaving," Mike said.

"Mmm mmm."

"We're going downtown, just Lonnie and me. I'll get them some presents or something."

Brother Greg nodded. He swung the door open. There on the desktop was the cross with the beaten man pinned to it, and, wrapped around its base, the skull-rosary with the *Padre Nuestro* staring at Mike from the abyss. He looked away, to the chessboard. Sure enough, the black queen was gone. But so also were nearly all the white pieces, and the white king was left alone, defenseless, naked, with nowhere to hide.

"I threw my queen away," Greg said.

"Yeah, I see that. The book's over here somewhere." He walked to the shelves on the far wall and bent sideways as if to read the spines of the books.

Greg closed the door behind him and stepped towards the shelves past Marco's desk to put Mike's book back, examining its cover as he did so. He stopped and opened the book to Padre's marker, just as Mike had hoped, and immediately became absorbed in it, lost to the world of animate things.

Mike slipped the weighty oriental volume out of its place on the shelf and reached behind it.

* * *

When he pushed aside the curtain and entered Lonnie's room, he saw Lonnie lying on the bed, his head propped on his pillow, his ankles crossed and his hands behind his head. On the tabletop beside him were three upside-down cups.

"Take your chances," he said.

Mike turned and started away.

"Okay, okay. Hang on. I'm coming."

CHAPTER 46

MIKE LOWERED HIMSELF INTO the front seat of the taxi and looked hard at the *narco-taxista*, who avoided eye contact.

"*Por fin*," Lonnie sighed as he settled into his place in the back. "Catch that *español* there, Mikey? *Por fin*."

"Yeah Lon, I got it."

"That means 'finally', right?"

"Yup."

"Downtown, Rodrigo. *Por fin. Por fin*. How do you say downtown in Spanish?"

"*El centro*," Rodrigo said. He smiled back in the mirror at Lonnie. "You like go *el centro* okay?" he said.

"Right now, we like go anywhere okay, hey Mikey? *Por fin*."

He rattled on and Mike ignored him, riding with his shoulder against the window and his backpack on his lap, his forearms resting atop it. When they came to the intersection with the road that led to Pilar's house, Mike strained to see down it. The *barrio* was quieter than before, as if the funeral mood lingered over it still. Even Lonnie seemed to feel it.

"I mean, the *hombre* died a natural death," he said. "That can't happen too often around here, right?"

"What?" Mike said.

"The old man. Pilar's buddy."

"He died of typhoid fever," Mike said.

"Well, that's pretty natural, isn't it? I mean, compared to being hacked to death, for example. And he looked pretty sharp in there, I thought. The old pervert."

Mike said nothing.

"Ah, but you're just thinking of her again, aren't you? You can't keep her out of your head, I know. She put the voodoo on you good. Nah, don't deny it. I see it. But I have to say, I'm kind of proud of you for that comfort-by-the-graveside thing. I thought my flower-in-the-hair act was good, but that comfort-by-the-graveside bit —"

"Keep talking, Lon."

"And you even worked in the flower thing, to boot. *Una rosa.* That was the stroke of genius, there, even if you did steal it from me."

Within a few blocks of the main square, Mike turned to Rodrigo. "Take me to the bus station," he said in Spanish.

Rodrigo turned back to look at Lonnie.

"Never mind about him," Mike said. "Just take me there."

"What's going on?" Lonnie asked.

"Nothing."

Rodrigo turned left on to a street choked to a single narrow lane by buses idling on either side and crowded with people crossing between them. He came to a stop halfway down the block, parallel to a ticket window. Beside it stood a Watcher.

Mike got out his wallet, extracted a stack of red bills from it and gave it to Rodrigo.

"This isn't the way," Lonnie said.

"I'm going to try to be back by five o'clock," Mike said to the *taxista*. "Come here and wait for me, okay? If I'm not here by six, I'll call you tomorrow. But you can keep the money."

"Fair enough," Rodrigo said.

"What's going on?" Lonnie said.

Mike turned back to him and switched to English.

"I'm going to Tamilito."

"No one go Tamilito," Rodrigo said.

"Yeah, you hear that, Mike? No one go Tamilito."

"You have to do something for me, Lon."

"Anything – I'll do anything. You know I will. Tomorrow, like I said. But meanwhile —"

"You have to go back to the mission and tell Padre I went to find her."

"Her who?"

"He'll know who."

"What's going on? What did Padre say to you in there?"

"And tell him I'll be back tomorrow before dark, at the latest. Tell him that I'll be safe, that if it gets too late, I'll find a hotel. Tell him to not worry. Make sure nobody comes to look for me. Tell them I'm not going to do anything crazy."

"You are doing something crazy, so don't ask me to lie to a priest, okay? Don't ask me that. I just went to confession. Hell, you know that, Mikey – you were the one who heard it. And what about our deal? We get all the monkish stuff out of the way in the morning, and then, hie we downtown in the afternoon. We had a deal."

"Something changed."

"What changed?"

"Just tell them I'll be back tomorrow before dark."

"What changed?"

Mike opened the door.

"I'm coming with you," Lonnie said. "I can help you find whoever her is." He started to open the door.

"No, Lon. You have to stay here and do this for me."

"Well I'll be damned. I'll be damned. All right, all right, but someday, in the unlikely event I ever see you again, maybe you can explain all this."

"I will."

"And you can tell me who her is."

* * *

As Mike stood at the ticket booth a miserable, smiling little boy approached him and held out his hand.

"*Señor*," he said. "Ticket, *señor*."

"Yeah, ticket," Mike said.

"For me."

"You want me to buy you a ticket?"

"*Sí.*"

"Where are you going?"

He shrugged.

"Tamalito?"

"*Sí*, Tamalito," the boy said.

"*Sí*, Tamalito, huh? What's in Tamalito?"

"Tamalito," the little boy repeated.

He bought two tickets and gave one of them to the boy, who led him to the Jocotenango-Tamalito bus, as if to earn his fare. The bus was small, old and beaten-up, the worst of the five parked along the curb, but like the others it was properly outfitted with a decal on its windshield – a large image of the thorn-tortured head of Christ. A line of blood ran down the side of his face and his eyes were lifted, as if he were rolling them in disbelief that anyone would choose to go to Tamalito. Beneath him were the words in Spanish, "Behold, I Make All Things New".

"All things but this bus, huh?" Mike said to the boy in English.

He climbed aboard, took a seat near the back, and shoved himself over to the window, thinking he might be alone there, and so could check to see if the thing was loaded. But the boy had followed him down the aisle and now flung himself down in the seat at his side.

A thick diesel smell permeated the bus. Mike slid his window open and tried to gulp some fresh air.

"So, what's your name then?" he asked the boy. "If we're going to be hanging out like this, I should know your name. It's not a secret, is it?"

He shook his head. "Abraham," he said.

"Abraham. How old are you, Abraham?"

He held up seven fingers.

"Yeah, me too."

The bus half filled with passengers, each seeming to contribute his own degree or two to the already oppressive heat inside. Finally, the driver climbed in and sat, levering the door closed behind him. He honked his horn, swung out into the traffic and began snaking the beast through the teeming streets and the tight blind corners of Jocotenango. From his perch in the bus Mike could look down at the people hurrying by or loitering at the corners, could see inside the petty shops crammed with merchandise.

"Do you live in Tamalito?" Mike said.

The boy shook his head.

"Do you have family there?"

He shrugged.

"Why are you going there?"

The boy shrugged again. "Why are you going there?" he said.

It was a good question.

Mike took his wallet out and opened it to the photo of Suyapa in her graduation gown, sitting erect with her chin tipped up, staring directly into the camera. She wore a tiny compressed near-smile, a mere hint of a smile. Her black hair fell out of the red cap, curving in two shiny folds along her cheeks. He could barely make out the cruel little crescent scar.

"Who is that?" Abraham said.

"Nobody. That's nobody. Do you know where this school is?" Mike said, pointing to the banner at the bottom of the photo.

"No. I don't know anything about Tamalito."

"Okay." He put his wallet back into his pocket. "Well, listen: I'm going to rest for a while." He was weary and descending hard from the miserable white buzz. He crossed his arms, slumped down in the seat, and closed his eyes. But as he tried to sleep, there was her image in front of him, with those dark eyes staring out at him, with that little brown scar branded there on her cheek, with that almost unbearable, questioning look. What did she want? What could he do for her? What could he possibly do?

Suddenly her mouth opened and she spoke: "We could be a family," she said. "Father, mother, daughter."

He was jolted awake when the bus turned left on to the two-lane road, the driver gunning it across the lane of oncoming traffic.

"Tamalito", the sign said. "Twenty-nine km."

Abraham was smiling at him.

"I kind of fell asleep there," Mike said.

"Snoring," the boy said.

"I don't snore."

The boy nodded his head. "*Sí, señor. Mucho,*" he said.

Mike picked up the backpack from the floor beneath him and unzipped it just enough to fit his hand in. At the top of the pack was an extra shirt, beneath that, a little shaving kit and the book he'd taken from Marco's shelf, as a decoy. At the bottom he could feel the hard wooden handle and the cold steel tube. Beside it, in the corner of the pack, he felt the remaining pieces of candy, mingled with coffee beans. He took out one of the beans, rubbed it and put it in his mouth. He took two of the candies, put one in each hand and shuffled them together.

"Take your chances," he said.

Up front, a large, dark-skinned man rose from his seat, bowing his head so as not to hit the ceiling. He turned to face the crowd, looking down the aisle and out the back window, avoiding eye contact with the other passengers. He held an ancient black book with ribbons of different colors streaming out from its bottom.

"Brothers and sisters," he began, his voice deep and strong against the diesel noise. "I am here today only by the grace of God…"

Mike shook his head, and Abraham, copying him, shook his. "You can't get away from them," Mike said.

"And no matter where you are in your own life," the preacher said, "you too can be saved like I was..." and he started in on his life story, one that, from Mike's perspective, was of only middling depravity, considering where they were.

He reached into his pack again and drew out the book, looking at it for the first time. He cursed in English. He zipped the pack up again and put it on the floor, tightening his shins around it.

"What's it about?" Abraham said.

"The book? You won't believe it." He opened it and read aloud:

> *A human being is spirit. But what is*
> *spirit? The spirit is the self. But*
> *what is the self?*

He stopped and looked at Abraham. "You'll never guess the answer."

"...and I did some bad things in my life, my brothers. And I fell. I fell. I saw some people die, and they died for nothing, and they died with nothing, and they died to nothing, for they died without Jesus on their lips, without Jesus in their hearts, in that hour when Jesus was what they needed most, for they did not know Him. One of them died, my brothers - I am ashamed to say it - one of them died by these same hands."

He held his thick fingers out in front of him, staring at them as if they were no part of him, as if they had betrayed him, as if he were astonished at them and at what they had done.

He remained motionless, waiting, waiting, staring at his hands, until it seemed to Mike that he was contemplating doing something desperate to them or with them, again. Finally, his face slackened and he spoke again. "But there is forgiveness," he said, and he raised his eyes towards the back of the bus. "Even for this there is forgiveness."

Mike looked around to see the reactions of the others on the bus; they were all studiously ignoring the man.

"Many are called," he said, "but no one's listening."

"What?" Abraham said.

"Nothing. Do you go to school?"

"No."

"Did you ever go to school?"

The boy nodded uncertainly.

"That's all right. School's overrated."

He rested his head against the window. The drone of the man's words and the gentle swaying of the bus, the sedative effect of the diesel fumes and the wearing down of the drug's buzz put him asleep again, a sleep such as he had not yet had in Cortes, and he was gone until awakened by the first *túmulo* of San Jose.

"Snoring again," the boy laughed.

On the edge of the highway he saw a woman with three-quarters of a broken pallet balanced on her head. She was stooped under its weight and shuffled slowly forward – God knows how long she'd had to walk with her little treasure there, riding atop her. And that would be Suyapa soon, he thought. A little further along an old man dressed in dirt-brown strained against his shabby two-wheeled cart, pushing it up the hill towards the town. That was Suyapa too.

The preacher had finished his pitch and was working his way down the aisle, holding up a rack of trinkets, shifting his glance from side to side, looking for takers. Just a junk salesman, after all.

They passed through San Jose. A scattering of lonely-seeming people meandered about the fairgrounds, and the square seemed abandoned by all but a single man lying on his side on the first step of the pavilion, his legs dangling to the ground, his pant cuffs hiked up to expose his bony shins, his hands wedged under his head for a pillow. On the stones beneath him an empty *ponche* cup rolled in an arc, pushed along by the breeze.

At the far edge of the village the bus made a stop. The preacher thanked the passengers and got off, and a crone got on, a hag, dragging a little girl behind her and carrying a baby in the crook of her arm. Shabbily dressed, tired, worn and badly used, she looked too old to have such small children. But as she passed her eyes met Mike's and he could see that he'd been wrong, that she was just the right age, no more than thirty. Suyapa.

Ten miles further along, the road intersected with a worn asphalt lane, and they turned on to it. A wooden sign announced the town of Tamilito. Beyond the sign was a cemetery with plastic flowers adorning the gravestones. A funeral or memorial service of some kind was going on amidst the tombs, and the people attending it stood motionless in rows, looking themselves like tombstones.

The road grew busier as they lurched along it, until they came to a crossroads at the entrance to an open-air market. In the middle of the intersection was a life-sized statue of a camouflaged soldier mounted on a pedestal. He was frozen in mid-charge, a rifle in his hand, as if ready to invade the marketplace and put an end to the madness. Two Watchers flanked him from opposite corners.

The driver swerved the bus to the side of the road and brought it to a stop. "Tamalito!" he growled.

The air brakes gasped.

CHAPTER 47

ABRAHAM FOLLOWED MIKE OFF the bus and stood beside him, looking up into the chaos of the market.

"You can't come with me from here, I'm afraid," Mike told him. "Do you have somewhere to go?"

The boy squinted up at Mike and shrugged.

"Come on."

Next to the small hut that served as the bus station was a pavilion with picnic tables and a small cooking shack to the side of it. Mike led the boy to one of the tables, sat him down and brought him a plate of food and a Coke. Watching him attack the meal Mike suddenly felt hungry himself, but decided against eating. He drew out a decent stack of *pesos* from his wallet and slid them under the boy's plate.

The boy looked up at Mike. He was chewing with his mouth open. Two grains of rice clung to his cheek.

"All right then. Take care of yourself," Mike said, as if a seven-year-old could take care of himself.

The boy smiled and nodded.

Mike hailed a cab. As he told the *taxista* the name of the *barrio*, he watched him for some reaction, some hint of surprise or fear. But like everyone in Cortes, he maintained a straight face regardless of the outrage being perpetrated. Without a word he ground his car into gear.

They rambled along the streets of the town for a few miles until the driver brought the cab to a stop sideways across the mouth of a dirt road.

"Is this it?" Mike said.

He nodded once.

"*El Campo?*" he said.

He nodded again.

"I need to go to a school somewhere in there." He took out his wallet to read the banner at the bottom of Suyapa's picture. "*Belén de la Meseta.*"

The cabbie shook his head. "Because the road," he said, and he pointed down it. It ran a hundred yards through an open, littered space before hooking to the right and climbing a rise, straightening back out and running away into God knew what. It was indeed a miserable thing, and Mike would never dream of taking his own car down it, but Mike wasn't a cabbie in Cortes. Mike was an American.

"I'll pay you double," he said.

Staring forward, his mouth set in a rigid line, the man shook his head.

"Triple."

There was no reaction.

"How far is it?" Mike asked.

"Not far."

"I could walk it?"

"*Sí.*"

"Is it safe?"

"It's daytime."

"*Sí*. It is daytime. But..."

Mike paid up and climbed out onto the gravel of the road. The taxi sped away, with, he thought, too much eagerness.

He began walking, sidestepping rocks and hopping over crevices in the road. He moved across the open space, feeling exposed and vulnerable, and climbed the rise, pausing at the top. He could see directly down the road now, running straight and narrow into the *barrio*. People were scattered along its length; men walking and riding bicycles, kids in school uniforms, women sweeping. Power lines crisscrossed overhead with round clumps of moss clinging to them like nests and an occasional pair of shoes dangling by its laces.

Mike took a deep breath, put a coffee bean in his mouth, and started out again.

Little two rut alleys bisected the main road, some of them twisting their way across to a parallel street a hundred feet off, others petering out to grass and brush. One was blocked by a pile of dirt, as if someone had planned to build a house in the middle of the road, but had gotten drunk and forgotten about it.

Though Mike felt utterly foreign and out-of-place, and though it could not happen very often that a white man walked into their *barrio*, the passers-by took no particular notice of him. Most avoided eye contact until Mike said good morning, after which they would look at him, smile kindly and return his greeting.

"*Bueno*," they would say, and Mike quickly adopted it.

There were groups of older men, survivors, standing under the awnings of some of the *casas* piled up along the side of the road, and they, too, seemed friendly enough. He called *bueno* to one pair, sitting on a wooden bench in the shade, and they nodded their heads and smiled back as if they'd been waiting there all morning for some *gringo* to greet them. A third man – flabby, with long pants and no shirt - was standing beside them, sliding his hand across the curly white hair of his barrel chest.

Mike approached them.

"I'm looking for a school, *Belén de la Meseta*," he said.

"Ah, Padre Teófilo's school," the shirtless man said. "*Sí.*" He gestured down the road with the back of his hand.

"Is it far?"

"No."

"How many blocks?"

"Not far."

"Is it safe?"

The man looked at the two others with a closed-mouth smile. He nodded. "*Sí*. Safe. All the bad one's are in jail, or in the ground," he said, and the three of them laughed together, as if they themselves had just finished burying the last of the bad ones.

"I see," Mike said.

"Here, they get two warning shots, and then…" The man put his hand in front of him and made a single short horizontal cutting motion.

"What do you mean?" Mike said.

"That's the rule. If someone tries to steal, he gets two warning shots, and then…" He made the hand motion again.

"I see."

"But sometimes we lose count." He looked at the other two again, and they laughed and shook their heads, as if they had just now lost count themselves, and were mildly embarrassed by it.

"All right. Well, I'll keep that in mind," Mike said, and started away.

The street that had been broad and roomy enough at its start now began to close in, its width seeming to shrink with each miserable block. The *casas*, too, became progressively smaller and poorer, closer together and huddled to the very edge of the road, as if they, too, feared what lurked behind. The barbed wire fences surrounding them were more meager and desperate, and some of the *casas* themselves were abandoned or never completed, roofless, with stands of trees growing within them. Jagged slashes of graffiti marred them.

Rib-cage *barrio* dogs panted about the streets, sweeping their lowered heads back and forth cautiously, as if on the alert for the next rock coming their way. Gutter chickens pecked about. A cream-colored kitten – impossibly small, too small to be alive – stalked about the foliage at the side. From a manhole a branch rose like the gnarled outstretched arm of some ancient Cortesian sewer god.

He heard laughter and footsteps coming from behind him and turned to see three boys in school uniforms, carrying backpacks and chasing each other down the dirt. They passed him without a glance. The school must be close, he thought with relief.

Every crossroads had its own *pulperia*, with Coke signs plastered on their walls and windows cut through them and barred over, with slots beneath where merchandise and money swapped hands.

He was relieved when he came to a school – a low, long cinderblock building with barred windows all along its walls.

But the place was empty and it reminded him of how late it already was. He did not have too much daylight left. He did not want to be caught in this place in the dark. He wanted to get to Rodrigo in time. He wanted to get back to his own *barrio*.

At the corner of the schoolyard was a large sign which at one time must have contained the name of the school, but was now peeled away and covered over with graffiti. On the road in front of the sign a pair of girls played *cantillos*. He showed them the photo of Suyapa.

"*Bélen de la Meseta*?" he said.

"No no no," one of the girls answered, wagging her finger in the air. Mike's heart sank.

"Do you know where it is?"

She pointed down the road.

"Is it far?"

She shook her head.

"Do you know this girl?"

She shook her head again. "She's pretty," she said.

"*Sí*, she is."

"She's sad," the other girl said.

"Yeah."

Mike reached into his backpack and gave them each a piece of candy. The girls tossed the wrappers behind them, put the candies in their mouths, and began to play again. Mike plugged a coffee bean into his own mouth and started away, thinking longingly of his own lucky *cantillo*. How much he needed it now. What a *tonto* he'd been to give it back to Belkis.

Up ahead a pile of bones in the middle of the road gathered itself together, rose slowly and rattled away, its skull hanging down between its shoulder blades.

THE CHILDREN OF EVE

On the next block he passed a gang of tough-looking teens, *los malos*, passing a joint around in front of a deserted *casa* set back from the road. Three of them were sitting on the stoop and another was standing alongside them, one foot up, leaning over to rest his forearm on his thigh. They were slack-looking, careless-looking, doing nothing but making bad plans. They eyed him malevolently.

What were they doing there, free and unburied? How had they escaped the attention of the shirtless man at the head of the barrio?

One of them said something in Cortesian *barrio*-slang that Mike couldn't make out and didn't try hard to. The others laughed loosely.

Nothing, Mike thought, they cared nothing for life, and so had the advantage of him, who only pretended not to.

He wanted to turn around – his entire being cried out for him to turn and run, but he was irretrievably deep in the *barrio* already, and there was something ahead that he must do – though he wasn't sure what - and, in any event, to turn back now would only show *los malos* that he hadn't been up to it, after all, that he'd succumbed to his fear, his cold, miserable, unappeasable fear. More dangerous, he thought, to go back than forward. He tried to walk faster without appearing to.

It had been many years since he'd fired a gun, and then only at tin cans and paper targets; to aim at another human being would be something altogether different. Nonetheless he was happy to have the pistol, loaded or not.

Half a dozen black buzzards slid about effortlessly above him, and lying up ahead in the middle of the road was a small pile of black and brown fur. As he approached he saw that it was a puppy, dead, splayed out in the dust, a grisly, sneering, wet look on its face. Mike stepped around it.

A boy passed by quickly on his bike. He was griping his handlebars tightly as his tires banged against the bumps of the road, and from each of his fists a skinny plucked chicken swung back and forth by the neck.

On the next side street, in front of a *pulperia*, a teen-aged girl stood on the edge of the curb, leaning back into the street, holding herself up with a finger looped around the bar of the caged window. She looked over at him as if she, too, knew he would never get out of *El Campo* alive. He stopped in the crossroads.

"*Bueno*," he called to her.

"*Bueno*," she said.

He glanced as if casually back up the road. Sure enough, one of *los malos* had come out into the street and was looking at him, a cell phone to his ear. When he saw Mike look back at him, he turned to where the others were sitting, said something, and laughed.

"Is the *pulperia* open?"

"*Sí*," the girl said.

He walked over to the window and peered inside. The room was illuminated only by the light from the window. A little table was butted up to the wall in front of the cage and on it was a wire rack with bags of snacks clipped to it – chips of different shapes and flavors. Two tall shelves made of unpainted pine boards stood end to end in the middle of the room. They were sparsely filled with boxes of candy and trinkets. Amidst the junk was a pair of unpainted *trompos*. In the middle of the shelf were cheap molded-plastic statues of the radioactive lady, three of them, standing in a perfect line, multiplying their indifference.

A door in the back wall led to some interior room. On one side of it was a chest freezer and on the other an old, round-shouldered refrigerator. Pallets were stacked against them and on the floor in front of the refrigerator was a crate half filled with empty soda bottles.

There was no one in the room.

"A coke?" Mike asked the girl.

"¡Mamí!" the girl shouted through the window. "A coke, mamí."

"Sí," came from beyond the interior door, shouted over the noise of a television.

They waited a few moments in silence, the girl trying not to pay any attention to Mike, Mike doing the same to her. She turned to shout through the cage again, "¡Mamí!"

"Sí, sí."

But again, no one appeared.

He showed her the photograph. "I'm looking for this girl," he said.

She examined it and shook her head.

He pointed at the little banner with the name of the school. She nodded, leaned around Mike and with a flick of her hand indicated the direction he'd been headed.

"Padre Teófilo," she said.

"Sí, Padre Teófilo. Is it far?"

She shook her head and leaned towards the grill again. "¡Mamí!" she called.

Finally, an enormous woman in a stained white sack of a sundress came limping through the door in the back wall, looking like a third appliance.

"A coke?" she said.

"*Sí, mami.*"

She took out a glass bottle from the refrigerator and opened it with a key hanging from a string tied to its handle. The cap fell to the ground and clinked twice against the concrete floor. The woman limped over to the window and stuck the bottle through a slot in the grill. The girl took it before Mike could, relayed it to him, and held out her palm.

Mike paid her and took a swig of the drink. It burned in his mouth, cold and sweet and strong. He glanced over at the corner from which *los malos* would appear, if they were indeed following him.

"He's looking for Padre Teófilo," the girl told the woman.

"The padre?" she said. "Down the road."

"I know, *mami*. That's what I told him," the girl said.

The woman leaned over towards the slot, as if she would crawl through it, and took a look at Mike with a wry smile. She stuck her hand out and flicked it down the road.

"I told him, *mami*," the girl said.

"And not very far?" Mike said.

"No," they both said together.

"*¡Mami!*" the girl whined.

"Thank you. Your daughter is very pretty," he said to the woman. This made her beam. Her daughter, too, smiled shyly and looked at her feet.

He downed the drink with one more gulp and handed the bottle to the girl, who passed it through the grill to her *mami* without looking at her.

He took out his wallet again and held some money out to her. "Have one for yourself," he said.

She smiled so that her perfect white teeth showed, and she opened her eyes wide and put her palm against her chest. "For me?" she said, as if no one had ever given her anything before.

"*Sí*. For you."

She glanced at her *mamí*, who smiled at her affectionately and nodded her okay. She took the money and thanked Mike.

"Do you want me to bring you to the padres?" she asked.

"No, that's okay."

The old woman stuck her hand through the grill and motioned with her wrist again.

"*¡Mamí!*"

He returned to the intersection and looked as if casually back up the road. There was no sign of *los malos,* and he now realized that this was even worse than if they had still been there.

Another block, and another, deeper and deeper into the undredged depths of the *barrio*. He surprised a dog on the side of the road that was biting fleas off itself, and it bared its teeth and growled lightly at him. He shifted a step to the side.

At the edge of the road in front of a hut a woman braided the hair of her daughter, dressed in a neat school uniform and impatiently looking up the road. "Okay, okay," she cried, and she twisted free and began skipping away, glancing up and smiling at Mike as she passed.

An entire family went by on a small motorcycle, a large man driving, his woman behind him, clutching at his sides, a child behind her, balanced precariously, pressing her cheek to her back, an even smaller child on the man's lap facing him. Working the bike carefully around the scars in the *barrio* road, the man smiled cheerfully at Mike, as if to say, "Can you believe I'm really doing this?"

He came upon a woman at the side of the road sitting in a vinyl chair in front of an abandoned *casa*. She wore makeup and the makeup worked: She looked pretty and, Mike thought, older than she probably was, maybe much older. Her chestnut hair was bunched together and pinned up high and with great care; wisps of it fell perfectly over her temple and cheek, and a carefully prepared swirl of it was pasted to one side of her forehead. She had a large white flower in her hair and enormous, dangling white hoop earrings. The top buttons of her blouse were undone and her collar flared back, showing a string of white beads lying across her shiny soft-brown skin. Her feet were propped up on another chair in front of her, her ankles crossed atop it. Around one of them, beneath the high cuff of her blue jeans, was an anklet of white beads. Her feet were bare; a pair of high-heels sat next to them on the chair. The nails of her toes were polished a sharp red to match those of her fingers. In her lap a furry white dog with a white collar slept.

She was slowly working on a piece of gum, rolling it around in her half-open mouth, looking as out of place as he was there in the barrio.

Mike greeted her and she answered in a soft voice. He took Suyapa's photo out of his wallet and as he leaned over to show it to her he smelled perfume. She put her hand gently on his bicep. He flexed, and let the hand linger there.

She shook her head - she did not know the girl. He pried himself away and continued on, finally coming to open country. To his right was savannah – a meadow with tall dull yellow grass and clumps of skinny trees. To his left a soccer field, even shabbier than that of the brothers, surrounded by a sagging chain link fence whose poles were pushed over in half a dozen places. Between the meadow and the field, the road ran another fifty yards, directly up to the black metal doors of a single story red brick building, low and long, like a warehouse. Painted above its doors were the blessed words, *"Bélen de la Meseta"*.

The building ran the entire width of the soccer field, and at the far end was another, smaller entrance. Across from it and just inside the fence was an old swing set with a boy swinging wildly, his head rising up to the level of the thick rust-colored support. Beside him was an open space where two other swings must once have been, but they were gone now, and in their place two girls dangled from their knees, their arms limp, their hair hanging downwards.

Mike walked to the corner of the fence and turned left on the rock-strewn lane, towards the swing set. The lane, he could see now, extended beyond the building to twist away into some low woods.

As he approached, the smallest of the girls shouted to him: *"Hola, gringo."*

The bigger girl elbowed her.

"Hola monkey," Mike shouted back. "Does Padre Teófilo live here?" He pointed to the entrance.

"I'm not a monkey," she said. "I'm Paola."

"Oh, okay. Does the padre live here?"

"Sí," she said. She looked at the older girl, hanging there beside her, and laughed again. With a motion rapid, fluid, and terrifying, she gripped the crossbar with both hands, pivoted her body around so that her legs swung down in front of her, and let go, completing her turn in mid-air and dropping to the ground. It seemed to Mike like an incredible distance to fall for such a tiny child, but she landed like a bird, straightened up and

skipped to the fence, hooking her fingers through the chain link and smiling out towards him.

Her face was dirty and her long hair was undone and wild. Her bare feet were rough and filthy black around the edges. She was *barrio*-lean, wearing jeans that were too short for her, with the zipper broken and bulging half open. Her t-shirt, though, was brand new, dark blue with yellow printing on it. A necklace of large wooden beads hung down her neck.

The boy on the swing wore the same shirt.

"Right in there," Paola said, pointing to the entrance behind him. She had shining eyes set wide apart and a wide mouth with thin lips. When she smiled a little horizontal fold appeared above her lip.

"*Gracias*, Paola."

"*De nada.*"

"I thought you were a monkey there, but now I see that you're almost more like a little girl."

"I am a girl."

The entrance was secured with a black metal grill. Behind it was an entryway about six feet long, on the other side of which was a wooden door.

Mike reached for the button high up on the brick wall.

"Be careful of the dogs," shouted the older girl, who had now joined Paola at the fence.

"And the padre," said Paola.

"Shh," the older girl said.

"Why's that?" Mike said.

The girls looked at each other and laughed.

He pressed the button and heard from within a bell ring and a pack of animals rush to the door and start to scratch at it, barking sharply and growling. He turned back to the girls.

"Do you guys know Suyapa?" he called to them.

"*Sí*," Paola said.

"Which Suyapa?" the older girl said. "There are lots of Suyapas."

"Yeah, which Suyapa?" Paola said. "There are lots of them."

"A girl, about your age," he said. "Not you, Paola. You. What's your name?"

"Soledad," the older girl said.

"She's about your size, Soledad. I don't know where she lives."

"The one whose mother died?" Soledad said.

"She didn't die. She just left, for the United States. That doesn't mean she's dead."

The girl shrugged, obviously electing to believe her *mami*, rather than this *gringo* stranger.

The door unlocked behind him and he turned to see a man peering out. He was short and a little stocky, almost bald, wearing a filthy, faded gray robe that hung to his sandals. With his legs he blocked the dogs.

"Padre Teófilo?"

"*Sí?*"

"*Bueno.*"

"*Bueno.*"

"Can I talk to you? I'm from the United States." He didn't know why he'd added that fact, as if he were bragging, and he felt foolish for having said it, but it seemed to reassure the padre, who kicked the dogs away behind him and slipped out into the entryway, closing the door on them. He opened the grill and stepped outside.

CHAPTER 48

THE PADRE SCOWLED OVER at the girls. Paola let go a little artificial scream and they both ran back to the swing set.

"They bother the dogs," he said to Mike.

He looked up and down the little lane.

"Did you walk here?" he asked.

"*Sí.*"

He shook his head. "*Problema,*" he said.

"*Problema?*"

"*Sí.*" He spread his arms in the air, palms upward; one look around, he seemed to be saying, and any *idiota* could see *el problema.*

"It's not safe?"

He wagged his finger in the air. "*Problema.*"

"Not even in the daytime?"

"No."

"They lied to me then."

"Ah-ha-haaaaa!" the padre said. He folded his hands behind his back and began to sway back and forth on his heels, looking up at Mike, awaiting his response.

Unsure what it all meant, Mike showed him the photo.

"Do you know this girl?"

He barely glanced at it. "No," he said. He chopped the word short, giving it an air of finality, but nonetheless he repeated it. "No."

"Look," Mike said, and he held the photo up closer to the man's face.

The padre pursed his lips, held his hands in the air again, palms upward, and began raising and lowering them against each other, out of phase, as if they were the pans of a balance. It was unclear what this signified.

"She went to school here," Mike said. He pointed to the little banner with the school name on it.

"Ah-ha-haaaaa!" he brayed. He folded his hands behind his back again and looked up at Mike with a smile or a grimace – Mike wasn't sure which. He seemed to be waiting for a reaction.

"You know her, then?"

"*Síiiii!*" he sang. He seemed surprised at having to repeat himself.

"She was living in Joco, Jocotenango, with the Sisters of Charity. She wanted to become one of them. But her father came and kidnapped her. And he drinks, and…I'm thinking he probably lives in this *barrio*. Do you know him?"

He nodded.

"Do you know where he lives?"

He made a motion as if pulling a zipper across his lips and looked up at Mike.

"You do know where he lives?"

He nodded his head in an exaggerated way.

"Will you take me there?"

"*Problema*," he said.

"Why *problema*?"

"*Problema*," he repeated, and he gritted his teeth at Mike in a way that was apparently meant to fully explain the *problema*, for he said no more.

"Can you tell me why there's a problem?"

The padre put one hand against Mike's elbow and made a drinking motion with the other.

"*Sí*," Mike said. "He drinks. I know. I said that. But I need to find him."

The padre pinched his thumb and index finger together, brought them to his lips and inhaled noisily.

"Marijuana. *Sí*. I suppose he does that, too. I suppose he does a lot of things."

The padre made a fist and punched it against his palm. "His own wife," he said.

"I see. Well, look, if you can't take me to him, I'll just have to go ask around until I find him."

"*Problema*," he said, shaking his head slowly. "*Problema*."

"But I'll do it," Mike said.

The padre thought over the *problema* for a moment before seeming to come to a resolution. "*Bueno*," he said, and started off along the lane towards the little woods. Mike followed.

"*Adios, gringo*," Paola said from the swing.

"*Adios*, monkey," Mike said.

The padre glared at her.

They slipped into the woods, following the path down through a little hollow, muddy at the bottom. They emerged on the other end, where another road intersected the path, and they turned left onto it. There were more trees along this road, with tiny *casas* interspersed among them.

Women watched as the padre approached and children stopped playing on the roadside, grew quiet, and stepped off to the side.

They passed an old man coming the other way, carrying a huge round bundle of sticks strapped horizontally across his shoulders. A little girl, her hair braided in tight black knots running like rope down her back, pushed along the road a homemade wooden wheelbarrow with wooden wheels, holding two large containers of water.

"Over here," the padre said, indicating the right side of the road. "No water. No lights."

From behind a stand of trees a column of black smoke rose into the air, and when they'd cleared the trees Mike could see that it was coming from the pipe chimney sticking up from the roof of one of the *casas*. An old woman was standing beside it, bent over, shoving a broom – an old tree branch with a bundle of straw tied to its end - down the opening.

"Should we help her?" Mike said.

"No *problema*," he said, and indeed, the woman appeared to know exactly what she was doing. She poked about with the broom, pulling it out of the chimney, looking down the pipe, shoving it in again. The padre pointed to the *casa* on the opposite side of the street, on the no-water, no-lights side.

"That's it?" Mike said. "That's his?"

"*Sí.*"

It was set back from the road behind a barbed wire fence propped up with posts of crooked unbarked tree branches cut to rough height. The front wall of the *casa* was constructed of dried-out, bleached planks tacked together on a slant, so that the whole house seemed to lean. The side wall that was visible from the road consisted of a blue tarp, its bottom fixed to the ground with boulders. The roof was cobbled together with overlapping sheets of corrugated metal held in place by rocks strung along the seams.

The doorway was open. Inside all was black. The padre went to the narrow opening in the fence that served as an entrance and stopped, standing sideways.

"*Hola*," he shouted. He hung his head, clasped his hands behind his back and rocked on his heels as he awaited a response.

The old woman on the roof - who hadn't seemed to notice them before - now looked over, shook her head, and jammed the broom down the chimney again. From one of the shacks further up the road a woman was haranguing a crying baby, her voice sharp over the noise from a television.

The padre called again in the direction of the *casa*, a little louder this time. Still there was no response.

He turned to Mike and put his palms in the air, shifted them about three times, and started forward through the gap in the barbed wire. Mike followed. They walked along the ash-gray dirt of the yard to within a couple feet of the doorway. The padre turned sideways and put his head down. "*Hola*," he called again, and waited. He looked up at Mike, shrugged, put his palms up and balanced them in the air again.

Mike stepped around him, walked to the threshold of the *casa* and peeked in. Pinholes in the roof let needles of light stab through the gloom, and Mike could see a dirt floor, a sagging single bed, a table with bottles and dishes stacked on it, and in a corner a pile of clothes. It all reeked of mold and urine. Darkness, dirt, despair.

He was about to take a step inside when the woman from the roof shouted out, "He's gone, Padre."

Mike turned and followed the priest back to the road.

"Do you know when he'll be back?" the padre called to her. The smoke from the chimney was reduced now to a thin gray wavering column, and the woman was backing down a home-made ladder propped against the wall, holding the broom in one hand. She stepped on to the ground, turned, and hobbled toward them without answering. The padre repeated the question.

"Never," she answered. "He'll never be back." She flicked her hand in the air to indicate his goneness. "That's what I think. They were here this morning. They packed a bundle of things and left."

"Was there a girl with him?" Mike held out the photo to her.

"*Sí, sí.* His daughter. *Pobrecita.* She was with him. 'Where are you going with that little one, you runt?' I said to him. He spit in my direction, the *cabrón.*" She took a couple token swipes at the ground with her broom. "*Pobrecita,*" she said. "She was going to be a sister, *sí*?"

"*Sí.*"

"And now..."

The baby up the road wailed again, and the mother started in on it with renewed vigor.

"Where would he take her?" Mike asked.

"I don't know." She swept at the road again. "Maybe to find the woman, his wife."

She scoffed as she said the word "wife".

"She left him," he said.

"*Sí.* Five, six days ago. While he was out drinking somewhere. When he got home he came to my house, looking for her. I said I didn't know anything, but he called me a liar, and I was, too, and he tried to hit me, but he was drunk, the little runt. He gave me a note she'd left and told me to read it to him. It said she was going to the United States, and don't try to look for her, because he wouldn't find her, and she hated him and always had. He said I was lying, and I wasn't, either. He tried to hit me again, but he was drunk, and he fell over." She looked at them with pride.

"'Bah'," he said. 'She was getting too old anyway' and he gave me the evil eye – he's an ugly little *cabrón*. I laughed at him again. Then this morning he came back, dragging that poor girl with him, and they packed, and..." She motioned down the road. "Maybe he took her to the mountains," she said. "He's from the mountains, I think."

"Which mountains? We're surrounded by mountains."

The woman shrugged. "The mountains," she said.

The padre shifted his palms up and down.

"I wish she'd stop nagging at that damn baby," Mike said.

"He doesn't need her anymore," the woman said. "Now that he has the little one..." Her voice trailed off.

"What's that?"

"He has her now. *Pobrecita*."

Mike turned to the padre. "You see?" he said. "She'll be his little slave now."

The padre nodded. He stuck his hand out and pretended to be receiving money from an imaginary person in front of him, then put it in his pocket. He made a sweeping motion with his other arm, as if he were moving the purchased item towards the imaginary customer. And he looked at Mike and nodded knowingly.

"What do you mean by that?" Mike said.

"His own wife," the padre said.

"What do you mean?"

"His own wife," he said again.

"You mean he sold her? He sold his wife?"

"*Mujer público.*"

"Public woman?"

The padre nodded. "*Prostituta,*" he said.

Mike stared at him for a moment, then turned back to look at the empty house with its blackened doorway. "*Prostituta,*" he said.

The padre pursed his lips, folded his hands behind his back and bobbed his head.

"*Pobrecita,*" the woman said.

"That's not what this is about? Tell me that's not what this is about," Mike said to the priest. He cursed in English, turned up the road, walked eight paces, turned around and walked back.

"*Prostituta?*" he said.

The padre juggled his palms.

Mike cursed again, turned and marched to the *casa* where the screaming was coming from. In the doorway there was a little girl dressed in a dirty white dress. When he turned into the entrance to her yard, she was gone, like a gecko. He marched to the doorway and stuck his head in. The baby was lying on its back on a blanket on the dirt floor, kicking its legs and screaming. The mother, flabby and slack, sat on a bed over it, flicking a towel back and forth in the air at the side of her head and watching an ancient little television that was hooked to a car battery, set on a plank shelf tacked to the wall. When she saw Mike, she stopped berating the baby and smiled up at him.

He cursed at her. "Stop it," he shouted. "Leave the damn thing be."

CHAPTER 49

WHEN THEY ARRIVED BACK at Padre's building, Mike could see children in school uniforms issuing out of the double doors at its far end. The padre told Mike to wait at the near entranceway while he got his truck so that he could give him a ride to the bus station. Mike didn't refuse.

The priest unlocked the grill, stepped into the entryway, and with the flat of his hand banged three times on the wooden door. In a moment it was squeezed a third of the way open by a woman in an apron. He wedged inside, blocking the growling dogs with his legs.

The three swing set children had watched in silence until the door was shut. Now Paola shouted to Mike, "Did you find her? Did you find Suyapa?"

He started walking towards her, and she dropped from the bar, skipped through an opening in the fence, and came to him.

"Did you?" she said.

Mike shook his head and got down on his haunches.

"We didn't find her yet," he said. "But we're going to." He could see her t-shirt better now. Across its front were a representation of the tablets of the Ten Commandments and, in small letters beneath it, the words *"Sirvientes de Cristo"* in Spanish and "Cortes Mission" in English. The necklace she wore was actually a rosary, made of hard beans of some kind, with a wooden crucifix hanging from it.

"If I see her," Paola said, "I'll tell her that you were looking for her."

Mike took off his pack and dug into it, shoving the gun aside. "Who wants a treat?" he said loudly. Immediately Soledad flipped over and dropped from the bar where she'd been hanging and raced towards him. Seeing her go, the boy went flying off the swing set, arcing through the air and landing on the run. In a moment they were standing in front of Mike, their palms extended.

He handed a piece of candy to the two oldest while Paola watched silently. They unwrapped them, stuck them in their mouths, and tossed the wrappers to the ground.

"And now you, monkey."

"Paola."

"That's right, Paola. You have to earn yours, though."

He held out his two fists, turned downward. "Take your chances."

She smiled over at her siblings, sucking their candy. Her sister pointed at Mike's right hand, and her brother, seeing her do it, pointed at it, too.

"Well, it might be there," Mike said. "I suppose it could be in that hand, I guess."

Paola bit her lower lip, and looked at the other two again before finally tapping his left hand.

"Are you sure?"

She nodded once, her eyes firmly planted on the hand. Mike turned it over and slowly started to lift his fingers. He stopped and looked up at her. She stomped her feet and looked over at her sister.

He opened his hand the rest of the way, exposing a single brown coffee bean. She frowned at him. Her siblings laughed.

"I told you," Soledad said.

"I thought monkeys liked coffee beans," Mike said.

"I'm not a monkey."

"Hold on. You haven't checked the other one."

She stabbed his other hand with her finger, and Mike began opening it slowly. As soon as there was enough of a gap, she snatched the two candies from his palm. She laughed and turned to look at her sister again. "Two," she said.

Soledad stuck her tongue out at her.

Mike put the coffee bean in his mouth and zipped up his pack.

"You guys aren't in school today?" he said.

Paola looked back at Soledad, who dropped her eyes and swept at the gravel of the road with her bare foot, her arms folded. "Next year," she said.

"No truck today," Paola said.

"No truck?"

"When the truck doesn't come, we get to play," the older girl said.

Mike nodded, trying to assume an air of nonchalance. Of course they could play today; on the days the truck didn't come, they could play.

"You, too?" Mike asked Paola. "You work too?"

She nodded proudly.

"She only picks one can," Soledad laughed.

"Two," Paola said.

Soledad looked at Mike and shook her head. Paola lunged at her and tried to hit her with an overhead swing of her arm, but she dodged away, laughing.

"Paola of the one can!" she said.

"Two," she said.

"Two's a lot for a little monkey," Mike said. "A lot."

He looked away, towards the field beyond, and then down at his sandals.

"Are you all right, *Señor*?" Paola said.

Mike nodded. He took into his hand the little wooden cross hanging at the end of her necklace.

"Where did you get it?" he said.

"I made it. With them." She pointed at the lettering on her t-shirt.

"Who are they?"

"Other *gringos*."

"I see. Other *gringos*. Do you like the other *gringos*?" Mike said.

"*Sí*," Paola said. "*Mucho*."

Mike turned the crucifix over in his fingers. It had the figure of Christ glued to it, rough-cut and featureless, but suffering there, nonetheless, just as he was in the chapel at the mission, in the little church on the way to the petrified woman, on the windshields of the buses, on the statue on Marco's desk – suffering, everywhere suffering.

He held it up to her. "Do you know what this is?" he said.

"*Sí*. It means God."

"Yeah, that's right. It means God."

He heard the noise of a motor and saw a small, dusty pickup come out to the road from the far corner of the building, beyond the school.

Mike waved at it and turned back to Paola.

"So, tell me," he said. "Is he in you?"

She squinted up at him, her head tilted, questioning.

"Is he in you, Paola?" he repeated.

She looked down at the crucifix and suddenly smiled. "*Sí*," she said. "*Sí*. In you, too." The little crease appeared above her lip.

He took her by the shoulders and pulled her into him. She was light and hollow - it was like hugging a doll - and he could feel her noodle-arms wrap around his head and squeeze. The beads of her necklace pressed against his chest.

"Maybe her mother isn't really dead," she said.

The padre beeped his horn; it was off-key and sour sounding.

Mike stood and picked up his backpack.

"*Adios*, monkey," he said.

"*Adios, gringo.*"

* * *

The padre's truck was dented and scratched and layered with dust. It had no hubcaps and no rear bumper. There was a crack in the lower right side of the windshield that was webbing its way across the glass, which was milky and hard to see through. The engine tapped loudly. There was no crank for the passenger-side window, just a gear poking out of the door panel. When the padre saw him looking for it, he detached the handle from his own door and handed it to him, and he jimmied it onto the gear and rolled open his window, waving back at Paola just as they passed out of sight.

"Lifters," Mike said in English, not knowing the Spanish word. "Your lifters."

Padre looked at him.

"Your engine," Mike said.

"*Sí*," he said.

"You should really get it looked at."

He pressed his thigh up against the bottom of the steering wheel and balanced his palms in the air.

They came to the girl in white sitting at the side of the road. She stared in front of her as the truck tapped past, her jaw still slowly working the gum in her mouth.

Padre leaned over to Mike as if to tell him a secret. "*Mujer público*," he said.

* * *

They arrived at the bus station five minutes before the four o'clock bus was to leave. Mike gave Padre the phone number of the mission and asked him to call if he saw Suyapa, though he had little hope for it. The padre took Mike's arm as he was opening the door.

"You must pray for her," he said. Mike nodded, got out of the truck, and walked to the Tamalito – Joco bus.

Such an easy thing it was, to ask someone else to pray.

CHAPTER 50

RODRIGO WAS WAITING AT the Joco station. Mike got in the cab and swung the door towards him, but it banged against the frame. He cursed.

"Lift," Rodrigo said.

He pressed his palm up against the window frame and closed the door. He sat back silently as they moved through the clogged side streets and turned on to the main road leading back towards the mission.

"How was Tamalito?" Rodrigo said.

"The same," Mike said. "It was Cortes. How about you? How was your day? Move any drugs today?"

"No," he said. "But if want you —"

"No," Mike said. "I don't do drugs."

"Okay. But if change mind —"

"I won't."

"Okay. I just say."

He drove another block before he spoke again: "I take him a place, though."

"You took him some place?"

"But not allowed to tell."

"Where did you take him, Rodrigo?"

He thought for a moment. "Hotel," he said.

"You took him to a hotel?"

"*Sí.* Is because Brother Marco come back and make him leave. He tell me take him there, to hotel."

"Good," Mike said. "I'm glad. To hell with him." Let him rot there in the gloom of the *Segundo Cielo*.

"But other thing," Rodrigo said, and he glanced at Mike, unsure whether to go on.

"What is it?"

"The girl from *Los Ángeles*."

"What about her?"

"He take her."

"He took her? What do you mean, he took her? To the hotel, you mean? She's with him at the hotel?"

"But he tell me not say anything."

"Turn around. Take me there."

"No, I promised —"

"I'll pay you double."

He thought for a second. "Okay," he said. "Double." He wheeled the car around the block and headed back towards the plaza. "Fair enough. But Marco, he say he need talk you, too. He not happy."

"No, I bet he's not," Mike said. "But who is, right?"

"I happy."

Mike laughed bitterly. "Yeah, and that's the hell of it," he said.

Rodrigo parked in front of the hotel.

"Stay here. I'll be back in one minute," Mike said.

THE CHILDREN OF EVE

A beggar at the side of the hotel door looked up blankly at him. Mike stepped over him, opened the hotel door, and marched to the counter. The clerk looked up at him with a glint of fear.

"Where is he?" Mike said.

"Who?"

"You know who. What room?"

"He not here."

"What room?"

The clerk shrugged.

Mike turned, went to the staircase, and started up the steps.

"No allowed," the man said weakly.

Mike reached the landing and was about to knock on the first door – he would try each of them in turn until he found what he was looking for - but he heard the popping of bongos from down the hall, and followed it to the last room.

The door was locked. He banged on it and it shuddered under his fist. The bongos stopped.

He banged on it again three times.

"Lonnie," he shouted.

From inside the room he heard the voice: "Mikey. Good. Good. I thought it might be…well…"

Mike punched the door again.

"Hang on, now. Don't go breaking the damn thing down." The lock clicked free and the door began to swing open. "But look, man, don't be pissed." The scent of marijuana rolled out into the hallway. "I know you said you didn't like the sharing thing, but…"

He had pajama bottoms on and his chest was bare. His hair was splashed over his brow and he squinted though its blonde strands. The corner of his mouth was turned up into a sheepish grin.

Over his shoulder Mike saw, standing at the corner of the bed, Sara, wearing Lonnie's bright yellow sailboat shirt, and nothing else. She held his Panama hat in her hands, as if she had just taken it off. She smiled weakly at him.

Mike turned to Lonnie. "You son of a bitch," he said. He pivoted and marched back down the hall, Lonnie calling after him. He flung himself down the steps.

"He tell me say no to everybody," the clerk said.

Outside, Mike tripped over the legs of the hollowed-out beggar and cursed. He climbed into the cab and slammed the door, but it thudded against the car frame and rebounded away. He cursed again, grabbed the door again, pried it up with his palm, and closed it.

"Always lift," Rodrigo said.

"Just drive."

But before Rodrigo could enter the line of traffic, the hotel door opened again and Sara stumbled out, barefoot, still dressed only in Lonnie's shirt and carrying her blue jeans bunched up in her arms. She opened the rear passenger-side door and slid into the car without saying a word. Rodrigo looked over at Mike.

"It's okay," Mike said.

He glanced back at Sara, who had shut the door and was looking away out the window as she wiggled into her pants. "We'll get you home," he said. "I have to talk to Pilar anyway."

Rodrigo shook his head. "I no go back there," he said. "Not after he do that."

"I'll pay you double."

"You already pay double."

"Triple."

He shook his head.

"A hundred dollars. I'll give you a hundred dollars."

"*Dollares* - not *pesos?*"

"*Dolares, sí.* But I'll have to pay you later. I don't have it right now. But I'm good for it, I swear."

Rodrigo thought for a moment. "One hundred *dolares*. You swear. But I no wait there. I go. Fair enough?"

CHAPTER 51

NO ONE SAID A word until they turned onto the road to *Los Ángeles*, when Mike looked back at Sara and asked her if she wanted them to take her to her *casa*.

She was thinking about something else. "My shoes are back there, at the hotel," she said, and then, more quietly, "And my shirt, too. My own shirt."

Mike stretched back to look at her feet. "We'll have to get them later," he said. "Do you want us to take you right to your house?"

She shook her head. "Drop me off a block before Pilar's road. Maybe she won't see then."

When they let her out, she started down the rocky side road, picking her way along gingerly on the balls of her feet, hunched over a bit, trying to avoid detection, the bright yellow shirt blazing out in the midst of the greens and browns and grays of the *barrio*.

Mike asked Rodrigo to go slowly, to give her more time to get around the block, but Rodrigo shook his head. "Here dangerous," he said. He turned on to Pilar's street, dropped

Mike in front of her gate and executed a quick three-point turn at Sara's corner, hurrying back past Mike, throwing dust in the air.

Mike stood at the gate, watching the corner, hoping to see Sara go by before anyone came out.

In a moment, though, Ana appeared in the doorway, not smiling.

He stuck his finger in the air to ask her to wait, unzipped his backpack and, as if looking for something, slowly fished around in it. The metal of the gun, nestled in amidst the remaining dozen or so pieces of candy, touched his hand, and he nodded as if he'd found that for which he'd been looking. He zipped the backpack up slowly and hitched it up onto his shoulder.

He glanced to his left again, to the intersection with Sara's road. Ana shook her head at him, as if disapproving of his lingering there when there was so much to be settled within.

Behind her shoulder Pilar appeared, wearing a frown, but a frown shot through with youth and innocence, almost a pretend frown, like a little girl playing at frowning.

Mike felt better seeing it.

She leaned in to her mother and whispered something. Ana shook her head once more, but slowly shifted to let her daughter slip past. Pilar started towards him.

Mike looked to the right, as a decoy, then to the left once more, and finally there was Sara, still bent over, tip-toeing rapidly across the intersection in the direction of her house, like the sun in some far northern zone trying to sneak across the horizon. She glanced at him and smiled, as if they were playing a game. She disappeared behind her corner just as Pilar came out the gate.

THE CHILDREN OF EVE

She had her arms crossed and was looking out beyond him, and for a moment he thought she would walk right past him.

"Pilar," he said. "I'm sorry."

She wagged her head. Tears had come into her eyes and now began dropping down her cheeks, but not real ones, Mike thought.

"Lonnie," Mike said dismissively.

"*Estúpido,*" Pilar said.

"*Sí, Estúpido. Imbécil.*"

"*Imbécil.*"

She looked back at Ana in the doorway, to show her that she was smiling now, despite the fake tears, and that it was all right. Ana shook her head and turned back into her *casa*, dragging along with her by the sleeve Naila, who had appeared alongside her in the doorway.

Mike led Pilar down the road, in the opposite direction from Sara's intersection.

"I went to find Suyapa," he said. "Her father kidnapped her."

"I know. Did you find her?"

"No. I couldn't find her. I don't know if anyone's going to find her, Pilar. I'm going to keep looking, though."

"But you're leaving," Pilar said.

Mike didn't answer.

"You have to go back to Michigan."

At the *pulperia* they turned around. They walked half the distance back to the *casa*, stopped, and faced each other. Pilar looked up at him with her cat eyes and her mouth slightly open.

"She liked you, you know."

"Who liked me?"

"Sara."

"Sara. Yeah, Sara. I liked her, too."

"But you didn't love her?"

"No, I didn't love her."

She nodded her approval of his not loving Sara and leaned forward slightly, not an inch, and he took her in his arms and kissed her on top of her head, on the seam of her wiry black hair. She looked up at him and he kissed her mouth.

She purred. He wanted to purr back.

"Do you think it's funny, what she said?" Pilar asked.

"What who said?"

"Suyapa."

"No, I don't."

"Do you remember what she said?"

"*Sí.*"

"So we have to find her then."

He kissed her again, softly at first, then harder. She raised herself on her tip-toes, her body sliding up his, her mouth rising to his ear. "Chark," she whispered.

"What's that?"

"Chark."

"Are you calling me a shark?"

"Chark," she said, and then more loudly, as if calling for help: "Chark! Chark!" She took hold of his arms and pretended to push him away.

They heard giggling and looked over to see Naila leaning out the gate. Pilar, trying to frown again, shooed her away with the back of her hand.

"*Tonta,*" she growled, and she glanced at Mike, and they laughed until they stopped, and there was a moment's quiet. She was looking down now at the ground between them.

"Pilar," he said.

"I know you're not a chark. I know it." She tilted her head up to look into his eyes, and in that look was everything that he'd done nothing to earn. The incongruity would have made him laugh if it hadn't frozen him.

"I know you love me," she said.

As the words left her mouth her eyes shifted away to look over his shoulder, and alarm sprung up in them. She jerked back from him, her hands still on his biceps. As he turned to look he heard the slapping of feet, quick and light, and he felt Pilar pull him towards her, and then a flash and an explosion, and then he was on his knees, he was looking at Pilar's arm, and his head stung, and behind Pilar someone was running away towards Sara's corner, looking back at him. A kid, a little boy, wearing a black *policia* mask that was too big for him. Fear shot from the eyeholes – why was he so afraid?

In front of Pilar's gate, not ten feet from Naila, the boy tripped, sprawling forward in the dust and dropping something on the road. He scrambled to pick it up, stopped for a moment and looked Naila in the eye, turned and began running again, swinging the thing back and forth in his hand.

Well Mike had one of those, too, if that's how it was, though he wasn't sure if it was loaded. If only he could reach his backpack, lying there on the road beside him. If only he could move his arm. But it didn't matter. It was just a boy, after all, running away, looking back with terror through that ridiculous mask. It was okay, he wanted to shout to the boy, he'd missed. There was no reason to run away. But he couldn't seem to speak.

If the boy would just come back and help him up, everything would be okay. If he would hand him his backpack, then they'd see...

415

Someone was screaming – Naila. Naila was screaming. He tried to lift his head to see Pilar, but could only raise his eyes, and now she must have stooped down, because her face was in front of his. He saw her lips move, the fine pale lips, the lips that were his now, because he'd just kissed them. He heard his name in Spanish. She'd been kind enough to say his name. He felt a surge of tenderness towards her, and he tried to raise his hand to touch her mouth, but the feeling overwhelmed him and he collapsed backward onto the dirt.

CHAPTER 52

HE WAS LYING ON SOMETHING hard and being transported slowly along a bumpy surface. He forced his eyes open but it was as if they had been shattered, cracked in half; a jagged line ran horizontally across his field of vision, so that there was an upper world and a lower world. Along the crack all was blurred, and only at the top and the bottom could he see anything clearly.

Someone was bent over him, and as in a fog he heard a voice, insisting that someone wake up. It was his name, he was the one the voice was talking to, he was the one who must wake up. He tried to respond, to tell the voice that he was awake, to tell it to stop the bumping, to ask it where they were taking him, why they were holding him down like this so that he couldn't move his arms. But his words came out broken and blurry, like his vision, and he stopped trying and fell again into the void.

* * *

He merged into and out of consciousness. The bumping seemed to be gone, mercifully, and he wasn't being moved anymore. Much time might be passing or none at all. At times when he came to there seemed to be great commotion around him and many voices, but it was as if his ears were plugged, as if it were the others now who were talking gibberish. At other times he seemed utterly alone and abandoned, and he felt as if he must be crying.

* * *

He heard his name in Spanish and he opened his eyes to find that his vision had improved. He was lying in bed, covered with white sheets, the whitest he'd ever seen. He was staring up at a white ceiling, and there was a humming coming from alongside him.

He shifted his eyes and there was Pilar. She was sitting on the edge of the bed, facing the window, and the sunlight was pouring through it and onto her face, outlining the curve of her cheek. Her hair was fixed up in back, and stray strands of it reached out into the sunlight. Her voice did not sound at all like a *sapo's*; it was beautiful, high and clear and sweet. No, it was Mike who was the *sapo* now, dull and slow and stupid.

He wanted to sit up, to better hear her singing, but he couldn't move. She seemed to sense his turmoil and turned to him, smiling, as if nothing, after all, was wrong. "Don't worry," she said. She leaned over and stroked her hand over the side of his head, where it seemed to be hurt.

She smiled at him as he tried to talk to her. "Shh," she said. She looked back away to the window.

"Don't you think it's funny," she said, as if to the sunlight, "what Suyapa said?"

He'd told her that already, but he tried to say it again, tried to tell her no, it wasn't funny at all, but he couldn't speak. He struggled to hold on to consciousness, to remain in her presence, so he could tell her his revelation, tell her that it was all possible now, after all - everything was possible. All things were new. He'd become a *sapo*, sure, blunted like a *sapo*, but there'd been stories about that, about *sapos* and princesses.

But again, she seemed to anticipate what he was thinking.

"I know you love me," she said.

Yes, he loved her. Of course he loved her; any *tonta* could have told him that. He loved her, had loved her, from the first moment. He would always love her. They would be a family.

But there was something else, something wrong with their plan, though he couldn't recall exactly what. Something about Suyapa - something bad. He tried to ask Pilar about it, but nothing sensible came out.

Again, she seemed to know just what he was thinking, and she turned back to him, still smiling. "Don't worry," she said. She stroked the side of his head once more, where the pain had been. "Just sleep."

He tried to talk again but nothing came out. He tried to raise his hand to touch her cheek but his arm wouldn't move. There was so much he couldn't do now.

"Just sleep," Pilar said. "For a little while longer."

CHAPTER 53

WHEN HE CAME TO again, he recognized where he was - in one of the recovery rooms in the mission; he could tell from the crucifix hanging on the immaculate white wall. He tried to turn his head to look about the room, but it made him dizzy. He moved his eyes, instead, and it was better.

Pilar was nowhere in sight. In her place was Brother Greg, nurse Greg, sitting beside his bed, his glasses slid down on his nose, glaring down hard at a book on his lap as if he were angry at it.

A phrase popped into Mike's head: "The eternal silence of these infinite spaces". He wondered why it had appeared. He remembered that he had almost understood it once. It had been in a book, a book Greg had given him.

He tried to ask him about it but his words came out weak and dry, and the brother didn't move his eyes from the pages. He said it again as loudly as he could, and Greg finally lifted his head, at first seeming annoyed at the interruption. He rose and leaned over to look at Mike, who tried to say the brother's name.

"It's okay," Greg said. "Just rest."

"My book," he tried to say.

"That's all right. Rest."

He laid his head back on the pillow and closed his eyes. His head was throbbing. It felt like there was something wrapped around it, and he tried to reach up to feel it, but there was a tube dangling from his forearm, and he was afraid to pull it out.

"Book," he said. But he felt the weariness sweep over him, and fell quiet.

* * *

An indeterminate amount of time passed, and he awoke again. His vision was clear now and he could speak, though it was difficult. It was the padre watching over him now. He and Greg and Pilar were apparently taking shifts.

"What happened to me?" he asked.

"You were shot."

"No. He missed. He missed me."

The padre nodded. "Well, something grazed you pretty good, anyway."

He closed his eyes and tried to remember. He was there at Pilar's house, in the street. He was holding her, kissing her. Naila was at the gate, laughing, and Pilar growled at her. "*Tonta*," she had said, and they had laughed at the word. And he was about to tell her, he was about to say it, but then the shock on her face, the footsteps from behind, her pulling him towards her, the world exploding and the little boy tripping in the dirt and dropping the black thing in his hand. Yes - that's what had happened.

He reached up towards his head, his arm pulling against the tube, but the padre took his hand and gently put it back at his side.

"My head?" Mike said.

"Yes. But it's not too bad. You were lucky."

"A kid."

"What's that?"

"Just a kid."

"Yes, it was a child."

"Why would a little kid —"

"Don't worry about it," the padre said. "Just lay back and rest."

"And there was a book," he said.

"You have to rest."

"How long have I been out?"

"Just overnight. Some of the men from the *barrio* brought you in on a truck. Our doctor came out, and he and Greg cleaned you up and put that bandage on you, hooked you up to that machine."

"I don't remember."

"No, you wouldn't. You were pretty bad. We were worried about you for a while. We had people praying upstairs all night."

Mike felt infinitely touched, and tears welled up in his eyes.

"Pilar, too. Did she go up there and pray?" he asked

The padre looked surprised. "No," he said. "Not Pilar."

"Do you know when she's coming back?"

"She was never here."

"Yes, she was. Right there," he moved his arm to the side, tugging it against the tube, to indicate where she'd been sitting. "I saw her."

"No, Mike, she hasn't been here."

"You just weren't here," he said.

The padre shook his head.

"Maria let her in, then. She was sitting right there. You just don't know."

"Pilar was never here, Mike," he said.

The old priest looked into Mike's eyes with that heaviness in his face.

"Right there," Mike said, trying to put a tone of finality to it. "She was right there."

"No, Mike."

"Why are you lying to me?"

"She couldn't have been here."

"What do you mean, she couldn't have been here?"

"She chased after him, Mike. She chased after the kid who shot you."

"She chased him?"

"And she was fast."

"She's fast, yeah. I know. So?"

"And the kid must have tripped or something."

"He tripped?"

The padre nodded slowly, still staring into Mike's eyes.

"And she caught him?" Mike said.

CHAPTER 54

HE WAS IN AND out of sleep for the entire morning of the next day, drowsy, nauseous, angry and sad when he was awake. In the early afternoon Brother Luke looked in at the doorway, saw that Mike's eyes were open, and entered. He was carrying a plastic glass with a straw in it. Mike tried to sit up for a moment, but the room shifted violently and he lay back down.

"Take it easy," Luke said. "Try a little of this." He held the glass to Mike's chin and bent the straw to his lips. Mike sucked in a small mouthful and rolled it around with his tongue. It was thick and cold and fruity.

Luke set himself down on the chair at the bedside. He was quiet for a long time.

"So what happens now?" Mike said when the silence became unbearable.

"Now you get better."

"I mean about Pilar?"

"Pilar's not ours anymore. She's in better hands."

"Better than mine, I hope." He felt the emotion running up in him. "And her family?"

"We're doing what we can for them."

"I need to help them."

"What do you have in mind?"

"I need to talk to them."

"That's out of the question."

"But I can't just leave it like this."

"We'll take care of it," Luke said.

"How can you take care of it?"

"How can you?" he said, but immediately he softened. "You just need to rest," he said.

There was something else Mike wanted to ask, but he couldn't remember what it was. He thought for a minute, tried to concentrate, tried to drag it forward through the muck of his *sapo* brain. But he couldn't grasp it.

"I'm sorry about it all, Luke," he finally said.

The brother nodded. Mike continued. "Tell me what happened."

"Someone shot you."

"To her, I mean, to Pilar. Afterwards, after she was shot. What did they do for her? They didn't just take care of me and leave her there, did they? They didn't just leave her there to die?"

"I don't know. They brought you here, but I'm not sure what they did with her. I didn't even know she'd been hurt until later."

"She pulled me away," Mike said. "That's why it wasn't worse. She pulled me out of the way, then they say she ran after the kid. Then…"

"Yes," Luke said. They were quiet again for a long time.

"They thought you were him, you know," Luke said. "That's why —"

"Yeah," Mike said. "I know. I know. When can I see the kids again, the orphans?"

"They're gone."

That's right. The orphans were leaving. Someone was taking them away, to a new place, far away from him, far away from Mr. Aquirre.

"Already gone?"

"Marco is taking them to their new home."

"Is it far?"

"Yes."

"Is it safe?"

"Yes."

"Are they all together?"

"Yes."

"What about the boy Greg took to the hospital? Is he with them?"

Luke shook his head. "Maybe later," he said.

"Maybe later. Okay. I wish I could have seen them again, though."

"Why don't you get some rest," Luke said. "There's someone from the police coming to talk to you, and the doctor will be here again at about three."

"Will they know what happened to Pilar?"

"I don't know."

* * *

In the afternoon Luke returned and woke Mike. There was a man with him.

"This is Mr. Alverenga from the police department," Luke said. "He'd like to talk to you."

426

That was right – the police. He'd forgotten. The police were coming to get him. And later, someone else, too. Someone important, too. Someone who might know what happened to Pilar. He couldn't remember exactly who.

The man did not have on a Watcher uniform, as Mike had expected, but wore a neat gray suit. He pulled the chair away from Mike's bed, as if to comply with some regulation regarding proximity to criminals, and begin asking questions. Mike told him all that he could remember.

"I know who paid the kid," he said. "The kid who shot her."

The man didn't seem interested, and Mike didn't press the issue. Revenge was senseless after all; what further damage could the stalker do? And who could blame the kid, the triggerman, the trigger*niño*? It was all of fifty bucks worth of drugs, after all, and a poor *barrio* kid didn't run into that kind of windfall every day. It hadn't been Pilar he'd been gunning for anyway. It hadn't even been Mike himself. The kid just stumbled, that was all. He was an uncoordinated kid, the only one in this country of spider-children, of Paolas and Arnolds and Juan Carloses, running and jumping, skipping and kicking, hanging like monkeys from swing sets, without a slip, without a fall, without a thought for the future, aimed at them, cocked and waiting for them.

Life was so precious, so damn precious and so damn fragile. Anything could break it. *Between us and heaven or hell there is only life...*

If the kid hadn't been clumsy, if he hadn't stumbled...

"What were you doing with the gun?" the cop said.

"I was looking for a girl. Her name is Suyapa, and her father kidnapped her —"

"What did you do with the bullets?"

"I didn't do anything with any bullets. When I took it it must have been empty."

"Then why did you take it?"

"I didn't know it was empty."

"It doesn't work without bullets."

"Yeah, I know."

"So you went to the trouble of stealing a gun —"

"Borrowing a gun."

" — and riding all the way to Tamalito with it, but you didn't have any bullets. Where did you put them?"

"I told you. I never had any bullets."

Alverenga shook his head skeptically and stood. This was it, then, this was how it would end. They would take him now, bring him to prison, remove his head and sew it up in burlap.

But the cop just frowned down at him. "I think that's enough for now," he said, and he started towards the door.

Mike felt mildly relieved, and before the man got to the door he called to him. "What happened to her?" he said.

"To who?"

"To Pilar. The woman. What happened to her?"

"She was shot. The boy knew enough to put bullets in —"

"I know. But afterwards?"

The cop shook his head, as if he didn't know or wasn't going to tell. He left the room.

* * *

The doctor showed up at the promised hour. He was tall and angular, and spoke English with a strange accent. He removed the bandages from Mike's head and examined the wound, cleaned it with some stinging liquid and rewrapped it.

He asked some questions and listened to the answers without much interest. He tested his reflexes with a rubber hammer. He moved a pen back and forth in front of his eyes, peering into them intently.

He seemed utterly unimpressed by Mike's condition, as if he were used to much worse.

"You were lucky," he said.

"I don't feel lucky."

"Well, you should. If that bullet had been a hair to the side, this would be a different conversation, because you wouldn't be part of it." He packed up the little hammer and the stethoscope and his other stuff, shaking his head. "The guy's got you point blank, he misses, and you don't feel lucky."

"It wasn't luck. I was pulled away," Mike said. "She pulled me away."

"Who?"

"Pilar. The woman I…the one who died. She saved my life."

"I see," the doctor said quietly.

"Did you treat her, too?" Mike asked. "When she got shot?"

He shook his head.

"Where'd they take her?"

"I don't know."

"Did they take her anywhere?"

The doctor pursed his lips and shrugged. He stood.

"You're doing fine," he said. "You should try to get out of bed for a while tomorrow. Use that wheelchair to get around if you have to, walk a little if you can, but rest when you get tired. If things get worse, if you start vomiting or your vision goes again, let them know and they'll call me. Otherwise, I'll stop by in a couple of days."

"I think I'm forgetting things," Mike said. The only things he remembered were the things he didn't want to. "And I get confused."

"That's to be expected. That'll improve."

CHAPTER 55

IN THE MIDDLE OF the morning of the next day, Greg entered the room and approached Mike's bed.

"Time for a little walk," he said.

"What? Did you say walk? You might as well tell me to fly, Greg," Mike said. "I can't even raise my head."

"Nonetheless…"

He detached the tube from Mike's forearm and peeled back his covers.

"Sit up first," he said, and he took Mike's hands and pulled him up. "Now swing your legs around." Without waiting he took his ankles and pulled them towards him, swiveling Mike around on the bed.

"Hang on," Mike said, for he felt dizzy again. He took three large breaths. "Are you sure about this?"

Some part of a smile appeared on Greg's face.

"There's a little sadistic side to you, isn't there?" Mike said.

"Perhaps. Perhaps."

He took Mike's hands and pulled him forward so that he slid slowly from the mattress onto his feet. He tried to straighten up but fell forward, so that Greg had to catch him.

"One minute," he said. He stood for a moment, bent over, his ears buzzing and his breath thick. His head felt like it was filling from the inside.

"I've got to lay down."

"Uh huh. You have to at least stand a little. Just give me twenty seconds."

Mike started counting, one, two, three…but the feeling kept coming on, and he tried to fall back onto the bed, but Greg held him up.

"I tell you, I'm going to throw up," he said.

"Go ahead."

"On you."

"Hmm mmm."

* * *

Later that day, Mike was able to take a half a dozen steps without losing it, and the next day, a dozen more, and could hold down solid food. He still had trouble when first standing and he avoided sudden movements, but he hid what he could from the brothers, and on the third day after the shooting he moved back to the dorm.

The children had left things for him on top of his bed: scribbled notes on scraps of paper with the words run together; a pencil drawing of what might have been a *sapo*; some marbles; even a *trompo*, old and battered, but without a doubt someone's treasure. The girl with the eyepatch had left one of her plastic cups there, together with a little rock.

There was an envelope that had initially been addressed to someone named Gerardo. A line had been struck through that name, however, and beneath it was Mike's name, in Spanish, written in all caps in an uneven hand. Inside the envelope was a white feather folded inside a card, on which Gerardo's name had also been scratched out, together with a birthday greeting. At the bottom of the card, in the same childish hand were Mike's name again and the words "*Te Amo*" – "I love you". It was signed "Wendy".

Without the orphans there, though, the place felt desolate, and Mike spent much of the day sitting in the *pasillo*, feeling dulled, suppressed, slowed. The world was gray, his movements awkward and clumsy; even sounds were muffled, and he could no longer detect the citrus smell that he'd come to look forward to. To distract himself he tried to read from the only book he had left in his possession:

> "*Easy there, girl*" *I said. "This is a —*"
>
> "*A classic, yeah, so you told me.*"
>
> "*That's right. '69 GTO ragtop.*"
>
> *As she crossed in front of the car she shook her head. "Whatever," she said.*
>
> "*Just so long as you know,*" *I whispered to myself.*
>
> *She walked towards the door of the tavern, and I could see she was trying to restrain it, but really – how could it be restrained?*
>
> *The perfect weapon.*

But no. He threw the book down and stared blankly at the empty courtyard. Hours passed, and nothing moved. Even his brother *sapos* seemed to have deserted him.

And always the thought of Pilar. Always the leaden fatigue and the sorrow and the regret over Pilar.

How had she died? What had really happened to her? The kid had tripped, he knew that much, and then had picked up the gun and scrambled away again. He'd gone towards the corner, the corner that led to Sara's house. And Pilar, Pilar had chased after him. Maybe Sara knew.

Maria was workman-like around him, lowering her eyes as she passed by on her rounds, all the smiles and the chumminess gone. He was just another obstacle now, something that had to be worked around.

With the orphans gone and no need for lessons, no one from the Missionaries of Charity came. He tried to reach Sister Rosario from the mission phone once, but there was no answer.

He had still not seen Marco, and wasn't sorry for it.

No one knew anything more about Suyapa.

He would have called Sara and asked to talk to Ana, but he'd never gotten her number from Lonnie. He tried to write a note instead, but struggled with it; everything he wrote seemed reasonable as he penned it, but hollow, insincere, insulting when he reread it. And his handwriting, never good, was even worse now, barely legible even to himself, no matter how much care he took with it.

Finally, he tore out a sheet from his notepad and as slowly and carefully as he could, he wrote:

"Ana, Naila: I'm sorry for your
loss. I don't know how to make it
mean anything, but I'm sorry. If I
could trade places with Pilar, I swear
I would."

He hesitated a moment, and added the words:

"I loved her."

He read it again with something like disgust, but could think of nothing else to say. He removed the card from the envelope that Wendy had left him, and on the envelope scratched a line through his name. Beneath it, he scribbled "Ana & Naila". He retrieved his money from under the mattress and counted out a hundred dollars in American bills – enough, with his credit card, to get him home. He set that money aside and stuffed the remainder – a mix of firm American *dolares* and flimsy blue and red *pesos* - into the envelope together with the note. He tried to reseal the envelope as best he could and put it in his back pocket without thinking of how he might get it to them.

Later in the day the doctor arrived, did his tests, asked a few questions, appeared satisfied. Mike didn't tell him about the problems he was having when he made sudden movements or when he stood - or about the confusion he was having over little things, a confusion that seemed to be getting worse and that now had begun to terrify him.

"I'll call again in a couple of days," the doctor said. "If you're still okay, I think you'll be free to fly. You've got to get to your doctor first thing when you get back home, though. Understand?"

"Yeah."

"Don't forget it."

It was the obvious next step, going home, the only next step. But he realized now that he'd been avoiding the thought of it.

Halfway to the door, the doctor turned. "I did see her," he said.

"What do you mean?"

"I did see the woman."

"Pilar?"

"Only after she was gone, though."

"Did she suffer a lot?"

"I don't know," he said, but Mike got the impression he was being lied to again.

* * *

Late in the afternoon Rodrigo came, and they let Mike shuffle out front to see him. The cabbie had Sara's shoes – hot pink tennis shoes with no laces - and her shirt – the frilly one she'd worn in the water line, when he'd first met Pilar. He had an envelope from Lonnie, too, who, he said, he had taken to the airport two days earlier.

"Not good man," Rodrigo said.

"Me?" Mike said.

"No. Him."

"No, not good man. Neither of us."

"You okay," he said. "With you I go north. Tell police what happen for sure. Help you. Help me. Help each other."

"For sure, huh? The only thing for sure is that you weren't there."

"Almost I was there."

Mike reached around to stuff Lonnie's note in his back pocket and felt another envelope there. He took it out and looked at it. A note for Gerardo - no, for Ana and Naila; now he remembered - he'd written a note for Ana and Naila.

He thought for a moment.

"Can you take me to Pilar's *casa*?" he said. "Just for a minute?"

"No."

"I'll pay you twenty dollars."

"Already you owe hundred."

"What?"

"To me. To take you there. You promise pay me one hundred dollars."

"To take me where?"

"To girl's house."

"To Pilar's house? I said that?"

Rodrigo nodded once, unsmiling, and Mike could see now something hard and implacable, even threatening, something that belonged on the front page of a Cortes newspaper, not on the face of their friendly *narco-taxista*. A hundred dollars. Had he really promised him that? He searched his memory but could find nothing.

"A hundred *pesos*, you mean."

"No. *Dolares*. One hundred *dolares*, American. You swear."

"I said a hundred dollars?"

"You swear."

"All right. All right. Wait here." He started back towards the door, carrying the tennis shoes, the girly white shirt slung over his shoulder.

Rodrigo took the toothpick from his mouth and pointed it at Mike. "But return," he said. "Must return."

"Okay, okay. It just takes me awhile now."

He carried Sara's stuff to his room, moving as fast as he thought he could without triggering the dizziness, hoping that no one would spot him. He bundled up the shirt and put it on the shelf and kicked the shoes under the bed. He took the remaining money out from under the mattress and with his thumb flicked through the edge of the sad little stack. One hundred *dolares* to the penny, the last hundred he had to his name. Decisions would have to be made.

He thought about stiffing Rodrigo some, offering him fifty or sixty, telling him it was all he had, leaving himself something to get home on. But he recalled the look on the man's face.

He took Ana's envelope out of his pocket and turned it over. He hadn't counted it, but there had to be two or three hundred in there. He rubbed at the corner of the flap, where it was so imperfectly sealed. He could just borrow some, until later, though of course there would be no later, and how could he steal it from them? And inside the thing, too, besides the money, was the shameful note, and how could he bear to see it again?

He took up the bills, returned to the street, and handed them with Ana's envelope to Rodrigo, who counted the money twice, rapidly and smoothly, as something he'd done many times before. He nodded in a business-like way and jammed the stash into his back pocket. He turned over the envelope and frowned at Mike.

"Can you get that to Pilar's mother for me?" he said.

"No. I no go back there," he said.

He handed the envelope back to Mike.

"And remember, help me get back to states," he said, now smiling like the old Rodrigo, the old, friendly, non-drug dealing, non-extortionist *taxista*. "Okay?"

He stabbed his toothpick back into his mouth.

CHAPTER 56

THE NEXT DAY MIKE was wasting time on the *pasillo* when Brother Greg came from the front.

"There's someone outside asking for you," he said.

"The cop?" Mike said.

"No, the woman from *Los Ángeles*. The other one."

"Sara? Sara's out there? Can I go see her?"

He tried to rise, but stumbled. Greg caught him by the elbow and lifted him. He stood bent over for a moment, fearing that the feeling would overpower him again, and he found that his head was bobbing, and that he was counting. Eight, nine, ten...He tried to straighten up, but had to abandon the effort. Twelve, thirteen...

"Are you all right?" Greg said.

"Yeah, I'm okay," he said. Fifteen, sixteen...

When he was ready, he started forward slowly, trying to act as if nothing had happened.

"So I'll be leaving soon," he said.

"I'm going to talk to the doctor about that."

"No, I'm okay. Doctor said it's fine. It's getting better. It's just going to take some time. It's going to — Hang on. I just remembered…"

He turned back to his room, returning a moment later with the pink tennis shoes, one in each hand.

"And those are hers, I suppose?" Greg said.

"Yeah. It's a long story."

"Hmm mmm. And an interesting one, I imagine?"

"Wait a minute," Mike said. "Can you hold these?" He handed Greg the shoes and went back to his room, returning with the frilly white shirt.

"Maybe it's better you're leaving, after all," Greg said.

They took three steps towards the front before Mike stopped again.

"Now what is it?" Greg said. "Not more of her clothing, I hope."

Mike went back to his room, stuffed the note to Ana in his pocket and returned to the *pasillo*.

"You got everything you need now?" Greg asked. "We can go, then?"

They started towards the front again, Mike carrying the shirt, Greg the pink shoes.

"Listen," Mike said. "I just want to say I appreciate you —"

"The gun wasn't loaded, you know. The gun you stole."

"Okay."

"You have to put bullets in it to make it work."

"Yeah, so I've heard. Look, I didn't mean to —"

"How did you get it from the library?"

"I took it when I returned the book you lent me. I didn't know what —"

"This one?" With his free hand Greg extracted a book from the pouch of his robe. With its gray cover and its tiny black lettering and its loose binding, it seemed to Mike like an old friend, his only friend - 194.9, P27.

"Yeah, that's the one."

"Was that your plan all along, to take the gun while I wasn't looking? Did you read any of it at all?"

Mike knew how to answer this one; he had the quote ready, memorized, the one the padre had book-marked for him, so long ago.

"'There are only two reasonable types of people in the world'," he said. "'Those who love God because…'"

Because…because…He'd forgotten the because. He'd had it down pat once, but now he couldn't remember: Why would anyone ever love God?

"Because they know him," Greg said.

That was it; because they know him. *Eso.* "'Those who love God because they know him, and those who hate God —'"

"'Those who seek God…'"

"'Those who seek God because they do not know him.'"

He looked proudly over at Greg.

"And this," he said, "from a guy who can barely remember his name."

"So tell me, do you consider yourself a reasonable man?"

"No. No, I don't. I was trying to be, but…"

They were at the front door now, and before unlocking it Greg paused, tapping the book against the soles of the pink shoes in his other hand, examining Mike from over his glasses. Finally, he unlatched the door and handed the book to him.

Mike reached for it but stopped. "'Ah, I better not," he said. "I'm out of here in a couple days, and with my memory the way it is, you'd never see it again."

He started out the door.

"Hey," Greg said.

"Oh yeah." Mike draped the white shirt over his shoulder and took the shoes from him. Greg reached down to stuff the book in Mike's thigh pocket.

"Keep it," he said as he turned and walked away. "For your trip. I took your Trent York Private Eye."

"What?"

"You know, it's really not all that bad."

"You're reading Trent York Private Eye? Hang on. You're reading Trent York Private Eye?"

He turned his head without breaking stride.

"No, not really," he said.

"No? That was a joke then?" Mike said. "That's even better. You know that was a joke, right?"

The brother disappeared into the atrium without responding.

Mike swung open the door. Sitting on one of the concrete benches out front, facing away from the building, was Sara, her black hair dropping down her neck in a thick, shiny ponytail. She turned to look at him, rose, and waited as he made his way to the gate, but as he opened it she started away quickly.

"Sara," he called to her. "You're going to have to stop. I can't run after you. I can barely even stand. Please."

She halted and paused for a moment before turning to face him.

"Look," he said. He held up the shoes and tipped his head towards the shoulder from which her shirt hung. "They don't fit me."

She shrugged as if indifferent to them. She took a couple of tentative steps toward him before breaking into a run.

"Careful," Mike said. As she approached he leaned back against the gate, bracing himself for impact, but she pulled up just short. She looked him over as if surprised to see that he was actually injured, reaching up to the bandage on the side of his head and letting her hand hover over it without touching it, as if by magic to heal it.

"Does it hurt?" she asked, and suddenly she was just another curious, eager little girl. Mike had to smile.

She dragged her shirt off his shoulder and with her head lowered slipped it on over her t-shirt, leaving it unbuttoned. She tugged at the lace fringes of the cuffs so they half-covered the backs of her hands. She took the shoes, one in each hand.

"Come on. Sit with me," he said. "I have to sit. I get tired kind of easy."

She led him to the bench.

"I'm sorry about Pilar," he finally said.

She nodded. "I'm sorry about Lonnie."

"Ah, Lonnie. *Ignorante.*"

She almost laughed.

"You don't have to be sorry, Sara."

"Are you leaving?"

"*Sí.*"

"New York?"

"No, Michigan. I live in Michigan."

"Take me with you."

"What?"

"When you leave take me with you."

"I can't do that, Sara."

She furrowed her brow and looked down. "It was a joke," she said.

After another long silence, Mike spoke: "How is Ana doing?"

She shook her head.

"How's Naila?"

She turned away to hide her face.

"Have you talked with them, Sara? Have you seen them?"

He watched the back of her head as it shook, but he knew she wasn't telling the truth.

Belkis came out of her *casa,* scowling over at Mike before walking to her tree and leaning her shoulder against it. Mike called to her but she didn't answer.

"She doesn't like me anymore, either," Mike said.

"I still like you," Sara said.

"You shouldn't. Listen, Sara - what happened, after...after this?" he said, and he pointed to his bandaged head. "To Pilar. What happened to her?"

She shook her head.

"I need to know, Sara. Please."

She looked into his eyes and swallowed. "I was lying on my bed," she said, but stopped.

"You were lying on your bed..."

"And I heard something - a bang, and a scream, but it wasn't loud, and you hear so much. And then people were running on the road, but that, too - you hear that, too. But then there was another shot, closer, and I knew it was a gun, and I looked outside, and from around the corner, the other corner, I saw her coming, trying to run. She was bleeding. From here." She put her hand on her right shoulder.

"Her shoulder?"

"But there was so much blood. I took her into the house, but there was so much blood."

"Did an ambulance come?"

"I wanted to get help, but she wouldn't let me. 'Stay here,' she said. 'Don't let him in. Don't let him shoot me again.'"

She stopped. She was rubbing the lace on her cuff with the fingers of her other hand, staring down at it.

"What then?" Mike said.

"I put her on my bed and I sat there with her, but she just stared up at the ceiling, trying to breath. I told her I was sorry, but she just stared like that, and her eyes, they were... Do I have to go on?"

"Please."

"She tried to talk again, but...her eyes..."

She had begun to cry now, and she turned away again.

"So much blood," she sobbed.

"And no one came to help?"

"Only when it was too late. Only when...Is it really impossible?"

"I'm sorry."

She nodded, composed herself, and stood. "I have to go," she said. But Mike caught her by the hand, rose, and took her in his arms.

"It wasn't your fault," he whispered, "none of it. I should have stopped the whole thing. I was the only one who could have, and I didn't."

"Okay," she said, as if to sooth him. "Okay."

She detached herself and turned to go, wiping her cheeks with her sleeve.

But he remembered now - there was something he had to give her, something for Pilar – no, no - for Ana. A note. He reached in his back pocket, took it out and handed it to her.

"Can you give this to Ana? It's just a card, but..."

She wiped her cheeks again and took the note. She walked half a dozen steps before turning back to him.

"Is snow really real?" she said.

"It is."

She frowned and started away again.

"You deserve better," Mike called after her. "Better than us. You're good *ponch*...you're a good person, Sara."

She twisted her head back to smile at him, her eyes still wet with tears.

"And you sing like a bird."

Now the smile broadened, and a hint of the Sara swagger returned. He watched as she moved away along the road, clapping the soles of the shoes together in rhythm to some song she was singing in her head. When she disappeared down the dip to the river, he crossed the road and squatted in front of Belkis. She glanced at him but quickly returned her gaze to her hand as it picked at the bark.

"I have to leave soon, Belk."

"That's not my name," she said.

"All right. But I just wanted to let you know that I'm going to be leaving."

She shrugged.

"I'll see you again someday, though."

She pursed her lips and shook her head once, still avoiding eye contact.

"I will. I promise you."

"How?" she said.

"I don't know how, but I will."

He heard the clank of metal behind him and turned to see the familiar, robed, muscle-bound figure closing the gate of the mission behind him.

"I've got to go," he said.

Without looking at him, she stuck her fist out at Mike. He put his hand beneath hers and she dropped the green *cantillo* into it.

"You can have it back," she said. "It doesn't work."

He rolled it in his palm. "No, I guess it doesn't. I'm sorry, Belk."

"Not my name."

"Okay. But I'm sorry anyway. And I will see you again. I will." He stood and took three steps towards Luke, waiting for him at the gate, until he heard her voice.

He turned. Finally, she was looking at him.

"What did you say?" he said.

"'Pilar'. I said 'Pilar'."

He strode back to her, dropped down, and took her in his arms, his hand holding her head tightly against his shoulder.

"Don't cry, Belk," he said. "Don't cry."

She struggled away from him and ran back into her casa. From his haunches he stared at the blank doorway, his back to Luke.

When he was ready he rose and crossed the street.

"How are we doing out here?" Luke said.

"Belkis was her cousin."

"Yeah." He glanced up the road to where Sara was just disappearing over the rise.

"And that was Sara, her friend."

"I know. She's been here looking for you a couple times."

"She's a good person."

Luke nodded. "She's a beautiful woman."

Mike looked at him, wondering what kind of trap was being set for him, wondering what he could say to evade it. He decided that his best move was to remain silent.

"It's a great thing, the beauty of a woman," Luke said. "It's a gift."

"Yeah, I believe it is," Mike said warily.

"The love of a woman is a gift from God. I mean, not the way you do it, of course."

"I know you don't believe me, but I did love her, Luke. Pilar, I mean. I really did love her."

"Yeah, well…Have you confirmed your flight yet?"

"No."

"They'll only hold it one more day."

"What if I get worse, though?" Mike said. "The doctor said if I got worse, I shouldn't fly."

"Are you getting worse?"

"Not yet. I don't think so. But I'm not getting any better either."

"You do want to go, don't you?"

"What else is there for me to do?"

"Stay here."

"Oh, I think I've done enough damage here, don't you? Worked enough of my special brand of magic?"

"No, I don't." He turned to look Mike in the eye. "I don't."

He started towards the gate and Mike followed.

In the atrium they ran into Padre Zeppi, who told Luke that he had a call. "It's Marco," he said.

Luke hurried away, leaving Mike alone with the padre.

"Is he coming?" Mike asked. "Brother Marco?"

Padre ignored the question. "How are you feeling?" he said.

"Not any worse, I don't think."

"Good," he said, and he started towards the stairway.

"Padre," Mike said.

The old man stopped with his foot on the first step and turned to face Mike.

"I think I'm ready."

"You're ready?"

"I think so. If you are."

"In the chapel," the padre said. "Five minutes."

CHAPTER 57

MIKE APPROACHED THE LITTLE door in the side wall of the chapel. He reached for the knob, paused, and withdrew his hand.

He turned and looked around him at the silent, empty room. The little pearl half-shell of holy water hung next to the door through which he'd entered. The dark, paneled walls encircled him, deepening the solemnity of the place. The old straight-backed pews, arranged in perfect rows, looked forward attentively. The candles flickered at him from the sides of the bare altar.

His eyes were drawn to the glowing woman standing there in her frame; from where he stood now he could see her more clearly. She was balanced on a black upturned crescent held aloft in an unlikely fashion by a miniature angel. Under her cloak she wore a white garment with a faint, intricate pattern, and from her waist hung two short hanks of black material. Her forehead was high and smooth, untroubled, and the lids of her eyes drooped, giving her a sleepy aspect. Calm, maddeningly calm, when just above her, just above her, just over her head…

Finally, he could bear it no longer, looked up, and beheld the man, hanging there on the cusp of the great moment, the moment that would change everything, that would redeem everything, that would make all things new - his clay-colored flesh racked out between the spikes, his ribs showing through his skin like those of a *barrio* dog, his side ripped open, his mouth agape, desperate for breath, the crown of thorns biting into his forehead like some strange bleeding hat. Suffering, suffering.

He'd been wrong - he wasn't ready, after all. He didn't believe in it yet, not enough, not completely. No, he would not go in there, he would return to his room instead, to his chair in the *pasillo*, where he would do more nothing, believe in more nothing. He took a step to go.

But now he remembered - the padre was in there, waiting for him. He would have to go in and tell him he'd changed his mind, or the old man might be there all night. He'd have to tell him that he wasn't ready, after all. Tell him he would never be ready.

He opened the door. Inside it was all just as he remembered from childhood. Tight and dark and hushed, with a screened-over window, shuttered with a panel, and a kneeler beneath it. Behind the panel, the silent priest.

"Padre," he said.

"Close the door, please."

He obeyed, swinging the door shut and lowering himself onto the kneeler; he felt the wood give under his weight. Why had he done that? Why had he knelt? He had not meant to kneel, had not meant to act as if he were really going to go through with this thing after all.

The panel slid open. Through the screen he could discern the outline of the old man, his head bowed, his chin in his hand. All just as it had been so many years ago, after so many of what he used to know as sins.

The padre waited for a moment, seeing if Mike could remember the formula. Finally, he prompted him. "Bless me Father, for I have sinned."

Mike felt agitated and imposed upon, but for some reason he repeated the padre's words: "Bless me Father, for I have sinned."

"My last confession was…" the padre prompted him.

"Ten years ago," Mike said brusquely.

The priest waited a moment and started again. "These are my sins."

Goading him, trying to get him to cough up his secrets, his shabby, shameful, nasty little secrets, the kind of stuff that would not pique the interest even of a voyeur. Well, he had a surprise for him then.

"I killed someone," he said, and with great satisfaction he thought of the old man behind the curtain, stunned now by how wrong he'd been about Mike, a great sinner after all.

But just as he was getting up to go the voice came from behind the screen, not betraying the least hint of surprise. "It wasn't all your fault," the voice said. "It wasn't just you who killed Pilar."

Mike dropped back onto the kneeler.

"But you were careless, you were reckless with her life."

He nodded, as though the padre could see him.

"As if her life didn't mean anything. As if it had no value. And now she's gone."

And now she was gone, and it *was* his fault. Out of love, out of lust, out of pride, out of vanity, he didn't know anymore, he just knew that it really had been him who had done it, as surely as if he'd pulled the trigger.

"Mike?" the padre finally said.

"Padre," he said. "There can't be forgiveness for a thing like that, can there?"

"Yes, there is."

"I don't believe it. What penance could possibly —"

"You'll fast for a week."

"Fast?"

"Bread and water."

"But I can't do that. I'm recovering." It was possible, anyway, that he was recovering.

"You'll start when the doctor says you're ready."

"I don't trust that doctor. He doesn't even know —"

"And after that, you'll stay here for one year."

"But I fly out tomorrow."

"You'll work with us, with the brothers. You'll do as we say. You'll go to sleep when we do. You'll rise with us. You'll work with us. You'll pray with us."

"I can't do that."

"You have more important things to do?"

"I can't stay here."

"If you're not serious about it, don't pretend to take responsibility for it."

"I am serious about it."

"Then stay."

"I can't."

"What did you come here for? Three Hail Marys?"

"I don't know why I came. It was a mistake. I'm just not ready for it, that's all. I'm sorry."

He stood and turned towards the door. He tried to take a step but stopped and dropped his head. He bent over, put his hands on his knees, and started counting to himself. Two, three, four...

He was fading away, he was being extinguished, and he dropped to one knee and felt his head bobbing. Five, six, seven...He braced his knuckles against the floor. Eight, nine, ten...

"Mike?"

"One second."

He heard the man start to rise.

"No, no, I'm okay, Padre" he said. Slowly he stood and straightened up.

"Mike?"

"I'm sorry," he said, and he walked out of the confessional, leaving the door open behind him.

CHAPTER 58

HE LISTENED TO HIS own breathing, heavy and thick, like a foreign thing, and could feel his heart thumping hard and sharp, like a door slamming shut in his chest, again and again and again. A thousand thoughts crowded his *sapo* brain, and he could not focus on any one of them. He cursed aloud, rolled over, rose slowly and went to the shelf. He glanced at the yellow flower, dried and shrunken now, but it was too painful to look at. Beside it was the little square envelope – Lonnie's note, still unopened. He took it and dropped it into the wastebasket. He picked up Suyapa's drawing, brought it to the bed, eased himself back onto the mattress, and held the paper up to his eyes to see it more clearly in the gloom - the upright rabbit, the bundle of flowers, the silly grin, the tiny signature.

So innocent and naïve, she'd been. So vulnerable, condemned to a place that did not forgive the vulnerable.

He folded the paper in quarters, slipped it into his thigh pocket and went outside. It was the hour when the day has not quite yet resigned itself to the advance of the night, the hour of brown air and waiting, the time of day he'd always found to be most powerful and lonely. The ferns and palms in the courtyard were still and quiet, as before a storm. Overhead a hook of a moon looked down, small, hard, sharp.

He started toward the front, his sandals in his hands, his feet bared to the coolness and smoothness of the tile. He passed through the atrium and trudged up the steps to the second floor, but at the landing stopped and stooped over, bracing his hands on his thighs. Three, four, five. He was driven to his haunches. Seven, eight, nine. Hoping no else would come along.

When he felt strong enough he rose, straightened up, waited a moment, and moved on, passing by the chapel and stopping at the library.

No light showed from under the door. He leaned forward until his head almost touched the wood. Inside was silence. He raised his hand as if to knock, but decided against it, turned and started back down the hall.

He pried the door of the chapel open and peeked inside. In the front pew, silhouetted by the glow of the candles, was Maria, on her knees, her head bowed and veiled. She was singing a hymn softly, the music seeming to come from the candles themselves. He could not make out the words, but the melody was simple and beautiful, like all their hymns, he thought, like Maria herself.

He slipped inside and eased the door shut behind him, but the locking mechanism clicked and Maria turned towards him. She was just a shadow against the candlelight, and he couldn't make out her expression.

"Go on," he said to her in a loud whisper. "Keep singing, please."

She turned back to the front and began humming aloud in her soft, high, slightly flat voice.

As quietly as he could, he went to the last pew and sat, but the wood creaked under him and the singing stopped, and all was silence once more; he could almost hear the candles burning.

He bowed his head and tried to concentrate, but his prayers turned into worries and regrets. He lowered himself onto the kneeler, and as he did he heard paper crumpling in his pocket. He reached into it. That was right, that was right – Suyapa's drawing. He'd folded it up and put it in his pocket when he'd left his room.

He unfolded it now and laid it on the bench. As quietly as he could he swiped his hand across it, pressing it against the wood to straighten it, but the sound of the paper filled the air, and he stopped.

He stayed on his knees for another two minutes before giving up and sitting down. He was surprised to see the drawing on the bench beside him. But that was right, he'd taken it here in his pocket, and he'd just now found it and unfolded it and put it there beside him and tried to straighten it, but it had made too much noise. He picked it up and held it to his eyes, straining to see in the gloom. The lettering – "God loves you" - seemed to mock him now. And the rabbit happier than any rabbit had ever been or ever would be. And at the bottom somewhere, though he couldn't make it out, the tiny signature – "Suyapa". And "God loves you." And the happy rabbit. And, somewhere, "Suyapa". Suyapa.

He put the paper back down on the bench and glanced at the glowing woman in the picture frame, and then at the crucifix above her. "Oh Lord," he said, but he couldn't think of what should follow.

"Oh Lord," he repeated, aloud this time, and Maria looked back as if he had been calling her. He noticed in the candle light that she was wearing a finely threaded veil that lay delicately over her cheek. She seemed to smile at him and turned back.

What was she praying about? There was so much to pray for; what was she praying for? Why couldn't he do it?

Lonnie had been right, damn him: To have faith was a blessing. The minute-by-minute grace and beauty of those who had it - Padre, Brother Luke, Rosario, Ibekwe, the other sisters, Suyapa, all of them, even Greg - were proof enough of that. How they acted toward one another, how they acted toward him, toward everyone. What they cared about. What they loved. What they did. And he'd been right, too, about not everyone getting to have it, though he'd once felt close to it himself. He'd thought he'd been on the right path, anyway, or had at least sensed that a path was possible.

He'd had hope, and he'd had love – no matter what Luke said, he'd had love – but they hadn't been enough.

Something in his other pocket was poking at his thigh, and he reached inside. The *cantillo*. He remembered now. It was lucky. Somehow, it gave one luck. It had brought him someone once, but now she was gone.

He rolled it around in his hand and felt its spikes dull against his palm.

He put Suyapa's drawing under the bench and lay down on his side, pulling his knees up, closing his eyes and crossing his arms over his chest. Maria had begun to sing again, and though he couldn't make out the words, he let himself be submerged in the lilt of her voice.

"Oh Lord," he whispered. "Come to my assistance."

* * *

He woke to the sound of the phone going off below him, somewhere on the first floor. He was disoriented, and only at the second ring – sharp and jarring in the quiet of the night – did he remember where he was. A blanket lay over him from his shoulder to his feet. He stretched up to look over the back of the pew in front of him, to where Maria had been, but she was gone, and only the candles flickered up front. Mike felt a boundless affection for her. She, too - one of the blessed.

The phone rang again, high and sharp and ominous. The policeman, probably, the policeman who hated him, calling to arrange the time of the arrest. He waited in suspense for the next ring, but someone answered it, or the person on the other end gave up, for it did not ring a fourth time.

He rolled his shoulder so that the blanket covered it and he closed his eyes, only waking again when the padre shook him gently by the shoulder.

"Mike," the old man said. "You should come with me."

He sat up, lowered his head and waited. Padre put his hand on his shoulder.

"Sorry Padre," he said. "I'm still a little…What's going on?"

"Brother Marco's coming."

"I see," Mike said. He stood, paused for a moment as the padre waited at the door, and then followed the old man out, genuflecting on the way as the priest had done, though he was faithless, crossing himself with holy water like the priest, though he had no faith. Silently they went down the stairs, through the empty atrium, past the medical rooms and outside, past the dorms and the room where Ibekwe had taught the orphans, along the far side of the pens, rustling with animals, to the driveway in back.

The truck was gone. Luke was sitting on the retaining wall on the other side of the drive, hunched over with his thick forearms on his thighs, staring at the ground in front of him. Greg sat on one side of him, gazing slightly upwards, over his eyeglasses and out into infinity. Joe was on his other side. He looked at Mike as if he had something to tell him but didn't dare.

Padre walked over to them, they shifted to make room, and he sat between Luke and Greg. He said something in a low voice. Luke nodded.

Mike dropped on to the wall opposite the others. He looked down at his feet and saw that they were bare. His sandals - where were they? And the drawing – what had happened to the drawing? He was sure he'd taken it with him from his room. Yes - he'd folded it in quarters and put it in one of his pockets. He checked them, but all he found was the *cantillo*, which had been lucky, once.

"The *barrio's* quiet tonight," Joe said.

The padre nodded, but there was no other response.

Mike noticed a flicker of motion to his left, and looked over to see a gecko clinging to the wall of the garage, a third of the way up. It froze there for ten seconds before transporting itself two feet higher. It chirped. As if in response a rooster outside the walls crowed, and crowed again. Someone in the *barrio*, right next to the mission wall, it seemed, called to someone else with a high-pitched, rapid burst of words that Mike could not understand. He waited for a response, but none came. A flurry of fireworks in the distance, and somewhere far away a helicopter thumping at the air. A sudden concussive boom, like an artillery shot.

The chapel. While he was in the chapel he'd taken the drawing out of his pocket, and when he'd tried to straighten it out it had been too loud. And the sandals; he must have left his sandals there, too.

"I have to get something," he said. But as he rose, his head grew light and he found himself gasping for air. The sensation of being sucked down into the abyss returned, the intimation of some ultimate change, and he leaned over and started counting.

Padre stood and said Mike's name.

At that moment he heard a vehicle approaching along the *barrio* road. The noise grew, and then stopped. The sound of a car door clipping shut.

Luke moved to the door and stood with his head bowed. What seemed like an hour passed. What was he waiting for? Why didn't he open it? Mike was as ready as he would ever be, ready for whatever Marco had in mind. He was already packed for the flight out in the morning. He could take a bus to the airport, though he didn't have any money to pay for it. Or maybe he would just melt away into the *barrio*; no one had money in the *barrio*. He just needed his drawing, his drawing and his sandals. Just those two things. Where had he left them?

He put his hand in his pocket again and pressed his palm against the *cantillo*.

Finally, there was a sharp, metallic rap from outside, a pause, two more knocks, another pause, one more knock.

The chapel. His drawing and his sandals were in the chapel.

Luke unlocked the door and swung it open. In the circle of light outside, a man stood. He was rough and unkempt, and it appeared as if he hadn't slept in days, in weeks; he had bags under his eyes and three or four day's growth of beard. He was out of monk's garb and wearing blue jeans and a t-shirt, from the sleeves of which hung long powerful arms. And though all Mike had ever seen of him was a blurry image in a tiny frame, he could have picked him out of a crowd; there was no mistaking him. He had the regal air that Mike had expected, hoped for, feared.

He nodded at the brothers, and his eyes briefly landed on Mike, seeming surprised to see him there.

At his side was a girl, half his height and a third his size, gaunt, starving. She wore brown linen pants that were too small for her; their ragged cuffs climbed her boney shins. An old hooded sweatshirt hung loosely on her shoulders, the collar drooping at the neck, exposing the fraying trim of a white t-shirt beneath. Her hair was gathered back behind her right ear and to the left fell alongside her face, almost as far down as her chin, and a black wisp of it arced across her cheek, intersecting the little sickle scar burned there. She stared directly at Mike with her piercing black eyes, testing him, questioning him.

He dropped to one knee and spread his arms. The girl ran to him, ran into him, knocking him off balance so that he had to drop one hand to the ground behind him to brace himself. The *cantillo* clinked against the cement of the drive.

Brother Marco strode through the doorway and turned to the old priest, his look softening.

"Padre," he said, "can you confess me now?"

Made in the USA
Middletown, DE
12 May 2018